Benjamin Hallowell, Henry C. (Henry Clay) Hallowell

Autobiography of Benjamin Hallowell

Benjamin Hallowell, Henry C. (Henry Clay) Hallowell

Autobiography of Benjamin Hallowell

ISBN/EAN: 9783337119454

Printed in Europe, USA, Canada, Australia, Japan

Cover: Foto ©Raphael Reischuk / pixelio.de

More available books at **www.hansebooks.com**

AUTOBIOGRAPHY

— OF —

BENJAMIN HALLOWELL,

WRITTEN AT THE REQUEST OF HIS DAUGHTER,
CAROLINE H. MILLER, FOR HIS CHILDREN
AND GRANDCHILDREN, IN THE SEV-
ENTY-SIXTH YEAR OF HIS AGE.

———

— "I (here) retrace
(As in a map the voyager his course)
The windings of my way through many years.
Cowper.

———

PHILADELPHIA:
FRIENDS' BOOK ASSOCIATION,
1020 ARCH STREET.
1883.

TO ALL

WHO FEEL THAT THEY ARE THE BETTER

FOR HIS HAVING LIVED,

THIS AUTOBIOGRAPHY OF BENJAMIN HALLOWELL

IS RESPECTFULLY DEDICATED

BY HIS CHILDREN.

PREFATORY NOTE.

In the following account of my life, which I began in the early part of last month, and have finished as far as I am capable this morning, I wish all who may read it, to endeavor to put themselves in sympathy with me as I then was, to whom the events and incidents related have all been a sober and sometimes a painful reality, and to understand that, to the very best of my knowledge and belief, it is a true picture of me and of my then condition ; that they therefore may study it as representing the environments that have evolved my character, and the "*me*" that makes this record.

I wish it understood, also, that it is written only from the impressions that remain, so that, in relating a conversation, where there are no quotation marks, what is given is just the impression upon my memory; but where quotation marks are placed, some or all the words were used by the person as there given.

BENJAMIN HALLOWELL.

Rockland, 2d mo. 26th, 1875.

CONTENTS.

CHAPTER I.

1799.

CHAPTER II.

1811 — Age, 12.

CHAPTER III.

1814 — Age 15.

CHAPTER IV.

1818.

CHAPTER V.

1821.

CHAPTER VI.

1822.

CHAPTER VII.

1824.

CHAPTER VIII.

1831.

CHAPTER IX.

1835.

CHAPTER X.

1842.

CHAPTER XI.

1845.

CHAPTER XII.

1846.

CHAPTER XIII.

1859.

CHAPTER XIV.

CHAPTER XV.

1840.

Convention of the friends of Education — Difference between work and play — Letter on the subject of the Alexandria water-works — A kind intention — Closing reflections.

CONTENTS OF PART II.

AUTOBIOGRAPHY

OF

BENJAMIN HALLOWELL.

CHAPTER I.

1799.

Parentage and birth — Family separated — Lives with his grandfather — First recollections — Goes to school — First mathematical reasoning — Notices the stars — Death of his brother
Joseph — Feeble health — Anxiety of his mother for his
education — Aversion to school — Anecdote of hiding his
hat — First experience in teaching — Visit to Philadelphia
— Hearing the watchman "cry the hour" — Attending
market— Anecdote of the cow.

I was born in Cheltenham township, Montgomery
county, Pennsylvania, on the 17th of the Eighth month,
1799, as the records of Abington Monthly Meeting, where I
had a birthright in the Society of Friends, show. My
parents were Anthony and Jane Hallowell. My father
was the oldest son of William and Mary Williams Hallowell. My mother was the daughter of Benjamin and
Mary Comly Shoemaker.

My parents had five children, viz.: James S., who was
about five years my senior, father of Caleb S. and James
S. Hallowell; Benjamin, who died young; Joseph; Benjamin, jr. (myself), and Mary S., now Mary S. Lippincott,
who has two daughters, Jane S. and Margaret W.

1

I was deprived of a father's care when about two and a-half years old, and have no recollection of ever being at a meal with him. The family was broken up. Joseph went to live with his uncle, John Brumfield, in Columbia, Pennsylvania, and my mother and her other three children, went home to her father, who had lost his wife some years before. He had a farm of over one hundred acres. She performed all the housework for the family for many years, besides spinning wool for stockings on the big wheel, and knitting them, and also spinning flax and tow on the spinning-wheel, for sheeting, shirting, etc. In addition to this she prepared material for blankets, coverlets, and winter wear for the men and for herself and daughter. She made, also, striped linsey, the colored material of which was the result of her own labor, and check for aprons.

Her father, my grandfather, after whom I was named, lived at the north-west corner of the Old York road and Chelten avenue, then called Grave-yard lane, inasmuch as it led to the burial place, about eight miles from Philadelphia, left by my ancestor, Richard Wall, to Friends of Cheltenham, for a grave-yard.

The house in which I was born was on the adjacent farm, near that in which my uncle Benjamin, who was a tanner, lived and died before my memory. Uncle Benjamin's house had a fine spring in one corner of the kitchen, which spring is the only thing that remains to mark the place where I first saw the light. By going up Chelten avenue, and turning to the left at the first lane beyond the present residence of Robert and Ann Shoemaker, and going a few hundred yards to the first hollow, a stream which supplied the tan-yard with water, will be found crossing the road. A short distance up the stream, and a little to the right, is *the spring* which used to discharge its waters into the forementioned stream. It is now covered up, and the water is used to supply the establishment of John W. Thomas (of No. 1022 Chestnut street, Philadelphia), on a hill near by, on the same farm that was my uncle Benjamin's.

The first consciousness that I can recall to memory, was sitting on the kitchen step of stone, in a feeling of very great discomfort, crying for bread and butter; which I think must have been the time of our moving to grandfather's, where everything was strange, and all so busy that the child did not receive its ordinary attention. This was when my sister was about six months old, and I nearly two and a half years. I can still recur, vividly, to the then existing feeling of distress and discomfort with which I commenced my life in a strange place.

The spring before I was five years old, I commenced going to school at Abington, to my cousin, Nathan Shoemaker, afterwards a prominent physician in Philadelphia, his sister Martha, who lived on my way to the school, kindly taking charge of me. I had previously been taught to spell and read by grandfather. Indeed, I do not remember when I could not read, nor do I remember any incident connected with learning to read, so early and gently did the good old man perform this kind and important office. He also taught my little sister to knit and spin when she was too small to do much other work.

When about six years old, I was assisting my brother James to carry a bucket of milk to the pigs, one of us having hold on each side of the handle, when he said, "Thee takes more steps than I do, why does thee not get along faster than I?" The query took hold of my mind, and when we had finished what we were then about, I sat down on a board that lay across a ditch, then dry, and filled with leaves, my feet in the ditch, my head resting on my hand, and my elbow on my knee, studying out the problem. I well remember my feeling of delight, when I saw that his steps must be longer than mine, and ran to give him the solution. This is the earliest instance of mathematical reasoning that I can recall, although, as we were much together, and my brother was possessed of a very active mind, he was daily doing or saying things calculated to exercise my reasoning powers, and I have no doubt assisted in my intellectual development.

When I was about seven years old, my uncle Atkinson Rose, his wife, Rebecca (my mother's sister), and some of their children, came in a sleigh from Philadelphia (eight miles), to make an evening visit. Sister Mary and I, whose invariable custom it was to go to bed before dark, (getting our suppers of bread and milk ourselves), were allowed on this occasion to stay up to be with our little cousins, and when I went out with the older people about 9 o'clock to get the horses, I saw, for the first time that I can remember, the night sky and the stars, which were very bright from the clearness of the atmosphere. I well recollect the impression of delight the magnificent spectacle made upon me.

In the year 1808 my brother Joseph died. My cousin, Richard M. Shoemaker, told me of his death at Abington Meeting, which we scholars attended. Mother and her brother, Comly Shoemaker, had been at Columbia, where he lived with his uncle Brumfield, about a year before, to see him. When I returned from school that evening and saw the evidences of my dear mother's grief, I felt as if further happiness would be unknown. She was expecting him home on his first visit, when she received the intelligence of his death. His uncle, with whom he lived, kept a store, and Joseph was weighing some gunpowder from a canister the evening before Christmas, when a boy threw at another boy a lighted cigar, that fell into it, causing the powder to explode, shattering the door and windows, and breaking through the floor where he stood, so that he was found in the cellar. His face was entirely black from the effects of the powder, but he lived till next morning in great suffering, and explained to the family how the accident occurred. All the reference mother ever made to it afterwards was to say, " Poor Joseph," and weep.

Samuel Mifflin, who lives at Columbia, and married a daughter of William and Phebe Wright, of Huntington, Pennsylvania, told me within a few years, that he well remembered hearing the circumstance spoken of, and could point out the place.

Mother, although so industrious, rising by day-break, and many times before day, having the clothes hung out on washing-day by sunrise, would on Seventh-days get all her work done before dinner. In the afternoon she would dress up with a nice clean cap, white apron, and nankeen mitts coming up to the elbow (her gown having short sleeves), and would look over the farm, garden, orchard, etc. After Joseph's death, she would frequently sit down by the front window, with her face towards the turnpike, and say " Poor Joseph," while the tears would stream down her cheeks from the memory of him, and perhaps other tendering reminiscences of the past! It made my young heart ache!

At that day farmers' children generally drank milk for breakfast and supper, which was the invariable rule with us, except that on First-day mornings we were each favored with a cup of coffee. My health was then feeble, and I was affected with a bleeding at the nose almost daily, especially if I ran or used any violent exercise, which made me weak and pale, so that my mother was told many times in my hearing, that she would "never raise that child," which I thought must be a true prophecy. I had heart-burn and nausea after my milk breakfast, almost every morning, but no excuse would induce my mother to let me remain from school. She would sometimes intimate unmistakably that the desire to stay from school might have something to do with my morning sickness. It happened that I was unable to retain my breakfast one First-day morning, and I then reminded her that *that* sickness could not be from a desire to remain from school, as there was no school on that day. Dear woman! She was very earnest and untiring in her efforts to keep me at school, in order that I might be a "good scholar," and I now venerate her for it, and see that she had some grounds for believing that feigned sickness might be one of the many devices I tried to find as excuses for staying at home.

On one occasion the men were a little short of help and wanted me to "rake after the wagon" in hauling hay. Delighted, I ran to tell her, when, to my great disappointment, she said, "*I* will rake after the wagon, my son; here is thy dinner" (handing me the basket), "go to school, and be a good boy." Another time the men wished me to "pull back," in cleaning wheat with a fan or windmill. On telling her, with hopeful feelings, she said as before, "I will pull back: go to school."

I tried every expedient I could devise, to gain the privilege of staying at home, for which it is but justice to myself to say, there was some excuse in the severity of the teacher,* who went about the school-room carrying under

---

* Our father did not give his name; he was one of several that succeeded his loved cousin, Dr. Shoemaker.

his arm a large rod or switch, which would resound from a back here and another there, every little while, and sometimes on a whole bench-full successively, from which I did not escape. Being very sensitive and nervous, the sound of a stroke on another hurt me almost as badly, it seemed, as if it had been on myself. I dreaded going to school *exceedingly*, and thought any expedient, which was not criminal, would be justifiable, that would relieve me from a day of such agony. We had school six days in the week, except Monthly Meeting day, and when school was dismissed on Seventh-day afternoon, I would walk home with a light heart and enjoy the evening greatly — but a sadness would rest on me the next morning, from the dark shadow of the approaching school-day.

One morning, under a strong pressure of these feelings, I thought I would make one more effort, and hide my hat. When the time arrived to go to school, mother brought me my basket of dinner and said, "Now, my son, it is time to go to school." I told her I could not see my hat anywhere. She told me to look again. I replied, I had been looking a long time. She then came to assist me in hunting it, and whether or not she suspected I had hidden it, I never knew; but she went deliberately and got her black silk bonnet, and said, "Thee can wear this to-day," and without changing a muscle of her face, began to tie it on, I looking steadily into her eye, where, child as I was, I could see a look of determination that I knew to be irresistible. I exclaimed, "Oh, mother, I *think* I can find my hat" (but she kept on tying the strings of the bonnet); "I am *sure* I can find it, mother, it is in the dough-trough," by which time the bonnet was well tied on and her countenance still unrelaxed. This circumstance is strongly impressed on me to this day. I went with a quick step to the dough-trough and got my hat, and said, "Here it is, mother; please take this bonnet off," which she did, to my great joy, and I felt that I had made a narrow escape, and never tried it again. This was one turning point in my life. With my disposition and capacity for expedients, had she then yielded, the consequences cannot be told. I fully believe her firmness on that occasion saved me. The school seemed pleasanter after I had satisfied myself there was no remedy, and from that time I got on rapidly with my studies, and I think, became a favorite with the teacher.

My mother's earnest and determined effort to keep me at school caused me to go in the summer time, when I was, by contrast, one of the "big boys" and most advanced scholars, so that for several summers the teacher would get me to hear some of the classes, boys and girls, in an adjoining apartment. Here I gained my first experience in teaching and it delighted me.

About this time, 1809, there were two sisters, with an orphan niece younger than I, from Philadelphia, boarding in the neighborhood. Mother, as was her custom when strangers were in the neighborhood, invited them to take tea with us, which they did. The two sisters sat at the side of the table, their niece at the corner, and I at her right hand. When the little girl had finished her supper, she put her hands together, her fingers extended, and said, in the sweetest accents I almost ever heard, "Thank the Lord and Mrs. Hallowell for my supper." What a sermon that was to me! I have never seen her since, but have very, very often thought of her and her sermon.

In 1809, brother James went to Philadelphia as an apprentice in uncle William Hallowell's hardware store, No. 197 North Third street. Uncle William also had a store on the southwest corner of Third and Arch streets, with his brother-in-law, Abel Satterthwaite. This suited and pleased him greatly, and he soon made himself useful. He left home for his new situation in the early fall, and at Christmas I received permission to spend Christmas day and two nights at Uncle William's with him. It was a delightful and memorable time to me. We slept together, and I told him in the evening I wished to hear the watchman "cry the hour." After I had got to sleep, he nudged me, and in an undertone said: "Ben, Ben, hear the watchman!" I soon listened, and heard faintly in the far distance the cry, "Ho — past — twel-ve o'clock." Then all was still — then the same cry, a little nearer — then the sound of his staff, and then his step could be heard, and the cry, more and more distinctly, as he drew nearer, with his heavy tread and knock of his staff on the pavement, till he seemed almost under the window. I felt a little alarmed, and huddled up close to my brother for safety. Then the cry became fainter and fainter as he passed, till at length it died away in the remote distance. I can recollect the scene and the attendant feeling as if it had been yesterday.

My brother was all love and kindness, having outgrown or corrected entirely his disposition to tease, and I have always looked back to this visit as one of the pleasantest incidents in my life. I walked home the next morning, eight miles, in just two hours.

My mother and I used to attend Philadelphia market from grandfather's, with the produce of the farm, leaving home about two o'clock in the morning, and returning before dinner-time. In the fall of 1809, as there was need of a cow for beef, we went down to the cow market, near Walnut street, where one was bought, and I left to drive her

out of town, mother going for the market wagon, to follow.
I got her along very well to the corner of Fourth and Vine,
I think it was, where, I suppose, she had been accustomed
to turn off, when she started up Vine street, I after her, to
get before her and drive her back. The weather was very
hot, and the then unpaved streets were extremely dusty.
On coming to Fourth street, she turned down back again,
when another race was required to get before her and
bring her back to Vine street, up which she turned
again, and all had to be repeated. I was almost overcome with exhaustion, yet could not give up and leave
the cow, when a gentleman coming down Vine street on
the sidewalk, seeing me, and seeming at once to comprehend my situation, went through the dust into the middle
of the street, stopped the cow, and assisted me in getting
her started out Fourth street, after which I had no further
trouble, and arrived with her safe at the place at which
mother and I had agreed to meet.

Now, the form of that gentleman, with his blue coat
and shining metal buttons, stepping out into the dusty
streets to assist an unknown child, is before my mind vividly as I write, after the lapse of sixty-five years. How
glad I would be to know who he was! But he taught me
a lesson I have steadily acted upon — never to pass a person whom I see in difficulty without rendering him all the
assistance in my power; for the double reason, that I know
from experience how grateful such assistance is to the recipient, and the recipient may be a descendant of the gentleman to whom I feel under lasting obligations.

In the fall of 1810, one of my schoolmates, Jonathan
Paul, whose mother, Esther Paul, was a cousin of grandfather Shoemaker's, and, I think, a sister of George Shoemaker, came home with me from school, to stay all

night. It was delightful to me; he was the first guest I had ever had. We were put to sleep in the guest chamber, over grandfather's room, and enjoyed it greatly. The next morning we were up early, before the moon and stars had disappeared. The beautiful bright day, and his imitating the crowing of. the chickens, are vividly impressed as among the pleasant recollections of my early life.

CHAPTER II.

1811 — Age, 12.

Death of his grandfather — Assists his mother — Anecdotes of early times, related by his grandfather — Family again separated — Uncertainty as to his future — Goes to live with his uncle Comly Shoemaker — Quickness at calculations — Begins the study of geometry—Solves the problem of "The Three Steeples"—Constructs a quadrant—Lesson learned from an accidental picture — Sorrow at the sudden death of a schoolmate —Alarmed by a soldier — Love of nature — Raccoon supper — Childish faith — Conscientiousness — No Young Companions.

On the 16th of Third month, 1811, my dear grandfather closed his long and eventful life, aged eighty-four years. His wife died on the 17th of Third month, 1793. She was very hard of hearing. They had fourteen children, twelve of whom lived to be young men and women. Grandfather outlived all his children but three, Nathan, Jane, and Comly. As before mentioned, I was named after him, and slept with him several years, and to the commencement of his last sickness, which was nine days before his death. I always felt safe in his presence.

In 1809–10, my mother having no help, and my sister being nearly two years younger than myself, I used to help milk, set the table, make the coffee, bake buckwheat cakes, etc., etc., and this part of my education I have valued very much, and have found very serviceable to me to this day. It was a good training of the muscles, too, for my work afterwards in the laboratory and lecture-room, and there is no part of my life to which I look back with greater interest and pleasure, than those days when I was assisting my dear mother in her household duties, she, grandfather, my sister Mary, and I, constituting the family, except the laboring men. As mother rose very early, we would get the milking and other work done in time for school, which was never neglected, except on hog-killing day. The school was vacated in harvest time, when I would work in the field, gathering sheaves, raking after the wagon, handing sheaves on the barrack or mow. I often assisted the men in the mornings and evenings when I went to school, by which I learned to do many things that were afterwards of use.

As already stated, on the 16th day of Third month, my grandfather Shoemaker died. It was Seventh-day morning, and I had gone with uncle Comly to Philadelphia, to market. Uncle had gone over to grandfather's about midnight, it being but a short distance, and although it was manifest that his father's end was near, there were no symptoms of a sudden change.

About 7 o'clock, Benjamin Harper came down to Philadelphia with the sad intelligence that grandfather was dead. It was very unexpected to uncle. Although he remained calm, I could see he felt deeply, and seemingly more, because he was not with him at his close. After considering for some time (I can see him yet, distinctly, as he stood in deep thought, occasionally taking a step or two forward and then back), he concluded to take the horse that Benjamin Harper had ridden down, and return home, leaving us to dispose of the marketing, which we did, and then followed. Dear grandfather's close was very peaceful and quiet, so that those who were sitting up with him did not know when he breathed his last. They had been to his bedside a little time before, when he appeared to be sleeping, but, returning a few minutes after, all was still in death! not a sigh or a groan, or the least struggle, having been witnessed. He was buried in the grave-yard near by, the next afternoon, First-day, the 17th of Third month, the eighteenth anniversary of the death of his wife.

Before leaving the account of my dear grandfather, there are two incidents of his early life, which he related to me, that it seems proper to preserve, as showing the difference between those times and the present. At that time, wolves, catamounts, bears, and other such animals were abundant, and scarcely any man went far from home without his gun or rifle. Nor was it safe to walk after night on account of them.

A company, of whom my grandfather was one, were belated on one occasion and climbed up into a barrack six or eight feet high, to take shelter for the night, each with a loaded gun beside him. In a little time all were asleep but my grandfather. His hearing was very acute, and he heard something come softly, tread, tread, tread, and at length, with one spring, mount the barrack. My grandfather had got his gun ready when he heard the tramp, and the instant the animal lighted he fired at it, which of course aroused his comrades, who inquired what was the matter. He told them something was about to disturb their slumbers, and he gave it a hint not to do so. In the morning they found a large catamount lying dead at the foot of the barrack.

In the other incident, he was returning from Philadelphia one very cold winter evening, and stopped to warm at the " Rising Sun," about three miles from the city. It was then the only tavern on the road. He had been in the tavern but a little time, when another farmer, who had been down with a load of hay, came in, telling what sum he had received for it, and that he had been attacked by robbers, who demanded his money. He took a candlestick that he had in his wagon, and holding it towards them, told them he would give them the contents of that, if they attempted to rob him. They, thinking it was a pistol, immediately disappeared. As soon as he had finished his statement, three rough-looking men, strangers, got up and went out. The landlord told the hay man that he thought from their looks and manner on leaving, there was evil intention, and insisted on his taking a loaded double-barrel pistol with him, which he did. He had gone but a little way before he was stopped, and a demand made for his money. He presented his pistol and told them he would give them the contents of that if they attempted to rob him. "Ah," said they, " we are not afraid of your candlestick," at which he fired one barrel and then the other (not aiming at them), and he saw no more of them, and got home safe.

The time succeeding grandfather's death was a sad one for dear mother and me. The family had again to be broken up, and everything sold, to be divided among grandfather's heirs. He bequeathed to mother an annuity of eighty dollars a year, the interest of five hundred pounds, Pennsylvania currency, to be secured on the farm during her life.

Uncle Samuel Shoemaker of Horsham, about eight miles further up the Old York road from Philadelphia, then invited my mother to live with them, in the same capacity in which she had lived with her father, and she, accepting the invitation, went there with my sister and found a pleasant and kind home, but I never afterwards had the pleasure of a home with her. Her standing injunction, however, was, "Be a good boy," and I well understood what this meant and included.

There was some difficulty in deciding what was to be done with me. I felt deeply interested as I heard this question discussed. Mother wanted uncle Comly to take me, but he already had four of his nephews with him, and there seemed to be no room for me.

John L. Williams, who was a first cousin of my father's, was spoken of, then Isaac Michener, and several others, farmers, and industrious, hard-working, thrifty people ; but dear mother, knowing that though I was well grown for my age, I was not strong (for the bleeding at the nose, and occasionally heart-burn, and sick stomach, still continued), seemed as if she could not consent for me to go to any one of the places named. At length, influenced, as I have always believed, by my mother's tears and entreaties, uncle Comly consented to take me on trial. I have reason to believe he never regretted it, and I know it was a great blessing to me. It was another turning point in my life, in which I have often thought I could see the workings of the "Unseen Hand" that has guided and assisted me all through the many windings and changes of my pilgrimage.

But my situation in my new home was rather a trying one. I was as tall as either of the two older boys, and it seemed only reasonable that I should take my full turn with them, which I did, though my strength was inadequate. Although I was without any companions, the two older boys associating together, yet I determined to bear it and do my part, and I experienced instruction and pleasant seasons when alone, and in the company of my dear uncle. The training my dear mother had given me in housework enabled me to make myself useful to my aunt, assisting in milking, doing the churning, and helping in many ways about the house, so that I gradually gained in her confidence and love, and she soon became as kind to me as a mother.

After some time, aunt Sally's niece, Amelia Bird, came from Philadelphia to live with her aunt. Amelia had been brought up with Caleb and Margaret Shreve, in the city, and the business and ways of country life being new to her, my training enabled me to assist her and be useful to her; she acknowledged her obligations, and became my true and lasting friend.

I was very ready at mental calculation, even then, and when aunt Sally went to market, as she frequently did in busy times, she always took me along to do the calculations for her, as did uncle also, and when he would go to market or to other places on business and sell anything, as a quarter of veal, or a ham, so many pounds at a given price, he would turn to me to know what it "came to," and the purchaser, frequently, would test it with his pencil and always find it right, which pleased uncle.

On one occasion we took a load of oak bark to Thomas's tan-yards, about two miles down the turnpike, where they measured it, reading off the length, breadth, and height in feet and inches, which I kept in my mind. As we rode home, standing up in the wagon, I calculated "in my head" how much was in the load. Uncle took off his hat and chalked on it the result. When we went with another load, he asked one of the two Thomas brothers how much the previous load contained, and when he obtained the result by calculation with the pencil, uncle showed him on his hat that it was the same I had made it, which pleased them both. Uncle told this circumstance to many persons, and it all tended to improve my comfort at home and develop and strengthen the mathematical faculty.

Benjamin Harper and John S. Rose, two of the nephews, soon after went to trades, and I was advanced to the general care of things around the house, barn, etc., and everything was very pleasant. The school was not neglected for as soon as the fall work was done, which was early in the Eleventh month, I was started off to school, to go steadily until the 1st of Fourth month, making five months.

I had got through the arithmetic in the winter of 1810-11, before grandfather died, and the teacher said I must now have surveying and geometry, so uncle Comly bought me Gibson's Surveying and Simpson's Geometry (both of which I have yet, and they have been of the greatest service to me), a case of mathematical instruments, and a box of paints, containing twelve cakes of water-colors, with all of which I commenced school in the fall of 1811.

The teacher, who had been a scholar of Enoch Lewis's, gave me, as an extra, the problem of the "Three Steeples" (now in "Gummere's Surveying," which was not then published). I succeeded, after some days' trial, in obtaining quite an accurate construction to it, which pleased him, and he then showed me how to obtain the point where the observer stood, on the geometrical principle that "angles in the same segment of a circle are equal." This delighted me greatly, the more from the

2

preparation for understanding it which my previous efforts to solve it had given me.

I constructed a quadrant of wood, marking the degrees with ink, with which I took the height of the school-house at Abington, of the sycamore trees at uncle Comly's spring-house, and of numerous other objects; which was interesting and improving "field-work" practice.

After taking the height of the school-house, which was of two stories, and measuring its dimensions, I drew a picture of it, painting the roof of a dark color. While finishing the chimney, I accidentally let the paint-brush fall, the brush part foremost, just on the top of the drawn chimney, making an exact representation of a colored boy's curly head coming out at the top, his features seeming perfect. When I took the ciphering-book home containing this picture of the school-house and of the colored boy, and told them the likeness was made by accidentally letting the paint-brush fall, it was unmistakably manifest that my statement did not receive full credit. Uncle Comly showed it to a number of persons, and when I would tell them that the picture of the head was made by accident, I could see the same evidences of doubt, so I concluded it best to say nothing further about it. I felt somewhat uncomfortable at my word being thus doubted, but I saw there was an excuse for them in the seeming miracle of the accidental correct representation, in every respect beyond anything I could have drawn by effort. The lessons I learned from this incident are: It is not best to discredit the statements of children; and, we should be careful not to tell *too marvelous stories.*

An incident occurred at this time that impressed me very deeply. My most familiar friend at school was James Benezett. He was a little older than I, but slender, delicate, refined and retiring, and I loved him. He sat next the wall, and I next. Like myself, he was very punctual at school, and I inferred he had a good mother. One day in the winter he was not there, and we heard in the evening he had been sent to the post-office on horseback, when the ground was icy, and was found dead in the road, there being evidences that the horse had fallen with him. Poor, dear James! The school felt desolate when thou wast gone! I thought I should never enjoy anything again. For weeks he was almost continually on my mind, at home and at school. But the great soother, Time, came to my relief, and gradually softened the deep grief into tender recollections of the departed one, which abide deep and strong to the present writing.

In the fall of 1812, at the commencement of the war, when I was thirteen, there was a company of soldiers formed in the neighborhood. I had an instinctive dread of war and of soldiers, thinking it was their business to kill people. I was returning to uncle Comly's one evening after dark, and just as I was leaving the turnpike to turn into the lane, I heard a clattering of a horse's feet, and when he got opposite me, the rider, who I could see was a soldier in his regimentals, jumped off, and presenting a large pistol against my leg, said: "Which shall I kill, you or your horse?" There was a boy scared! I plead like a good fellow for the life of both. I seemed to feel the sensation from the touch of the pistol running up my leg, and even yet, when I think of it, the twinges seem revived. He saw that I was much frightened, and told me his name, that of one of our neighbors, whom I well knew, and he asked me to excuse him, as he intended it for a joke, thinking I would have known him by his features, which I should probably have done, had it been daylight. I excused him, and we parted good friends. On getting home, I related the circumstance to uncle Comly and brother James, who thought his conduct was unjustifiable.

It is said that "character is the result of organism, acted upon by environments," and the pressure of my surroundings thus far in life had given sharp outlines to mine. When I went to live at uncle Comly's, having no associates, as already stated, I spent much of the time alone, but never felt lonely. When at leisure, especially on First-days, I rambled into the woods and among the flowers and irrigating streams in what had been grandfather's back meadow, near uncle's, where sister Mary and I had wandered, careless and happy, in former years. It was a beautiful meadow, where grandfather had conducted a stream for a long distance, from a large spring in one corner, along the upper part of a slope. From this stream little branches were permitted at different places to flow and spread over the bank, imparting to the grass a vigorous growth, a "livelier green," and luxuriant appearance, that I have many, *many* times since revisited in my dreams.

I was very fond of watching and listening to the birds, observing the waves on the growing grain and grass, and was charmed with the motion of the trees, and the roar of the wind through a woods or a large pine tree or around the house. All nature pleased me. The moon and the stars delighted me, as did frequently the splendor of the heavens at sunset or sunrise, which last I then had an opportunity of observing more times in a year than I have done since.

A little incident occurred about this time, which so illustrates the character of the middle-aged people of that day, who were actors in it, that I will endeavor to relate it.

A company of them happened to meet at uncle Thomas Shoemaker's, among whom were his brother-in-law, Thomas Thompson, uncle Comly, Samuel Rowland, and perhaps one or two others, and they were talking over old-time pleasures and enjoyments, and among other topics, the relish they had had for a raccoon supper, wondering if it would relish as well now that they were older, and all agreeing that they would like to have an opportunity of trying it. Aunt Hannah at once told them if they would procure one she would cook it, as she used to do, and they should all meet and have the supper there. Uncle Comly said he frequently saw them for sale in the Philadelphia market, and he would procure one for her to dress and cook, and word was to be given to them all, for them and their wives to meet there to supper.

The raccoon was bought; aunt Hannah had it cooked, and all met to partake. They sat down and spoke of how very nicely she had prepared it, how good it was, and how it reminded them of "the days of other years." She urged them to take more — said she feared she had not "prepared it as nicely as they expected." "Oh," they said, "it could not have been better," and they had "eaten very heartily." They "could not eat any more."

She asked them to enjoy themselves around the table for a few minutes, and had the dishes all taken to the kitchen, and a nice baked chicken-pie, with a cup of coffee, and its accompaniments, set on the table. The dear people all set to work as if there had not been a raccoon in the neighborhood, while a mischievous smile played on aunt Hannah's countenance. No one praised the second supper by *words*: it praised itself.

My mother and brother had both drawn my attention, carefully and earnestly, to the everywhere presence of the Good Father, and said, that what we asked of him, *in faith*, we would receive. This was confirmed by the New Testament, which was one of our school-books. Our other reading-books too, which consisted of Murray's Introduction, English Reader and Sequel, and Cowper's Task, all tended to elevate the feelings in religion and inspire trust in God. But the point of difficulty I experienced, was, how to ask "in faith." I was confident in the belief that if I could only *do that* I would obtain what I asked for. I am willing to mention in this connexion, that on several occasions when alone, I first thought, "I have faith;" then said it in a whisper, then *said it aloud*, and in every instance I received what I asked for.

I will mention two cases. One morning uncle and aunt were going in a sleigh to Germantown, about four miles distant. I had never been there, and had a great desire to go; so, when alone, I asked the Good Father to help me in the way I have stated. We went to breakfast, the two older boys sitting next to uncle, on his left, I next below them, and aunt Sally on the opposite side of the table to uncle's right. I was quiet, but felt *confident* I would get to go. While my mind was dwelling on it, aunt Sally said, "Suppose we take Ben along!" Uncle turned to me and said, "Would thee like to go?" "Indeed I would," I answered, and he told me to get ready. I have always believed it was the Good Spirit that moved my dear aunt to make the proposition in my favor. I can see us all at the table as plainly as if it had been yesterday.

Another time there was to be a "cellar-digging" at Joshua Paxson's, who owned the place where I was born, just back of uncle's. Uncle was going after an early dinner, in order to make a long afternoon, and I wished very much to go too, but said nothing on the subject to any one, only to express my desire and faith to the Good Father, in the manner before stated. Soon after we sat down to dinner, arranged as we had been at the breakfast I have mentioned, uncle said, "Which of the boys shall I take with me?" "Oh!" said aunt Sally, "take Benny-boy; he would like to go, I am sure;" and he did, to the rejoicing of my heart. The Good Father, as I fully believed, again prompted her heart and my uncle's too, perhaps, in my favor.

The remembrance of these incidents has been very instructive and encouraging to me. This cellar-digging was on the 1st of Fifth month, and on my way to it, I had to cross a rye-field, and observing the rye was in head, I was reminded of what I had heard my grandfather say, that "There never was a first of May without a head of rye."

I have mentioned we had an early dinner. I was placed with some others to fill the carts with earth, as they came back after being unloaded, and we worked very hard, and by sunset, which is pretty late at that time of the year, I began to feel weak, but the carts still came back, and had to be filled. So they came one after another till it was nearly dark. One of our company was an Irishman, named James McGuire, sent by neighbor Leech, to help. On one of the sons bringing another cart back, James spoke up, "Wullet, why didn't ye bring a *candle wid ye?*" "Oh," said Willet, who took the hint, "let us turn out." I was obliged to Jimmy, as we called him. How plainly these incidents are all before me as I write!

I sometimes said things, or committed acts, that were not right. Then I found no peace at heart, till my mind was brought into a condition to endeavor to avoid a repetition of it, and if I had wronged an individual, to make all the amends in my power, to correct the wrong. Then I would feel reconciled to the Good Father. This was heart-work between the Good Father and my soul.

I was very conscientious and sensitive at this time, and feel it right to relate two incidents where I was checked. I was sent one morning on an errand to Joseph Rover's, who lived on the other side of the county line road from uncle's, and I had to cross a field of well-grown grass. As I went I came across a bird's nest with beautiful blue eggs in it. I wanted them very much, and saw no bird, but when I went to take them I felt a check, as saying, "They are not thine." I went on, and after I had finished my errand and was returning through the same field, I thought, Now if I *happen*, in this large field of grass, to pass over the same nest, without the least design, I will regard it as an evidence that I may take the eggs. In a little time I did come across the same nest with the same blue eggs in it, and felt rejoiced at my good luck, but on stooping down to take them, I felt the same check as before, "They are not thine," and I went on home thoughtful. This too has been of great instruction to me.

Having little to amuse me, and uncle having a gun which he allowed me to use, there was some danger of my becoming fond of gunning. One morning I saw a bird on the top of a large walnut tree. I took my gun, fired at the bird, and down it came. I felt gratified at my success, but this was soon changed to pain. It was a beautiful dove, its eyes bright and clear, with one wing badly broken. What shall I do with it? was the thought. I would have given anything I possessed, could it have been on the tree-top as it was before. The idea of the pain it was suffering from my thoughtless sport, wrung my heart. My feelings would not let me kill it, so I threw it into the pig-pen near by, and the hogs soon put it out of its misery. But I had no more comfort that day, thinking of my cruelty, and I have never taken an interest in a gun since.

At my present home I had little opportunity for social intercourse. There were no young persons there, and no neighbors' children with whom I could associate, and I was not invited to take a meal from home, in the settlement, more than once or twice in the year; then uncle George Hallowell would ask me to go with him from meeting and take dinner with him, aunt Sarah, and their children. This is the only place I can call to mind, of taking a meal in the neighborhood, in the three years and more that I lived at uncle Comly's.

I was permitted to walk on Seventh-day afternoon to see my mother at uncle Samuel's, about eight miles, once in three or four months, perhaps, as often as I wished to do so, and return the next afternoon. Besides this, I was allowed to go about once a year to Philadelphia, to stay over night, at my uncle William's or uncle Atkinson Rose's. I would go to Philadelphia with the market wagon, and walk home, eight miles. This was the extent of my visiting.

I had no opportunity of making anything, and consequently my store of pocket-money was small; but then we lived well, and I had everything I needed, and did not feel the want of more. When I went to see uncle William he invariably gave me something; a Barlow pocket-knife, a "levy," and sometimes a "quarter," which would make me feel rich. Uncle Comly too, when I went with him to market, would get me to drive as we rode home, while he counted the money he had received for the marketing, and he would occasionally ask me to make some calculation in regard to what he had sold by the bushel or pound, and after he was done, he would always give me a "fip" or a "levy." My finances, traveling, and my intercourse with the world, were so far very limited. After my grandfather's death I was sent on an errand to Doylestown, the county-seat of Bucks county, about eight miles further up the Old York road, to get an advertisement of the sale of the farm put in the paper. This was the first time I had seen a printing-press. I was then about twenty-five miles from Philadelphia, northward, and sixteen from uncle Comly's and the place where I was born, which was the greatest distance I ever was from home, until I went to John Gummere's school, at Burlington, New Jersey, when I was eighteen years old. The extent of my journeyings up to that time were, from Philadelphia to Doylestown, northward, and as far as Germantown and Plymouth, six or eight miles east and west. But my mind was not idle, and I had sources of enjoyment in the varied objects of nature, and was never lonely, preferring to be by myself, unless I could be with those from whom I could learn something. The impress of all this was not favorable to a life of social enjoyment, and a deficiency in this respect has been felt ever since, and is to this day.

CHAPTER III.

1814 — Age 15.

Desires to learn a trade — Goes to Nathan Lukens's to learn
carpentering and cabinet-making — First impressions discouraging — Finds himself useful and is reconciled —
Pleased with the business — Articles made by himself —
Reflections — First chemical experiment — Fall from ladder
and consequent suffering — Old colored woman's advice
— Anecdote of colored clergyman — Unable to continue
his trade — At his uncle Comly's — Concludes to qualify
himself for a teacher — Goes to the village school — Solves
difficult problem in geometry — 1817, goes to John Gummere's — Enraptured with chemical experiments — Delightful experiences at Burlington — Favorite sermon by George
Dillwyn — Leaves Burlington.

I wanted very much to learn a trade, to use tools and
be a builder, and many inquiries were unsuccessfully made
for a situation of the kind in Philadelphia. At length,
Nathan Lukens, of Horsham, my mother's first cousin,
offered to take me as an apprentice. He was both a carpenter and joiner, and I was much pleased with the idea
of living with him. I would then be within two miles of
my mother and sister, would belong to the same meeting,
and there would be a probability of my seeing them more
frequently.

It was therefore arranged that I should go there to
learn the trades, and on First-day morning, Tenth month
8th, 1814, I packed up my wardrobe in a pocket-handkerchief, and walked with my bundle up to Nathan Lukens's,

eight or nine miles. I was very tired when I got there.
I had never seen the place, although I had several times
seen him at Uncle Comly's. He was a pleasant man, very
tall, and I found his residence was a tall, narrow, three-
story house, on a high bank called Murdick Hill. The
shop had an open basement, in which his hearse was
standing, ready to convey coffins at funerals. I stood for
some time contemplating it. The aspect of things did not
make a very favorable impression, but after a little while
I ventured into the house and introduced myself to Matilda, his wife, Nathan not being then in, and they not expecting me that day. I found she had a little daughter,
Rebecca, about two and a half years old, which pleased
me, for I had never lived where there was a child since I
lived with my little sister. Nathan came home soon, and
things began to look and feel a little more pleasant and
comfortable.

After tea a neighbor came over, and I was introduced
to her, and when she understood the arrangement, she congratulated Matilda on having me to help her. She could
soon teach me to milk, she said, and that would be a great
relief. I told them that my mother had taught me to
milk years ago, and that I had frequently helped my aunt
Sally to milk, and that I would be glad to give any relief
and assistance to Matilda in my power. How the training my dear mother gave me enabled me to make my way
favorably with those amongst whom I was thrown! Matilda had no help whatever, and it was a pleasure to me to
milk, and to assist her whenever I could. The shop was
near by, and she would send little Rebecca for me whenever my assistance was needed.

I was pleased with the business. Nathan had a lot of
about twenty acres, in which was corn, etc., and when it

was needed we worked on that, where I could make a full hand now, and we would then work in the shop by candle-light.

The hardest part was when we would have to sit up till midnight or after, making and polishing a coffin for a funeral next day, I having to hold the light.

But the business of the trade suited me. The winter was employed in joiner-work in the shop, which was kept warm and comfortable. I made a knife-box for Aunt Sally, dove-tailing the corners nicely, and a self-sustaining lever for uncle Comly to take off the carriage or wagon wheels in order to grease them. Nathan made a fine large secretary of mahogany, with secret places for deeds, bonds, etc., very ingenious and very handsome. Any part that I could do, on that or his other works, he put me at.

Not long after I went there, it was proposed by Nathan that he, his wife and daughter, should go, after an early Seventh-day dinner, to spend the night at his sister's, twelve or fourteen miles distant, and return the next evening, and I would milk the cow and take care of things in the meanwhile. Matilda made me a nice chicken pie for my First-day dinner, and left everything I needed in abundance. Nathan told me what to do in the afternoon, and while I had something to employ me the · time passed pleasantly; but after the milking was done, my lonely supper eaten, and the dishes washed and put away, the prospect ahead of staying in that tall, unshapely house all night alone, was not very comfortable. I went to bed before dark, and, thanks to youth, I did not wake till morning. The day ahead looked so long, with nothing to do! I prepared my breakfast, but had not much appetite. There were no books to read. I went to Horsham meeting, about a mile south, which helped to pass the day;

went home and ate my chicken pie, and after dinner I felt better from the prospect of their soon being back. I had a good fire and a nice supper prepared for them, and it was truly pleasant to have them home again.

They made this visit about once in a month or six weeks while I lived with them, and although it was always dreary in their absence, it was never so much so as at this first time.

In the incidents of my life thus far, there had been little or nothing to develop or strengthen a healthy self-respect, which depends much on a conscious recognition by others of obligations and benefits conferred; and such self-respect is an element of character in which I have always been painfully deficient, partly, as I believe, from my environments in my early life. Still, by the faithful performance of my duty, my actions showed that I respected myself morally, and by Cowper's rule, I was worthy of respect.

One Seventh-day afternoon, in the early spring of 1815, I walked down to see them all at uncle Comly's, and had a delightful visit, and the next afternoon walked back, carrying in my handkerchief six goose-eggs that aunt Sally kindly gave me to put under a hen that was about to sit. Five of them hatched, and they pleased little Rebecca and her mother highly. All five lived, and in eight months they were as large as old geese, and it was very gratifying to Matilda to have them.

In the same spring we worked about at different places, doing carpenter work. We put up a building about two miles off for Nathaniel Richardson. While there, he collected some gas by stirring the leaves, etc., in the bottom of a pond, transferring the gas to a gas pistol, and exploding it, which was the first chemical experiment

I ever saw performed, and it pleased me highly. We did some work for aunt Grace Conard, and all seemed to be progressing very finely.

About the first of the Seventh month, uncle Samuel Shoemaker, with whom mother lived, wanted a new roof put on part of his house. There was to be a great celebration on the "4th of July," at the Billet, which I was desirous of attending, and Nathan said if we got the roof put on I might go. So on Second-day morning, the 3d of Seventh month, we got up and walked, with our tools, over to Uncle Samuel's, two miles, before sunrise, ready to go to work. But the long ladder was needed, which was at Dr. Gove Mitchell's, near by, and I was sent with a horse and cart to bring it. The doctor said there was a board off the gable end of his barn (which was one with stables under), above the square, that he wished nailed on before the ladder went away. I told him if he would let me have a hammer and some nails, I could soon do it. These were procured, and the doctor and Thomas Ackley were holding the ladder, while I went up with the hammer and nails and board. It was so high that I was obliged to stand on the round next to the top one and steady myself by putting my fingers through a knot-hole in the board above. I got all fastened but the extreme end on the left, and was reaching over to drive the nail in it, when they let the ladder slip at the top. I held with my finger to the board above, when *it* came off, and there was no alternative but to tumble head foremost or jump. I chose the latter. The distance was about twenty feet, the ground very hard, and oh! it *did* hurt me! My ankles were both sprained, and the cartilages between the bones of the joints were bruised and swelled so that my laced boots had to be cut to get them off. My back, too, was very much injured. They took me home to uncle Samuel's, with the ladder, and when my mother saw them bringing me back in the cart, she, perhaps naturally, imagined I was killed, and anxiously exclaimed, " Is he dead?" They answered, " No, but he is a good deal hurt by a fall."

There was the greatest amount of pity for the "poor boy," as they called me, from uncle Samuel, aunt Agnes, and the rest. They had a nice lounge fixed up for me in the parlor, and one after another of the old people would sit by me by the hour, to keep the flies off, with a look of the tenderest compassion. Dear mother, too, gave all the spare time she had from her household duties to attend to me.

But, badly as my ankles and back hurt me, my mental sufferings were even more severe. I could not understand it in the dispensations of Providence. I regarded it as a "judgment," while I had been doing the very best I knew, and had not to my knowledge done one wrong thing for over three weeks. There was no one to whom I could make these troubles known, they seeming to be a matter to be kept between me and the Good Father alone, who, I thought, was offended with me, and I kept my head under the cover of the lounge and wept, and wept!

That evening of the 3d I suffered very much with my ankles and back. Dr. Mitchell was very attentive to me. He left some opium pills for me to take. I could not then swallow a pill, but it being cherry-time, I suggested that if they would remove the stone from a cherry and put the pill in its place, I could swallow it readily, which was done. But the skin of the cherry prevented the stomach from acting on the pill, and it produced no effect whatever, so that I passed a very painful and sleepless night. The doctor prescribed long cotton bandages for my ankles, and that water should be pumped on them for ten or fifteen minutes every day, previous to their being bandaged. This was a very painful operation. The cold well-water falling on my ankles caused them to ache exceedingly. After continuing this treatment about three weeks, an old colored woman came by while we were so engaged, and said, "You kill dat chile — pumping cold water so long on his sore feet; let him set on de board over de creek, and hole his feet in de runnin' water, and his ankles *soon* git well." This speech pleased me greatly. Her prescription was followed, and I was carried daily to the creek, instead of to the pump, and my feet and ankles were held in the running stream. They began to gain strength immediately, so that in about another week I was able to walk a little on crutches, and to return to Nathan Lukens's. My back still hurt me, however, but I gradually improved, and got so that I could sit up and churn, and plait straw for hats, and do many little things for Matilda, so that I felt I was not in the way.

Soon after I returned, Nathan's sister Agnes came to stay with them a while, and Joseph Lukens (brother of Dr. Samuel Lukens, of Sandy Spring), and his wife Elizabeth, who was a sister of Isaac Briggs, came to board with them a few months. Joseph and Elizabeth had just returned from a visit to Sandy Spring and Baltimore, and brought home some chinquapins, the first I ever saw, and a smart, active colored boy. They told about the elder Roger Brooke having a pack of hounds and going foxhunting, and of the Patuxent river being so small that at times a man could jump across it, while my idea of a river was obtained from the size of the Delaware and Schuylkill at Philadelphia. They told also of a Balti-

3

more dinner at Yearly Meeting time being "ham and cabbage," while a Philadelphia dinner was roast beef and sweet potatoes. All these things interested me very much, and made my confinement to the house more pleasant. They were very nice people! Everybody loved them. They had sold their place to Nathaniel Richardson before they left for Maryland, and they were now intending to settle in Philadelphia.

One day, while we were at dinner, Nathan came home with his shoulder dislocated. Poor Matilda turned as pale as a corpse. Joseph immediately got up, called for some napkins, got me to help him, and had the shoulder in place in a short time, when Nathan joined us in finishing our dinner.

An incident had occurred just before I was hurt that I neglected to mention, and I will do it here.

Word was given out that a clergyman from Philadelphia, a colored man, would hold a meeting at Loller Academy on First-day afternoon. I obtained permission to go. The house was full. On the bench immediately in front of the preacher's desk were some half dozen persons who had come with the manifest intention of causing a disturbance. One of them had on an imitation of spectacles, cut out of sole-leather; he had these low on his nose, and, with his arms folded across his breast, stared over them at the preacher, who did not seem to notice him. The disorder occasioned by him and his associates seemed to be spreading and engrossing general attention, when the preacher stopped, straightened himself up amidst a profound silence, and, in a calm, distinct voice, said, "We need not be discouraged by such things as we now sorrowfully observe; they are nothing new; for we read of old, when the children of God were gathered together" (raising his voice and shaking his long finger at the leather-spec-tacled man) "*Satan was there also.*" He then resumed his discourse, with the closest attention of the congregation, during which the disturbers slipped quietly out, and we had a solemn, good meeting; the better, probably, from the power the preacher had evinced in the severe and merited reprimand he had given at the commencement of his discourse; from the calm manner in which it was done, and the manifest effect it had had on them, we all felt its power. I have since heard Clay, Randolph, Webster, Calhoun, McDuffie, Burgess, and Benton, all powerful in severity when occasion required it, but I have never witnessed anything like the *power* and *telling effect* of the quotation from Job on this company.

As soon as I was able to get about pretty well on my crutches, I wanted to go down to Pleasant Valley to see uncle Comly and aunt Sally. It seems a little remarkable, with the distinctness of my recollection of other incidents, I cannot remember at all how I got down there. But I did get there, with my crutches, and never returned, except to go up when strong enough (which I remember well) to get some things that I had left, and to bid farewell to the family, it being thought I was such a cripple that I would never be able to resume work at my trade.

Uncle Comly, aunt Sally, and their niece Amelia were particularly kind to me, and seemed pleased to have me back. I could do many little things sitting down, as shell corn, churn, and help in various ways, which it gave me pleasure to do. My ankles and back continuing so weak, it was thought I would never be strong enough for farm work, or any labor, and the idea was suggested that I should qualify myself for a teacher. Accordingly, as soon as I was able to walk so far, I commenced to go to school again at Abington, to Thomas Williams, my father's first cousin.   He was a very nice young man about twenty-one, a Westtown scholar, and fond of literature and science.   It was in his case, as it had been in Dr. Shoe-maker's, my first teacher, that at the earnest solicitation of the school-committee, he consented to take the school (his father living near on a good farm), and it was a blessing to the scholars that he did.

He gave me a mathematical problem that I puzzled over for some time, continually, in my effort, becoming acquainted with some principle in geometry that I had not before known, and at length I succeeded in solving it, which pleased him very much.   It was on a barrack of hay at his father's (I remember it all as if it were yester-day), where I showed him my solution, and he showed me another and neater way, which delighted me.   I will give the problem and both solutions in the appendix.

I advanced in my studies, surveying, algebra, etc., etc., very pleasantly, and I now liked to go to school.   I was a good speller and reader, but a *very* poor writer, which I partly attributed to the treatment I had received from a former teacher, who had some of us scholars who did not write well, to write *two* lines and take them to the teacher, holding the copy-book open, which I did tremblingly, and when he would get time to look at my book — the capital letters particularly — I would sometimes get a box on my ears, and at other times have to hold out my hand to have it paddled with a ruler.   One or the other of these occurred almost every day.   The scholar who sat by me, Thomas Paxson, who was older than I, had a daily difficulty about his "sums" in arithmetic, so we ulti-mately had a standing agreement that I was to do his sums and he to make my capital letters, and in that way

we got along harmoniously with our teacher, if not so im-
provingly to ourselves.

But with Thomas Williams the school was delightful.
His successor, Henry Twining, too, was a pleasant, good
teacher. I never went to any school but Abington, till I
went to John Gummere's when I was eighteen. The
teachers I went to were in this order, in which they taught:
Nathan Shoemaker, Benjamin Moore, his younger brother,
Isaac W. Moore, Joseph Jacobs, John Cavender, Thomas
Williams, Henry Twining, and for a short time, Thomas
Paxson, who had been my former school-mate.

In the early part of the summer of 1817, it was
thought I ought to go to John Gummere's boarding-
school, as a means of becoming better qualified for what
was now looked to as my future avocation, that of teacher.
The proposition for me to go to Burlington school originated with my brother James, and was warmly supported
by his wife, Amelia Bird Hallowell. But where were the
means to come from to pay the expenses? James soon
solved that problem. As already stated, grandfather had
bequeathed to my mother in 1811, eighty dollars a year.
By economy, she had managed to add enough to it, out of
what uncle Samuel paid her, to put one hundred dollars
annually at interest. James immediately proposed that
sufficient of this money at interest should be taken to keep
me at John Gummere's school a year, and provide me with
clothes, to which mother cheerfully consented, as she often
said, " All I want with it is to assist my children."

Now, I have often thought how things come round, as
if the Unseen Hand of the Good Providence were guiding
events, which I have no doubt whatever is the case. The
kindness and generosity of my brother and his wife, in
getting me to Burlington school, were the means of

enabling me to take care of both their sons, and give them a good education, by which they were rendered well-known and useful citizens.

As soon as all was fixed for me to go to Burlington, uncle Comly and aunt Sally went over to enter my name as a student. The school was then full, but they told uncle they would write to him in a few days to the care of Kimber & Sharpless, Philadelphia, informing him when there would be a vacancy. How well I remember my feelings and the suspense, awaiting that letter! At length it came, fixing the time, and uncle went with me punctually, on the day named. We carried a large trunk, containing my books and clothes, from the steamboat wharf up to the school — one of us holding each handle. Uncle did not stay long after he had paid my entrance fee. He bade me farewell, and left me, among entire strangers, and further from home than I had ever been before. Everything was new. I had never before been across the Delaware. It was on Seventh-day too, the very worst time to take a student to school; the time seemed so long before I could get to work. But I well remember feeling some quiet self-respect, from a consciousness that when I got into school I would gain the respect of my classes and the approbation of my teachers, which proved to be eminently the case.

John Gummere was lecturing in his course on natural philosophy, illustrating his subject by experiments (the first I had ever seen) with a large air-pump, electrical machine, magic-lantern, etc., etc., and his brother Samuel on chemistry, with the gases and the compound blow-pipe, of which I had never heard, and I was perfectly delighted, *enraptured* with the unfolding of what appeared to be a new life, in a new world of great beauty, and filled with wonder and magnificence, of which before I had had no conception. And now, for the first time, I began to see that my fall from the ladder at Dr. Mitchell's barn, three and a half years before, was a " blessing in disguise ; " and although I have experienced much bodily suffering, and do to this day, from its effects, I am deeply grateful to the Good Father for giving such a turn to my life, as brought me into a better acquaintance with his works, and a higher appreciation of "the true, the beautiful, and the good."

Burlington was an improving place to me in more respects than in the school opportunities. The delightful walks on Green Bank along the shore of the Delaware river, and out Main and Broad streets, where were the fine residences of George Dillwyn and Elias Boudinot (author of "The Star in the East"), and others, surrounded by a great variety of flowers and ornamental shrubbery, the impress of all of which, it being new to me, and I of an age to appreciate it, was very favorable to my feelings and the culture of my higher nature. I well remember the thrill of delight I would experience in my rambles (which were generally alone), when some new beauties, or sweet fragrance wafted from the flowers, would gratify and enliven the senses.

I became very fond, too, of attending meeting, where were George Dillwyn, John Cox, and some half-dozen other ministers, of more than ordinary eminence, one or more of whom favored us with an interesting discourse at every meeting.

We all liked to hear George Dillwyn and John Cox, portions of whose discourses I remember to this day. One of George Dillwyn's has been so instructive to me through life, that I will here give it in nearly his own words; he never said much at a time. "When I was a young man I "wrote a little book" (*Dillwyn's Reflections*), "and in it "I put a little *varse*" (he spoke it very broad), "which con-"tains the sum of the practical truth needed by man: 'Do thy best and leave the rest.'" I was fond of poetry, and when he spoke of "a little verse," I fixed myself for remembering it, expecting it to be *four* lines, at least, and when it came out the simple "Do thy best and leave the rest," I felt almost provoked, but the solemnity and emphasis with which it was delivered made a deep impression, and the latter part of it, to "leave the rest" to the Good Father after we have "done the best" we could, has been a strength and encouragement through my life since.

But the time came for me to leave Burlington. This was done with regret for two reasons. I had formed some very pleasant acquaintances among the students; with Reynell Coates, Thomas Cook, David Ogden, Jesse Wilson, and others; and then I had no home to go to.

I went to uncle Comly's, and spent my time there and at brother James's (being made cordially welcome at both places) for some weeks, but I was not yet strong enough to enter upon farm work, and the uncertainty of my being able to find anything to do to make a living weighed heavily upon my feelings. This was a trying period of my life, perhaps the most so I had then experienced. I would take a book and spend most of the day in the woods, reading and thinking. Things passed on in this way for some time, when one First-day, John R. Perry, from Westfield, New Jersey, a cousin of my mother's, was at meeting, and on seeing me, inquired who I was, and came to speak to me.

I think, from what afterwards occurred, some one must

have given him some account of me, and told him that I would like to find a school to teach, for two days after, he and Abraham Lippincott came to uncle Comly's and invited me to go over and take the Westfield school, then without a teacher. This proposition, as may be judged, I cheerfully accepted. I have often thought the " Unseen Hand " of the Good Father came to my aid in this emergency, by influencing the hearts of others in my favor, and cast my lines in pleasant places.

CHAPTER IV.

1818.

Takes the Westfield school — Pleasant winter — Efforts to improve his handwriting — Applies for position of teacher at Fair Hill Boarding School — Meets school commissioners in Baltimore — Receives the appointment — Difficulties of journey to Fair Hill — Attends Sandy Spring meeting for first time — Duties and responsibilities — Lonely walks and poetical address to the Cedar — Death of Anna Thomas — Meets Margaret E. Farquhar for the first time — Reminiscences of Samuel Thomas — Sickness of Samuel Thomas — Goes home on a visit — Sad experiences — Death of his brother James — His sister Mary returns with him to Fair Hill — Death of Samuel Thomas — Trying times for the school — Deborah Stabler's assistance — Mournful thoughts — Poem.

I went to Westfield that same week, the fall of 1818, when I was a little over nineteen. It was the Monthly Meeting school that I was placed in charge of, and I was under a nice committee of men and women Friends. For a short time I boarded with Abraham and Abigail Lippincott, near the school-house and meeting-house, and afterwards at John R. Parry's, whose wife Letitia was a sister of Oliver H. Smith, of Indiana, who married my first cousin, Mary Brumfield. I passed a very pleasant and improving winter, and continued the school (which was large, sometimes having as many as eighty scholars of both sexes, some young men and women older than myself), till the summer vacation. Charles Lippincott came to study surveying, and when the school was large he assisted me for his schooling, and I found him a very efficient assistant and pleasant companion. Mary Smith, Letitia's sister, was also a pleasant companion at home.

I felt now that I was doing something for myself, and the kindness of the Friends where I boarded and others in the neighborhood, and the respectful manner in which I was treated by them, all made a very favorable impression.

The residence of John R. Parry, with whom I boarded, was about a mile from the school-house, with a pine woods almost the entire distance, through which was a foot-path. It was my practice to spend my evenings at the school-house, pursuing my studies, reading, etc., and walk home about nine o'clock through these pines, which was a source of great enjoyment to me, especially the "green pines' waving top" and the shadow it made by moonlight. My friends with whom I boarded felt an apprehension that I might be waylaid and robbed of my watch, but I entertained no fear, and was never disturbed.

At the close of school I parted from these kind and valued friends, those with whom I had boarded, the school committee and others, with reluctance. I felt that I had developed very much within the two years just past, and that a new world had been opened to me.

As I have before stated in this memoir, I was very deficient in my handwriting, and I resolved to use the first money I had earned in an endeavor to improve it. Accordingly I went to Philadelphia, and entered the celebrated writing-school of Benjamin Rand, boarding with Ann Burr and her mother, where I was pleasantly situated. I kept up a correspondence with some of my Burlington schoolmates, David Ogden, of Swedesborough, New Jersey, and Jesse R. Wilson, of Loudoun county, Virginia, and with my sister Mary, who was a scholar at Westtown boarding-school.

About the time my term of writing expired, in the early fall of 1819, I received a letter from Jesse R. Wilson, who was then teaching a school in Alexandria, Virginia, advising me to apply for the situation of teacher in Fair Hill boarding-school, then recently opened, which I did, accompanying my application with a letter of recommendation from Charles Shoemaker, who had once lived in Occoquan, and whom the committee all knew; also, one from the school-committee of Westfield, where I had taught the previous winter. My letter was addressed, by Jesse's advice, to Samuel Thomas, superintendent, who made a very respectful reply, and invited me to meet the school-committee in Baltimore, at the time of the then ensuing Yearly Meeting. This I informed him I would do, and accordingly, a week or more before the time of the Yearly Meeting, I went down to Alexandria to make a visit to Jesse, whose company was very congenial to me, as I believe mine was to him. I boarded with Mahlon Schofield* (Andrew's brother and William and Ann Scofield and Elizabeth Hopkins's father), at the upper end

---

* Now spelt Scofield.

of King street, which was in that day thronged with four
and six-horse wagons. Jesse introduced me to a number
of Friends, the widow Hartshorne and her family, Friend
Wanton, George S. Hough, Rachel Painter, who taught
school there, and several others.   This was my first
acquaintance with Alexandria, and I found it a very
agreeable place. When I was going to Alexandria, I
stopped all night in Washington, and as I was walking by
the President's house in the evening (James Monroe being
President), there was a most brilliant display of the
Aurora Borealis, the first I ever saw, and I was willing to
interpret it as an omen in my favor.   On my way back
from Alexandria to Baltimore, I spent some time in Washington city, and happened to fall in with a person from the
south, at the "Indian Queen" (now Brown's) hotel, who
seemed to take a liking to me, and was going in a hack
around to the Capitol, Navy Yard, and other places of
interest, where he had been well acquainted a few years
before, and he invited me to accompany him as his guest,
which I cheerfully did.   It was a day of great interest and
instruction to me.   Under his guidance I saw a vast
amount that was new.   Among others of the notables, he
pointed out to me General Jackson on horseback, the out-
line of whose tall, spare form I have with me to this day.

There was one incident with my new acquaintance
(whose name I am unable to recall), which I have always
been surprised at, when the remembrance of it has come
before me.   In the evening he invited me to take a place
in his bed, which I accepted.   As we were preparing to get
into bed, he showed me a belt around his body in which he
carried his money, and it then contained a great many
thousand dollars.   He was a Southern merchant going
North to pay debts and buy goods.   What induced him to

show his money, and where he kept it, I never could imagine. But all was safe when we arose. The next morning we set off together in the stage for Baltimore. General Winder, who had been in the battle of Bladensburg, was in the stage, and my friend knew the General, though the General did not know him, revived some reminiscences of the battle as we passed the battle-ground, which it was evident the General would be glad should be forgotten, as for instance bullet-holes in the *top* of a high house, shot by the American soldiers at the British when they were *crossing* the bridge.

We reached Baltimore, and I met the school committee at Elias Ellicott's (I think it was). There were Edward Stabler, Gerard T. Hopkins, Samuel Thomas, Isaac Tyson, and several others present. They asked me very few questions; seemed well satisfied with my recommendations, especially with that of Charles Shoemaker, which was pretty full, and told of my having been at John Gummere's school. It appeared to me that they left the decision of the case very much to Samuel Thomas, the superintendent. I remember Edward Stabler's saying emphatically in the committee, that if I was appointed teacher, he would send his son Robinson, who was then well-grown.

It was ultimately concluded that I was to enter on duty at Fair Hill, on the 1st of the Twelfth month, then ensuing, as mathematical teacher, that being the time fixed for the girls' school to open, under Margaret Judge. Samuel Myers was the teacher already there, under whom the school had been opened, on the 1st of the preceding Fifth month, 1819.

In the latter part of the Eleventh month, 1819, I left my old neighborhood at Cheltenham, Montgomery county,

Pennsylvania, for Fair Hill, Montgomery county, Maryland.

My expenses for board and schooling in Philadelphia, and getting a suitable outfit for my new home, and some books, as Cowper's and Ossian's Poems, of David Allison, in Burlington, had pretty much exhausted my savings at Westfield, and I borrowed twenty-five dollars from brother James, to pay my expenses, for which I gave my note, with interest.

On arriving at Baltimore I went to Isaac Tyson's to inquire how I should get to Fair Hill. " Why," said he, "there is *no* way ; it is the most out-of-the-way place in the world." I felt much discouraged, which perhaps he perceived. He walked the room for some time, seemingly in deep thought, and then sat down and wrote a letter to Samuel Snowden, of Indian Spring, which he read to me, telling who I was, and asking him to assist me in getting to Fair Hill. He then told me to take the letter to Samuel Snowden, who lived not far from the hotel he named, where the stage stopped, and Samuel would take or send me up, a distance of fourteen or fifteen miles. This I at once *felt*, but did not *say*, I could not do. I took the letter, thanking him for his kindness, but resolved to make further inquiry at the stage office, to ascertain whether I could not get there by public conveyance. I found a person who *seemed* to know all about the country. He told me to take the stage to Washington, and that a stage went from there to Rockville, which was near Fair Hill. On this advice I paid my fare to Washington and took my seat in the stage, but did not feel quite easy.

We stopped to change horses at a hotel, near where Laurel is now, and seeing a company of men, I made known to them my situation, where I wished to go, and what I had been advised to do. They appeared to know the country, and said I would be nearly as far from Fair Hill when I got to Rockville as I then was, after a stage travel of nearly thirty miles. There was but little time to deliberate, so I explained the matter to the driver, who seemed interested in my favor, had my trunk taken off, and kindly returned me the difference between the fare to Washington and to that place.

In the little time I had to decide to have my trunk taken off the stage, I never thought to inquire whether I could find a conveyance to take it and me the fourteen miles I still wished to go, and I was greatly disappointed and surprised to find there was no such thing as a carriage or carryall to be had in that neighborhood. It was Seventh-day afternoon, and *that* was wearing fast away. I was greatly perplexed, but at length a man said he had a horse and cart that would take my trunk, and I could either ride or walk, as I chose, and he would send a boy to take me and my trunk for five dollars. It seemed the only thing I could do, so I accepted his terms. He said the boy knew the way. I urged him to get us off soon. He started off on his horse in a gallop (I can see him yet leaning forward, his feet dangling below the little horse's body), but it was nearly sunset before he came back with the horse and cart and a colored boy, who looked to be about fifteen. The boy had but one line to his horse, and it was truly a very poor and unsightly outfit. But I paid the man his five dollars, and we set off, I walking. It soon became dark, when I found the boy was uncertain about the road, it being through old fields and pine bushes, and no house to be seen, or person of whom to inquire. Soon our road led to a stream, which I suppose was the Patuxent. The boy wanted to cross it. I told him I was confident from

the directions I heard his master give him, that we were
not to cross so large a stream. He took my advice not to
cross it, and wound his way deviously through pine bushes
and old fields a long time, which seemed longer probably
from the uncertainty in regard to our making any way towards the place I desired to reach, till at length, near
nine o'clock, I saw a light in a house not far from the road,
the first house we had seen since we set off on this journey,
and we had not seen a single person. I went up to inquire the way. It proved to be William Thomas's, and I
was rejoiced to find that we were within three or four miles
of Fair Hill, with a good plain road leading to it, so that
there was no danger of getting lost again. The person I
saw there told me how to know Fair Hill when I came to
it. I called at Sandy Spring store as I went by, to have
my instructions about the road renewed and confirmed.

It was near ten o'clock when I arrived at Fair Hill.
Samuel Thomas was the only one of the family up, and he
was just about retiring. The boy assisted me to carry my
trunk in, and Samuel showed him where to put his horse
and find feed for it. I was very tired, but I felt brightened
up on seeing a person I had met before, so, after explaining
"the journey of the day," and why I came in that style,
all of which, from knowing the place where the stage had
stopped, and the country between, he seemed fully to comprehend, I was glad to retire.

The next morning (First-day), we all met at the break-
fast-table, there being two tables. Samuel Thomas sat at
the end of one of them and his wife at the other end. He
placed me at the other table, near him, to his left, Margaret Judge being opposite to me; then the scholars filled
up the other part of the tables.

As was customary at the school, breakfast was taken

without conversation; then there was a silence, after which the scholars left two by two. I was pleased with the order. When they had all gone I walked to the other end of the table to shake hands with the women Friends. Such was my introduction to Fair Hill, which is all distinct in my recollection.

A little incident occurred on this First-day, that I think it proper to relate, as illustrative of the characters of both Samuel Thomas and myself. We had some free, pleasant conversation before meeting, and when meeting time came, we set off, Anna Thomas and Margaret Judge on the back seat, and I by Samuel on the front seat. When we went into meeting he showed me where to sit, under the gallery next the women, facing the meeting (where Robert R. Moore sits now), and, to my surprise, he went up into the gallery, and after a little while, to my still greater surprise, he arose and preached! I had always had a profound reverence for preachers, there never having been one with whom I was well acquainted, and my feelings were much solemnized. I looked carefully over all the conversation we had had to see if there had been anything too free and light.

In this condition of mind, I took my seat by him in the carriage to return to Fair Hill, when, after riding a little way, he suddenly clapped his hand on my knee, and said, "How did thee like the sermon?" What reply I made, I know not, but, after the shock it occasioned was over, his genial manner, consideration for my situation, and kindness of heart, gained my fullest confidence.

It was about the same time of year that I had entered Burlington school as a scholar, that I now, two years after, entered Fair Hill as a teacher, and what great changes had occurred in the intervening two years!

4

I felt lonely at Fair Hill. My associate teacher, Samuel Myers, was a married man, and at all spare time was with his family at Sandy Spring. Of all the inmates of the large family, or of the inhabitants of the neighborhood, Samuel Thomas was the only one I had ever seen before I went there to live. The duties and responsibilities that I felt to be resting upon me, in the care and instruction of the scholars, several of whom were older than myself, seemed heavy, almost to oppression! With feelings such as this state of things was calculated to produce, I used to wander through the fields and woods in the evening after dark, or sit alone in my school-room.

When I walked out, my favorite resort was a thick clump of bushes, in the centre of which stood a large cedar, at whose foot I passed many hours in thoughtful, and I have reason to hope not unprofitable, reflection. Some time afterwards I learned that this venerable cedar was the centre of the former private burying-ground of the Dorsey family, who had owned the property, and whose remains were mouldering into dust around it. It was to this cedar I wrote, in 1820, an "Address," which was published in 1821 (in the second volume of the "Rural Visitor," page 226), by David Allison, in Burlington, New Jersey. Some one has torn the leaf containing the "Address" out of my copy of the Visitor, and I can give from memory only the opening and closing lines :

> I to the cedar sing, whose dark green boughs,
> Extending wide into the open field,
> And, as with melancholy stooping low,
> Wave in the breezes o'er the slumbering dead.
> Thou first received my notice, as I strayed
> At evening's stillness through the lonely fields,
> With thoughts contemplating a future life,
> And various scenes that troubled us in this ;

Till by thy beauty, viewed at distance, led
T' approach still nearer thy majestic height,
(Not knowing, then, what lowly lay beneath),
I found thy shade congenial to my mind.

*   *   *   *   *   *

Yes, sombre cedar, when I pass thee by,
Or morn, or noon, or in my evening walks,
May'st thou e'er bid me think, life soon will pass,
And I, if not beneath thy outstretched arms,
Will somewhere else a bed of earth demand,
That thus I may be blessed my life to pass,
Pleasing to God, and gainful to my soul.

The following four lines were written about the same time under similar feeling:

Soothed with the pleasing calm of solitude,
To lonely valleys, woods, and wilds I stray,
Where naught disturbs my contemplative mood,
And hours, as moments, pass improved away.

I have ever since regarded it as an unspeakable favor, in which I have often thought the guidance of the Unseen Hand was manifested, that so early in life, I had the wise counsels, pure example, and religious influence of those three precious Friends and devoted servants of the Most High, Samuel and Anna Thomas, and Margaret Judge. They were much beloved by the inmates of the family, teachers, scholars, and domestics.

The winter of 1819–20 passed on pretty pleasantly. We had a good many nice students, David Brown, John Smith, Henry S. Taylor, Thomas Stabler, and Samuel Peebles, all older than myself, and Robert Crew, George Winston, Isaac Briggs, Artemus Newlin, Robinson and Thomas Stabler, and others about my own age; all was harmonious and pleasant.

But soon this happy condition of things was broken. In the latter part of the winter 1819–20, dear Anna Thomas was attacked in the night with paralysis. She had collected with the boys on the previous evening, First-day, and had spoken to them very impressively. Her husband was in Baltimore, attending Quarterly Meeting. A little after midnight, Margaret Judge called me to go over to Brooke Grove to get some one to go to Baltimore for Samuel, which I did, and he arrived before sunset that evening. She lingered under the effects of the stroke until relieved by death on the 19th of Fifth month, 1820. This was a great blow to the school and to all its inmates, and especially to her loved and devoted husband. She was a lovely woman, and the life of her husband seemed buried in her grave. He attended to his duties, but never seemed the same man afterwards. To him the light of the outer world seemed extinguished.

In the spring of 1821, the girls' school increased so much that another female teacher was needed, and the committee obtained Margaret E. Farquhar to fill the situation, and take part of the scholars in a separate room. She had been to the school on a visit during the preceding winter, and she and her cousin Mary Briggs (now Mary B. Brooke) came into my school-room to see the "new teacher." On their leaving the room, Margaret said to her cousin, " He is no beauty, anyhow."

Samuel Myers, who had accepted the situation only temporarily, then leaving, Charles Farquhar, Margaret's brother, was appointed in his place. They both entered upon duty as teachers at the same time, about the 1st of Third month, 1821. The school was well filled, and everything appeared to be proceeding satisfactorily and harmoniously.

I have already mentioned an incident illustrative of the character of Samuel Thomas, which was an original one. I have never since met with one like it; open, deep, philosophical, social, and profoundly religious. He would frequently come into the upper parlor when I was there alone, and enter into conversation. One day he said, " Benjamin, I was a Methodist preacher once" (he talked very fast), "and on one occasion I rose and preached, and the words flowed to my astonishment, and I preached with such power that I felt sure I had preached some persons to heaven. After I sat down, I thought I could see where I could mend it, and I stood up and preached and preached and *preached,* till I felt sure I had preached them back again. Why," said he (putting the ends of his thumbs and fore-fingers together, forming a ring on each hand), " the two sermons would not fit together any more than two rings or links " (rubbing the rings he had formed together). " Ah," said he, " it is a great thing to learn to let ' well done ' alone; by attempting to mend it you spoil it."

Another time he came in and sat by the front window. After a little time he said, " Benjamin, if a person blusters or gets angry, when an opinion is expressed different from his, it is certain evidence that he is not *sure* he is right. If he *knows* he is right himself, he may feel pity for the other's ignorance, but he would have no feeling of anger or displeasure. To illustrate: Yonder is a peach-tree ; I have just eaten a peach which I pulled from it. If I point to it, and tell a man that it is a peach-tree, and he contradicts me, and says it is an apple-tree, it may provoke a feeling of commiseration for his positiveness and ignorance, but nothing like hostility or anger."

On another occasion, he sat down and said, " Benjamin,

I once owned slaves. I thought I could not get along without them. After a time, it was impressed upon my mind, that I ought to set one man free. He had served me faithfully. I put it away,—he was the very one I could not spare. It *would* come up again — kept me awake — I could find no peace — the wakefulness night after night increased. One morning I got up before day, having slept none, rode down to Annapolis, brought home the man's 'freedom papers;' told him he had served me long and faithfully, and giving him his papers, informed him that he was now free. Benjamin," (stroking his hands over the region of his heart), " I did feel *so* comfortable, and I slept that night. A few months after my mind became troubled in the same way about another slave, a woman, and I had to pass over the same ground again, and found no relief till I went to Annapolis and brought home and delivered to her her ' freedom papers ;' then I did feel relieved, and thought the work was all accomplished, but in this I was mistaken. It kept on in the same way, one at a time, until I had liberated six or eight, all but one boy about sixteen. *He*, I thought, certainly would be left to me, and I was confirmed in this opinion by my feeling no uneasiness for a longer period than on either of the other occasions. At length symptoms began to appear. I resisted them, thought I could not spare *him;* he slept near my room ; saddled my horse ; waited on the table. *I could not spare him.* With such reasonings I could keep it off in the day time, while I was blustering about, but at night the thought of him and his bondage and his uncertain condition if I should die, would come and take away my sleep and my peace. So one morning before daylight, I started down to Annapolis and got his 'freedom papers,' and gave them to him. Then, Benjamin, I *did* feel confortable, and have never had any slave sickness since. How kind the Good Father was, in not laying all this burden on me at once, which in all probability would have crushed me, but he just moved in it gradually, as I was able to bear it, and I cannot express how grateful I now am to him for the blessing and favor."

As already stated, the happy condition of things at Fair Hill was soon to be broken. It was decided that I was to take my two weeks' vacation about the middle of the Ninth month, and I had looked forward to this, my first visit home, with great interest and the anticipation of much pleasure, particularly in seeing my brother James, and my mother, who was then living with him and his wife Amelia; also in seeing uncle Comly and aunt Sally.

Deborah Stabler, whom the committee had appointed in Anna Thomas's place, gave me what assistance I needed in getting ready.

Before the time arrived for me to go, Samuel Thomas was taken seriously ill with bilious fever. I had written to my relatives that I expected to get to Philadelphia on Seventh-day evening, but Samuel Thomas was so ill that it was thought best for me not to leave. He seemed to like me to sit up with him, which I did the greater part of three nights. He quoted portions of the Psalms almost continually. He repeated the tenth verse of the 90th Psalm with great emphasis: "The days of our years are threescore years and ten; and if, by reason of strength, they be fourscore years, yet is their strength, labor and sorrow; for it is soon cut off and we fly away." His quotations and expressions were all encouraging and hopeful, yet resigned to whatever way his sickness might terminate; though, if it accorded with the Divine will, it seemed to be his choice to follow his beloved wife to the land of spirits.

On First-day night he seemed better, and it was thought I might venture to set off on my vacation on Second-day morning, which I did. I arrived in Philadelphia on Third-day morning, when I immediately (there being no stage running out at that time of day) walked out to uncle Comly's, nine miles from the wharf. I found aunt Sally in the house as usual, but soon there seemed to be something the matter. She told me uncle was at the barn. I went there, and when he saw me he burst into tears! As soon as he could compose himself, he told me how very sick my dear brother was. James, he said, had gone to Philadelphia to meet me on Seventh-day, although not then well, and had stayed till nearly dark, when the last Baltimore boat arrived for that day, and I was not there, which was a great disappointment to him.

I endeavored to comfort dear uncle, and told him I hoped James would soon be better. "Ah," said he, "thee does not know his condition, nor how ill he is;" and he proposed that we should go up to Shoemakertown and see him and the others, which we did. Dear mother met me in tears, but said nothing. Sister Amelia said, "Ah, brother, if thee had come on Seventh-day as we expected, how glad we would have been! James did want to see thee so much." I tried to encourage them to hope for the best, and sister Amelia and uncle went with me to his room. I found him under a high fever, talking incessantly in wild delirium. He knew me; called me by name, and asked me why I did not come on Seventh-day. He said he was going to die. I told him I hoped not. He looked me sternly and inquiringly in the face, and said, "Is thee willing to die for me?" I could not say I was.

I found what dear uncle had told me was correct. I did not know how ill he was, nor his condition; so restless, talking so loudly, and not being able to sleep at all.

In a few days, perhaps a week, he died. Two young men had offered to come and sit up the night before the burial. I told the family, who were all worn out, to go to bed, and I would remain with him till the young men came. The family retired. There was to be ice and camphor put on some parts of the body every hour through the night. From some misunderstanding, the young men did not come (for which they afterwards expressed great regret), and I remained with him alone, attending to these services all night, and it was a night of great thoughtfulness and solemnity to me. He was buried the next day, in the grave-yard at Abington meeting house. I turned from his grave with a heavy heart. A kinder brother no man ever had. He was buried toward the latter part of the Ninth month, 1820, and his second son, who was born the following First month, was named James S., after his father.

The time of my vacation expired before his funeral, and I wrote to Fair Hill that I would be delayed two or three days in getting home, and explained to them the reason. I had thought a great deal about Samuel Thomas in the two weeks that had elapsed since I left him, but there being then but one mail a week between Sandy Spring and Philadelphia, I heard nothing from him, but hoped he was better.

It was concluded that my sister Mary should return with me and enter Fair Hill school as a scholar, although she had been at Westtown a year. On our way down the Chesapeake at night, our boat ran aground in a great rain storm, which alarmed the persons in the ladies' cabin very much. They, understanding that Mary had a brother on board, sent her to inquire of me what was the matter. I saw that she was somewhat alarmed, and wishing to indicate by my answer, that I thought there was no danger, I told her to tell her companions we had stopped out of the rain.

We arrived safe in Baltimore the next morning, and I hired a hack to take us to Fair Hill. When we got a little beyond Ellicott's Mills, from Baltimore, we met a hack with Gerard T. Hopkins and some others in it, who told me that Samuel Thomas was dead, and they were just returning from his funeral. This intelligence seemed almost more than I could bear. I was never more to see that noble face. He was one of the best men I ever knew, and one of the kindest friends I ever had, and the main support of the discipline of the school. He died on the 30th of the Ninth month, 1820, aged about fifty-five years. (See in Friends' Miscellany, Vol. 6, pp. 130 and 133, the memorials of Anna Thomas and of Samuel Thomas).

We arrived safe at Fair Hill, and met with a cordial reception. They all seemed glad to have me back again to assist in bearing the increased duties and responsibilities which these severe and mysterious dispensations imposed upon the teachers, and which brought them all into a feeling of lasting unity and near sympathy, which nothing but death could dissolve.

These were trying and sad times for the school. The heads of both the girls' department and the boys' department, being thus removed in the very infancy of the institution, only a year and five months after it was first opened, was a great shock to it, and a break upon all the arrangements of the concern.

As already stated, after the death of Anna Thomas, that valued Friend, Deborah Stabler, whom we all loved, consented, on invitation of the committee, to take her place temporarily, as superintendent of the girls'· department, which was a great comfort and strength to us all.

The duty had several times devolved upon me, at that early age, to sit head of the meeting on the men's side, in Samuel Thomas's absence, and I felt the weight and responsibility of the position, under which the desire was that I might be favored with right qualification The impress was favorable.

Philip Dennis, who owned the farm where Roger Brooke, jr., lived and died, was invited by the committee to take charge of the farm and out-door affairs. In Deborah Stabler we men teachers found a wise and safe counsellor; and although we felt deeply the loss that we and the school had sustained, and had it brought daily to our remembrance, when we needed advice or assistance, yet we still got along very comfortably and harmoniously through the fall and winter. I spent a good deal of my time in my school-room (which was in the northwest corner of the main building), especially in the even ings, when the remembrance of the loss of my dear brother would come before me, in seeming harmony with the dirges of the winds around the house. It was at this time (winter of 1820–21), that I wrote the following stanzas, which were published in the " Rural Visitor " in 1821, volume 2, page 206:

> I love, at eve, the solemn moan,
> Of winds, as 'round my walls they're blown,
> 'Tis music of the loveliest tone
>   Of all I know :—
> It minds me of the time that's gone,
>   Long, long ago!

Once blessed with friends, with hope, with peace,
Each day beheld my joys increase,
Delights, I thought, would never cease
     Round me to flow ;—
But they to care and grief gave place,
     Long, long ago !

I saw my kindred round me fall,
My brother mantled in his pall,
Then deemed terrestrial things were all
     An empty show :—
I'll fit me for the heavenly hall,
     And to them go.

The first three lines of the second stanza have reference to the latter part of the time I lived at grandfather's, which was the most free and happy portion of my life.

CHAPTER V.

1821.

The wren's nest — Books read at Fair Hill — Resignation as teacher — Return to Pleasant Valley — Anecdote of Fair Hill — Visit to John Gummere, where congenial occupation is found — Applies for situation at Westtown and is accepted — Visit to relatives — Reflections — Introduced to future scholars — A stroke of diplomacy — Successful management of unruly student — Anecdote of the key — Reading Addison's Spectator — A small legacy and the use made of it.

In the spring of 1821 I frequently sat at the west front window, in the upper parlor, when there would be nobody else there, and noticed a wren was building its nest on the string-piece that supported the lower end of the rafters over the front porch, and having nothing to light on, it found great difficulty in accomplishing its undertaking. Margaret E. Farquhar (my future wife) observed the trouble it daily had, and either at her suggestion, or voluntarily, I cannot now remember which, I nailed half a flat ruler for the wren's accommodation, which ruler is still there. The bird seemed to enjoy the convenience, and it was a comfort to me to see how much it was aided by it.

During the time I was at Fair Hill, I read Clarkson's "History of the Abolition of the Slave Trade," which I found very interesting; his "Portraiture of Quakerism," then recently published, several copies of which were presented to the school; "The Mountain Muse," from the Brookeville library, by Daniel Bryan, whom I afterwards knew favorably at Alexandria; and Cowper's Poems in three volumes, Ossian's Poems in two volumes, and some other books, which I bought at David Allison's, in Burlington, and have yet, they having been my companions in my various places of abode since.

I kept on the best I could with my many duties, till the meeting of the committee in the Ninth month, when I believed it to be right and best, for various reasons, to resign my situation as teacher at Fair Hill, and look out for a home elsewhere, which I did. My resignation was accepted, of which Roger Brooke and Gerard T. Hopkins very respectfully and feelingly informed me, and I left the next morning.

I felt my being again adrift in the world, having no place to which I could of right go. My brother was dead; my mother had gone to keep house for uncle George Williams, my grandmother Hallowell's brother; I had no

home! I knew, however, that I would always find a
welcome with my valued uncle Comly and aunt Sally
Shoemaker, who felt like father and mother to me, and
where I knew how to make myself useful. I did not
feel discouraged, for I had gained valuable experience,
and I never doubted having done right in leaving Fair
Hill. So I made my way to Pleasant Valley at once.
Uncle did not quite like my giving up my place at Fair
Hill, where I was getting four hundred dollars a year,
but he was none the less kind, and soon became satisfied.

One incident at Fair Hill I ought to mention for the
instruction it contains, as well as to show the discernment and tact of superintendent McPherson. The boys
had been noticed, for several days, to be very busily engaged beyond a clump of trees in the "bounds," but as
there was nothing there that could be injured, no notice
was taken of it. One day two students came running to
the superintendent, almost out of breath, and said, "Oh,
superintendent, the old sow is in a deep hole down in
the 'bounds;' come see." He went with them, and on
arriving there, at once took in the whole situation. The
animal would weigh some three hundred pounds, and the
hole was five or six feet deep, so that it would be attended with no little difficulty to get her out. After
reflecting a little time, he said, "Now, boys, you have dug
a grave for the old beast, now *bury* her." This was a
grand idea for them. At it they went in fine glee, pushing in the earth with spades, paddles, shingles, and those
who could not obtain either of them pushing the earth
in with their feet. But the old beast would not stay
buried. As they put earth in the hole on her, she would
rise above it, and when the grave was full she quietly
walked out. This was all play to them. Had he *ordered*

them to fill up the hole they had dug, in order that she might get out, this would have been *work*, and it would have been a long, time in all probability, before it was accomplished. Everything can be moved if we touch the right spring.

After visiting my mother and sister Amelia, and my two nephews, her children, I went to Burlington to see my highly esteemed teacher, John Gummere. He seemed truly glad to see me, and when I informed him I had left Fair Hill, and gave him a little statement of my reasons for doing so, which he could readily comprehend, and in which he evidently sympathized with me, he said it would suit him exactly, for he was just in want of a good calculator to assist him with the Astronomy he was then writing. So, without going back to uncle's, I set right to work at astronomical calculations at Burlington, about a week after leaving Fair Hill.

Very soon after this I received from George Ellicott, who had heard of my having left Fair Hill, an invitation to take the school at Ellicott's Mills, but the locality not harmonizing with my feelings, I thought best to decline, and did so in a respectful reply.

My situation and occupation at Burlington suited me exactly. It was only temporary, to be sure, but from former experiences I had ground to hope that if I did my duty as I went along, some way would open for me. I occupied John Gummere's private study for my calculating, where I abridged the "Solar Tables" of Delambres, for the "Tables of the Sun," in his treatise on Astronomy; and the Lunar Tables of Burkhardt, for those of the Moon; and calculated the "Tables of Second Differences;" "Changes in Right Ascension," and many other tables, besides making most of the calculations of the problems in

the Second Part. I worked nearly all day and until nine
o'clock in the evening, which pleased John very much, for
he was anxious to get his book out.

While engaged in these problems of the Second Part,
a little incident occurred that I have frequently thought of
since, with interest. John went one morning with his
family to Quarterly Meeting, at Crosswicks, some fifteen
miles distant, above Burlington, and left me to calculate
the parallax of the moon in longitude and latitude, which
requires the finding of the longitude and altitude of the
Nonagesimal degree, or the highest point of the ecliptic.
This I was to do by a new rule he had formed. It is a long
process, and I worked at it faithfully, and satisfied myself
fully that there was something wrong in the rule. About
three o'clock they returned, and John came immediately
up into his study to see how his new rule worked, when I
showed him the indications I had observed of something
being wrong in the rule. He sat down by the fire without
taking off his hat or surtout, or having any dinner, with
my work and the rule before him, and, as was his habit in
hard study, with his little finger hooked in his mouth, and
thus remained for an hour or more. How plainly I can
see his countenance and form yet, for I had nothing to do
but to observe him ; and I loved him.

At length he saw he had made a mistake in his rule by
saying "take the difference" instead of "subtract such a
quantity *from* such a quantity, adding twelve signs or a
whole circle to the latter when necessary," and he was delighted. He then went to his dinner, while I made the
calculations with his rule thus corrected, which I found to
work right. There was not much of the calculation to
alter, and it was quickly done. He soon returned, and was
highly gratified. He said he would not have failed to de-

tect that error, in time to have the correction inserted in
the errata, for any consideration. The correction will be
found in the errata, first edition, 1822, at the last of the
book. The preface is dated Twelfth month 21st, 1821,
about a month after I left him.

Seth Smith, a particular friend of John Gummere's,
having given up his place as teacher at Westtown, to open
a school of his own in Philadelphia, John Gummere advised and encouraged me to apply for the situation, and
said that he would give me a letter of recommendation to
the Westtown Committee on Teachers. He gave a good
many reasons in its favor, having himself been a teacher
there; the good society, the nice walks, opportunities for
improvement, and the acquaintance it would lead to with
many of the most interesting and valuable members of our
religious society. I took his advice, made the application,
and met the Committee on Teachers, in Philadelphia. It
consisted of George Williams, Israel W. Morris, and
Charles Townsend. I presented the recommendation John
had given me, and they told me they would inform me of
the result of my application, soon after the General Committee met, which would be in about a week.

In the meantime Josiah Tatum and William Cooper
came up to Burlington to invite me to take the Friends'
school at Woodbury, New Jersey, the same school that
Henry R. Russell now has.

I told them of my application for the place Seth Smith
had left at Westtown, but they wished me to go down and
look at the place, so that I might be ready to decide, in
case I did not get the appointment at Westtown, of which
I was to know in a few days. This I consented to do,
John Gummere offering to lend me his horse.

I was very much pleased with things at Woodbury,

5

where I spent the greater part of a day ; the Friends, the committee, the school-room, and the village or town. We talked matters over. There were some little things I would wish altered from what had been their arrangement, as, for instance, to have the reading-books furnished to the scholars, instead of each one having his own, so as to admit of a better classification of the scholars, and giving them a greater variety of reading; to which the committee cheerfully consented. I found it would be a nice place to live, too, in case I should wish to change my situation, to which my mind had been turned, having become engaged to be married to Margaret E. Farquhar before I left Fair Hill.

Altogether, I felt almost a wish that my Westtown application might not be successful, but still hoped whatever was best might be.

When I returned and told John how much I had been pleased, he said, " Yes, but Westtown would be the most desirable and improving place for thee," and I had great confidence in his judgment, particularly as he knew both places well.

In the latter part of Eleventh month I was informed by the committee that I had been appointed teacher at Westtown, to enter upon duty on the 1st of Twelfth month, of which I informed my Woodbury friends, and as I had about finished my calculations for the Astronomy, I began to make preparations to leave Burlington. John asked me to tell him what compensation he should pay me. I told him I could not do it. I had not thought of any. My situation had been pleasant. He said I must name what sum he should pay me. I said *I could not.* Was I right? He then concluded to pay me at the same rate I would receive at Westtown, and asked if that would be satisfactory. I told him, perfectly, but I have never felt satisfied, when I have thought of it since, believing it was too much, for the advantage was *fully half* in my favor, having such a pleasant home, when otherwise I should have had none, and the training I had received in astronomical calculations was quite equal to spending that much time at boarding-school. Besides it was entirely through his advice and influence that I obtained the situation at Westtown. This was the only difference there ever was between us.

I made a short visit to my relatives in my old neighborhood at Cheltenham and Abington, and went out to Westtown in the stage on Seventh-day, to be ready for duty on Second-day, according to appointment, Twelfth month 1st, 1821. It was just about three months after I had left Fair Hill, just two years after I had entered on duty at Fair Hill as teacher, and four years since I entered Burlington school as a scholar. What a great variety of incidents had intervened, tending to form and establish character! The most prominent impress the review had upon my feelings seemed to be the manifest care of the Good Father, and the guidance of the Unseen Hand or Good Angel, leading me in a way I knew not and could not otherwise have found.

Once more I had to make my way among entire strangers, but I had learned more of human nature than I formerly knew, and this knowledge made it somewhat easier to me. Seth Smith, or "Master Seth," as they all called him, had been a great favorite with all — superintendent, teachers, and scholars. It was easily to be seen that the teachers did not regard me as capable of filling Master Seth's place. They left me to myself all First-day, which I spent in my school-room, No. 24, the one

Seth had occupied, which was relieved by attending meeting twice, and I had some interesting reflections, with ardent desires that I might be favored to do my duty in what I felt to be a very responsible position. The scholars eyed me closely through the (to me) long day. In the afternoon two of the larger boys, Ellis Middleton and Joshua Husband, picked out some walnut kernels, brought them to me as I sat at my desk, and asked me to accept them, which I did gratefully, regarding it as an indication that I was making my way. At school-time the next morning, the superintendent, Philip Price, went with me to my school-room. He introduced me to my future scholars. After he left I made a brief address to them, the import of which I cannot now call to mind.

I had noticed the day before, and noticed again that morning, a certain boy who was very active, observant, and influential, and seemed to know everybody and to see everything about the school. I called him to me at my desk, and after inquiring his name, which was Jesse Corse, from Delaware, I asked him what exercise Master Seth had first in the morning. He told me, and that exercise we began with. I then asked him what Master Seth did next; and *that* we did, and so through the whole day and every day, what Master Seth did, we did, so that by the time the week was out I had their confidence, and they seemed almost to think Master Seth had got back again. Master Seth's plan did not suit me exactly throughout, and I gradually made some alterations, which attracted no evident attention, as they did not know but that Master Seth would have made them had he continued in charge of the school. By the close of the first week I was sensible of having gained the confidence of the scholars, which I believe I never lost while I was there.

It having been over a month since Seth left, and the other two teachers, Jacob Haines and Pennock Passmore, having had "first and second care" alternately, every week since, they proposed that I should take "second care" the next week, to which proposition I cheerfully consented. I got through with my duties that week very satisfactorily. The next week, two weeks after my arrival at the institution, I had to take "first care" and have the general charge of the students, between school, in the dining-room, etc., etc. The responsibility felt heavy, but I had got along well so far, which gave me ground to believe that, with continued watchfulness, I would get through the duties of that week pretty satisfactorily also.

The week started quite pleasantly. All were as orderly as usual in the dining-room, where the girls and boys were seated at their respective tables, which I had dreaded, and they left the dining-room quietly and in beautiful order.

There was one boy amongst the largest of them, who, I several times through the week saw, was disposed to cause trouble; but I took no notice of it, and with this single exception we got through the week very comfortably, distributing the clothes after dinner on Seventh-day included.

It was the custom in pleasant weather, after distributing the clothes on Seventh-day, for the students to collect in a kind of semicircle in the east yard, standing according to height, when permission was given to those that had done well through the week to "go out of bounds," a privilege that they much valued and enjoyed.

When so collected I made a brief address, and referred to the very satisfactory deportment of the students through the week, with a single exception, whom I named, and that all but he might have the usual privilege of going out of bounds. The excepted student then made use of very insulting language to me. I calmly remarked, "Bad leads to worse," and requested him to take a seat in my school-room. After he left, in compliance with my directions, I again addressed the students, appealing to what they must have observed of his improprieties of conduct through the week, and that I *could not*, with propriety, have granted him a privilege for good conduct. I saw distinctly that I had their sympathies, and then dismissed them, and they set off in high glee.

The remark of the student had not disturbed me in the least, but I thought it right to report the case immediately to the superintendent and the other teachers. The other teachers looked awe-struck in sympathy for me, and said the boy must be severely whipped or sent home, or my authority would be irretrievably lost. The superintendent looked sad too. I said to them, "I am not in the least discouraged. This is only one boy out of nearly eighty. I am convinced I have the confidence of the others, as I am sure there are none among them that sympathize with him in his conduct. This is my first case. If you will let me manage it I think I will succeed without the boy being whipped or sent home. If I fail and lose my authority, I will at once withdraw." They all consented to my proposition, though seeming to feel some apprehensions for the result.

I then went into my school-room where the boy was, spoke kindly to him, asked him if his mother was living, and expressed the deep regret I felt, which was sincere, that he should have exposed himself as he had done before all the students. There must be some cause for it. There had been nothing but kindness on my part towards him, and I could think of no other cause for his conduct through the week and this last great outrage on decency and propriety, but that he was not well. " Thou must be sick ; such conduct and language could not come from a well boy. I will go with thee to the nursery." So I took him to the boys' nursery and put him to bed, and told the nurse that I had taken a patient to her room to whom I wished her to pay careful attention. She was soon there to know what was the matter, but he was ashamed to explain to her.

It happened to be on the Seventh-day that the Visiting Committee came out, and the women Friends of the committee had great regard for the nursery, and were soon there to see who were sick. The boy's mother was a prominent Friend, and known to many of them, and they expressed great regret at finding him in bed.

That evening I was still "in care," and could not be much with him, but I was free the next day, and spent most of the time between meetings in his room, reading to him and conversing with him kindly. Never, probably, was a boy more broken down and penitent than he was that First-day evening. He begged that I would not let his mother know what had happened, nor John Cook, who was one of the committee and a particular friend of his mother's. He said he would be willing to do anything if I would only excuse him, and he wept bitterly. He said if I would only let this pass I would never have any more trouble with him. So we closed the day without his knowing what was depending.

On reporting the case to the Faculty, after the boys had retired that evening, they were highly gratified with my success, and thought I might safely let him come into school the next morning, which I did, and a better boy

than he was, from that time till he left school, there was
not at Westtown. So, at a little after the end of my third
week, I had gained the confidence of my fellow-teachers
and the superintendent, which I believe I retained while
I remained at the institution.

The boys all slept in one chamber in the attic, the
framing of which made three divisions, so that three lights
were needed, candles then being generally in use. The
teachers were in the practice, which had continued for a
long period, of putting out the lights before they left the
chamber, and after waiting a while in the dark and not
letting the boys know when they left the sleeping-rooms,
coming down in their stocking feet, bringing the candle-
sticks with them. When I came into care the first week,
I was advised to adopt this course, but I *could not do it.*
I came down with my shoes on and the lights burning,
relying upon their individual honor, and not fear of me,
to preserve order, and I continued to practice this course
all through the three years I was at Westtown, and it
was acknowledged that there was quite as good order in
the chamber the week I was in care as at any other
time.

Pennock Passmore married one of the teachers, Sarah
West, soon after I went there, and went to live in the
"Infirmary," where Jacob Haines and his family already
lived. This left me the only single male teacher, and I
very generally went into the chamber to receive the boys
on their coming up to bed, even when the other teachers
were in care, in order that when they had dismissed the
boys from the collecting-room they could return to their
families, so that I had charge of the chambers pretty much
all of the time.

The second winter I was there, 1822–23, was a protracted one, with much snow and ice, and the east door was for a long time kept locked to prevent the snow from being tracked into the hall, or getting in by snow-balls being thrown at boys as they entered. When this door was locked the boys were obliged to go a long way around through the dimly-lighted gallery to get to the school-rooms, collecting-room, meals, or chambers, which was a great inconvenience and very disagreeable to them.

One day, when the door was unlocked, the key in some way got out of it and was lost, so that it could not be found. This was a great trial to the superintendent. This key, as all others in the house, had been imported from England at the time the house was built, and was a very peculiar and valuable one. Inquiry and search were made in every conceivable way and place, but no trace or tidings of it were to be had. When the super-intendent and teachers all collected in the library after meeting one Fifth-day, the topic of conversation, of course, was the lost key. Superintendent expressed himself as being very sorry and worried. "Well," said I, "Friends," if you will give me a chance, I think I can find the key."—"What chance dost thou want?"—"This after-noon."—"Very well, thou canst have it."

I immediately went out among the boys, and, taking out my watch, said, "Boys, there is elegant skating on the pond, and there is nothing in the way of our going this afternoon but that key. It is now near dinner-time, and if that key can come back before dinner, we will all go skating immediately after." I should state that the superintendent and older teachers did not like the boys to go skating on the mill-dam for fear of accident.

It was not over five minutes before the long-lost key was in my hand. It had been found in the bottom of the dust-barrel, where the sweepings were thrown. I returned to the library, where the others of the Faculty, and the librarian, Thomas Williams, still were, and held up the key, the sight of which brightened up their countenances beautifully, particularly the superintendent's. "Now," said I, "the boys and I are going skating this afternoon, on the dam." On hearing this their countenances were almost as much shaded as before, it being a way of *having* the afternoon that they had not thought of; but they let us go cheerfully, and we had a delightful time and returned all safe. Everything can be moved if we touch the right spring ; adapt the means to the ends.

One day when in care, I sent for a boy who had been doing something amiss. He was in Pennock's room, and appealed to Pennock to let this be an excuse. "No, no," said Pennock; "as James the First, of England, said to a man who claimed protection of the king's presence, from arrest, when Lord Coke sent for him, 'Tut, tut, mon, gang along,— if old Coke were to send for me I should go quickly;' so if Benjamin were to send for me, I should soon be there. Go along." The boy came.

I was the only unmarried teacher in the establishment, and my colleagues had families and lived at the Infirmary, so I volunteered to take their respective places when they were in care, to keep order at the table of the waiters, who ate after the other scholars and the teachers were all done. This allowed my associate teachers an additional half hour three times a day, the week they were in care, to attend to their domestic concerns. By this arrangement, I attended at the waiters' table three times every day, the whole year, and having nothing to do but to preserve order by my presence, I kept a volume of Addison's Spectator on a shelf by the place where I sat or stood in the dining-room, and read a paper in it, which was from four to six pages, while the waiters ate each meal, which made twelve to eighteen pages a day. When I closed the book I thought over the import of what I had just read, and before opening it, on picking it up at the next meal, I ran over this again in my mind, so as to keep the connexion, and thus continued, till in these small portions of time, which otherwise might have passed as waste, I read thoroughly the whole twelve volumes of the Spectator in which my copy of the work is printed, in one year. It was among the most profitable reading I ever did; so that by accommodating my fellow-teachers, I did a kindness to myself, by gaining valuable information and intellectual improvement, and knowing experimentally the value and importance of occupying small portions of spare time in some useful and systematic engagement. Four pages, read three times a day, requiring from fifteen to twenty minutes, will in a year make twelve volumes of three hundred and sixty-five pages each.

A little before this time the estate of my grandfather Hallowell had to be divided. The will had been made many years (he was over eighty-four when he died), and it so happened that the deeds of far the greatest part of the property he held at the time of his death were dated after the date of his will, and such property is not willed, and has to be divided according to law.* The legal settlement of an estate, under such circumstances, is by an administrator with the will annexed, and under an administrator who takes care of the part not willed, and the law *requires* any *previous gifts* to any of the children or heirs to be deducted, including lawful interest. Grandfather

---

*In 1822.

had given to my father, about 1794, one thousand
pounds, Pennsylvania currency, which is two thousand six
hundred and sixty-six and two-thirds dollars, and the interest for twenty-five years would be four thousand dollars
more, making the amount to be deducted from our share
six thousand six hundred and sixty-six and two-thirds
dollars, which absorbed nearly all the share coming to us,
leaving us about fifty dollars apiece.

All this is to prepare me to tell of what great use
this money was to me. I laid it all out in scientific
books, before I left the city. My studies at John Gummere's, with the lectures by him on Philosophy and
Astronomy, and his brother Samuel on Chemistry, had
awakened me to a great interest in these sciences. I had
procured, while there, "Vince and Wood's Course," consisting of Astronomy, Hydrostatics, Mechanics, Optics, etc.,
to which I was able to add, with these fifty dollars,
Cavallo's Philosophy, two volumes; Thompson's Chemistry, four volumes; Henry's Chemistry, two volumes;
Parke's Chemical Catechism, and some others (all of
which I have now), which came into immediate use, and
have been of great value to me from that time to the
present. The Philosophical Notes in Darwin's "Botanic
Garden," which I read carefully at Westtown, gave me
the first real insight into the beauty and extent of natural
philosophy, and other branches of science. If I had been
heir to one-third of six thousand six hundred and sixty-
six and two-thirds dollars, as my grandfather intended,
it is doubtful whether it would have done me as much
good as did those fifty dollars.

CHAPTER VI.

1822.

First lecture at Westtown — Two requests granted — " The Circle " — Conundrum — Grammatical discussions — Social Suppers — Extending his mathematical knowledge — Accumulating works on mathematics — Revising Bonnycastle's Mensuration and preparing a key to it — School committee very accommodating — Boys' parlor established and matron appointed — Offers his library for use of the boys — Begins to study French and Botany — Conscientious scruples — His sister Mary enters on duty as teacher at Westtown — Plans to leave Westtown — Resignation regretfully accepted — Three happy and profitable years.

It had been Seth Smith's department to lecture on Natural Philosophy, Pennock Passmore lecturing on Chemistry, and it was decided that I was to continue his course, which had proceeded as far as Light and Optics. My first lecture was upon Optics, and I do not know what I would have done without Cavallo's Philosophy and Darwin's " Botanic Garden." They gave me the very information I needed. I got through the lecture to the boys, which was on Second-day evening, very satisfactorily to them, and with considerable ease to myself, but I very much dreaded the one to the girls and the female teachers, which was to be the next evening, although it was to be the same lecture, or rather from the same notes.

There was a little laboratory where the lecturer stood, connecting by sliding shutters with the collecting room, where the classes, who attended the lectures, sat. In this little apartment the lecturer could adjust his apparatus, and prepare what he needed, unseen. From this place I heard the girls and their teachers coming in, and the

attendant bustle and murmur; then all was still, and it
seemed as if I *could not open those shutters.* Can you see
me? *At length* I mustered courage to do it. There was
the room, crowded with girls (there being at that time a
good many more girls in the school than boys) and their
teachers, Sybilla Embree, Abigail and Mary Passmore,
Elizabeth Walton, and Sarah West, all with white aprons,
caps, and neckerchiefs. I well remember, but cannot
describe, the feeling. I had uttered but a few sentences,
when I found pencil and paper being brought into
requisition by teachers and scholars (thanks to Cavallo
and Darwin), which was a new source of embarrassment.
But I got through alive, and was glad of it. The teachers
expressed themselves well satisfied, and Mary Passmore
told me, that one of the girls in her class, who was required to form a sentence containing the word "agreeable," wrote, "Master Benjamin is an agreeable lecturer."

Jacob Haines taught reading, writing, and geography
to all the boys, while Pennock and I each had classes
in arithmetic, mathematics, English grammar, and history,
which at that time constituted the curriculum of the
Westtown course. The history used was "Whelpley's
Compend." When the committee met, I asked permission to have one-third of the scholars assigned to my
care, permanently, for instruction in all the branches
taught in the school, and that I might substitute "Blair's
Natural Philosophy" for history. I drew the committee's
attention to the fact that almost the whole of "Whelpley's
Compend" consisted of statements of when and where
battles were fought, what generals commanded, how many
men and officers were killed on each side, who gained
the victory, and such facts connected with battles, without any information in regard to trade, commerce, the

products of the different countries, or their physical and geographical features, which it would be beneficial to the students to know and remember.

On hearing me through, examining Whelpley, consulting with the superintendent and the other teachers, and considering the subject, both of my requests were granted, to my great gratification.

The "Circle" in superintendent's parlor, where the teachers of both sexes, not "in care," would collect in the evening with superintendent and his wife, became very pleasant and instructive, as I got better acquainted.

Questions on science, grammar, etc., would be asked and discussed, as well as the current news generally remarked upon. Superintendent took "Walsh's National Gazette," of Philadelphia, which was the most advanced paper of the time, containing much scientific information, and the most important domestic and foreign news. Through it and the Congressional speeches it contained, I first became acquainted with Clay, Webster, etc. Webster's speech on the Greek question, President Monroe's message to Congress, which became the basis of what has since been known as the "Monroe doctrine," I read in the Gazette, with great interest.

The Gazette contained a conundrum, which it was said the Prime Minister Canning sat up a whole night to solve: "Why is an egg overdone, like an egg underdone;" his solution being, "Because they are *both hardly* done." The brightness and comprehensiveness of this answer was much admired by the teachers, but I maintained that it was not grammatical in regard to the overdone egg, which is done *hard*, and should have an *adjective* and not an *adverb* to express its condition. This and its connections became an object of pleasant discussion for weeks, in which the general distinction between adjectives and adverbs, resting on the definition of each, came to be fully understood. Many other questions in grammar were discussed, as Young's line, "Sleep, like the world, his ready visit pays, where fortune smiles." Was world in the nominative case, subject of the verb "pays" understood? or objective case, governed by "to or unto" understood? I maintained the latter position, believing the intention of the author was to draw a comparison between *sleep* and the *world*, and not between what or how sleep did, and what or how the world did. This was all very agreeable and improving to me, and these are only specimens, the topics having been very varied and embracing a wide range.

Breakfast and dinner the teachers took with the scholars, to help them to the relish, meat, soup, vegetables, or whatever might be on the table. The suppers were plain, bread and milk, mush and milk, or pie and milk, so that the scholars needed no waiting on, and the teachers all ate (a little later than the scholars) at the superintendent's table in a small room on the same floor.

It seemed a great treat to have this little remembrancer of domestic life and the family circle, once a day, where all were pleasant and free.

One little incident that occurred at these suppers, I feel like relating, although there were many others very interesting and instructive to me, as when, after my quoting from Lalla Rookh,

> "Oh! ever thus, from childhood's hour,
>   I've seen my fondest hopes decay;
> I never loved a tree or flower,
>   But 'twas the first to fade away;

I never nursed a dear gazelle,
To glad me with its soft black eye,
But when it came to know me well,
And love me, it was sure to die :"

Pennock said, "All people are like pendulums, swinging backwards and forwards, having their ups and downs; but Benjamin's vibrations are longer than most."

But to the incident: One evening the conversation turned upon names. Rachel Price's name before she was married was Kirk. Her ancestors were English, and named Church, and they moved to Scotland, where the hard sound as k is given to ch; it became Kurk, and finally Kirk, which she said was such a beautiful name, she always admired it. One of the teachers said, " If thou admired it so much, how came thou to change it ?" "Oh," said she, " I would not have done so, only" (patting her husband, who sat to her left, affectionately on the back) "I got such a *good Price* for it." We all laughed heartily, the superintendent, who never raised his eyes, fairly shaking his sides. It was a beautiful scene, and is vividly before me as I write.

I employed myself closely between schools (having then a good deal of leisure, when not in " first care "), in extending my knowledge of mathematics. I calculated a number of eclipses of the sun and moon, and devised a method of a parallactic construction of the transit of Venus for 1882, taking the apparent semidiameter of the sun for the "radius of the circle of projection," what had never, to my knowledge, been done before, and the results agreed very nearly with those obtained by calculation. This pleased Pennock very much. I also constructed all the problems in the latter part of the school edition of Bonnycastle's Algebra, that

6

were capable of construction, having no other assistance than Simpson's Geometry, which uncle Comly had bought for me when I went to school at Abington, in 1811. It is the the only copy I have ever seen.

One day when Enoch Lewis (who had been John Gummere's teacher) came to see us at Westtown, as he frequently did, I showed him a construction I had invented to a certain problem, which I told him I thought was ingenious and beautiful. We were down in the dining-room, sitting by the stove, while the waiters ate. He looked at it for some time, and then said, "It is very beautiful and neat, but Simpson has preconceived thee. In his 'Select Exercises,' he has constructed the same problem, in much the same way." This was an English work that I had never before heard of, and on his recommendation I sent immediately for it and obtained it.

By John Gummere's advice I procured also Simpson's Algebra, containing constructions of many geometrical problems, several of which I had already constructed, which constructions were as original with me as if they had never been constructed before. I was much interested in comparing my own with his, and to find that his were generally superior, but in *some* few instances, mine were decidedly preferable, being shorter and neater.

John Gummere, at my request, imported for me also "Leybourn's Mathematical Diary," in four volumes, containing questions, with their solutions, proposed and published in "The Ladies' Diary," from 1704 to 1816, also "Lacroix's Differential and Integral Calculus," "Peacock's Examples," adapted to Lacroix's work, and "Herschel's Calculus of Differences," so that I was accumulating a good mathematical library.

Enoch commended the evidences of mathematical

talent my constructions gave, and his commendation was highly gratifying. All this tended to form my character.

We used Bonnycastle's Mensuration as a school book, which, besides containing many typographical errors, gave rules without their demonstrations, so that solving the problems was just a mechanical process of performing the four primary rules of arithmetic, following the direction the rule gave, without any intellectual benefit. This did not suit me, and I proposed to Kimber & Sharpless to revise the book, correct the errors, add some new problems, and restore and give demonstrations to the rules, all gratuitously, if they would print it, and I would also read and correct the proofs. They cheerfully acceded to my proposition. The rule and its demonstration for finding the length of a circular arc were kindly prepared for the work by John Gummere, and I obtained some assistance in the same problem from Seth Smith.

This afforded me interesting and congenial employment. Calculation was a pleasure to me, and my training at Burlington in assisting John Gummere with his Astronomy had rendered me accurate. I finished the Mensuration to the satisfaction of all parties. Then Kimber & Sharpless desired me to prepare a Key to it, containing solutions of all the unsolved problems in the work, and exhibiting the different processes with their results. For this Key I solved every unwrought problem in the Mensuration, and set the work down on paper, ready for the printer, in one week, between schools, it being a week in which I had neither first nor second care. Kimber & Sharpless were much pleased with both works, and, although I had volunteered to do it all, and read the proofs, gratuitously, they made me a present of a large Family Bible, Cruden's Concordance, both bound in calf, and a volume of the plates of the Bible, they having understood, from some source, that I did not like the plates bound with the Bible. The value to me of this present, particularly the Concordance, is incomputable. I have read that Bible entirely through, Apocrypha and all, several times, and have found use for the Concordance from that time to the present, it having been a great aid and convenience to me. I have consulted it, I suppose, thousands of times.

The committee were very accommodating to me. I much wanted an orrery or planetarium, to illustrate to the students the phenomena of eclipses, the seasons, and the retrograde motions of the planets; and on representing the case to them, they told me I should have it. John Cook imported a beautiful one, the sun gilded, and the moon and planets of ivory, with several ingenious appendages, all moved by a crank and wheel-work.

The committee had a case made for the instrument in my school-room, which I regarded as quite a compliment to me. It was of great use in the lectures, and in the class exercises on Astronomy.

Enoch Lewis, much to our gratification, came and illustrated a lecture on Astronomy with it, in which he beautifully explained the retrograde motion of the superior planets, by regarding the earth as a superior planet to Venus, and observing what would be the motion of the earth when in opposition to the sun at Venus. This ingenious method, for which the appendages to the orrery were well adapted, pleased Pennock and me highly. I was always both ready and willing to exhibit the orrery, and to explain any principle to those who desired it, and a number availed themselves of the opportunity.

It was my custom to open my school in the morning by reading a chapter or part of a chapter in the Bible previously selected, and seemingly adapted to the occasion. One morning while the committee were on a visit to the school, the sub-committee appointed to visit my department, principally women Friends, came early, before I had read to the scholars. I was at first disposed to omit that part of the morning exercises, but that idea did not seem pleasant, and I performed the reading as usual. They asked me if that was my practice. I told them it had been since I first had a class of scholars to myself.

We then went on with the school exercises, grammar, philosophy, geography, reading, mathematics, etc., they spending the entire day and part of the next. They expressed themselves very much pleased with the school, and gratified with the sprightliness and accuracy with which the students recited. When they reported to the general committee, they made a full statement, including my reading some Scripture at the opening of my school, and to this they attributed the good order observed in it, and the proficiency of the scholars, instead of looking to the principle that lay behind this and prompted the reading and the corresponding effort for the students' improvement; so the committee made a rule requiring all the teachers, male and female, to open the morning session in the same way, by reading some portion of the Bible. Here was a mistake, though the intention was good. The minds and feelings of some of the teachers did not sympathize with the engagement, and even to me it was a very different thing when *done under authority*, from what it had been when it was a voluntary private act, done under a concern for the boys' good.

I ought to mention that a concern was awakened in the mind of one of the female committee that visited my school, by my asking the question of the class in philosophy, " How much larger the earth would appear to a person at the moon than the moon does to us?" After the school closed she invited me and a woman Friend, member of the committee, to meet her, and she expressed a concern, extending the caution, as she " felt convinced I would occupy a position of influence in society, not to indulge the opinion that it is possible that any other planet is inhabited besides our earth." I heard her through, but I fear not so patiently as I ought to have done, for the dinner-bell rang during her discourse, and I being in care, knew that I ought to be in the dining-room.

There was no woman on the boys' side of the house to exert a favorable influence upon them, and I had felt a concern for some time that the boys should have a parlor on their end, with a suitable matron to whom the little boys could go and get a cut finger wrapped up, and who could fix their collars, smooth their hair, and produce a humanizing, civilizing, and motherly influence upon them generally. When the committee met I laid this concern before them, giving my views fully in the belief of its beneficial effects on the boys, from the influence of a home feeling. To my surprise and gratification, my views were *at once* united with, and it was decided to have a " boys' parlor" established immediately, and Elizabeth Sykes, a nice Friend from Burlington, New Jersey, was appointed matron to have charge of it.

My library, which I kept in a closet in my school-room, had increased considerably. Besides the books that I have already mentioned, I had " Locke's Essays," "Stewart's Philosophy of the Human Mind and of the Moral Feelings," " Watts on the Mind," " Milton's Poetical Works," " Young's Night Thoughts," " Lalla Rookh," " Lady of the Lake," "Beattie's Minstrel," "The Wreath,"

"Falconer's Shipwreck," "Mavor's Universal History," twenty-five volumes, " Johnson's Dictionary," four volumes, " Classical Dictionary," " The Ocean Harp," and " Byron's Farewell to England," by John Agg, and some other books. In another interview with the committee I proposed that if they would procure a book-case, I would put my library in the boys' parlor, and let them have the privilege of reading the books when there. The boys had united themselves into companies in working their flower gardens, where they had seats arranged, and then when any one of them received a box he shared its contents with the others of his company, and by letting them go into the parlor, one " company" at a time, on successive days, all the boys would have the privilege of the parlor one day in every week. There being six companies, it would not be on the same day in successive weeks, and thus it would avoid its being the lot of some to be there two Seventh and First-days in succession. This proposition was united with also, and dear John Cook offered to furnish the book-case. It was soon there, and a beautiful one it was, of mahogany. It contained a desk with a lid to let down, where the boys could write, two at a time, drawers, where Elizabeth Sykes could keep various needed things, and a book-case above, with glass doors, of sufficient size to hold all my books on the different shelves. John wrote me a beautiful, witty letter to accompany it, saying it was old, like himself, but he had learned not to think less of things simply on account of their age, if they could perform the purpose desired, as he was of the belief this would. The boys assisted me in moving and arranging the books, and they made quite a handsome show.

The parlor was well furnished with carpet, settees,

chairs, tables, etc., and it proved to be all that was expected of it, and even more. It was near the foot of the " up-stairs" and the head of the " down-stairs," so that all the boys had to pass the door of the parlor in going to their chambers or to their meals, and the changes in the in-creased order and quiet in that part of the establishment were very gratifying, almost marvellous.

Friend Rachel Price used to come there occasionally and sit and talk with the boys, and the women teachers, one or more of them almost every day, came to sit with Elizabeth and converse with the students, who had the " privilege of the parlor" for that day, so that the boys' parlor, with its arrangements, was regarded as a very useful appendage to Westtown, and the wonder was expressed that it had not been established before. There were many expressions that I had improved the condition of West-town. There was certainly a great improvement in the order and domestic feeling on the boys' side of the house.

I had a great desire to have a practical knowledge of the French language, so as to write and speak it, and also a knowledge of botany. Pennock was a good botanist, and could *read* French pretty well, and he gave me some assistance in both studies very cheerfully and efficiently. Pennock named after me his second son, Benjamin Pass-more, who is a fine man. At length a Frenchman, an excellent teacher, came to West Chester, and we made up a French class among the teachers, I making ar-rangements to send for him to West Chester, four miles, every week, and send him back the next morning. We were all delighted with him, both as a man and as a teacher. We congratulated ourselves upon the good opportunity we were about to have for accomplishing the purpose which some of us had long desired. On sending for him the next week, lo! he was in jail, and all our bright hopes vanished.

I fell back on Pennock's kindness, however, and kept vigorously at work, during my leisure hours, on both studies, declining the nouns and pronouns, and getting the names of species and orders of plants, till I translated a brief "Life of Fenelon" into English pretty creditably, and was getting on quite well with my botany.

At length, I found these studies were getting an undue hold on my mind. They *would* come before me in meeting. The declension of the French pronouns, the conjugation of the French verbs, and the long botanical names, as *liriodendron tulipifera*, *would* "steal between my God and me," in my retired moments, and I thought it right to give up both studies, and I accordingly did so.

Although I knew I did right in so doing, it being my highest conviction of duty, with the knowledge I then possessed, I have since seen that, while it was right to correct this obtrusion into my thoughts at unseasonable times, there was another way of effecting this object without relinquishing the studies, which were in themselves right and proper. This way was, to bring my mind and thoughts under that mental discipline which would render them obedient to the will, so that I could withdraw my thoughts from one object and fix them on another, when I felt it to be my duty to do so.

Had I only known this *then*, and made the necessary effort, in which I feel confident I should have been successful, what an advantage it would have been to me! Besides having a creditable knowledge of French and botany, which I could readily have acquired under Pennock's instruction, I should have secured that healthful mental discipline in the government of my thoughts, which I have so much needed, and of which I did not know the importance till I was too old to gain it to the extent that would render it fully beneficial. I record this experience, in order to give evidence to my belief that the government of the thoughts, as indicated, is a most important part of intellectual training.

In the winter of 1822–23, Sybilla Embree's health failed, and it was deemed necessary for her to leave school, take a sea-voyage, and travel in England and other parts of Europe, which she did. Ann Mifflin, from Philadelphia, one of the committee, was appointed to take her place temporarily, but to her the situation was not at all congenial. She became very tired of it, and frequently expressed an ardent wish that the committee would obtain a permanent teacher to take her place.

In this condition things continued for about five or six weeks. I had several times thought that my sister Mary, who had been a scholar at Westtown, and afterwards at Fair Hill, and was then teaching a private school at Cheltenham, might suit well, but I had not felt like mentioning the subject to any one, and did not. One Fifth-day in meeting the subject came impressively before me, and I resolved that, if Ann Mifflin asked *me*, as I had heard her ask others, whether I knew any one who I thought would suit, I would frankly mention my sister to her. When I went out of meeting and got to the foot of the stairs, there stood Ann Mifflin. She said to me, " Benjamin, doesn't thee know of some one who would do to take my place!" The coincidence seemed to me remarkable, but I simply told her I *had* thought of my sister Mary in that connexion. She clapped her hands and said, "That is the very thing. I wonder I had not thought of her before." She knew Mary, as they all did, and when she mentioned it to the female teachers and the superintendent, they all approved of it.

Ann went to Philadelphia that afternoon, and the next day she and another woman member of the committee went to Cheltenham to see my sister Mary. About a week from the time it was first mentioned to Ann Mifflin, my sister entered on duty as a Westtown teacher, Second month 8th, 1823, on the fifty-second anniversary of which I make this record, and all the incidents seem fresh before me. Here she became acquainted with John Mott, who afterwards invited her to assist him in opening a boarding-school at Rensselaersville, New York. When the committee met, one of them remarked, " A new thing has happened in Israel: a brother and sister are teachers at Westtown." When our mother came out to see us, she was treated with additional respect in consideration of her having two children, a son and a daughter, teachers there.

In the Eleventh month, 1823, Jacob Haines resigned his place as teacher, after having served in that capacity eight and a half years. I knew of his prospect to resign, and encouraged Charles Farquhar, who had been there as a scholar, and also my colleague at Fair Hill, to apply for the situation, which he did. Samuel Bettle made some inquiries of me about him, and the committee appointed him. Jacob left on the 6th of Eleventh month, and Charles entered upon duty in his place on the 10th of Eleventh month, 1823.

It was truly pleasant to me to have a congenial companion and an old acquaintance in the new teacher, and the good order and pleasant feeling that now existed among the scholars, with the establishment of the boys' parlor, etc., rendered Westtown a very comfortable and homelike abode.

The pleasant companionship of Charles did not increase my progress in my studies, but rather the contrary. Nevertheless, it was a very agreeable respite to me.

On one occasion, word was circulated that William Forster, from England, was expected to attend Goshen meeting on a particular day, and as I had seen him at Fair Hill, where he spent some time while I was there teaching, it was concluded that I should attend the meeting and invite him to visit Westtown. As soon as I spoke to him after meeting, he remembered me and where he had before seen me, although it had been more than two years since, and said to me, "Do you still keep that big negro (Washington White) to wait on the table? He would do very well in the corn-field, but he is out of place in the dining-room."

William came to Westtown and spent a night. I was in care, and could not be much of the time with him. At the time of collection in the evening, he went into the girls' part of the building. Visitors of the Westtown family, who staid all night, went to the "Infirmary" to lodge, and when this was proposed to William, the name alarmed him, and it was not till after he was assured that the building had never been used in the capacity that its name would seem to imply, that he consented to go there to spend the night.

I began now to feel that the time had nearly come for me to change my condition of life. I had been engaged to Margaret E. Farquhar since 1821, before I left Fair Hill, about three years. My pecuniary circumstances had not heretofore permitted of a change, such as I felt willing to make, for it did not seem right to me to take Margaret to Westtown, though to the school, the place, and the people there I was much attached. . Charles Farquhar (Margaret's brother) and I consulted about the matter for some time, and we ultimately concluded to unite in establishing a private boarding-school, if we could find the right place and the right time to begin to move in it. I thought of Richmond, Virginia, as a suitable place, although I had never been there, and I made a journey to Sandy Spring to consult Margaret, and to advise with my valued friend and counsellor, Deborah Stabler, who knew all about Richmond, and felt a great interest in both Margaret and me.

When I opened my prospect to her, she sat a little time silent, and then looked at me and said, " Benjamin, Friends do not thrive in Richmond." That settled the matter in regard to Richmond, at once; not only her *words*, but the weight that accompanied them, produced a conviction of the correctness of her judgment.

I returned to Westtown, and some time after, the subject being weightily before me, desirous as I was of finding the right place and the proper time, while sitting in meeting it presented to me, with a clearness that I could not doubt, that Alexandria, D. C., would be the place for our school. Edward Stabler and many other nice Friends resided there, among whom was my cousin Nancy Shoemaker Janney, widow of John Janney. On writing to Sandy Spring, it met the approbation of all concerned. I decided to leave Westtown early in the Ninth month, and the day before Willistown Monthly Meeting, in the Eighth month, I wrote a note to Pennock Passmore in No. 25, which was just across the passage from my room, inquiring of him how he would word an application for a certificate on account of marriage, were such a thing necessary. He returned the form by the same boy that took my note, and in a few minutes came to my door, called me out, as was the custom when important business required it, with the greatest gravity, and preceding me to the collecting-room, shut the door and stood with his back against it. (I can see him yet, so plainly). He then said, with a pleasant inquiring smile, "I can stand it no longer. What does this mean? Who is it?" I then made "a clean breast" of it to him. The next day the matter became public by the reading of the application in the Monthly Meeting. Everard Passmore gave the news to his sisters at dinner, and they carried it to the school, where it was a universal surprise. There had not been an idea of anything of the kind entertained amongst them. When the committee met, I tendered my resignation, to take effect on the 8th of Ninth month. They spoke very prettily and kindly to me, and of the fidelity with which I had performed my duty; said they had hoped to have me as a "fixture" for many years to come, that I had made some improvements at Westtown, and would leave it better than I found it, but they supposed they must accept my resignation.

It seems like a singular coincidence, that Oliver Paxson, who succeeded me at Fair Hill in 1821, was appointed to take my place at Westtown three years after.

My three years' sojourn at Westtown was, take it all together, the happiest, most congenial, and most improving period of my life. It was like a little world in which I felt that I was doing good, and possessed the confidence, affection, and respect of those among whom I daily moved, which was a very encouraging and grateful feeling to me. There was a system, regularity, and order that

I loved; a dignity, and a quiet, staid manner, universal kindness and respect, and a united purpose for what was best, on every important subject and occasion.

This training was admirably adapted to form my character, so as to meet successfully the exigencies I was about to encounter, and on this account I have dwelt longer upon the incidents and experiences at the institution.

CHAPTER VII.

1824.

Preparations for opening school in Alexandria — Difficulties in getting a house — Kindness of friends — Marriage — La Fayette — School fills slowly — Lectures — Confidence of ultimate success — Unhealthy location — Change of residence — Temporary financial anxieties — Girls' school — Private lessons — Prospects brighten — A benevolent society — Mathematical correspondence.

It now became necessary to make preparations and arrangements for opening a boarding-school in Alexandria. I went down to rent a house for the purpose, and with the assistance of my Fair Hill student, Robinson Stabler, I found a very nice place; a frame house on the west side of Fairfax street, below Prince street, fronting south, and a little back from the street (where Thomas Sanford, I think, afterwards lived), belonging to Charles Slade, who was about to move from Alexandria. He drew up the articles of agreement, which we both signed, and I returned to Westtown. About two weeks after, I received a letter from him informing me that he had an opportunity of selling the property I had rented, to advantage, if I would give up the lease, and it would be a great accommodation to him if I would do so. On thinking over the matter, I concluded it would only be " doing as I would be done by " to comply with his request, and I accordingly sent him the lease by the next mail. I have never seen him since, but Robinson Stabler said he was greatly obliged to me.

It then became necessary that another visit to Alexandria should be made, which was done by Charles Farquhar, who rented the brick house and half a square of ground on the north side of Orinoco street, near Washington street. I ordered some chemicals and chemical apparatus of Daniel B. Smith, of Philadelphia; an air-pump, with its appendages, an electrical machine and its appendages, the mechanical powers, and hydrostatic apparatus, of the Mason Brothers; and of McAllister a large magic lantern, with astronomical slides, etc., etc. I also got Seth Smith to superintend the making of a pneumatic trough or cistern, with gasometers for the compound blow-pipe, on a plan that his experience at Westtown had suggested as the best. It was oval, with one gasometer at each end, leaving a space or well between them for collecting and transferring gases, the top of the gasometers serving as shelves. The gasometers were open at the bottom, and the gases were to be introduced below by a leaden tube from the retort. It cost fifty-five dollars.

I may say here that with Daniel B. Smith and W. & A. Mason I had a running account for many years, adding to my stock of chemical and philosophical apparatus, annually. They were very liberal and accommodating to me, which was a great convenience, and I remember their kindness with gratitude.

On the 8th of Ninth month, 1824, I bade farewell to

all at Westtown, to make a new start in life, with a feeling of heavy responsibility and some uncertainty of success, which can be better imagined than described. I had accumulated some funds at Westtown, my dear mother gave me some, and uncle Comly lent me two hundred dollars, which he increased at times of pressure afterwards till it became four hundred, for which I gave him my note to be paid with interest. This was all the assistance I ever had, except some that my sister Mary returned for what I had paid for her boarding and schooling at Fair Hill, which I have always regretted my necessities at the time compelled me to take; but I endeavored afterwards to make it up to her fully.

Uncle Comly was very kind to me; he never would take more than five per cent. interest on the money he lent me, that being, he said, what the Norristown bank paid him.

My dear mother kindly went to Alexandria with me, to assist in getting the house, beds, etc., ready. Charles Farquhar was to come about the first of the year 1825. Mother and I put up at the hotel, corner of King and Royal streets, then kept by Edmonston, if I remember right. After mother had retired for the night, which was early, Mary Stabler, wife of Edward Stabler, came to call on her, having learned through Robinson, whom I met in the street, where we put up. Mother saw her in her chamber, and Mary insisted on mother's going to their house and making it her home until we got the one on Orinoco street prepared to go into. This was a kindness my dear mother remembered with gratitude to the close of her life, and she frequently spoke of it, and of what a relief and comfort it was at the time. It seemed to remove a burden from her mind.

7

I got Elisha Talbott to make two large cases, with four glass doors each, for my apparatus, to stand in my lecture-room, which was the west front room on the first floor, one case each side of the fire-place; and to make a platform, teacher's desk, and desks for twenty-five scholars, in the school-room, which was the east front room on the second floor; and to have all ready for the school to open on the 1st of Eleventh month, 1824.

I also got Robert Brockett to build a brick oven and make some repairs about the kitchen, etc., and engaged Nancy Gordon (colored), as a housemaid for Margaret. Nancy was then staying with a kinswoman "Nelly." In speaking with Nancy in "Nelly's" presence, I said, "Thou wilt find Margaret easy to please and pleasant to live with." "Nelly" looked up very significantly, and replied, "*Ah! you don't know yet.*"

My apparatus, books, clothes, etc., were to come by vessel, and I felt some uneasiness lest they might not be there in time, the day of the marriage having been fixed for the 13th of Tenth month. They came safe, however, and in time to have all the apparatus nicely arranged in its place, and it made a very respectable appearance.

It was arranged that we were to be married at the close of the Monthly Meeting at Sandy Spring, Maryland, on the 13th, and go down to Alexandria the same afternoon. I obtained a nice hack of John West, telling him of the occasion, and that he might take his time in going up on the 12th, but I would like him to drive down pretty brisk-ly. On arriving at Fair Hill on the 12th, I found that Stephen and Hannah Wilson, by whose residence we had to pass in going from Sandy Spring Meeting House to Alexandria, had kindly insisted that we should stop there and take a lunch as we went down. They thought a great deal of Margaret, and she had accepted the invitation. Philadelphia was then a great distance, in *time*, from Sandy Spring, and none of my relations came to the wedding. My mother thought it right to remain in Alexandria to receive the bride, her new daughter, whom she had never seen. I had, at my leisure, written the certificate in Alexandria, on parchment, and it looks well yet. Roger Brooke read it at our marriage, and read it well. Eighty-six persons signed it, many of whom were Fair Hill scholars. A large number of the signers have passed to the spirit world. Phebe Farquhar and Catharine Leeke (now of Cincinnati), went down in the hack with us, we four constituting our entire wedding company, and all four are still alive.*

Hannah Wilson's lunch proved to be a very nice and bountiful dinner. After dinner we started, and Margaret not feeling very well, we stopped at Lovelace's, six miles from Washington, to rest awhile. While waiting I wrote to my uncle Comly. It was just in the midst of preparations at Alexandria for the reception of General La Fayette, and everything was running in that channel, so I wrote,

> Each lover of liberty surely must get
> Something in honor of La Fayette.
> There's a La Fayette watch-chain, a La Fayette hat,
> A La Fayette *this*, and a La Fayette *that*.
> But I wanted something as lasting as life,
> And took to myself a La Fayette wife.

Margaret soon got better, and the man drove on rapidly and we arrived safe, and well at our home, where dear mother received her new daughter and all of us very kindly. She had invited Edward and Mary Stabler, Mar-

---

*All have died since the writing of this Autobiography.—EDS.

garet Judge, Rachel Painter, Phineas and Sarah Janney, Jonathan and Betsey Janney, and a good many other Friends, to take tea with us.

Mother and Nancy, with the kind assistance of some of the Friends, had prepared a very nice supper. After tea, Margaret Judge, in the goodness of her heart, took the Friends to see the lecture-room, and asked me to exhibit the magic lantern, and particularly the astronomical slides, which, tired though I was, I could not well refuse to do, and the exhibition seemed very gratifying to the company.

The next morning General La Fayette came to call on the widow of General Harry Lee, and mother of Robert E. Lee, who lived next door to our house. Margaret and I stood in the front door as he went by, and when he got opposite he looked at us, took off his hat, and made us a graceful bow, not knowing it was to a lady who had been married the day before, and whom her husband had named, after the wedding, his La Fayette wife.

Washington street in Alexandria is one hundred feet wide, each sidewalk being eighteen feet. There were three spans of arch erected in honor of La Fayette across it, just north of King street, two of eighteen feet span over the sidewalks, and the central one sixty-four feet span. They made a very handsome appearance. Appropriate mottoes were on each side of each arch. I remember the two that were on the central arch. On the side of his approach was, " Welcome La Fayette! A nation's gratitude thy due!" On the other was an extract from a speech he had made in the Paris Tribune, " For a nation to be free, it is sufficient that she *wills* it."

Colonel Mountford, keeper of the Alexandria Museum, had fastened one of his live eagles on the crown of the arch, with its head in the direction of the approach of the procession, and he and others said that just as the General was passing under the arch, the eagle rose, spread out his wings to their full extent, then gracefully folding them, resumed his former position.

My school filled slowly. I had advertised that it would open on the 1st of Eleventh month, but no scholar came during that month.

It was concluded that Margaret's brothers, Granville and William Henry, should come on the 1st of Twelfth month, at the same price they were paying at Fair Hill, twenty dollars per quarter each for board and tuition, forty dollars of which was paid in advance, and this was the only money received for schooling till after New Year. I had never been used to having *much* money, but I had never been in debt, a thing of which I had great horror. On the 1st of Twelfth month Andrew Schofield entered his nephew Thomas, Mordecai Miller his son Joseph, and late in the month Abijah Janney sent his son Richard, and Obed Waite, of Winchester, his ward, Thomas Page. These four were all the day scholars I had till after New Year, 1825. The price of tuition of day scholars, in the common branches, was six dollars a quarter, and in mathematics, ten dollars a quarter, and for board and tuition, thirty dollars a quarter.

It was thought proper early in the Twelfth month to begin a course of lectures on Chemistry, Natural Philosophy, and Astronomy, as I wanted something to do, and thought probably they might give some notoriety to the school, so I advertised them in the paper ; one dollar for a single ticket for the course, and five dollars for a family. The day the advertisement appeared, Hugh Smith sent for a family ticket, with the money, and soon after Jonathan Janney did the same.

My first lecture, which, according to custom, was free to all, was a memorable occasion. It was the first time my pneumatic cistern, that Seth Smith had made for me, was brought into requisition. From the description I have given of its construction, it will be seen there was no way of getting the gasometers filled with water, but by filling the whole tub. Our maid Nancy carried the water for the purpose all the way from the "diagonal pump," over five squares, on her head. She said it "did hold so much." I wished, in my introductory lecture, to show the "compound blow-pipe," and it was therefore necessary to have both the gasometers filled.

I had never had any practical experience in chemical manipulations. I had never seen gases made, except in small quantities, in the lecture-rooms at Burlington and Westtown. There was no one from whom I could obtain any information or assistance, and I had a *very hard time of it.* The great difficulty I experienced was in getting the leaden tube attached air-tight to the glass or iron retort. As will be understood by the construction of the cistern, the leaden tube had to be taken down through the water to the bottom of the cistern, and there introduced into the gasometer, and of course it was necessary to overcome the pressure of the column of water, which gave that much more pressure upon the interior of the retort, and caused a leak in the connection, or "luting," as it is called. I found the directions given in Henry's Chemistry and in "Faraday's Chemical Manipulations" very serviceable to me, and eventually, with great perseverance as my only assistant, I got them both filled.

Then came the evening of the lecture. Margaret

Judge had taken great interest in the lecture, and had invited many of her friends, Parson Norris, Parson Wilmer, Townsend Waugh, Edmonds Hoffman, Elizabeth Cooke, Doctor Fonerdon, etc., etc. The room was crowded, a thing very unexpected to me, and so many being strangers, I was somewhat embarrassed at the commencement. I had arranged to have an "experiment," so as to give a little breathing place early in the lecture, and Margaret Judge, who I think perceived my condition, under pretence of changing her seat to the other side of the room, came by me and said in an undertone, "Thee is doing admirably !" and went on. Dear woman, how deeply interested for me she was! Her remark seemed the very encouragement I needed, and was truly a "word in season." I got through quite creditably — exhibited the compound blow-pipe, some experiments with the air-pump and the magic-lantern, and was, after the lecture, introduced to Parsons Wilmer, and Norris, who congratulated me on my success.

My pneumatic trough not serving a practical purpose, Thomas William Smith planned and made for me the most complete one I have ever seen.

About the first of the year, brother Charles Farquhar came, and we had some addition to the number of scholars, and one more boarder, James P. Farquhar, sent by his guardian, William Shepherd. Edmond I. Lee sent his son Cassius, and Thomas Swann his son Wilson, who were ten-dollar scholars. Samuel M. Janney and Townsend Waugh came to night-school to study mathematics, all in the First month. In the Second month Robert E. Lee came to study Mathematics, preparatory to going to West Point; also William S. Young, son of Elizabeth Young. In the Third month Ann Swift sent her son Foster, Jonathan

Janney his sons Isaac and Richard, and Edward Stabler his son Edward H., a mathematical scholar. He had been my scholar at Fair Hill. In the Fourth month Jonathan Janney sent his nephews, James and Israel Janney. Bathurst Daingerfield sent his son John, and Dubre Knight, who had been a teacher at Fair Hill, entered as a boarder. In the Sixth month John Wood sent his son John, so that, by the end of the first six months of 1825, we had about twenty scholars, including four boarders. The school and the income from it were small, but I had confidence of ultimate success.

On the 1st of Ninth month, 1825, our son James was born, and seemingly with the bilious fever. His mother was very ill. Then, for the first time, we heard that our situation on Orinoco street, on the edge of the town as it was, had always been regarded as unhealthy. Doctor Washington (who attended Margaret), Edward Stabler, and others, so considered it. This brought a new trial and responsibility on me. I could not bear the idea of my wife and family continuing in a place that was thought to be unhealthy, or of my inviting boarders to such a situation.

Margaret continued ill through the fall and winter, · and Dr. Washington was discouraged about her recovery, especially in that place. I endeavored to find a suitable situation in a more central part of the town, but failed.

After some time I was offered by the widow Hooe the commodious brick house at the corner of Washington and Queen streets, a healthy situation, and admirably adapted to our purpose, and I immediately engaged it. We moved in the spring vacation, 1826. I obtained a hack, placed a bed in it, and carried Margaret in my arms from her chamber up-stairs, into the hack, and placed her on the bed.

She was exceedingly emaciated. Nancy carried little "Jimmy." On arriving at our new home I carried Margaret from the hack to the chamber, and felt greatly relieved by the hope of her now being better.

Cousin Benjamin Shoemaker, who was there as a boarding scholar, assisted me in moving, and it was very pleasant to have him with us. He was always very congenial to me.

My school-room was on the first floor, north end, all across the house, I having obtained permission of my landlady, in our arrangements, to remove the partition on condition of replacing it by one with folding doors, when I should leave the property, which was done. My lecture-room was the back room over the school-room. The school-room was considerably larger than the one on Orinoco street, so that we could now take more day scholars, and the lecture-room was about the same size as the other one. Brother Charles soon after, left me to study medicine. Margaret's health was decidedly improved, which was a great comfort to me.

The very day the quarter's rent was due the widow Hooe's carriage was at the door, and this continued to be her custom as long as she lived. If I had not the money, which was generally the case, I would frankly tell her so, and add that the first money I should get, and could possibly spare, I would take to her, with which she was always satisfied. She never said a word like urging me or being disappointed in not getting the rent due, and I *did* take to her the very first I received, never permitting it to be in my possession over night. If I received it in the evening, I would take it immediately to her. I was favored never to let a second quarter's rent become due before the last one was paid. She was a truly good land-lady, and I possessed her confidence.

It was a very hard time with me financially through 1827–28–29 and 1830. I dreaded Seventh-day to come, it being the day that bills came in, people thinking I would be out of school. At one time I was three weeks without as much as three "fip-penny bits" in my pocket. One morning I did not know how I should get along, felt very badly, and on going to the post-office found a letter from Mary Rich, Thomas Winston's sister, with a thirty-dollar note in it (the first one I ever saw), on account of his schooling. This did seem like a God-send, and caused me to spend a happy day, as it supplied every pressing demand.

George S. Hough was very kind and liberal. He told us to get what dry goods we wanted at any time. John P. Cowman, in the same way, invited us to come to his store and get flour, butter, and groceries, whenever we needed. I would pay them part, as I had the money, but they never sent in a bill unless I requested them to do so, and I suppose I did not owe either of them less than one hundred dollars at any time for some years. I have often since thought, with gratitude, of their kindness and liberality.

One day I needed some money badly, and after calling with bills on several persons unsuccessfully, I went to Ezra Kinsey with a bill for his son Samuel, who was in Astronomy, and a "ten-dollar" scholar. I explained to him the necessity that induced me to call; that my purse was very low. "Well," said he, " you have come" (here I was expecting another rebuff) "to the *very right place*, for I have the money, and am willing to pay it. My son is making good progress." This was quite a wind-fall.

Mary Stabler had a concern for my Margaret to open

a school for girls; she wished to send her daughters, and on consideration Margaret consented to do so, in the front room, over my school-room, and she soon had the school full of nice girls. They attended my lectures, as did also a class from Eliza Porter's and Rachel Waugh's schools. Some difficulty occurred between these two schools, and Rachel Waugh urged me to give a lecture each week to her scholars, separately, for thirty dollars for the winter, which I consented to do. I could not afford to buy a stove for the lecture-room, so I carried the one from Margaret's school-room to the lecture-room, with faithful Nancy's aid, every lecture-night the whole winter, and back again the next morning, the arrangement with Rachel Waugh doubling the stove transportation labor.

Widow Hooe offered me the tobacco warehouse, just south of the sugar-house, and but a little way from my residence, for fifty dollars a year, which I agreed to take. This enabled me to accommodate more day-scholars, the school-room where I was being full, and gave me a fine large lecture-room, besides four more rooms in our dwelling house. This was a fine and very unexpected movement in my favor.

In the fall of 1828 I began to give private lessons to the daughters of Craven Thompson and Robert W. Taylor, at their respective homes, having definite hours assigned to me, between my own school hours, like their music and French teachers. This was humbling to me, but I was in debt, and I was desirous of doing anything that was honorable to get out of debt and make a living. I went to Thompson's and Taylor's immediately after my afternoon school.

Then after tea in the evenings I had a class of girls, consisting of Sarah Smith, Susan and Rebecca Stabler,

Rosalie Taylor, and some others, in Philosophy, Grammar, Arithmetic, etc. After this class left, which was about half-past eight o'clock, I would lie down a little while in my school-room where I heard their lessons, and then prepare the gases and get the appendages ready for my lectures. It was frequently midnight or after before I got through.

On the 17th of Ninth month, 1830, I commenced giving private lessons to Angela Lewis, daughter of Major Lawrence Lewis (who was a nephew of General Washington, and it was said a good deal resembled him in appearance). These lessons continued through the year, for which I charged fifty dollars, and the Major promptly sent me his check for the amount. Eleanor Lewis, Angela's mother, always attended at her daughter's recitations in English Grammar, Parsing, Natural Philosophy, etc., so that her influence, which she afterwards exerted in my favor, and her praise of my method of teaching, was of greater value to me than the amount I received in hand for teaching her daughter.

The ceilings of my school and lecture-rooms were low, and the windows were the longest horizontally, the sash revolving. I proposed to widow Hooe, my landlady, that if she would have the roof raised about four feet, and the windows put longest way up, and furnished with weights so as to rise and fall, I would double the rent and pay her one hundred dollars a year, to which she cheerfully consented, and she had the changes commenced promptly. This greatly increased the comfort of both rooms, my school became full, there being as many as one hundred scholars, and my lectures were well attended, by some of the most respectable citizens and their families—Hugh Smith, Anthony Charles Cazenove, William

Fowle, Phineas Janney, Jonathan Janney, Edward Stabler, and classes of girls from the schools of Eliza C. Porter, Rachel Waugh, Ellen Mark, and John West's wife.

A benevolent society was formed in Alexandria about the year 1827, of which Thomas Jacobs was President and I Secretary. Benjamin Lundy was there, and assisted in its organization, The object of the association was to render assistance to such persons as were slaves and willed to be free at a certain time, in which case, if they were hired out of the State, or from the District of Columbia, they were *at once* entitled to their freedom on that fact being established. Samuel M. Janney, George Drinker, Abijah Janney, Townsend Waugh, Presley Jacobs, Thomas Preston, Daniel Cawood, —— Shackelford, and a number of others, were members. Edward and William Stabler did not join, being fearful that the object of the society might be misunderstood.

We got a number of persons liberated, who were hired out of the State of Maryland. Francis S. Key* informed us by letter of the case of a whole family. I went to Upper Marlboro' upon the subject, taking my nephew, Caleb S. Hallowell, with me, and it resulted in the liberation of thirteen, most of them children. The object of the society was, not to interfere with slavery, but to secure to the slaves their legal rights. A number of communications, mostly written by Samuel M. Janney, were published in the Alexandria Gazette, in favor of abolishing slavery in the District of Columbia, and we prepared a petition to Congress, praying for that object, which was signed by all the judges of the courts, nearly all the gospel ministers in Alexandria, Washington, and Georgetown, and over fifteen hundred voters of the District,

---

* Author of the "Star Spangled Banner."- EDS.

which then comprised a county on each side of the Potomac. The petition was presented to Congress, but the prayer it contained was not granted.

This was the first society, of others than Friends, I was ever a member of. I had never known a decision by yeas and nays, where I was concerned, or heard the yeas and nays called. It was all new to me, but I was learning. Being only Secretary, my duties were plain, and my ignorance was not discovered. The society met every month, (and it was a *live* society), until the Southampton or " Nat Turner " insurrection, Eighth month, 1831, when, under the excitement this occasioned on the subject of slavery, it was thought to be most prudent to suspend the meetings, and they were never resumed.

In 1829, I had some mathematical correspondence, through the columns of the "National Intelligencer," with James Caden, a teacher who lived in Alexandria when I went there, but who had moved to Washington, which tended to bring my school into notoriety. The letters on both sides are in my scrap-book.

CHAPTER VIII.

1831.

Death of his valued friend Edward Stabler — Eclipse of the Sun — Family bereavement — Northern tour — "Celestial phenomena " — Surveying — Calculating an almanac — Revising Blair's Philosophy — Cholera — Meteoric shower — A move which begins in difficulty but ends well.

The year 1831, just mentioned, was a memorable one to me in several respects. On the 18th of the First month, my valued friend, Edward Stabler, departed this life. I was in the chamber with him when he died. His wife fell immediately on her knees in earnest and affecting supplication for patience and resignation to the severe and unexpected bereavement to her and to her now fatherless children. The previous Fifth-day, five days before, he had been at meeting. His disease was pronounced to be scarlet fever.

On the 12th of Second month was a very large eclipse of the sun, that I had calculated at John Gummere's, and had looked forward to ever since, with interest. The sun was eleven and a half digits eclipsed. On the 6th of Fourth month, our daughter Mary Jane died, twin sister to Henry, aged nearly twenty-two months. On the 9th of Seventh month, James, our oldest child, died of scarlet fever, after nineteen hours sickness, aged nearly six years. On the 17th of Seventh month, one week after, his next younger brother, Charles, died of the same disease, aged four years and two months, sick eight days.

Of our four children, three were taken in less than three months, leaving only Henry. When Joseph Mandeville met me first after these strippings, he quoted, feelingly, the following appropriate lines from Young's "Apostrophe to Death:"

"Insatiate Archer! could not *one* suffice?
Thy shaft flew *thrice* and thrice my peace was slain,
And thrice, ere thrice yon moon had filled her horn."

It was a hard stroke to me. I felt as if the light of the world was put out. I had not then learned that children are only lent, or to know this truth, to quote from Hannah More: "That is not true content which does not enjoy as the gift of infinite wisdom what is *has*, nor is that true patience which does not suffer meekly

the loss of what it had, because it is not in accordance
with the Divine Will that it should have it longer."

Upon the death of little Charles, Seventh month
17th, of scarlet fever, it was thought best to break up
the school. I took Margaret and Henry, our *only* child
left, to Fair Hill, the home of my father-in-law, and I
went on a visit to New York, Boston, etc. I left New
York in the evening, taking the boat for Boston, just one
week after Charles's death, and was walking alone on the
upper deck, thinking over recent events, with a feeling of
sadness, when I looked up and saw the heavens all tran-
quil, and many of the stars, of which I had known the
names for years, seeming like old acquaintances, and I
was favored to realize that *all* was not gone, but that
there was something still left worth living for. I was
much strengthened and encouraged by this outlook at
the stars.

I visited Cambridge college, where I was introduced
to President Josiah Quincy, and was delighted with their
large planetarium and rich cabinet of minerals; visited
the Athenæum, to which I had some difficulty in gaining
admission, being at first refused, having no ticket; but I
told the person in charge that I was from Alexandria,
below Washington, knew no one in Boston to whom I
could apply for a ticket, and looking him pleasantly in
the face, told him I would be very glad if he would let
me in; when, with a look as pleasant as mine could have
been, he asked me to enter, and was as careful to show
me all the many objects of interest it contained as if I
had had a regular introduction. I also called to see
Dr. Nathaniel Bowditch, who was then the actuary of a
life insurance company, and had some very interesting
conversation with him. John Gummere once had called

on him, John told me, and introduced himself in a similar way. They had both been contributors to a mathematical work called "The Analyst," and had learned to appreciate each other's intellectual powers, but had never met. John thought Bowditch did not manifest quite as much cordiality as he expected; when some turn was given to the conversation, by which Bowditch learned who his visitor was, (not having previously realized that he was his former correspondent), he rose from his seat and took him by the hand, saying, "Is your name Gum-me-re? I have always called it Gum-mere"; and afterwards he was most cordial and agreeable. My visit to Boston was delightful throughout.

I concluded to return to New York by way of New Haven. I arrived at New Haven on Seventh-day evening, and staid over First-day at the "Tontine Hotel." I attended chapel in the morning and church in the afternoon, where I heard a most interesting discourse from the Scripture account of Peter and Simon the Sorcerer, the import of which I remember to this day, and have been many times instructed by it, but it is too long to record it any other way than I am doing it, by my life. Between meetings I walked over the city and into the beautiful cemetery, where I saw the tomb of Eli Whitney, who made that great gift to the South, the cotton gin. I also saw the graves of three children of Professor Silliman lying side by side, whose ages did not much differ from those we had recently lost, and the coincidence was touching to me. I had known him by character for some years, and had taken his Journal of Science at John Gummere's recommendation, from its commencement, and as my visit to New Haven was principally to call on him, I went to his residence the next morning. He recognized

8

me as one of his Southern subscribers who had contributed to his Journal, of which I shall speak hereafter, and he seemed very glad to see me. I mentioned having seen the graves of his three children in the cemetery the preceding day, and related to him the coincidence of our having recently lost the same number at nearly the same ages, which seemed to touch his sympathies, and was the foundation of a warm friendship, that terminated only with his life. I was shown through the college, the cabinet of minerals, containing the largest piece of meteoric iron I had ever seen, and through the laboratory, where I saw an electro horse shoe magnet, constructed by Professor Henry, then of Rensselaer Institute, that would support the weight of seven men.

I returned to Alexandria and went up to our home intending to stay there till next morning. *It did look desolate.* Margaret and Henry, our only remaining child, were at Fair Hill.

The clock had stopped. Not a being was there. At last, in one of the rooms, I came across a half-starved cat, that mewed piteously when it saw me, which incident affected my feelings so much that I at once got a hack, and went to Fair Hill for Margaret and Henry. I found them both well, and also all the rest. My coming upon them, rather unexpectedly, brightened them up, and that cheered me, and we spent a right pleasant evening.

The next day, the 13th of Eighth month, the same day as the " Nat Turner Insurrection," I brought Henry and his mother to Alexandria, and in the afternoon, as I was walking down the street I observed a very unusual and remarkable appearance of the sun, in explanation of which I wrote an article for the National Intelligencer, which they headed "Celestial Phenomenon." Little Henry and I took this communication to Washington, Eighth month 20th, the afternoon of the day on which our daughter Caroline, at whose request I am writing these incidents, was born.

This communication was replied to by Dr. Robert Newman, of Romney, Virginia, which resulted in a correspondence through the columns of the National Intelligencer, that continued nearly a year and a-half, which correspondence is contained in my "Scrap Book."

I was appointed by the Common Council, City Surveyor of Alexandria (successor to William Yeaton), the fees of which office, if I had exacted them, would have amounted to a considerable sum in a year; but it afforded a fine opportunity to instruct my students in "Field Practice," with the theodolite and level, and I always took with me those of them who were qualified, and made it a class exercise, so that I did not feel willing, or think it right, to receive pay for it.

However, on Seventh-day afternoon, I did a good deal of field surveying in Alexandria and Fairfax counties, for which I made regular charges. After making a pretty extensive survey for Rozier Dulany, who owned and lived at "Suter's Hill," he sent me a check, with the amount in blank, for me to fill with what sum I chose, which I made not *over* the ordinary charges.

About 1830, I sent a communication to "Silliman's Journal of Science," giving a reason for the blue and dark appearance of the heavens; for the twinkling of the stars; why telescopes cause the stars to shine with a steady light, and enable the observer to see stars that are otherwise invisible; and the cause of large hail in warm weather. All the articles were published in the Journal, first series, and were copied into the Boston Courier, and from it into a paper published in Charleston, South Carolina, where James P. Stabler, of Sandy Spring, Maryland, saw it, and he sent the paper to me.

I also calculated the Alexandria Almanac for William A. Morrison, which was printed by Edgar Snowden for two years in succession, but what years I cannot recollect. For this, my training with John Gummere was of great service to me.

About 1830, I also revised Blair's Philosophy, in which I inserted the substance of my articles to Silliman's Journal, and some other original matter, and the book was very neatly printed by Kimber & Sharpless.

In Fifth month, 1832, brother Charles Farquhar returned to Alexandria, commenced the practice of medicine, and opened an apothecary store on King street, boarding with us. It was the year the cholera was in Alexandria, and he was appointed by the Common Council one of the physicians to the cholera hospital. On his visits to the hospitals I accompanied him, he fixing the time to suit my hours of school. There were many sudden deaths, immediately around us, and throughout the town. The scenes at the hospitals were heart-rending; some continually dying, and generally seeming indifferent whether they lived or died.

One day, a large, strong man, appearing to be about thirty-five years old, was struck down with the disease in the street, at noon, near my school. He remained entirely sensible. My interest and sympathy were keenly awakened, and I remained with him until time for school, two o'clock, when, as there were physicians and a number of others in attendance, I left him to attend to my school duties. But my thoughts would run to the poor man. About four o'clock, I went out to see how my unfortunate patient came on, and found that he was *not only dead, but buried!* All this in about four hours from his first attack! My feelings were shocked. For several days, his image, as he lay there pleading that he might live, seemed continually before me. I could not sleep. My heart was filled with discouragement. I had not then learned that, while there are many mansions in the Father's house, there are none for the discouraged, for discouragement implies want of faith and trust in the Good Father. So I found it. There was no peace in that state of mind. I strove to rise from it, and to feel assured that *all* being in the orderings of the good and merciful Father, it must be in wisdom and love. Thus with this thought "getting up to the entering in (or mouth) of the cave," like the prophet, I one night received an impression as distinct as if it had been with an audible voice, or written in letters of light in the firmament, " *death cannot separate from my Father's care, love and mercy.* " My feelings were overwhelmed with gratitude, not only for the relief and calm to my troubled spirit, but for the everlasting goodness and tender solicitude of the Eternal Father, and the renewed assurance that "his mercy endureth forever."

In Sixth month, 1832, our brother Charles Farquhar was married to Sarah Brooke, daughter of Roger Brooke. They boarded at our house for three weeks, while they got their own house on King street ready to live in. In the spring of 1837, they left Alexandria and settled at Olney, Sandy Spring, Maryland, where our widowed sister Sarah still lives.

In the Eleventh month, 1833, a communication appeared in the National Intelligencer of Washington city, headed, " A call to Mr. Hallowell," asking me very respectfully and complimentarily to give an explanation of the "Meteoric Shower" that had occurred on the thirteenth of that month, to which I replied, and both the communications are contained in my scrap-book, also a description of the shower of stars.

These all tended to make my school more known, besides being useful to myself, from the requisite thought and research, and they were among the environments that acted on my organism and evolved my character, and the "me," as I then was.

About the Eighth month, 1831, that very memorable year, my good landlady and true friend, Elizabeth T. Hooe, died. I had formed a warm friendship for her. She was a good, true, and honorable lady, and, although she was regarded as particular in pecuniary matters, the condition in which her husband had left the estate, which she had to settle, rendered this necessary. She never once urged payment of me, but only let me know, on the day my rent was due, that it would be a convenience to her to have it, when I was ready to pay, which was very reasonable.

I was just getting my school under good way, and now the property, both my residence and the house containing my school and lecture-rooms, would have to be sold. It was a great derangement of my plans.

The sale was not to be till the following spring, 1832, so I resolved to lay up all I could by that time for a first payment, and endeavor to buy it, in which proposition Phineas Janney and Robert I. Taylor, two of the trustees that had the selling of the property, encouraged me. They told me how high they thought I might safely go in my bids. The day of sale came. I felt anxious. It was a new scene to me. The house where we lived was first offered, and I ran it up to what Phineas Janney and Robert

I. Taylor had thought was a fair price, but the bidding kept on above that. I did not know who was bidding against me. I reflected that moving would be attended with a good deal of expense, as well as inconvenience, and as I was already nicely fixed there, I concluded to run it up to one thousand dollars beyond the limits these friends had named, and if the bidding went above that I would think it was not best for me to have it, and let it go. It *did* go beyond the extra one thousand dollars, and was struck off to John Lloyd. It was a great disappointment to me, my thoughts having been running on it for so long.

The sale was some time in the Twelfth month, and although I paid my rent quarterly, I rented the property by the year, and Robert I. Taylor, who was very kind to me, took the pains to let me know that I could not be disturbed in my possession, without having three months' notice before the close of the current year, which would allow me to remain where I was until Eighth month, 1833.

On the afternoon of the day of sale, Margaret and I went all over the town to try and find a suitable place for our school. We looked at a place nearly opposite Robert H. Miller's residence, on St. Asaph street, and I felt sick at heart,—almost thought we had come to an end. But I remembered it was done for the best. I thought it was not right to bid higher, and I was strengthened to believe that there would be some way to get along.

I could not sleep much that night. As I lay thinking of the day just passed, it was presented to my mind that the Bank of Potomac, that had the selling of the property, had bid in the lot running through the square on which the sugar-house and my school-house both stood, for three thousand dollars; and I saw how I could convert the sugar-house into a comfortable roomy dwelling. I got up

early the next morning and went down to see Phineas
Janney, and told him I would take the property at the
price at which it was bid in, to which he consented. I immediately engaged George Swain to do the carpenter work,
and Robert Brockett to do the brick work, for although
the law allowed me possession of the property till Eighth
month, 1833, I assured John Lloyd that I would get out
of the house at the earliest practicable moment. The
building containing the school and lecture-rooms remained
undisturbed.

My school was full, having one hundred scholars or
over; my lecture-class was large, and I was enabled to
meet the payment of the bills as they came in, to my astonishment, occasionally giving my note for a few months,
which never failed to be met. The bills from Margaret's
scholars, her school being full also, helped me considerably.

I did the planning as the work progressed, consulting
with Swain, which required a good deal of time and
thought. Teachers at that day had not the convenience of
metallic pens, but were dependent upon the "gray goose
quill." So, five days in the week, I made at noon one
hundred quills into pens, besides repairing the old ones, so
as to give every student a new pen when he began the
writing exercise in the afternoon, and to have some to give
them when the others needed repairs. I kept my knife
sharp, and learned to be very expert at this business, a
part of my education and training for which I since have
had no use.

The kind liberality of Daniel B. Smith and W. & A.
Mason, of Philadelphia, and of George S. Hough and
John P. Cowman, of Alexandria, which I have before
referred to, preserved me from feeling peculiarly pinched
or humiliated under a pressing debt. I feel grateful

to them all under a retrospect of their kindness to this day.

After the house was finished, A. C. Cazenove called one day, and I showed him all through the building, and when he saw how nicely it was arranged, and what a comfortable residence and how complete an establishment it was for a boarding-school, he stopped and looked at me with an expression of astonishment on his countenance, and said, "Well, Mr. Hallowell, how came you to think of all this? Did you do it by Algebra?"

The lumber materials were obtained of Benjamin Waters and George H. Smoot; the plastering was done by Tyler; the painting by Higden. George Swain engaged employees, plasterer, painter, slater, etc., and got the house finished so that we moved into it in Fifth month, 1833. George Swain and I had but one difference of importance in all the many changes that had to be made. It will be understood that all the inside wood-work, floors, etc., had to be taken out, leaving the four outside walls and a cross wall (all of which were good), standing, with the openings that had existed for doors and windows, and we had to arrange the stories and the openings for doors and windows anew. The cross wall was about one-third of the way across the building from the west wall.

The openings in the walls did not correspond, and to avoid too many cuttings that would weaken it, George proposed to have the passage on the second floor to go diagonally from one of the then existing openings to another, which of course would make it not parallel to the outside walls. This my mathematical organ could not reconcile, and I insisted upon having a new opening made, so as to avoid this unsightly appearance, which he reluctantly had done, and it harmed nothing. He afterwards acknowledged that mine was the right plan.

Although I was so much disappointed and discouraged at not getting the property I so much wanted, I was far better accommodated in every respect with my present buildings than I could have been with the one I desired to have, the present one affording comfortable rooms for so many more boarders, thus increasing the means of paying for it. The remembrance of the circumstances connected with this whole proceeding has many times been a source of encouragement and strength to me, proving that straightforward integrity of purpose will come out right in the end.

On the 8th of Eleventh month, 1835, more than two years after my purchase of the property, I received a characteristic note from Phineas Janney, one of the trustees, asking if I would please to calculate the amount of three thousand dollars, at interest for so many years, months, and days, the time being exactly that from the sale of the property to the then date. There had never been any writing, memorandum, or deed, on the subject. The note was handed to me in school. As soon as school was out I went down to the bank, and Phineas met me with one of those pleasant, meaning smiles, which showed the goodness of his heart. I told him I had taken his hint, and had come down to arrange matters, which he said would be all settled by my paying the interest up to date and giving my note at four months for the principal, which was very satisfactory to me. I did what he required, and the trustees made me a deed for the property.

CHAPTER IX.

1835.

Scientific use of cannon balls — Touching the right spring — Increase of school — Heavy responsibility — A Lyceum established — Wearing cases — Need of rest — Giving up the school.

My school increased in popularity and in the number of boarding scholars. Robert E. Lee, George Turner, Fisher Lewis, and several others, who had gone from my school to West Point, graduated in that institution with marked distinction, so that persons who consulted with the authorities at West Point in regard to a cadet who was preparing to enter there, were advised to send him to my school to get him prepared in mathematics. On one occasion, Senator Bagby, of Alabama, brought his son Arthur to enter my school, and said he wished me to prepare him to enter West Point. I told him I did not do that. I was a Friend, and disapproved of war. What they were learning in our school was practical knowledge of scientific principles, that would be useful in any calling in life, and if the students made any other than a good use of it afterwards, the fault was not mine. This was said very pleasantly. Colonel John J. Abert was present. He had recently returned from the Mexican war, and seemed to enjoy our conversation. His son William was a student with us. They wished to look over the establishment, and in going around we went into my observatory, which revolved on three cannon balls, rolling in an iron trough. "Now," said I, "*this* is the use I like cannon balls to be put to, a scientific purpose, and not to be sending them in an unfriendly way to our Mexican neighbors." They both enjoyed the joke. "Ah," said Bagby, patting me on the back, "Mr. Hallowell, if you will make a good scholar and a good Quaker of my son, it is all I ask." I was on the point of telling him that if his son was a " good Quaker" he would not go to West Point, but I thought it best not to check the evident flow of good feeling in which his remark was made, as such a reply from me might have done.

We kept as few domestics as would perform the ordinary family labor, and when there would be a fall of snow, inasmuch as there was a large extent of brick pavement to clean, the front pavement being ninety-five feet by eighteen, besides a great deal between the buildings and in paths back, I took it upon myself to have this done. I would get up early, a half hour before sunrise, and collect all the spades, shovels, brooms, etc., about the establishment, and place them out of sight, but where I could soon get them if wanted, and commence myself to shovel off snow. Soon one of the early risers would come and say, "Mr. Hallowell, let me have that shovel." I would hand it to him very politely, and get another tool. Another student would come and say, "Benjamin, let me have that broom." I would pleasantly hand it to him, and get another, and so proceed till every shovel, spade, broom, and hoe on the premises would be employed, "oven peel" and all. I never gave up the last one, but kept it for my own use. When a student would want it, I would tell him, "No, such a student has been at work a good while, get his shovel," and there would be a pleasant struggle as to who should have the *privilege* of using the tool. In this way, time and again, we had all the pavements cleaned before breakfast, the students enjoying it, and going in to their meal in the fine spirits that pleasant and useful exercise gives. *It was play.* Now, if I had taken an armful of tools out at once, and asked the students to assist me in cleaning the pavements, some of them would probably have done it out of respect to me, but all the animation, hilarity, and *zest* would have been wanting. *That would have been work.* Everything can be moved if you touch the right spring.

I now was out of debt. I took what I owed uncle Comly to him in gold, interest and all, and thanked him heartily for his kindness. It had been a great accommodation to me. I have already stated that he would never take more than five per cent. interest.

About 1835 the number of boarders had so much increased that I was induced to make additional accommodations for lodging and for the school. We had students from fourteen different States and Territories, from South America, Cuba, and England. For this purpose I connected the dwelling and school-room by a cross building, which gave us two additional class-rooms, a teacher's room, and three additional chambers, that would accommodate from sixteen to twenty more boarders. It also gave us a larger kitchen, and rendered our establishment very complete.

We had of course to increase the number of teachers. Besides those who taught French, Drawing, Latin, and Greek, there were three competent and full teachers of English, Mathematics, etc., including myself, and in addition two tutors. We had eighty boarders, besides the day-scholars, and about one hundred in family, including domestics. It had grown to be a large and heavy concern, and seemingly without my intending it, and against my wishes. It was my desire and effort to keep the number limited, and some years I had to refuse quite as many who applied as were admitted. From 1824 to 1842 I employed twenty-nine different teachers in all, four or five at once, much of the time, and four tutors.

While my school was smaller, so that I could become well acquainted with each student, study his character, and get him near my heart, and I get near to his, the school was delightful, kindness and mutual confidence between the students and teachers very generally prevailing.

I generally read some in the Bible at collection, before breakfast, sat a little time in silence at the opening and close of each session of school, and on First-day evenings either myself or Margaret read some essay, allegory, or poem. I continued these customs regularly throughout the whole course of my teaching at Alexandria. But when the school grew larger, and I had to employ a number of teachers, I could not know the students as well, and I would have more difficulty in sustaining the teachers' authority, than in any other part of the government, and it was more embarrassing, because I could not *always* approve of the course they had adopted, though I felt obliged to sustain them in it. Moreover, in my earnest efforts to get near so many students in feeling, day after day, and to get them near me, there was an exhaustion of nervous energy, which would diminish that patient forbearance and calm firmness, that are so important in the administration of discipline with young persons. The school would commence very pleasantly in the fall, but after it got so large, about Christmas, say three months after the term commenced, my nervous energy would become exhausted, and there would be a seeming change among the students. For some years, I believed that it was the interruption occasioned by Christmas holiday that made the change which invariably occurred about this time, but in a careful retrospect of all the circumstances, I am convinced it arose from too much wear and pressure on my physical and nervous energies.

I endeavored and labored hard to secure for my assistant teachers the same authority, deference, and respect from the students that I myself possessed, but in this effort I could not always succeed; and although it was done with the very best intentions, I can now look back and see it was a mistake, from not possessing a better knowledge of human nature. It must be the individual character that impresses authority and respect in the student, otherwise they will not be rendered, and this character cannot be transferred to another. "For a person to be respected, he must be respectable."

In the spring of 1838, brother Granville S. Farquhar, whose health had given way at the apothecary business in Washington, wished to go to the country and raise Multicaulus, which were then much in vogue, and proposed that I should build a house on the land I had bought the preceding year of William Birdsall, in Sandy Spring, Montgomery county, Maryland, and named Rockland. As mother Farquhar was about to leave Fair Hill, where a Yearly Meeting school was soon to open again, I was more than willing to build a house to accommodate the two families; Granville and his wife Emily to occupy one part, and mother Farquhar and her family the other. I had then no thought of ever living there myself. They and my wife's uncle John Elgar, who then lived with mother Farquhar, and who kindly assisted, planned the original building.

In the fall of 1838, mother Farquhar and Granville moved with their families into their respective west and east ends of Rockland, and settled there.

About 1834 a proposition was made by Thomas William

Smith, William Stabler, Robert H. Miller, Elias Harrison, John McCormick, Edward S. Hough, and myself, to found a Lyceum, and have lectures once a week on some literary, scientific, or historical subject, to be followed by a debate on some topic that was neither political nor religious. A public meeting was called at the Lancasterian school-house, back of my lot, which was well attended. It was decided to establish a Lyceum and to elect a President and six directors. I named Parson Harrison for President, with whom I had been very pleasantly associated in the " Board of Guardians" of the Alexandria free schools, of which board he was President, and I believe no other person was put in nomination. The election was by ballot. When the ballots were counted, to my great surprise, I was elected by a very large majority. At first I was disposed to decline the proffered honor, but Parson Harrison and the rest insisted so strongly on my serving, that I consented to do so. I had had no experience in an office of the kind; it was, however an improvement to me.

I delivered the first lecture, which was on Vegetable Physiology. It was the commencement of my attention being turned to that very interesting subject.

Caleb S. Hallowell soon after lectured upon Meteorology, which interested the audience very much. The debates, too, were well conducted by Benoni Wheat, George S. Hough, John McCormick, and many others, and occasionally by Parson Harrison and myself. The meetings for some time were held in my lecture-room, which would be crowded. Lectures were given by Parson Harrison, Dr. Murphy, etc., etc., and the Lyceum became a very popular and instructive institution.

At length a lot was purchased on the southwest corner of Washington and Prince streets, on which was erected a fine building, a little back from the street, with a pediment front supported by four fluted Doric columns, with a triglyph cornice, and surrounded by an iron railing, and a beautiful yard of flowers and ornamental shrubbery. In this building was placed the Alexandria Library, and there was besides, on the first floor, a large reading-room, and a room for a cabinet of minerals, and specimens in Natural History. On the second floor was a well arranged and handsome lecture-room, with marble busts of Cicero and Seneca, one on each side of the President's desk and seat. In this room lectures were given by John Quincy Adams, Caleb Cushing, Dr. Sewell, Samuel Goodrich (Peter Parley), Daniel Bryan, Robert H. Miller, William H. Fowle, and several others. I gave the introductory lecture (which was published), and several others afterwards. Attending the Lyceum was a very interesting and improving way of spending one evening in the week (Third-day evening), and the citizens would adapt their visiting and other arrangements so as not to have them come on Lyceum evenings.

My boarding-students all attended the Lyceum meetings, I paying the fee for admission, it being part of their education. I continued President until I removed to the country in 1842. The marble busts spoken of above were purchased in Italy in the time of Cromwell, by one of the Fairfax family; were brought to this country by Lord Fairfax, and had come into the possession of Daniel Herbert, whose mother was a Fairfax. I purchased them of him for the price he asked (one hundred and twenty-five dollars), but permitted them to remain in the Lyceum while it continued in operation. I then moved them to my study in Alexandria, and they are now in my study here, where I am writing. I value them *very highly.*

9

The wear of the large school, my lecturing twice a week, through nearly the whole term of eleven months, on Natural Philosophy, Chemistry, Astronomy, Geology, and Vegetable and Animal Physiology, besides providing for the large family, and principally keeping my own accounts and books, began to tell unfavorably on my physical constitution. *I needed relaxation, rest, and quiet.*

CHAPTER X.

1842.

Removal to the country — Farming — Lecturing — Minor trials — "Aunt Kittie's" sermon — Practical mathematics — Accepts a professorship — Chemical investigations.

In the spring of 1842, it was decided that my nephews, Caleb and James S. Hallowell, should take the school, and that I should take my family to our Rockland farm, where, after some additions to the house, we moved in the summer of 1842, and I commenced farming.

In compliance with my arrangement with my nephews, Caleb and James, to lecture for them upon the opening of their school in the fall, I went to Alexandria, twenty-five miles, every week on horse-back. At the close of my course with them, I accompanied my valued friends, Nicholas and Margaret Brown, from Canada, as driver and companion, on their religious visit to Fredericksburg, Richmond, Goochland, etc., in Virginia, for an account of which journey see my "Memoir of Margaret Brown," pages 91 to 131 inclusive.

In the spring of 1843, I commenced farming regularly, arranging the fields, putting up fences, planting trees, shrubbery, etc. Brother Granville, who had now moved to Calvert county, Maryland, to practice medicine, had planted both an apple and a peach orchard in 1839, during his occupancy of the premises. I now got my valued friend, Thomas P. Stabler, to assist me to plant some Seckel pear trees, which I had purchased of him, six in number, in our front lawn, near the house, where I had not long before planted a juniper bush, which our kind friend, Roger Brooke, had found in the fence corner on my place, and which is very rare in these parts. There was very little other shrubbery. One Fourth-day morning, Margaret wanted the yard mowed, and I got my man Samuel to mow it. I went around with him and pointed out each of the six Seckel pear trees, and a hen that was sitting by the juniper bush, and charged him to be particularly careful not to injure any of them, but to stop the scythe when far enough off to leave them safe. I then went to my chamber to get ready for meeting, and on my return in about one hour, going to see how "Sammy" came on, I found he had cut down five of the six pear trees, and had *cut the hen's head off!* I was glad it was meeting morning. I got right in my carriage, without saying a word, being afraid to speak, for fear, as it *was done,* and speaking could do no good, *I might say too much.*

Now, Samuel was a very good, obedient hand; is my neighbor at this time, and a fine man, with several children grown, but he was then a *great beau,* would sit up and sing and dance all night, and then sleep over his scythe in the day, swinging it mechanically, and only knew when he came up to the pear tree by the jar it occasioned, awakening him. It was this trait that rendered colored people, at that day much more than at present, *only muscle.* They needed an intelligent mind to direct them continually. *Now,* happily, the mind and muscle are becoming blended in the same person.

The same year, 1843, I commenced ditching, under-draining, and removing the bushes and rocks from eight acres of meadow land on a part of the place called Centreville, and had it plowed and prepared for seeding in timothy in the fall. The manures and work expended on it cost one hundred and thirty-six dollars—seventeen dollars an acre—which was thought by some of my neighbors to be more than the land was worth. I sowed the seed with my own hand, a little time before I went to Yearly Meeting. It was the first of *my* sowing. When I came home the timothy was up nicely. It looked like rabbit-fur over the meadow, and perhaps I was a little proud of it.

One morning, before breakfast, I rode my horse Cato to see my timothy, and lo! my colored neighbor Kitty Waters' pigs had been in the meadow all night, and had rooted it up dreadfully! It looked all over as if it had the small-pox. I had to pass her house in returning home, and stopped, and in a pretty loud tone told her that she knew what pains I had taken with that meadow, that I had been working at it all summer, had sowed it with my own hand, and now, when the timothy was coming up nicely, her pigs had been in and had rooted it up shamefully, what I would not have had done for any consideration! As soon as I had finished my hurried and loud speech, "Aunt Kitty," as she was called, in the most mild manner and kind, gentle tone of voice imaginable, replied, "Well, Mr. Hallowell, these things are good for us. If our patience did not get *exercised* it would never get *strong*. But the pigs ought not to have been there. I did not know they were there — they shall never trouble you again."

There was a man that felt badly and greatly humbled! I had just come from Yearly Meeting, and had thought I had made some progress, and this colored woman was away out of all reach above me, to know that the exercise of patience was essential to its increase of strength, while I had lost an opportunity that might have been beneficial to me, had I only possessed her wisdom. I set out and walked my horse home. I *could* not go in a trot—had not spirit enough; fastened Cato by the horse-block and went in to breakfast. Margaret said I seemed dull, and asked me what was the matter. I was ashamed to tell her, but said I did not feel much appetite.

While I was at breakfast I remembered that I had some seed left in a bag, so, after the meal, which was soon finished, I put the bag of seed and an iron garden rake on my shoulder, rode out to the meadow, hitched Cato, and sowed the rooted places over with seed and raked it in well. It grew so, that in a month after no one could have told where the pigs had been. This sermon of "Aunt Kitty's" has been of the greatest practical instruction to me from that day.

I may mention here that, although some of my neighbors thought I was wasting my money in the expense put on that meadow, I sold in each of the two succeeding years more from that meadow than the whole improvement cost me, one hundred and thirty-six dollars. The third year I was not here.

Two other incidents occurred at Rockland, which I will relate here (although I do not remember the time of their occurrence) as illustration of the mode of my managing the hands I employed.

My man Edward, colored, was hauling out the manure from the barn-yard, with a pair of oxen, and I observed he rode on the cart with every load. This I felt to be a wrong, but I wished to correct it without hurting anything. So, as he rode out with a load, an idea was presented to me, that answered my highest expectations. I placed myself in the way of his return, and as soon as he got near me, I said, "Edward, how much dost thou weigh?" He seemed a little embarrassed, and in a short time said, "About one hundred and seventy pounds." "One hundred and seventy pounds!" I responded. "How many loads dost thou take out in a day?"—"Twelve." "Well, now, suppose thou wast to put one hundred and seventy pounds more manure on the cart, and thou walk out. Dost thou think the oxen would know the difference?"—"Oh, no."—"Then there would be one hundred and seventy pounds more manure each load in the field, wouldn't there?"—"So there would. I never thought of that."—"Then in six loads there would be ten hundred and twenty pounds more, or half a ton more manure taken to the field, which is as much as another load. In twelve loads there would be a ton, or two loads more each day, and in six days twelve loads more, or a day's work, without being any harder for the oxen."—"So it would! I never thought of all that. I will walk out after this." He seemed pleased with the discovery, and even to think better of me afterwards.

I never held more than one office in Maryland, which was sub-supervisor, under Edward Lea, of about one and a half miles of road in front of my house, between the two turnpikes, for which the pay ran out of my pocket instead of in. During my administration, a law was passed requiring every able-bodied man to work one day on the road, furnish a substitute, or pay one dollar and twenty-five cents, thus requiring as much road tax of a laboring man as of one who owned a farm and many horses. The law was very unpopular with the colored people, and I did not like it at all myself. However, as it was the law, and the road needed mending, I accepted the forty days labor that were apportioned to my division of the road, and notified the persons in companies of six or eight a day, to meet me at the road. I was there punctually, but my hands came in very slowly each day, straggling along till nine o'clock.

One day I saw a man sitting for more than half an hour on the fence a little distance off. At length he got down, when it was at least half-past nine, and came slowly to the place where the others were at work. I soon saw he was going to do nothing that would be work, and I reflected a little time for a right way to meet the case. At length I said to him, " William, how old art thou ?"—" I am nearly twenty-four."—" So old ?" I said, " I thought thou could not be more than fourteen or fifteen."—" What made you think so ?"—" Why, thou seemed so weak, so very weak ; would just take a little earth on the point of the shovel, and after motioning two or three times, just toss that little earth a few feet — thou didst seem so *very weak.*" The others all smiled, for they had noticed him. " Why," said he, " I am as strong as any of these men, and can do as much work," and suiting his actions to his words, he started in, and by night he had done a *full day's work,* and was in the best of humor, as indeed were all my company that day, the little incident having seemed to do them all good.

In the fall of 1843, after the death of Dr. Hall, Professor of Chemistry in the medical department of Columbian College, I was strongly urged to accept the vacant chair, which I ultimately consented to do, spending three days in each week in Washington.

The class of students numbered some fifty or sixty, who met at eleven o'clock, Fifth, Sixth, and Seventh-days, and I had quite a large class of citizens in the evening on Sixth-day, which was pleasant. My colleagues, Drs. Miller, Sewall, Johnson, and Lindsley, were very agreeable, intelligent, and social, but my situation, being separated as I was so much from my family, was not very congenial to my feelings. Besides which, the students, regarding Chemistry as of less importance than Anatomy, Physiology, Materia Medica, etc., came to the college with comparatively little previous study, thinking they could gain what knowledge they needed on that subject at the lectures, which was simply impossible. The examination each day on the previous lecture showed great deficiency. The class preparing to graduate consisted of about fourteen, and I thought I would drill them thoroughly upon "Marsh's method" of testing for arsenic. When the examination came around, and the Faculty were all together, each Professor to examine every student upon the branch upon which he had lectured, there was *but one* of the class that could give the process and rationale of Marsh's method of testing for arsenic, or was qualified to graduate in Chemistry as a medical student. I told my colleagues as there were, one hundred years ago, as good physicians probably as at present, without a knowledge of Chemistry as a science, if the students were well prepared on the other branches of the profession, I would not let their deficiency in chemistry prevent them from graduating. This was approved by the Faculty, and when I had signed my name to the last diploma, I handed to the Faculty my resignation, which I had already written.

There were some incidents connected with my professorship that were interesting. One evening William W. Seaton, one of the editors of the "National Intelligencer," introduced to me John S. Skinner, the celebrated agriculturist and the founder of the "American Farmer." He interested me by his conversation very much. He was strongly in favor of sheep husbandry. He said, "A sheep can never die in debt to its owner. In its annual fleece and lamb it pays as it goes." The object of his visit was to get me to tell the composition of two powders from Germany, which were said to be a certain remedy for the murrain in cattle, and as he was writing a treatise on cattle disease, he very much wished to know of what it was composed.

He left both powders with me. I operated upon one and found it consisted of saltpetre and "Bole Armeniac," or Armenian earth, in proportions that I determined. I went to an apothecary and got him to mix me a powder of these ingredients in the proportion I mentioned, which he did. When J. S. Skinner called, I gave him the one the apothecary had prepared and the one imported from Germany, and in appearance, taste, or smell, he could detect no difference. They seemed exactly alike. He was very much pleased.

In John S. Skinner's edition of "Clater & Youatt's Cattle Doctor" the editor inserts the following, pages 91 and 92, in reference to the preceding analysis: "I received some months ago, from a Hollander, some powders for the cure of murrain in cattle, the receipt for the manufacture of which is a secret. I have thought that possibly the chief ingredients might be detected by the experiments of an accomplished. chemist. I send you two papers of the murrain powder, each being two doses."

"The two powders were placed in the hands of Professor Benjamin Hallowell, as eminent for scientific attainments as he is remarkable for simplicity of manners and benevolence of heart. In a few days he was good enough to return one powder with an exact duplicate of it, and the following memorandum:

"'The powder contains three hundred and eighty grains. It is composed of three hundred and forty grains of nitrate of potash (saltpetre), and forty grains of Bole Armeniac, intimately mixed. Be it remembered that the above quantity made two doses, and the Holland directions are, dissolve in a pint of hot water. Thus, we came to the following receipt for murrain: Take nitrate of potash one hundred and seventy grains, Bole Armeniac twenty grains, dissolve in a pint of hot water, and give.'"

A distinguished Washington physician brought me one evening a cake of a whitish substance, in shape of a Lima bean, and about the size of a silver quarter of a dollar, which had been found in a cavity in the stomach of a man who died very suddenly. The doctor thought it was calomel, as the deceased man, though wealthy, had insisted on being his own physician when sick, and always took calomel.

This hint naturally gave direction to my incipient investigations. I tried all the tests for calomel, but detected no mercury. I then tried the tests for lime, but there were no indications of a trace. I knew of no other whitish substance that ever accumulated in quantities in the human system. I tried different tests to no purpose. My piece, small at first, was fast wearing away, as was the night, which had now got into the small hours, and my character was at stake. I was to report in the morning. I thought if I could only bite a piece, to taste it, I could probably gain some clue to what it was by that means, but to taste what had been taken from the stomach of a dead man seemed revolting to me. There I stood in my laboratory, with a piece of the substance in my hand, in a situation more readily imagined than described, regard for my standing as well as for my friend urging me to do all in my power, and my feelings protesting against it. My elbow, seemingly, *would not bend*, to bring the substance to my mouth. But regard for my reputation got the mastery sufficiently to bring my will to my aid, when I took a bite, and found at once that it was magnesia. I then applied the chemical tests for magnesia, and discovered that my taste had determined correctly.

When the physician called in the morning, I showed him the test of its being magnesia, which he supposed the man had taken after the calomel, and, his stomach not being in a condition to dispose of it, it remained there, corroded its coats, and formed an abscess, of which he died. Pure magnesia is a very unsafe medicine.

CHAPTER XI.

1845.

Call to Philadelphia — Mental conflict — Lecture class — Pleasant friends — " Berzelius " — Lectures on Geology — Visitors from home — Interesting excursions — A profitable mistake — Dr. Bartram's inscription — Philosophical ideas on the art of writing — Farewell to Philadelphia and return home — Pleasant occupations and resources.

In the summer of 1845, I received a joint letter from James Martin and Dr. John D. Griscom, of Philadelphia, informing me that Friends there were about to establish a High School for the guarded education of Friends' children, although not to be strictly confined to Friends. They placed the subject before me rather on the ground of a religious duty, that I should accept the situation of Principal, assist in its organization, adjusting the philosophical and chemical apparatus that had just been procured, and in inaugurating a course of lectures in the corresponding branches of science. This presentation occasioned no little exercise of mind and embarrassment to me. I had greatly desired a quiet, retired, country life, with my family of five children, in order to bring them up to industry and mechanical training, as well as to agriculture, gardening, etc. I had fixed up a nice roomy carpenter shop with two work-benches and a full set of carpenter's tools, brace and bits, etc., for each, a pair of large shears for cutting sheet-iron, a large vise, and a superior turning-lathe, with all its accompaniments, and had also, with the valued assistance of my wife's uncle John Elgar, who was a skillful mechanic, machinist, and engineer, fitted up a smith-shop with anvil, bellows, and appurtenances. Under his tutorage I had already learned to weld, solder, turn, etc., so that I had made a tin-cup, had turned tops for each of my three boys, and had done many other things of like character, with a steady aim to get my sons interested in the practical use of tools, as well as in farming, it being my full intention that each of them should learn some mechanical trade.

To break off from all this, in which I was so much interested, and leave my family, to go to Philadelphia, seemed to be a sacrifice that could hardly be required of me. Yet I desired to do just what was right and best, and I earnestly craved that I might be able to see what this would be. I had a letter too from John Comly, placing the concern on the same ground that the other two Friends had done. I felt myself to be "in a place where two ways met," and how ardently I desired and prayed that I might be favored to be directed to choose the right way, I well remember, but I cannot express. But still I could not see. I had enough to live on comfortably, with my farm, and to educate my children, and what I most desired, as congenial to my feelings and higher nature, was quiet in the country, with full employment, which, in the improvement of my farm and the means I had prepared for pleasant and agreeable occupation in rainy or stormy weather, I would continually have.

I remained unable to determine the matter for some time. At length I concluded that I would ride over and see Richard S. Kirk, and if he would be willing to come to Rockland and take care of my family and carry on my farm while I was absent, it would remove *one* difficulty. He consented to do so.

Then I went to Philadelphia to endeavor while there

to see what was the right course for me to take. I saw
the beautiful school building on Cherry Street, near the
meeting-house, which was not far from completion ; went
all over it alone, conversed with some of the Friends,
and things looked and felt more comfortable. On carefully weighing the matter, the balance *seemed* to incline
to my complying with their request, and I eventually
told the committee I would be there on the 1st of
Ninth month, to enter upon my duties with the school.

I went on to Philadelphia a little time before the
school was to open, to make preparations for my arduous
duties. George M. Justice, whom I had known at Dr.
Mitchell's, at the time of my fall, kindly assisted me in
the putting together and arranging of the apparatus.
I valued his friendship very highly, and received much
benefit and instruction from my intercourse and conversation with him. Dillwyn Parrish came to see me on
Seventh or First-day at the school-room, where I spent
most of my time. The school was to open on Second-
day. He perceived I was under discouragement, and he
sympathized deeply with me.

Next morning the school opened with nearly seventy
scholars, from children seven or eight years old to boys
of fifteen or sixteen. I knew the names of but three
in the whole number, Francis Miller, Isaac Bond, and
Clagett Page, sons of old friends in and near Alexandria, Virginia. To examine and classify these properly
was utterly impossible under the circumstances.

I got Isaac Bond, who had been teaching school, and
had gone on to enter the High School as a student, to
assist me. I was not long in learning the names and
getting the school into some kind of order. James Martin kindly spent most of the first morning with me, and

rendered me all the assistance he could, but with such a beginning the order and discipline of the school were necessarily poor. All the character I had acquired by the success of my school in Alexandria, and which would have been of avail to me almost anywhere in the South, was here in Philadelphia entirely lost. I had a new one to form, and with such surroundings, the formation of an available character was necessarily slow.

After about a week my boarding-house was changed from Arch street to the house of Henry and Mary Pike, No. 222 Cherry Street, who, with their daughter Lydia and son Thornton, made it a pleasant home to me.

I soon commenced my lectures to the scholars of both the boys' and girls' schools in one lecture-room. These lectures were on Seventh-day forenoon, being the closing exercises of the week. William and Deborah F. Wharton, Dr. Shoemaker, and a number of others, attended. I would get the students to assist me sometimes in making preparations for the lectures, by which I gradually became better acquainted with them and they with me, and I found in them objects to which my affections could freely flow, which was so essential to my comfort and enjoyment, especially now in the absence of my family. In order for me to experience this comfort and enjoyment, I then discovered that it was not only needed that I should love them, but that they should respect me so far that my affections could flow on to their hearts, and not be checked at the surface.

Joseph Foulke, jr., came to enter as a scholar, and although he was young, yet as he had had some experience in teaching in his father's school, I invited him to assist me, and he accepted the invitation. We three, with Clinton Gillingham (who was my principal assistant), conducted the school for some months.

It was proposed to me by a number of Friends that they should form a class to attend lectures in the evenings, to which I consented, and these lectures were truly pleasant; they gave me an opportunity of becoming acquainted with a large number of valuable Friends, and, what was to me more important then, made them better acquainted with me, as I was confident I was not before them in my true character.

I never have had anywhere a more respectful, attentive, and appreciative class than the evening one at Cherry street in the winter of 1845-6, and I soon became sensible of making my way in their sympathies, and of my becoming better known to them. James and Lucretia Mott, James Martin and family, George M. Justice and family, George and Catharine M. Truman, Dr. Griscom, Dillwyn Parrish, Joseph Warner, Jane Johnson, Morris L. Hallowell and family, Dr. Noble, Thomas Longstreth, William Wharton and Deborah, Dr. Shoemaker occasionally, Charles Townsend, Ann A. Townsend, and many others, were among the number.

The room was generally full, and the interest evidently increased as the course proceeded. Much of the substance of the lectures was new to most of them, and they expressed themselves highly gratified with the opportunity of attending them.

With my lecture class I soon got to feel at home. It was very congenial to my feelings. I gave quite a course on Natural Philosophy, Astronomy, Chemistry, Geology, and Vegetable Physiology. I felt that I was doing good to some of them " by informing their understandings," which " corrects and enlarges the heart."

In preparing for my lectures John Townsend's son John assisted me some, a very fine young man of no ordinary ability. Also Dr. Hare's man, whom the medical students called "Berzelius," kindly volunteered to assist me, and he gave me not only assistance, but valuable practical instruction in Dr. Hare's methods of preparing and performing a number of interesting experiments. "Berzelius," whose real name I cannot now recall, was afterwards employed by Professor Henry at the Smithsonian Institute, where I several times had the pleasure of meeting him.

It was not my original intention to do more for my evening class than to lecture to them on Chemistry, Natural Philosophy, and Astronomy, but in these lectures I had several times referred to the facts that Geology taught, and when my original course closed, a proposition was made to me to have a new class formed for a course on Geology, issue new tickets, and have the lectures in the meeting-house. The object of proposing to issue new tickets was to give me additional remuneration, as they said they thought they had received the worth of the former one. I told them I would reflect upon the proposition and let them know my conclusion. Their proposition embraced three points: To give a course of lectures on Geology; to issue separate tickets for this course; and to have the lectures on Geology in the meeting-house. Upon reflection, the first point looked very pleasant, but the other two did not set easy; so I informed them I would with great pleasure give the course they desired, but it must be in the same room, with the same tickets. These lectures were the most satisfactory to myself that I think I ever delivered. Some sentences that were spoken extemporaneously, under the influence

10

of an intelligent and appreciative audience, I remember to this day. "Matter is found in space, in every stage of condensation, from the first collection of attenuated matter to the dense center of revolving worlds." "Wherever circumstances are favorable to vegetable existence, there are vegetables found to arise, either by the immediate exercise of creative energy or the universal diffusion of embryotic matter." So great is the influence of an audience that is fully in sympathy with the speaker!

In one of my lectures I spoke of the organic remains in the limestone rocks, of which many mountains are composed, giving evidence in the perfection of even the most delicate parts of the fossils that the animals died tranquilly where they are now, which, however deep, was then the surface, and that those above have been successively deposited upon them through long circling periods of thousands of thousands of years. An elder of Friends' meeting met me on Market street, the following Seventh-day, and expressed deep concern that I should hold out the view that the earth was older than the period assigned to its creation in the Bible, and we talked the matter over for nearly two hours, all very pleasantly. On my inquiring of him how he thought the fossils got there, he said they were placed there as they are, by the Almighty, at the creation. We separated in very good feeling. In my next lecture I went over the corroborating evidences pretty strongly of the two points, the *great age* of the world, and the present formation of rocks with fossils and other substances imbedded, illustrating by what is at present going on in the Gulf of Mexico, and instanced the fact of a brass cannon, which is now in the Museum of Montpelier in France, having been dug from a limestone rock of recent

formation, containing fossils, in the Mediterranean, near
the mouth of the Rhone. "We all must admit," I said,
"that this brass cannon was not placed there by the
Almighty at the time of the creation, and besides, it
had its maker's name on, and the year 'Anno Domini'
when it was cast." This lecture was one of the greatest and most satisfactory efforts to myself that I ever
made. I evidently had the audience with me in showing the great changes that the surface of the earth has
undergone through the agencies of water and fire, so that,
as Beattie says,

"Earthquakes have raised to Heaven the lowly vale,
  And gulfs the mountains' mighty mass entombed,
  And where the Atlantic rolls, vast continents have bloomed."

J—— had said nothing to me on the subject since our
conversation on the street. I had no idea, except from
the general favorable feeling, how he was impressed.
After I had finished my concluding lecture, and before I
had left the stand, he came to me with his eyes beto-
kening the deep emotion of his soul, and said, " Benjamin,
I wish thou wouldst write a work on Geology for our
school, containing the substance of these lectures." " Why,"
said I, "J——, is thee satisfied?" " Yes," he replied, "and
more than satisfied." There was another Friend there
whose soul was deeply stirred by this announcement!

Late in the fall of 1845 my dear Margaret came on,
and brought our three youngest children, Elgar, Benjamin, and Mary, the latter about six years old, to stay
till early spring, all of us boarding at Henry Pike's,
which gave it more of a homelike feeling. Our son
Henry went to school to Caleb S. and James S. Hallowell,

at Alexandria, Virginia, and our daughter Caroline to her aunt Mary S. Lippincott, at Moorestown, New Jersey.

After Margaret came on, a number of our friends kindly called upon her and asked us to take tea with them, and, could I have risen from under the constant pressure of my school, I should have enjoyed it very much. She was obliged to return in the early spring of 1846 to our home at Rockland, Sandy Spring. My friends in Philadelphia then seemed to increase their kindness. Thomas Longstreth took me to Moorestown, New Jersey, to see my mother, with whom he had been acquainted when he was a young man, and she had named her son Joseph after Thomas's brother, since deceased. They both enjoyed the visit, as I did the ride also. On my taking out my money, as was my wont, to pay the ferriage, he told me, "No, that is my part; it belongs to the carriage."

Doctor Noble, one beautiful First-day morning, took me a distance of about fifteen or sixteen miles, above Plymouth, to see his wife's brother, Judge Longstreth. We passed through Germantown, Chestnut Hill, etc., and he pointed out many objects and places of interest in connexion with the Revolutionary war. The Judge had a very fine farm, limestone land. We walked to a lime quarry at which there had been a "land-slide," that exhibited a clover root which had descended four feet below the surface, while, by a bend in it, its entire length was over fifty inches. His stock was some of the finest, I think, I ever saw.

The most interesting part of the visit to me was (although it was all very interesting) when I ascertained that the Judge's wife was the daughter of my old friend (one of the Westtown committee), who had been so kind to me, John Cook, of Philadelphia, and sister of my old schoolmate, Thomas Cook, one of my very dearest friends at that time.

Another of her brothers was on a visit to her at the time, who had traveled extensively in Europe, furnished with "scientific spectacles," and had been on Mount Vesuvius, ascended Mount Etna, and visited the ruins of Herculaneum and Pompeii. It was he who first taught me how to pronounce the name of the ruin, which I had called Pom'-pe-i, while it should, he said, Pom-pa'-ya. I have seldom in my life passed a day of greater interest.

On another occasion Dr. Noble took me to his farm in Delaware, some distance below New Castle, where he showed me a field of wheat, the thickest I ever saw, the heads seeming as level as a floor, and, like a floor, continuous, which had been seeded by a drill, with only three pecks to the acre. This was another day of great interest to me.

James Mott, one First-day, kindly took me to Byberry, where we attended meeting. We had intended to dine at John Comly's, but he being out of the neighborhood, we were invited home with Cyrus Peirce, where we dined with the celebrated Robert Purvis.

On another occasion James and I were riding pretty early in the morning, and we passed a man with his paint-pot and brushes, and soon after another with his gloves and gold watch-chain, and on comparing sentiments, after we had passed them, we found that with us both the stronger stream of respect had flowed out to the one with the implements of industry.

At another time Morris L. Hallowell took me to Byberry, when we went to John Comly's and had a very pleasant visit.

Dr. John D. Griscom took me to some place near Frankford, perhaps the Asylum for the Insane, and on the way related to me the circumstance of a man, whose residence he pointed out, who made a fortune by his ignorance. He was a very peculiar man, very immovable if he took a " set." He owned a property near Richmond, Philadelphia, that was almost indispensable to the railroad company (now Port Richmond), and they asked him to put down the very lowest figure he would be willing to take for it. He took his pencil and paper and intended to put down $80,000 (eighty thousand dollars), but ignorantly added one cipher too many, putting down $800,000 (eight hundred thousand). The company thought the price was high, but were glad to find he was willing to sell at all, and, knowing the character of the man, took it at the price he named, drawing up an agreement in which the price was written, which he signed, and the company afterwards paid.

Dillwyn Parrish took me to " Bartram's Garden," where I was highly interested in seeing the vast collection of trees, shrubs, and plants, that were entirely new to me, and I was always a true lover of the variety in the works of nature. He showed me too a cider-mill and press, which had been cut out of the solid rock, with a pool in the same rock to receive the juice. Above all, he drew my attention to the stone door-head, with the inscription, cut by Dr. John Bartram's own hand, Dillwyn said,

> " To God alone, the Almighty Lord,
> *The only one by me adored.*"

For entertaining such-like sentiments, he had been previously disowned by Friends. I had a good many thoughts as I stood there looking at the work he had done, thinking what must have been the depth of his convictions, that he was cutting there to perpetuate in stone, and I had a near and deep sympathy with him, for *I* was on the same platform as he, and am yet. I have never seen it since, but have frequently thought of it, and remembered the inscription from that day, and have felt greatly obliged to Dillwyn for taking me there and pointing it out to me.

There were many other evidences of kindness extended to me, in showing me through the different manufactories of machinery, soap, forming lead and tin tubes, etc., etc., of the extent of all of which, although I was brought up near there, I never before had had the least conception. The Academy of Fine Arts, the Franklin Library, the fine statuary by Thom of " Old Mortality " and " Tam O'Shanter," were all sources of real delight to me, tending greatly to compensate for absence from home.

Benjamin Eakins, the writing-teacher at the Cherry street school, was a true, *live* teacher. He possessed philosophical ideas of the art of writing and the object to be aimed at, rapidity with ease, and *thus* grace. He would take the hand-writing of an individual *as it is* and *correct* it, not change it *entirely*, unless it were of a person just commencing to write. In this his idea was greatly in advance of that of Benjamin Rand, to whom I went to learn to write in 1819. He entirely changed my hand, and had me to write exceedingly slow, training the muscles to new movements, while the old habits were striving for employment, till my hand-writing became like the speech of old Ambrose Vass, a Frenchman I used to know in Alexandria. He had learned English late in life, and when he was old he could not tell which words were English and which French, in the expression of his ideas, and mingled them all together in the same sentence.

When I asked Benjamin Eakins about changing my hand, he asked how long I had been writing. I told him about forty years. He said, " It will then take about forty years more to unform the habits thus acquired, and afterwards another forty years to acquire as ready a use of the pen as you now have. What you had better now do is to correct your present training in the movements of your muscles by aiming at rapidity and ease."

We had several trials at one of the standing exercises with his scholars, to see who could make the greatest number of a certain letter in a minute. He would exceed me in every letter but x. I had made so many x's that I invariably made two or three more in a minute than he.

I eventually got through the school-year, though by no means to my own satisfaction, but I was conscious of having done the very best I could under the circumstances. Love is stronger than fear, and the moral power is the only true governing principle among rational beings, but it makes its way more slowly than the physical force that induces fear; requires to be expended on a smaller number in order to get the hearts and feelings assimilated, and then these will assist in its extension, so that it will become a power that cannot be overthrown. To my unshaken and continued reliance upon this principle in my tried situation, I look back with great satisfaction.

I resigned to the committee my office of teacher, and returned to my family and farm at Rockland.

I have omitted to mention the interest and congeniality I experienced in M. Fisher Longstreth, in connexion with the observatory on the Central School building.

This structure was the result, I believe, of the united efforts of Fisher and George M. Justice, both of whom were enthusiastic in the science of Astronomy, and hence congenial associates for me. The observatory was supplied with a good transit instrument and a superior astronomical clock or clock chronometer, made by J. L. Gropengeiser, of Philadelphia.

On my leaving Philadelphia, my evening class presented me with a fine transit instrument, which I had learned how to use practically, at this observatory, and a Troughton's Circle, the method of using which I afterwards learned through the kindness of Lieutenant James M. Gilliss, U. S. N., superintendent of the National Observatory, Washington, and Captain Morrill, an old and experienced sea-faring man.

I procured a complete artificial horizon, the mercury (contained in an iron bottle when not in use) protected from the wind by plate glass of best quality, and all neatly packed in a mahogany box.

The transit instrument would be of comparatively little use without a chronometer. A little before this time, my valued and beloved uncle Comly Shoemaker died, and, having no children, left to each of his numerous nephews and nieces a residuary legacy, of which my share was two hundred and fifty dollars. I immediately requested George M. Justice to order of Gropengeiser an astronomical clock, similar to that at the observatory, which it seemed to give him pleasure to do. I paid for this out of my uncle's legacy, and I always regarded the chronometer as a present and remembrancer from my beloved uncle. With the balance of the legacy I obtained a drab broadcloth cloak for my dear Margaret, which looks well yet, after thirty years' service.

On arriving at Rockland, the first thing to do was to prepare a place for my transit instrument and astronomical clock, which I did, and mounted my two instruments, the transit and chronometer, as soon as they arrived.

Then, with my farm to occupy us in pleasant weather, the carpenter-shop, turning-lathe, and smith-shop to employ us in rainy, rough weather, the observatory of clear evenings, and the library, etc., of other evenings and at odd times, I would have everything I wanted to interest and occupy myself and children, and to give them a good practical education.

CHAPTER XII.

1846.

Interrupted plans — Resumes the charge of the Alexandria boarding-school — A well-spent vacation — Fitting up a laboratory — Lectures at Smithsonian Institute — Pleasant prospects interrupted by failing health — Disposes of his school property — Favorite ideas on education — Consulted in regard to establishing the Agricultural College — Elected President — Enters upon duty in 1859 — Arduous duties — Health breaks down — Resigns the presidency — Successful experiments at the college.

But Burns said long ago, "The best-laid schemes o' mice an' men gang aft agley." All this beautiful prospect had to vanish! I was again to be disappointed in my plans.

On reaching home from Gunpowder Quarterly Meeting in the Ninth month, I found a letter from my nephews, Caleb S. and James S. Hallowell, stating that they wished to give up the school property in Alexandria, on the 1st of then ensuing Eleventh month. With so short a notice there seemed no prudent way to do but for me to go with my family to Alexandria, and take charge of it. This was a severe and unexpected turn of affairs, to have to leave all at Rockland, just as I had got them fixed to my mind, but I was comforted in the belief that He who had been with me in former trouble, would not leave me now, and that there would still be a way to get along. I wrote to them immediately, that I would comply with their wishes, and this I tried to do in every respect, throughout the entire arrangements, returning to Alexandria, my family with me, the latter part of the Tenth month, 1846.

Using my experience when we had had eleven months' school, from the 1st of Ninth month to the 1st of the next Eighth month, I remembered that the most sickness we had in a term was in the first and last months, the Ninth and Seventh. I, therefore, determined to include these two months in vacation, and have the school term of nine months' duration. I also thought it right, from principle, to have it stated in my printed circulars that the use of tobacco in any form, while at school, would not be allowed, and that no one need apply for admission to the school who was in the practice of using it in any way, and was not willing to relinquish the use of it. I had certificates printed and sent out with each circular, for the parent or guardian and student to sign, previous to the student's entering the school, stating that they had read my rules and regulations, and would faithfully comply with all the required arrangements, to the best of their ability.

From my experience, as the subject is now seen in

the retrospect, if I had had less reliance upon printed rules and regulations, and made stronger effort to inculcate and cultivate principle on this point, in view of its hurtful effects, the result would have been more satisfactory. For several years after I opened school in Alexandria, I had but two rules. First, "Be good boys." Second, "Learn all you can." Every boy knew them by heart; all understood them, and moreover, all *felt* that they were right and ought to be observed, the obligation to which, also, I took frequent occasion to inculcate. My school never was in better order than when under these simple rules.

We commenced our school with a small number of scholars, of course, but it gradually filled up, and it was not long before we had more applicants than we could accommodate.

In 1847, I had an observatory built adjoining my school-room on the west, planned with the assistance of my valued friend, Thomas William Smith, and mounted my transit instrument and a fine refracting telescope, which I had purchased of my nephews. Gropengeiser himself came on from Philadelphia, to mount the astronomical clock, which was a most beautiful instrument, with a mercurial pendulum and a glass door, through which to see the vibrations. The observatory was a cylinder, about ten feet in diameter, revolving on cannon-balls, rolling in an iron trough, which enabled us to see in all directions. It was very convenient, and we endeavored to make it serviceable to ourselves and others, in the advancement of science. My son Henry has now a book containing drawings of the solar spots, made by him continuously, so as to show their changes for several months in 1848 and 1849, which Professor Holden, of the National Observatory, when he saw them at our house, pronounced valuable. In the vacation of that year, 1847, I went to New Haven and spent some time in the laboratory of Yale College, under Professor Benjamin Silliman, jr., in gaining instruction in practical analysis of minerals, soils, etc., the first instruction in practical chemistry I had ever received, and it was very interesting and useful to me. I then went to Boston, to the laboratory of Professor Charles T. Jackson, of " Ether" memory, with the view of getting an insight into the best methods of analyzing soils. He had known of me, and entered into my wishes with enthusiastic ardor. I never had had such a teacher, and I heard him tell his wife, who happened in his laboratory while I was there, that he had never had a student that learned so much in the same time. The fact was, I was prepared to learn.

My former experience and general acquaintance with chemical principles enabled me to classify every new fact or idea, and arrange it permanently in my stock of chemical knowledge, in harmony with the oft-quoted remark, that "the more a person knows when he leaves home to travel, the more he can bring back with him."

Dr. Jackson had made a geological survey of the State of New Hampshire, and he was afterwards employed by the National Government to explore and survey the copper regions, on the confines of Lake Superior. He gave me a finger-ring when on a visit to me at Alexandria, exhibiting beautifully the manner in which silver exists in copper, each metal pure to the line. I regarded him as the best-informed practical chemist in the country.

These two courses of instruction at Yale and Boston were of very great advantage to me. On my return I fitted up a room for a laboratory on the plan of Dr. Jackson's, with a " breast furnace," pneumatic cistern, sand-bath, separating bottle, washing bottle, and all the most approved appliances for chemical manipulations. I prepared the tests of Fresenius, made some chloroform, guncotton, etc., etc., and was ready to instruct the students pretty fully in chemical analysis. I had the pleasure, when it was completed, of showing my laboratory and its furniture and fixtures to Dr. Jackson, who was highly pleased with it, and regarded the imitation of *his*, complimentary.

I instructed the students in chemical analysis myself, until 1849, when my other duties required so much of my attention that I had not time for this, and then, at Dr. Jackson's recommendation, I employed one of his former students, George I. Dickinson, to take charge of the laboratory, and gave instruction to the students in practical chemistry.

I may mention here, that the last year of our school, 1857–8, we were compelled to refuse over one hundred applicants.

Edward H. Magill, President of Swarthmore College, was a teacher in my school during the term of 1848–9.

In the fall of 1849 it was proposed that my son Henry, and Francis Miller, who had been a student with me at Philadelphia, and afterward a tutor in my school in Alexandria, should join me in conducting my boarding-school; and as I desired they should receive the best possible qualification, to be of the most service to the scholars, it was decided that they should go through a regular course at Yale College. They entered the sophomore class in the fall of 1849, and on their leaving home, Mahlon Kirk, jr., George Newbold, and Samuel Conard, all of whom had been scholars in the institution, assisted me, in addition to Latin, Greek, French, and drawing teachers.

I think it but just to say that Mahlon Kirk was the most reliable and efficient aid, at every point where I needed assistance, that I ever had, it being his whole aim and steady effort to carry out my views in the interests of the students, and to render me practical assistance and relief, for which kindness and favor I feel grateful to him to this day.

I obtained a very complete compound microscope, with a Camera Lucida for drawing magnified images of small objects. I also procured a superior solar microscope, with polarizing apparatus, very complete, exhibiting some of the most beautiful and interesting phenomena in connection with the molecular structure of bodies, and the changes in their structure produced by pressure or heat, in order that the students should have every attainable opportunity of informing their understandings.

About 1854 I was invited by Professor Henry, Secretary of the Smithsonian Institute, to deliver a course of three lectures in that institution on Astronomy, which invitation I accepted. They were the first of that winter's course, and largely attended. I have reason to believe they were more satisfactory to the Secretary and to the audience than they were to myself. The hall was much larger than I had been accustomed to lecture in, so that I found it difficult to make my voice fill it, and those who have had experience in lecturing will know the unfavorable effect this has. Besides which, these lectures came at a time when I was particularly oppressed with my own lectures and school duties, and my mind and feelings were not in a condition to do justice to myself or the subject. However, all seemed to pass off satisfactorily, and I had the sustaining consciousness of having done the best I could do under the circumstances.

In 1854–5, I built a house on a lot I owned opposite the boarding-school property, with the expectation of *resting* there, and giving my influence and assistance to my son, Henry C. Hallowell, and my son-in-law, Francis Miller, who after their return from Yale College had joined me as partners and joint principals of the school in its management and duties, so that I could gradually withdraw from it, and ultimately give it up to them.

As I expected to end my days in this new building, I furnished it with every known convenience, and supplied it with all the modern improvements.

The house was built larger than it otherwise would have been in order to accommodate Henry, and in the event of his marrying, his family also, while Francis and Caroline were to have their home in the old establishment. Henry and Francis were gradually ingratiating themselves in the confidence of the students, acquiring their respect and gaining influence and authority, and I looked forward to a near time, when we would be there all together, with a well-furnished school, observatory, laboratory, philosophical apparatus, and all appliances to aid the students in acquiring a liberal and extended education. We moved into the new house in the Ninth month, 1855.

But this "air castle" was soon to vanish! Henry's health failed, and, it seeming indispensable that he should take a rest and recreation, it was thought best for him to go to Europe, where he spent eight months. On his return he married Sarah Miller, and they seemed nicely fixed in their new home, but it soon became evident that he would not be able to endure the confinement and arduous duties of a boarding-school life, so it was concluded for him and his wife to go to Rockland. This left Francis Miller and me in charge of the large board-ing-school establishment. My continuing with it had been wholly in order to get Henry and Francis established there, and as Henry had left on account of the failure of his health, and as I wished to retire, Francis Miller concluded, if he had to be by himself, he would rather have his school in the country. So I gave him a field of nearly thirty acres of Rockland farm, on which he built quite a handsome house for a boarding-school, called it Stanmore, and moved there in the summer of 1858.

When Francis decided on this change, I advertised the boarding-school property for sale, with the "good-will" of the establishment, and sold it to William S. Kemper, of Charlottesville, Virginia, who had been for some time connected with the University of Virginia, and his two sons had been well educated at that institution. They took charge of the establishment, I leaving all the school furniture, the school library, apparatus, telescope, etc. They opened their school after the vacation, 1858.

Myself, wife, and daughter Mary, our youngest child, were thus left alone in Alexandria, in that large house, with nothing for me to do, the worst condition possible for any one to be placed in.

The arduous and responsible duties that had rested on me for many years brought on a chronic complaint, which admonished me that I needed rest and a change of avocation.

William S. Kemper several times urged me to as-sist him in his school, and to lecture for them, for which he was willing to compensate me liberally, but I told him that besides other considerations, the condition of my

11

health at that time, was such that it would not be prudent for me to undertake it.

I had desired for over thirty years to be connected with an educational establishment in which the muscles would be trained simultaneously with the intellect, in the various mechanical industries, and agricultural and horticultural pursuits,—budding, grafting, and training fruit trees, vines, and shrubbery, the propagation of flowers, etc., on which employment the vast amount of waste energies that I had witnessed among boys, especially, which were the occasion of nearly all the rudeness and disorder, might be advantageously and pleasantly employed under skilled direction.

Indeed, my ideal of an educational establishment was a combination, may I call it?—of these different branches that I have mentioned, together with an education that would commence under skilled and enthusiastic instructors in Natural History, as soon as the student would set foot from the door-step. What kind of stone or pebble is that? What bird? Its habits? Is it permanent or migratory? If the latter, at what seasons does it appear and leave? What insect? (with similar additions). What plant, shrub, flower, tree? and so on with everything that comes into sight, as far as they go, the range getting wider and wider every day, and then, when anything new would occur, or be presented to them, it would be certain to be noticed and receive that attention that would soon class it among known objects. Possibly a Utopian theory.

When the Maryland Agricultural College was about to be established, I was requested by one of the trustees to write out pretty fully my views of what should be the location and the objects and aims of such an institution, and I complied with his request to the best of my ability. I recommended, as the result of my experience, that it should not be near a city, nor too convenient to a railroad station or steamboat landing. My idea might be gathered from imagining a very large ship or barge, with everything on board that could be needed,— President, professors, teachers, physicians, everything the very best in its line, farm and all,—and then push it out into mid-ocean, as a floating island, to come to shore *only* twice a year, and to have no communication with it at other times. I then gave my views of the subjects to be taught, and of the objects and aims, a little as I have already expressed them.

The trustees located the college near Bladensburg, about eight miles from Washington, and obtained on the premises a station of the Washington Branch of the Baltimore and Ohio Railroad.

In the fall of 1859, I was unanimously elected President of this Agricultural College, then about to open, without having been consulted, and my name was placed at the head of the faculty list in printed circulars at the inauguration of the college, when I probably should have received notice of it, but that I was, for several weeks, including this time, in Philadelphia.

The plan and objects of the college, though not its location, seemed to be a step in the direction of what I had long desired, and it took such a hold of my mind that I thought it best to go see the place, and especially to have a conversation with the President of the Board of Trustees, Charles B. Calvert, in regard to my duties.

The college was situated in the midst of a slaveholding community, and I first wished to know whether free or slave labor was to be employed on the farm and in the house. I was much gratified when informed it was to be free labor only.

I found nothing in their regulations that required duties of the President that I could not conscientiously perform, so I informed Charles B. Calvert that I would consider the matter, and give him an answer on the next Second-day.

In the meantime I was to come up to Sandy Spring, where my family then was, and so informed my friend Nathan Tyson. He, feeling great interest in the subject, and fearing something might have occurred to discourage me, drove from Baltimore to advise me to accept the appointment, which I accordingly did, and never regretted it. Though I was able to do but little, the appointment was accepted with the best intentions.

I entered upon duty in the college about the middle of Tenth month, 1859. The college had opened about six weeks before, at the time of the inauguration already alluded to, under three professors, who had apparently been waiting for me, the appointed President of the Faculty, as Calvert stated, to organize the college, and prescribe the studies, discipline, etc. From the six weeks that had elapsed without regular order or government, or a classification of the students, a very heavy burden and labor devolved suddenly upon me, and in the earnest effort that I made to effect a proper organization, and secure a healthy order and discipline, my health gave way in about a month, under my chronic complaint, irretrievably, as I then thought, and I resigned the Presidency unconditionally.

I gave to the institution a first-class barometer with attached thermometer of both Reaumur's and Fahrenheit's scales, hygrometer with wet and dry bulb, for determining the dew point, a pluvimeter, self-registering thermometer, and other meteorological instruments, which I had obtained in order to keep a record of the weather, which we reported for several years to the Smithsonian Institute. These I presented, that they might keep and preserve at the college a regular account of meteorological phenomena, regarding it as an important element in obtaining a full understanding of agricultural and horticultural questions.

I had an opportunity in the short time I was there of trying two experiments, which were an entire success. The students had each a regular working outfit, complete, kept on a pin, with hat above, and shoes or boots below, and such changes could be made in a very short time.

They went out daily, in classes, to their employment, for an hour at a time, with just as much regularity as the classes in the other studies, changing in the same way at the ringing of the bell when the hour was out. In this employment they were under a skilled director.

The first experiment was in constructing an ice-pond and ice-house. There was a small stream running through a thicket in a ravine in front of the college building, and a little distance from it. The students were shown a nice place to make a " breast " for the dam, and they were told if they would make a dam and excavate an ice-house they could have a good and convenient place to skate the next winter, and as much ice as they wanted with their drinking-water the next summer.

At it they went, class after class, with as much zest as they could have done to a game of cricket or base-ball. It was amusing to see the efforts of large students, who had never handled an axe before, cutting down bushes and trees six to nine inches in diameter, hacking them all around, and the awkward manner in which they would at first handle the spade or shovel, in loading a cart. But they improved rapidly, and finished the enterprise to entire satisfaction.

The next experiment was with a strawberry-bed. The students were told if they would plant an acre of land in strawberry vines, and divide the plat into two equal parts, they might take their choice of the portions and have all the strawberries that grew on it, subject to such regulations among themselves as they chose to adopt, the other division being for the family. They accepted this proposition with the greatest alacrity, went at it by turns in the classes with earnestness and under competent direction; and like the ice-pond, it was completed to the perfect satisfaction of all the parties concerned.

I became convinced that all the labor on a farm of 150 to 200 acres, except, perhaps, the original breaking up of the sod, could be performed by seventy or eighty students, under suitable direction, and also most of the farming implements made, if a wheelwright and blacksmith were among the directors, with proper tact, so that it would have a relish with students, ultimately, by the competition it would evoke, even greater than that which attends the ordinary college games. This idea remains with me as an abiding conviction; and how superior would be the result!

Such a plan would possess all the advantages in the formation of character, of independence, self-reliance, competition, invention, etc., that the college games now have, for, as we all know, some one or two at present assume to be leaders or directors, so that the large majority of the students are as much under a director in the college games as in the industrial employment.

CHAPTER XIII.

1859.

Return to Alexandria — Trip to Canada — Finally removes to Rockland — Journey to the west — Indian affairs — Visiting tribes in Nebraska — Literary work — Reflections.

After a month's absence, I returned to Alexandria, much enfeebled. We had been in the practice for many years of spending our summers at Rockland, moving up at the commencement of vacation and back again in the fall, of course not moving all the things either way. In this experience I found two homes were just one too many. ·

It was of frequent occurrence, that, when in the country, I would want a book, paper, or something that was in town, and when in town I would need a paper, book, etc., that was in the country. So I became convinced of the correctness of the conclusion at which John Quincy Adams arrived, and to which he referred in a lecture he delivered at our Lyceum in Alexandria. "Man's nature requires," said he, "in order for him to · fill his true sphere and be happy, three things: one fixed home, one wedded wife, and a belief in one God."

In the spring of 1860 my wife, my daughter Mary, and myself, which now constituted our whole family, decided to make a visit, for rest and recreation in part, to our valued friends Nicholas and Margaret Brown, in Canada, and some other persons and places in which we were interested. My niece, Jane S. Lippincott, joined us at York, Pennsylvania.

Before setting out from Alexandria on this journey, we held a family council. I gave it as my judgment, based on experience, that as Margaret and I were getting advanced in years, we were less able to bear the fatigue and change of moving twice a year, as it produced a continued unsettlement.

Besides the inconveniences just stated, in regard to books, papers, etc., our places in meeting could not be properly held, while we were members of one and so much of the time attending another. In conclusion, I told them we could move but once now at most. It would be for them to decide. Our home might be either in town or in the country,—we could not have both,—and I wished them, while we were on our journey, to think seriously on the subject, and make up their minds.

My dear Margaret soon decided that if it were to be our home all the year, she would prefer the country, where her three children and her grandchildren were.

We set off on our journey, and a delightful one it was, to Elmira, Buffalo, Niagara, etc., and arrived at the latter place just in time to see Blondin walk the rope, and perform the astonishing feat of wheeling a wheelbarrow, standing on his head, etc., etc., on a wire across the Niagara river, below the Chain Bridge. After spending some time at Niagara, we went to Toronto, and then to Nicholas and Margaret Brown's, at Pickering. They accompanied us on a week's travel to King county, to see John and Mary Watson, and William and Elizabeth Dennis, extending our visit to Lake Simcoe.

We returned from Canada, after stopping a day or two at Niagara, on the American side, by Catskill, Rochester, and New York city.

In our journey I had occasionally introduced the

subject to be decided on our return home. Margaret had already decided. On asking Mary for her decision, she said, if I would get her a riding-horse, she would prefer the country. William S. Kemper had just before asked me to buy his riding-horse, Selim, a beautiful blooded horse, well gaited, a bright bay, with black mane and tail, both of them thick and long, which I at once purchased. It was then unanimously decided that we were to move to Rockland for a permanent home.

I have many times since looked back at the seemingly little thing that determined this decision, and thought the hand of the Good Father was in it, for the next spring the civil war broke out, and I would not *then* have gone away and left my friends there, nor would I have been mixed up with and obliged to witness the incidents that occurred there, for any consideration. From the time I left Rockland to return to Alexandria and resume the duties of my boarding-school, the hope of being at some time able to return to my farm, and resume the improvements that I had begun in 1842, lighted up many a dark hour amidst my trials there. Now, this hope seemed about to be realized. I never had *one feeling* in sympathy with a city. My situation in Alexandria was a favorable one, however, because our residence opened to the country on the northwest. Still, like Cowper, in regard to the country:

> "I never framed a wish. or formed a plan,
> *That promised me with hopes of earthly bliss,*
> *But there I laid the scene.*"

We moved finally to our Rockland home, in the summer of 1860, our son Henry and his family living in one portion of the house. A kinder son, and one more attentive to what he thought would be best and most comfortable for his parents, no one has ever been blest with, and this can be said with equal sincerity of his precious wife.

During these last fifteen years, I have performed that long journey on a religious visit to the West, of which the journal I kept bears record, and in which I traveled three thousand one hundred and twenty-nine miles in my rockaway, going with it beyond the Mississippi river, and two thousand seven hundred and ninety-one miles by public conveyance, making in the six months, wanting two days, that I was absent, five thousand nine hundred and twenty miles travel.

I have been Secretary of the Indian Committee of Baltimore Yearly Meeting, and also of the General Committee on the Indian concern of the six Yearly Meetings, and have performed a vast amount of correspondence.

As one of a delegation from New York, Philadelphia, and Baltimore, I have visited all the Indian tribes, on their reservations in Nebraska, constituting the northern superintendency, and have written the report of the delegates, which was printed.

I have written the "Young Friends' Manual," and numerous communications to Friends' Intelligencer. I have written also, and published a work on Geometrical Analysis, besides conducting a wide general correspondence.

My communications to Friends' Intelligencer, together with some essays and paragraphs in a manuscript book, contain my highest and deepest religious convictions in unstudied language. The "Young Friends' Manual," too, with a little modification of a few sentences, which it is my intention to make in my copy, has the sanction of my present judgment.

I have thus brought the history of my life up to the present time, and while I have been writing, the feeling has several times rather singularly impressed me, whether the "Me" that was the actor through all the long series of incidents, was or is the same that now records them for my daughter and other children and grandchildren, and I have concluded that the only connection between the "Me" to whom all these varied incidents relate, and the present one, is the combined effect, favorable or otherwise, that they have woven into my character and constitution, physical, mental, and moral, by which the present "Me" has been evolved. Every right act, word, or thought, made its impress on my character, and every wrong one its impress ; and "character being the stamp or permanent impression by which conduct is regulated," these all combined successively in their influence and evolved as the resultant the "Me" of any particular period.

CHAPTER XIV.

Effects of inhaling Nitrous Oxide — A mysterious package — "Citizen Granville" — Story of a ten-dollar note — Experiences with an original character — An incident of travel — Visit to a Normal School — Verses for a May-day picnic — Management of domestics.

I will now refer to some facts and incidents connected with my schools, without much reference to the order of time.

We never lost a boarding-student by death. We nursed a student through that loathsome disease, the small-pox, and several times a number of students through scarlet fever, measles, mumps, etc. All recovered, and I believe all were returned to their friends as strong and healthy as we received them. We had one student who broke the small bone of his leg, and two that sprained their ankles, which were the most serious accidents that ever occurred among our boarding-students, as far as I can now recall, although we had for many years from sixty to eighty at a time. The retrospect is very pleasant, too, that neither at Fair Hill, where I was a teacher for about two years, nor at Westtown, where I taught nearly three years, did a single death occur among the students of either sex.

In 1830, Jonathan Ingham, son of Samuel D. Ingham, Secretary of the Treasury under General Jackson, was a student with us, and when I was lecturing on the nitrous oxide or exhilarating gas, he wished to take it. The lecture-room was always particularly crowded on the occasion of exhibiting the effects of the gas. He was a handsome, sprightly youth, about sixteen or seventeen years old, and of a very fine manner. He inhaled the gas freely, stood a little time, then in an attitude as well adjusted as it could have been by a finished actor, gave a quotation from Shakspeare. It was done with all imaginable grace, and the whole scene was much admired and applauded.

On the occasion of the exhibition of the effects of the gas in 1833–4, several of the larger students offered to take it, and I was prepared for what followed, a pretence of taking the gas and then the exhibition of some premeditated feats, which I partially defeated by seeing that each one had a pretty full dose. The previous bias given to their minds, however, caused them to manifest a very pugnacious disposition towards me, and, being prepared for it, and pretty strong, I put them success-ively on the floor, to the great amusement of the audience, part of whom, I had reason to believe, knew what was intended to come off.

The next student to take gas that evening was from Massachusetts, who had been a page in Congress. He was a tall, handsome youth, with gentle manners, and was a general favorite. He inhaled the gas freely, and then, with the greatest gentleness and affection of manner imaginable, put his arms around my neck and placed his cheek to mine, first one side and then the other, when I remarked that such evidence of affectionate re-gard was a full compensation for the pugnacious treat-ment I had before received, and, by the time I had en-tirely finished my sentence, he left *me* and embraced the stove-pipe with equal affection (fortunately it was mild weather, and we had no fire in the stove that evening). I observed to the audience that I had appropriated an affection to myself that I found belonged equally to the stove-pipe, which occasioned great amusement.

I never observed any inconvenience to the students from the inhalation of this gas, but there were some cases in which I was glad when the effects had passed off. Frederick P. Stanton, afterwards a member of Con-gress, who was at school with me as student and assistant for several years, inhaled it a number of times, and was always affected in the same manner. He stood straight and motionless as a statue, the blood would leave his face till he was as pale as a corpse, and his eyes had a vacant stare. This would continue, I suppose, for two minutes, and it would be quite a relief when the returning color in his face gave evidence of continued vitality.

Two of my students who were at school together, both nice, able boys, were in a class by themselves in their mathematical studies, because no others could keep up to them. On fixing the length of their next recitation, when finishing one, I would ask if such a length would be too much, indicating on the book a long lesson, and neither would say it was, so I put it on them "pretty strong" in Solid Geometry and Analytical, Plane and Spherical Trigonometry. I afterwards learned there was a boyish miff between them, and they did not speak to each other during the whole time, and neither was willing to say the lesson proposed was too long. I never had such rapid ¯progress made, nor such perfect recitations in this difficult part of mathematics, as by these two students. I have never seen J—— since he left school, and have heard from him but once, when he wrote me from Florida, not long after he left me, saying he was in the grocery business, "weighing weighables, wrapping wrapables, and tying tyables," which was not very congenial to him. Dear boy! I should like to know his history. He was no common youth.

For many years I thought I could not lecture without a white Marseilles vest and a red bandana handkerchief. One afternoon some *unknown* person left a small package at my house, directed to me, in which, on opening it, I found a bottle of cologne, six linen pocket-handkerchiefs, of superior quality, each one having on it a drawing of some experiment I had performed in the course of lectures, admirably executed, with a very respectful, courteous letter, neatly written, stating how much the writer was "interested in your lectures, and how much I would be gratified if you would use the cologne and handkerchiefs," believing they would be so much more comfortable to me than the bandana I was in the habit of using. There was no name to the communication. Here was a problem to solve. I must know who sent them. So I studied out and finally had my plans all arranged. I commenced my lecture, as usual, and was going on, when I took out my pocket-handkerchief, as I frequently did, held it in my hand a little time while speaking, without looking at it; then, when my eyes rested on it, I stopped with premeditated surprise, and in a lowered, slow voice, said "I am indebted — to — somebody — in — the — company — for — a — very — great —" and before I had gotten thus far, I saw a fan going faster and faster, the only one in motion, from which I drew the inference that there was some one behind that fan who was particularly interested in the topic. I observed who it was, rounded off the sentence, used my white handkerchief, and went on with my lecture. After the lecture I went to my friend and expressed my cordial acknowledgment and appreciation of her kindness. It was a lady named Cox, from Bermuda, who, with her husband (they were then recently married), was spending the winter in Alexandria, and attending my lectures. She never knew how I made the discovery till her daughter, Laura Cox, came to Stanmore school, from Bermuda, when my wife gave her one of the valued handkerchiefs, and related the circumstances, much to the daughter's interest and amusement.

About 1834 the Roman Catholics had a fair for the benefit of their church. It was held in a hall in the market house, under the charge of the priest. It had been continued for several days, when they had a sale to dispose of the remaining articles. The next morning after the sale, they were clearing up the room and emptying the sweepings in the street, the priest superintending. As I was going to market, I met Hugh C. McLaughlin, who was my Latin and Greek teacher, and also a Catholic. As soon as I saw him, I observed he was much amused. He said he had just witnessed a rich scene, their priest nonplussed by a colored boy. As the priest was looking out of the window, he saw the boy pick up a bank note from among the sweepings, so he ran down in great haste and called out, "Here, boy, give me that note, I lost it." The boy, as the priest approached, put his hand, with the note in it, behind him, and looking up archly, said, "Massa lose the note? How many dollar was it? What bank?" Seeing the priest was bothered, he stepped back, still holding his hand behind him, and, smiling, said, "I spec massa 'll fine de note dat he loss, in his pocket."

On one of my excursions from Alexandria to Philadelphia, about the time the feeling against the colored people began to run pretty strong, citizen Granville, as he was called, from Hayti, was on board the boat between New Castle and Philadelphia. He was a very intelligent, well-to-do colored gentleman, deputed by his government to make arrangements for colonizing some of the African race from the States, on the Island. Soon after we left New Castle the bell rang for dinner, and the steward showed Granville to his seat at the table with the rest of us. There were two Southern gentlemen at the table, who remonstrated warmly against this. There were not a great many passengers on board that day, so there was one table unoccupied, and Granville, perceiving the dissatisfaction, and judging the cause of it, requested the steward to set him a plate at the other table, as he wished to make no disturbance. The steward did so; Granville went over, and all the others, except the two Southerners, took up their plates and went to the other table, leaving the two gentlemen alone. They were mortified. They had not known the character of Granville. After dinner all went to the upper deck, and the two gentlemen went up to Granville to apologize. As soon as he understood their object, "Oh!" said he, with a manner suiting the language, "gentlemen, there is no occasion; *favors I write on marble, insults on sand.*"

In 1828, when our number of boarding-scholars was very small, a popular Episcopal minister, of Alexandria, came to my school to enter the name of his nephew, James A. Lewis, from near Charlestown, Virginia, son of Dr. John H. Lewis, as a boarding-student, to come in about two weeks. I told him I would place the name of his nephew on the student's register, and be glad to receive him. I was much gratified with this application, not only because it was another boarder, and he from a distance in Virginia, beyond the Shenandoah river, indicating that the knowledge of our school was extending, but also because the application was made by an Episcopal minister of Alexandria, at a time when there was a good deal of prejudice operating against our school, on account of what were termed "Hicksite proclivities." I felt considerably comfortable that evening. In about a week afterwards, the parson returned to tell me there was one thing he neglected to mention, which was that Dr. Lewis desired his son to learn music, and to have the privilege of practicing upon the flute, between the sessions of school. I told him at once that that would not harmonize with the plans and arrangements I had formed for my school, and it was a privilege I could not consistently grant; but that if it was his wish I would remove his nephew's name from the register. He said he would be glad for me to do so, and we parted kindly, but my feelings were not as comfortable as they were when he entered him. It did go right hard with me to remove his name, but I remembered it was a matter of principle with me, and independent of any other consideration, I wished the school-room to be kept quiet, so that the students could study, and if this privilege were granted to *one* student, it could not with consistency be refused to another. I therefore felt well satisfied that my decision was right, and gradually became comfortable under its results.

In about another week the parson came again, accompanied by his nephew, who, he said, had come to enter, and to comply with all my rules and regulations. My feelings can be better imagined than described.

We had a succession of Dr. Lewis's sons, Fisher Ames Lewis, who graduated with much distinction at West Point, Charles H. Lewis, John H. B. Lewis, Magnus M. Lewis, and William H. T. Lewis, the mother continuing to send them after the father's decease, from that time, 1828, till 1849, when the last son was entered, and he remained with us two or three years, making the whole time, since James first entered our school, about twenty years.

About 1835, one of the students came to my study and told me that a ten-dollar note had been taken out of his trunk, and he had no idea who could have done it. I asked him to give me a list of his room-mates, which he did, six in number, including himself. I then charged him to mention the subject to no one until I could examine a little into the matter. I kept a pretty close eye upon the movements of all the boarding students, and particularly of the room-mates of the one who had lost the money. One Seventh-day one of these room-mates, whom I will call James, went to Washington, as the students frequently did, by permission, when they had particular friends or relatives there, to return on First-day evening. James did not return with the others; this gave me a hint. I immediately set inquiries afloat, and found he had gone in the cars to Baltimore, and had put up at a prominent hotel, and I was impressed with a full belief that the bill was paid with his room-mate's money. Yet it required very careful proceeding. James did not return until Third-day evening. This was an occasion in which I felt I *must act*. He was about sixteen years old, perhaps over. I feel it right here to mention, and the retrospect of it is very comforting and encouraging, that it was my custom, on all those occasions of difficulty, in which I felt obliged to act, that before I would invite the student into my study, *to go in by myself*, the doors being constructed so that no one could then enter, and earnestly crave that I might be favored in the interview I was about to have with the student, that all might be for his good, without any regard to the interests or popularity of the school. And in no single instance, when this precaution was taken, did the interview fail to be satisfactory.

After such preparation, I invited James into my study, and the subject being an unusual one, and it having been for several days in my mind, I was favored with an unusual degree of calmness and strength. We sat some time in silence. I then inquired of him why he had not returned on First-day evening. He replied he had been

to Baltimore. "How didst thou go?"—"In the cars."
—"Where didst thou stay in Baltimore?"—(These questions
were put feelingly and very deliberately).—"At Bar-
num's Hotel."—"Where didst thou get the money to pay
thy expenses?"—"My father gave it to me."—"Is thy father
in Washington?"—"Yes, sir."—"Now," said I, "James,
this last is information that I value, as I see from it the
way of helping me out of a difficulty." Here I called my
man, and asked him to bring up my horse and buggy as
soon as possible, as I wished to go to Washington. I continued to say to James, that such a student (naming him)
had lost a ten-dollar note out of his trunk the week before,
"and thy not returning to school with the other students,
but going to Baltimore instead, and putting up at a hotel
there, naturally awakened an apprehension that *something
was not right*, and I am rejoiced at the opportunity of having my mind relieved on this point." I saw while I was
speaking that he was guilty. As soon as I ceased, he
arose, and with tears in his eyes, said, " Oh, Mr. Hallowell, I cannot go to Washington with you, I *did* take that
note. It was the first act of the kind I ever committed,
and if you will only forgive and excuse me, I give you my
word it shall be the last." We were both affected. There
seemed to be an unusual depth of contrition and humility,
and he had made no denial of the act.

I asked him to sit down, while I thought the subject
over a little while. After a few minutes I said to him,
" James, I am pleased with thy candid acknowledgment,
and with the evidence of thy regret and contrition. I can
forgive and excuse thee heartily on the terms thou namest,
and no one knows of it but thee and me, nor shall any
one know of it, as far as I am concerned. But the student
must have his money. I must pay him the ten dollars,

and charge it in thy bill as money advanced to thee in a particular emergency, and if thy father makes inquiry of me about it, I will refer him to thee, and thou must satisfy him in such way as thou thinkest right." After giving him a little consoling counsel, he left me.

I paid the student the ten dollars, and when I presented the bill to his father, who was then among the most distinguished and influential men in Washington, he paid it promptly, without making any inquiry, and so the matter ended. No student could have behaved better, or could have been more affectionate and respectful than James was, during the remainder of the time he was at school. I told *no one*.

About twelve years afterwards I was called out of my school-room to see a gentleman whom my man had shown into the study, and there I found a fine-looking large-sized naval officer, who took me in his arms and wept. It was James, with whom I had the interview in that same study. We both wept. He was a Captain in the Navy, and at that time had command of a prominent vessel. As soon as he could speak, he said, " Mr. Hallowell, you have been the making of me. *You have saved my character*," and his tears flowed profusely for some time. He is now dead.

About 1836 Judge ——, one of the Justices of the Supreme Court of the United States, brought his grandson to our school. He was, I suppose, about twelve or thirteen years of age, and an entirely original character, so that a new mode of treatment had to be invented in every case, like a new mould for different castings. But he was always *truthful* and *open*. I never knew the least department from strict integrity, when speaking soberly. There are two incidents I feel willing to relate of him:—

One day a student came to me in my study and said he had lost a dollar out of his trunk, and he thought M—— had taken it. "Why dost thou think so?"— "Why! I know he was short of funds last Thursday, and last Saturday he hired a horse at the livery stable, bought a whip, and rode up to Washington, and I think it was all paid for with my dollar." I cautioned him to keep this suspicion to himself, or he might do injustice to one of his school-mates, and told him I would see him again. In a little time I sent for M—— to come to my study, and he was soon there, with his pleasant smile and bright face. I had learned the necessity of two cautions in an interview with a student : first, never to make, even by insinuation, a charge that I could not substantiate, so that the student could say and think he was unjustly accused, when, if he was *guilty*, there would be the greater bluster. Second, never to express a doubt of a student's word. He would at once bluster up and say, "Why! do you think I'd tell a lie? I never told a lie in my life," and his bluster would be in the inverse ratio to his veracity. I felt the necessity of great caution with M——, for he was a boy of quick discernment. I introduced the subject at a distant point, and put the questions very deliberately. He had hired a horse last Saturday? "Yes." Such a student had lost some money out of his trunk. "Yes." Just then his mind seemed to connect the two facts, and see that there might be some ground for suspecting him, when, with great earnestness and boldness, he said, "Why, Mr. Hallowell, I can tell you all about that. My grandfather told me, when I wanted money, to go to such a man" (whom he named, and I knew, in Alexandria), "and he would let me have it. I went to him last Satur-

day and got a dollar of him. You may ask him."
" Well," said I, taking out my pencil and getting some
paper, " now, M——, tell me what thou didst with it?"
" I paid fifty cents for the horse, twenty-five cents for
a whip, bought ten cents' worth of cakes, of which I
gave part to such a boy, and here is the rest." I
counted it up, and it made the even dollar. " But,"
said I, " M——, where is the toll? There is a toll-gate
between here and Washington, and toll to pay both
ways." He straightened himself up, and, with a look of
bold independence, and almost contempt, for the idea of
his paying toll, said, " I never pay toll, Mr. Hallowell;
my whip does that. When I get near a toll-gate, I let
my horse have the whip, and *he* lets me through. *I
never pay toll.*"

On another occasion M—— had been very trouble-
some for several days, and one morning our man came
to me in school-time and told me that M—— had hidden the wheelbarrow, which he must have to bring the
things from market. I spoke to M—— and asked him
to get the wheelbarrow for Lucas. He was soon back,
and I called him to my desk, which was on the platform,
so that, as he stood by it, his face was a little lower than
my eyes. All the students were still and listening. I
said, " M——, didst thou find the wheelbarrow for Lucas?'
—" Yes."—" Where was it?" Here I could see his whole
countenance struggling with the incongruity of the idea
his answer would awaken, and his lip quivering with a
smile, as he said, " It was in the clothes-press," which
made the whole school laugh. I then asked him to go
into my study. After thinking the matter over a little
while, I went to see him, and, after recounting the number of cases in which I had had occasion to speak to him

for misdemeanors within the week just past, and we were now beginning a new one on the same tack, I told him I thought something must be the matter: he could not be well, and I wished him to go to bed and rest, for he had been very active, and I thought must be tired, and when he was ready to behave himself and be a good boy, to let me know. So I put him to bed in the guest-chamber, where he would be separated from the other students, and told Lucas to take up his breakfast, dinner, and supper, full meals, for he sat opposite me at table, and I knew he was a very hearty eater, though very thin and muscular. As soon as each session of school closed, I went up to see how M—— came on, and on asking him if he was ready to be a good boy, he would answer with quivering lip, half-hidden by the bed-clothes, with a most pleasant countenance, but without raising his eyes to mine, "No, sir." So it kept on, I going up three times a day till near the close of the week, and Lucas taking up his meals. I felt at a loss. It occurred to me to ask Margaret to happen in his room and see if she could make an impression on him. I knew if he would once say he would be a good boy, he would keep his word. The next day Margaret happened in, and went to the bureau drawer, and on turn-around she saw M——. "Oh, M——," said she, "I am very sorry to see thee there; I know thee must have been naughty, or thee would not be put to bed. It is always hard for people when they do wrong."—"I have not found it so, ma'am." This unexpected reply seemed to bring her purpose to a period, and she gave M—— up.

Things continued so over First-day, now nearly a week, the longest "case" I had ever had on hand. M—— occupied my thoughts much of the time throughout First-day. I was desirous of effecting his good, which was my single concern. He was eating very heartily, and using no exercise, and the mental inquiry arose, whether that was good for his health, which immediately suggested another plan of proceeding for trial. On Second-day morning, after breakfast, I went up to his room as usual, and asked him if he was ready to be a good boy. "No, sir." I then took out my watch, and said to him, "Now, M——, I have been coming up to see thee three times a day the past week, and every time receive the same reply, 'No, sir,' to my inquiry if thou art prepared to be a good boy. This is my lecture evening, and I have a great many things to attend to, and shall be very busy all the week. Now, this day week, next Second-day morning, about this time, half past seven o'clock, I will be here to see what answer thou wilt give to my inquiry." As soon as I said "this day week," I saw a shade on his countenance. I continued, with all the indications I could manifest of being in a hurry, as I was, "Now, M——, we must have regard for thy health. Thou hast been a week taking no exercise, and, Lucas says, eating very heartily of meat, etc. This is not good for thee, so I will direct Lucas to bring for thee as much bread and water as ever thou canst eat, and at this time, a week from now, punctually, I will be here again." I hurried out and down-stairs, but not till I beheld by his countenance that I had been favored to fall on the right plan. Very soon after school called I received a message from M—— that he wanted to see me. I sent him word I was busy and could not come. I would see him next Second-day. Through the day I received several messages from him that he wanted to see me, and to them all I returned the same answer. Towards evening, Lucas came and told me M—— was weeping, and wanted very badly to see me. This touched my heart, for I loved the boy, but I thought it best to wait ; so I sent him word that I was very busy then with making preparations for my lecture, but I would *try* to find time to see him in the morning.

In the morning I went to see him, and no boy could have been more broken-down and penitent. "Oh," said he, "Mr. Hallowell, if you will let me out this once, you will have no more trouble with me till vacation. I will be a good boy." Then I knew I was safe. I let him go down, saying very little to him, and he kept his word, there being no better nor more orderly boy in the school.

The vacation was about three months off, and as his promise was limited to vacation, I wrote to his grandfather that I thought it best that M—— should not return to our school after vacation, as nearly everybody in town knew him, and he knew everybody, so it would be better for him to be at some suitable school in the country, where there would be fewer incentives to mischief and tricks. His grandfather took my advice, and M—— and I parted the best of friends.

In 1847, after finishing my course in chemical analysis, in Dr. Jackson's laboratory, in Boston, on a very warm afternoon, I wanted to go to South Bridgewater, to visit the Normal School there. I went to the Boston station to take the cars, and on looking in the car, I saw every seat·was occupied by some one, coat off, fanning himself (it was dreadfully hot), and his elbows sticking out, looking as uninviting for a neighbor as possible, but so it was all the way to the far end of the car, where I found a double seat unoccupied, facing toward the door I had entered. I was scarcely seated before I saw a gentleman, appearing to be about sixty years old, with drab suit and white hat, in the same predicament in which I had just been, with unmistakable evidence that no one wanted him for a neighbor. I could see his confusion and appreciate it, so I stood up to my full height and said, audibly and deliberately, "Here is a seat by me, if thou wilt accept it." He came directly up, without seeming to look to the right hand or to the left, with his hat in his hand, and bowed most gracefully to me. I invited him to sit next to the window, as he seemed very warm, which he gladly did. We were the observed of the passengers for some time. Having done my part towards an acquaintance, as I was out studying character among other things, I waited to see if he would second the effort. I waited but a little while. He inquired almost immediately if I had ever been over that road before, and how far I was going. I told him I had never travelled it, that I was a stranger, from Alexandria, D. C., was out on a tour of observation, and was going to South Bridgewater to visit the State Normal School. This seemed to "open his mouth." He said he was very glad he had met with me, as it would afford him pleasure to point out to me the objects of interest on the road, as far as he went, which would be nearly to Bridgewater. He made himself very agreeable, pointing out the quarries of the Quincy granite, the residence of John Adams, the second President of the United States, a large mansion embowered in a thick grove, with a four-pitch roof, and the residence of his son, John Quincy Adams.

The heat of the day was forgotten in his conversation, and a more agreeable, instructive ride I never had. I gained information which I held to be of more value than one hundred dollars cash in hand would have been, and I feel it so now, for the money would soon have mingled in the common fund and disappeared, but the information this gentlemen so kindly gave me, and the impress of his appearance and manner, have been a real source of pleasurable enjoyment, whenever the incident has been revived in my remembrance, which has been very frequently.

I was highly pleased with my visit to the Normal School, and with the person at the head of it, whose name I am unable to recall. He gave me a great deal of information. All the students must have taught school at least six months before they can be admitted to the institution, in order that they may know their wants and deficiencies. There were about fifty of each sex in attendance, all neatly, but none expensively attired : the young men shaved smooth (didn't wear beards at that time), their boots nicely blacked, the girls' hair neat, shining, and plain, the dress corresponding, all mingling together in their studies and recitations, like brothers and sisters. I attended the recitations in Mathematics, Algebra, and Analytical Trigonometry. One student, say a young man, would recite at the blackboard till the teacher was satisfied with his knowledge of the subject, then the teacher would call a young woman to the board, who would continue the subject, and so on till the recitation was finished. I had formerly been much opposed to the co-education of the sexes, but this visit to South Bridgewater, and two subsequent ones to Earlham College, near Richmond, Indiana, which is conducted on the same principle, not only removed my opposition, but brought me in its favor, by convincing me that the co-education of the sexes would secure two objects, which I have found of the most difficult attainment with boys and young men, when educated alone,—the avoidance of rough, turbulent, boisterous conduct, and a careful preparation of their exercises for recitation, particularly with a judicious system of recording or "marking" for the class, so that a deficiency in one member will lower the whole, as no one would be willing to let his failure, if he could possibly avoid it, be the cause of lowering the standing of the whole class. This system embodies principles that are in harmony with man's nature, and must work favorably.

About 1848–9, my sister-in-law, Mary W. Farquhar (now Mary W. Kirk), had a school of girls in Alexandria, in Friends' old meeting-house, where Rachel Painter had formerly taught. It was her custom to give them every spring a "May-day picnic," at the close of which she would deliver to them an address. On one occasion, she requested me to write one for her, which I did, as follows :

> Again returns the joyous May :
>   Again this merry band I view ;
> Another year has passed away ;
>   But still 'tis spring-time, girls, with you.
>
> And would you wish this spring to last?
>   This beauteous May-day, mild and clear ?
> No clouds your mental sky o'ercast?
>   Nor winter follow, cold and drear?
>
> Then turn your tender thoughts above,
>   Whence all this beauteous season springs ;
> To Him whose everlasting love
>   One constant round of comforts brings.

He gives the light that gilds the flowers,
  The heat, the life, that makes them grow;
The fanning breeze and fertile showers
  From His unbounded goodness flow.

And, higher far, an eye to see,
  A heart to enjoy, He gives you too;
And then His love, so bounteously,
  To make you happy, good and true.

Oh, to His laws yield all your powers,
  His secret whispers prompt obey,
And He will strew life's path with flowers,
  And make your year one lengthened May.

It was received very favorably, and was *encored*, which, no doubt, was as much due to the recitation as the poetry.

We had to employ a good many domestics, often six or eight at a time, and, as I suppose is the case in most large establishments, and perhaps in smaller ones too, there would sometimes be little differences among them; some would not perform their duties to the satisfaction of the mistress of the house; and, as the plan I adopted looks pleasant in the retrospect, and has the sanction of my present judgment, I feel willing to relate it.

In the first place, from principle, I was always kind and respectful to them, regardful of their comfort and interest, and thoughtful of their condition, which I felt was one of many trials and comparatively few comforts.

Next, I made it a point to pay them punctually at the close of every month, so that they knew when they would get their money, and had not to ask for it. Those whose wages were not over five dollars, as was generally the case with the female domestics, I always paid in specie, purchasing it for them for this purpose, during the banks' suspension of specie payment. I generally had their pay in silver half-dollars. I always paid them in my study, one at a time, asking the last one I paid to send in another. Then, when there would be anything not satisfactory reported to me during the month, among them, I would treasure it up in my mind till pay-day, and when the delinquent would hold his or her hand for me to count the money in, I would place one half-dollar in, and then recount the deficiency or dissatisfaction that had been complained of to me, and then count another half-dollar, then more of the complaint and then another half-dollar, closing with the hope that, at the next pay-day, there would be nothing to complain of, which, indeed, was almost universally the case. I advised them too, at these times, about saving their money for a rainy day, if only a little each month, and how to invest it. It often made my heart ache to see the little the women had to save out of three, three and a half, and four dollars for a hard month's work, though these were then regarded full wages for the different employments.

Nancy Gordon Franklin, whom I have already mentioned as our first domestic, worked for us till we left Alexandria, thirty-six years, at which time she then owned three lots, all with good houses on them. She was a "woman of all work," washing, ironing, cleaning house, early and late. She was reliable and energetic, doing as much in one of her long days, and with her quick step, as almost any one else would do in two. She was always in demand, and had plenty of work. Her children, too, do well. Nancy is still living, and although older than I, was strong and active at last accounts. Nancy had been a slave.*

---

* Nancy died in the winter of 1880. EDS.

Nathaniel Lucas, colored, had lived with Edward Stabler till he died, in 1831, soon after which he came to live with us. He was a faithful domestic, who also had been a slave. He first bought himself, then his wife, "Aunt Monica," then a grand-daughter, and afterwards a lot on which there was a good two-story house, on South Washington street. He died at the school, and left his widow the house they lived in and two hundred dollars, which I had invested for her. I paid her the interest, a dollar a month, she preferring to receive it in this way, until after I left Alexandria, when I transferred the stock to my valued friend, Robert H. Miller, who continued the payment of a dollar a month, till her death. She died in her own house.

I feel much gratification, in looking back, at the comfort I had with the domestics, and in the belief that they found a pleasant and profitable home with me and in my family.

CHAPTER XV.

1840.

Convention of the friends of Education — Difference between work and play — Letter on the subject of the Alexandria water-works — A kind intention — Closing reflections.

Some time about the year 1840, I think it was, a convention of the "Friends of Education" was held in Washington, of which Professor Alexander Dallas Bache was President, and Dr. Thomas Sewall and myself were secretaries. Professor Durbin, President of Carlisle College; William Cost Johnson, M. C. from Maryland; Stanley, M. C. from North Carolina; Joseph John Gurney, from England; Francis S. Key, and a considerable number of the practical educators of the country, as well as of the friends of education, were present. The object of the convention was to compare sentiments in regard to the working of the public school system in the different States; to awaken public attention to its importance, and to make suggestions for discussion of modifications and improvements in the system.

William Cost Johnson spoke for Maryland, and Stanley for North Carolina, in both of which States the cause of education had been much neglected, and there was an amusing play of witticisms between them, each trying to establish the point that the most hopeful condition for the future belonged to his State. One of the speakers, William Cost Johnson, was a bachelor, at which class some hit had been given by his opponent, who said, as evidence of the hopeful future, that the ladies in his State now "smiled on education." The bachelor retorted that "in Maryland, the ladies not only smiled upon education, but upon bachelors too," which occasioned a good deal of amusement.

This meeting was in the hall of the House of Representatives. The information given, and the remarks and discussion it elicited, were exceedingly interesting. All agreed in the belief that it would be a great aid to the cause to hold meetings to awaken public attention to the subject, and Francis S. Key and I were appointed a committee to hold such meetings in Maryland, but, on making further inquiry, we ascertained there was really no school system in Maryland, and no foundation to build upon.

Joseph John Gurney gave a very interesting account of education in England, which he admitted was in a low condition, but it was gradually receiving more attention from their enlightened statesmen.

I offered a resolution to this effect: "*Resolved*, as the sense of this convention, that it is of the highest importance in a system of education that the muscles should be trained and educated to industrial pursuits, simultaneously with the mind, in order that they can ultimately execute the highest performances the mind can conceive, and the artisan and the artist shall be united in one person."

Professor Durbin, of Carlisle College, opposed it, but in very respectful, friendly terms. He said he had been for some time connected with a "manual labor" school in Pennsylvania, and it proved to be a failure. I said in my reply, "It is difficult to meet an argument based on the individual experience of the speaker, but from his own statement, the experience he gives has no connection whatever with the object of my resolution. It is no surprise to me that his experiment failed; the surprise would have been, had it succeeded. The name itself was sufficient to kill it. Manual labor would soon be, by boys, construed into hard labor, and it would be regarded as a juvenile work-house or penitentiary. Manual labor, mere work, with one's hands, is almost universally regarded as belonging to the lowest class of employees, while the industry contemplated by my resolution is of the very highest respectability.

"Then," I queried, "will the gentlemen please tell us the difference between work and play." I saw he was a little surprised, and I at once relieved him from his embarrassment, for it was all mingled with the best of feeling on both sides. I told him I had reflected upon that subject, and was willing to give my views. That is *play*, no matter how severe the exercise or labor, that is done of one's own free choice and direction; that *work*, however light the employment, that is done under the control, direction, and authority of another.

Before I concluded, I saw that I had the sympathies of the audience with me. What interested and gratified me very much was, that Professor Bache, the President of the Convention, called some one to the chair, and took the floor in support of the resolution. I remember some of his words: "The resolution possesses the length, breadth, and depth of philosophy, and I thank the gentleman from Alexandria for offering it." It met with no further opposition.

The following letter, which I addressed to my valued friend, Robert H. Miller, since deceased, in answer to one from him, gives a little history of the plans and successful termination of the effort to furnish Alexandria with a supply of good water, for which it had been previously dependent on water carts to bring it from the "Diagonal Pump," and perhaps one or two other pumps, or on having domestics carry it in buckets or tubs, on their heads. A charter of the company was obtained from the Virginia Legislature, Third month 22d, 1850.

SANDY SPRING, MD., *Fourth mo. 14th, 1873.*

DEAR COUSIN ROBERT:

The boring for water in the Market Square, in Alexandria, was not commenced till after I went there to live, Tenth month, 1824; but I cannot fix the time certainly.

About the time that project was given up the Chesapeake and Ohio Canal was commenced. John Quincy Adams, while President, moved the first spadeful of earth in that great work, after some difficulty which obliged him to take off his coat, from encountering what was stated to be a hickory* root,

---

* Hickory, or "Old Hickory," was the sobriquet for General Jackson. Adams' opponent for the Presidency.

about 1827. The corporation of Alexandria subscribed a quarter of a million dollars to that enterprise, on condition that the necessary arrangement and structure should be made for connecting with it a branch canal to Alexandria. One great benefit looked forward to from this Alexandria canal, by some of the citizens, and especially by our valued friend, Hugh Smith, was its being the means of supplying the town of Alexandria with water. This idea was adhered to, even after the canal was in operation, and seeing all manner of filth that was continually being thrown into the canal and basin by the boatmen, and from other sources, the idea of drinking that water rendered some fastidious stomachs qualmish.

Another plan proposed was to erect a mound for a basin or reservoir, and force water up from the Potomac river, which plan did not give much better promise for pure water than the canal.

A third proposition was to collect the streams from all the springs, in the valley northwest of the town, into one channel, and thus supply the town with water. Dr. Powell and myself spent some time on horseback reconnoitering the country in regard to this plan, and we were convinced that any supply that could be thus obtained would be wholly inadequate to the demands of the city.

My own attention had been for some time turned to getting "Cameron Run" to the top of Suter's Hill, and letting it pass thence by its own flow through our kitchens, bath-rooms, etc., to the Potomac river, and give us all a full supply of good water, as well as furnish a means for extinguishing fires, of which the city stood in great need.

When on a visit to my sister, Mary S. Lippincott, at Moorestown, New Jersey, while this subject was occupying my mind, I met with James S. Hulme, of Mount Holly, and in conversation with him, ascertained that his mill had recently been brought into requisition as a means of supplying Mount Holly with water, and I accepted the invitation he kindly gave me to visit him and examine the works. They were very simple and efficient. The crank that moved the piston of the forcing pump was attached to an iron pin in the water-wheel of the mill, and a supply of water for the town was forced up to the reservoir, with very little, and many times no perceptible, diminution of the previous working power of the mill.

This idea was at once transferred to Cameron Mills, as the source of power for the Alexandria water-works, and on returning to Alexandria I mentioned the subject to several of my friends, to thee, Edward S. Hough, and Thomas William Smith among the number. They all encouraged me. I told them if they would get up a public meeting of those in favor of a supply of water for the town, I would make a speech upon the subject in favor of using the Cameron stream. This was done.

The large company of citizens that collected in the Lyceum building, gave evidence of the interest they felt in the subject. I spoke of the feasibility of having the clear and pure water from Pebbly Brook (Cameron stream) conducted through all our houses on its way to the Potomac, and, referring to the motto on one span of the beautiful arch on Washington street, erected in honor of General La Fayette, when he visited Alexandria, Tenth month, 1824, taken from his speech on the Paris Tribune: "For a nation. to be free, it is sufficient that she wills it," so, I added, for Alexandria to have this great luxury, it is sufficient that she wills it. I cannot remember whether or not a subscription was opened at that meeting, which was held some time in the winter of 1850-1, or at a meeting held soon after. The shares were twenty dollars each. The subscription paper was first handed to some of the rich men, the largest subscription among whom was ten shares! I saw at once that with such a commencement among our moneyed men, the work would never be accomplished. On the paper being handed to me, I subscribed forty shares. The effect was electrical. Thou wilt remember it. I, a comparatively poor man, going so far beyond the wealthy ones, seemed to give *eclat* to the subject. Phineas Janney doubled his subscription at once, and recommended to others, "Do thou likewise," which many did. The shares were afterwards raised to twenty-five dollars each, which made my subscription one thousand dollars.

I have ever since believed that the life infused into the undertaking when my subscription was announced to the meeting, and made known among the citizens, was one great element of our success.   It gave evidence of an earnestness of purpose and of confidence in the practicability of the scheme, by one who had made it most of a study, and who was believed to be among those who were best able to judge, and thus inspired confidence in others.   I was appointed on the committee to obtain subscriptions, and no person I asked failed to subscribe at least one share.

The subscription got on finely, and a meeting of the stockholders was soon called to elect officers.   I nominated George D. Fowle for President, but he and others named me, and to my surprise I was unanimously elected, with the exception of my own vote.

I accepted the office upon two conditions :— first, that I was to have no salary ; second, that I was to have the privilege of selecting a competent engineer, who had constructed similar works, to the satisfaction of the companies by whom he was employed.

Both these conditions were acceded to.   I saw and felt the wisdom of them afterwards.

Frederick Erdman was mentioned to me by John Elgar, my wife's uncle, as a competent engineer for our purpose, he having been connected with the Philadelphia water-works for many years, under that distingished engineer Frederick Graff, and, moreover, had constructed water-works at Harrisburg, Pennsylvania, and Frederick, Maryland.

I immediately wrote to the President of each of these companies, making inquiries in regard to his success, and they both bore emphatic testimony to his competency and efficiency, and stated that, if they had similar works to build, they would have him for engineer, if he was to be had, at almost any price.   In answer to my inquiry, how much was the annual cost for repair of the forcing pump, made under Erdman's direction, the President of the Harrisburg company

said he could not tell the annual cost, for in the number
of years, some six or eight, it had been running, they had
uot paid the first cent for repairs.

Frederick Erdman, from this high testimony, was of course
elected by the Board our engineer, he proposing to superintend the whole work to completion, performing all the duties
of engineer, for the sum of fifteen hundred dollars, which
was satisfactory to the Board, and, as thou knowest, we had
many times afterwards cause to congratulate ourselves for
having been favored to obtain his valuable services.

As already intimated, I had always looked to Suter's
Hill as the site for the reservoir from which the water was
to be distributed through the city, and the Board had agreed
upon a spot in a conspicuous situation from King street.
The day Erdman first came, after his appointment, the Board
accompanied him there to show him what an eligible site
we had, the Board consisting of Benjamin Hallowell, President; Robert H. Miller, Stephen Shinn, George D. Fowle,
Thomas McCormick, John B. Daingerfield, and William N.
McVeigh, Directors, and Edward S. Hough, Secretary.

Thou wilt remember our engineer looking all around,
silently, for some time, when at length he said, in substance,
"Gentlemen, this place will not suit you at all for the reservoir. It is more than twice the height you need. You
will be able to get less than half the water at this elevation
than at a proper one. It would be a double strain upon
your service pipes, and cause a continued perplexity and expense from their breaking." I do not know how many other
convincing practical objections to our "eligible site" he would
have brought out, had I not interrupted him by asking if
he would please to point out to us the proper place for the
reservoir. After a little pause, in which he took an eye
survey between there and Cameron Mills, from which we had
told him we were to obtain the water, he pointed to the site
of the present reservoir, and said, "That is the knoll for
your purpose," and he proceeded towards it, the Board following, *one* of whom felt as humble as their "knoll" appeared beside Suter's Hill. But were we not all pleased

with our engineer, and highly gratified that we had the result of practical experience in time! It saved us many thousands of dollars. This is only one of many instances in which we found the value of his experience in constructing different parts of the work.

The following notice of "breaking ground" for the reservoir, appeared in the Alexandria Gazette in the spring of 1851:

"Having taken quarters at Sanders' City Hotel, where the illustrious Washington frequently sojourned, I proceeded at once to learn the passing events of the day. In the afternoon the President and Directors of the Alexandria Water Company had, in the presence of a number of their fellow-citizens, performed the important and interesting ceremony of breaking the first ground towards that noble work.

"This took place on the lot recently purchased of Peter Tressler, in the rear of Suter's Hill. The venerable Benjamin Hallowell, spade in hand, and with a degree of vigor and enthusiasm that would have reflected credit on a more youthful operator, took the lead, in which he was followed by our excellent townsmen, Phineas Janney, Hugh Smith, and others.

"Mr. Hallowell made a very neat and appropriate address, and at the conclusion the whole company walked to a house in the neighborhood, where they partook of an agreeable entertainment, in the shape of ice-cream, lemonade, etc., etc.

"May each and all who were there present long live to enjoy in their dwellings the pure streams of water from Cameron Run."

With the subsequent proceeding thou art as well acquainted as I, and therefore I need proceed no further with my narrative, unless it may be to relate a little incident connected with bringing the water-main from the reservoir across the "Stone Bridge."

Erdman, our engineer, proposed to cut a little distance into the arch of the bridge, so as to imbed a portion of the pipe, which he said would not injure the bridge in the least, but we thought it would be only respectful to consult Phineas

Janney, who was President of the Turnpike Company, that claimed ownership of the bridge. President Janney and his engineer refused permission, the engineer saying "it would ruin the bridge." Erdman told us (the Board) there was no other safe way to cross the ravine. What was to be done in such an emergency? I think it was thou who told me that, some time previous, when that bridge was carried away by a freshet, the Turnpike Company represented to the corporation of Alexandria that their road terminated at the west side of the stream, and asked the corporation to rebuild the bridge, which it did, entire.

On gaining this information, I immediately obtained an interview with Lawrence B. Taylor (a former student), who was then Mayor, and with Reuben Johnston, who was Auditor of the corporation of Alexandria ; explained the state of affairs to them, and they, remembering the correctness of what thou hadst told me, said they would sustain the Board in any course they and their engineer thought best and right to take.

We then made arrangements with William McLean, the energetic and faithful contractor for laying the pipes, to carry the pipes across the bridge "between two days," and he put the work under way accordingly by having his men to dig trenches on each side of the bridge, closer and closer. In the afternoon McLean saw Phineas Janney coming, and he jumped into an idle cart and lay there about two hours, the President remaining on the ground till near sunset. On asking the men what the plan was to cross the bridge, they told him they did not know, which was the case. They were just working according to orders. On the President of the Turnpike Company's going out there early next morning, he found the pipes all laid across the bridge, and covered up nicely for some distance towards town, without the least injury to the bridge, nor has there been any since, to this time.

It may be proper to add that neither *McLean* nor the *President of the Water Company* was there at the time the President of the Turnpike Company came out in the morning, nor did they meet with him for several days thereafter. When we *did*

meet, he was very pleasant, and he never afterwards said a
word on the subject.

Thy sincere friend,

BENJAMIN HALLOWELL.

ROBERT H. MILLER, Alexandria, Va.

The water was let into the pipes and conveyed into
the town on the 15th of Sixth month, 1852, just fifteen
months after the appointment of the Board and after
the commencement of the undertaking. There were but
two leaks in the whole seven miles of pipe, and these
were stopped in a few hours the same afternoon the
water was admitted; showing the faithfulness and efficiency of the contractor, William McLean. It was believed to be an unparalleled success.

It was acknowledged that in the Lyceum Building
and the Water-works, both of which were due to my instrumentality, as well as in the buildings erected for private use, I left Alexandria better than I found it.

Among the papers of my valued friend, Robert H.
Miller, who died on the 10th of Third month, 1874, was
found the following inscription, in his own hand-writing,
apparently of recent date, to be placed upon a tablet to
be inserted in the banks of the reservoir at Mount
Cameron, in pursuance of a plan that had long been on
his mind, and which he wished to accomplish at an early
day. But the hydrant of Cameron water, that is now
in the Market Square, with the evidence of the wish
and intention of my valued friend, which, I have understood, was shared in by the Water Board, are more
grateful to my feelings, and more in harmony with my
ideas of the fitness of things than would be a *monument
of marble:*

TO
BENJAMIN HALLOWELL,
FIRST PRESIDENT OF THE ALEXANDRIA WATER COMPANY,
WHOSE FORESIGHT DEVISED,
WHOSE INFLUENCE AND ENERGY COMPLETED
THE SIMPLE BUT EFFECTUAL SCHEME
OF SUPPLYING ALEXANDRIA WITH PURE WATER,
THIS MONUMENT IS ERECTED
BY HIS GRATEFUL FRIENDS AND FELLOW-CITIZENS.

ALEXANDRIA WATER WORKS COMMENCED 1851.
COMPLETED 1852.
ENLARGED UNDER THE PRESIDENCY OF GEO. H. SMOOT.
COMMENCED 1869. COMPLETED 1872.

"Now, what I wished is done.
By contemplation's help, not sought in vain,
I seem to have lived my childhood o'er again,"
as well as the many and varied incidents of my life to
the present time.

NOTE.—To make the picture as complete as possible,
it seems right to add the following:—I was recommended
as an approved minister of the Society of Friends by
Alexandria Monthly Meeting, and confirmed by Fairfax
Quarterly Meeting, Virginia, while I was President of
the Maryland Agricultural College, in the Eleventh
month, 1859.

Of our nine children, six are dead. Four died young, the oldest of them being under six years; the next four years and two months; the third twenty-two months; and the fourth, seven months. Five lived to be married and have families. Three of our children and their companions still live to cheer' and comfort us, besides eighteen grandchildren, who feel almost as near to me as our own children, of whom Henry has seven, Caroline four, Elgar left four, Benjamin jr. has one, and Mary left two.

The thought has several times presented itself, since I commenced to write this Autobiography, in the early part of last month, how many of those persons who have been brought so pleasantly into remembrance, as *they were then*, and many more than I have named, so that I can seem to see them and hear them distinctly, have passed on to the higher life!

The fact I have gained from the preceding minute and careful review of all the varied incidents of -my earthly career, that there is not a single person, living or departed, whom it does not afford me real pleasure to remember, or whom I would not feel rejoiced to meet in this stage of existence, or the one to which we are all passing, fully repays for all the labor of compiling and writing this history.

I have no feeling, *save of love*, for *any* person *anywhere*, nor do I feel that *any* person *owes me anything*, material or spiritual, or is under obligations to me; *all is fully paid*. I am conscious of never having *intentionally* wronged any one, although I may have done so by impulse, which I have continually striven, and with some success every year, to overcome. From a nervous excitable temperament, it has occasioned me more anguish and suffering than all the physical pain, sickness, and disease I have experienced, and I am assured the Good Father, in his love and mercy, has forgiven me for it. I therefore feel *at peace with him and with the whole world,* and ready to depart at his *earliest summons.*

BENJAMIN HALLOWELL.

Rockland, Sandy Spring, Md.,
Second mo. 26th, 1875.

PART II.

REMINISCENCES OF VARIOUS SUBJECTS.

INTRODUCTORY NOTE.

In the early part of the present year (1875), at the request of my children, and particularly of my daughter, Caroline H. Miller, inasmuch as I needed something to occupy me in the intervals of waiting on my dear companion, who was an invalid, I wrote for the benefit of my children and grandchildren an Autobiography. The object aimed at was to give a history of those incidents and circumstances in my life which had tended to form my character, and evolve, from the " Me " that was the actor in the transactions, the " Me " that is now relating them.

When I had finished that engagement, which was toward the latter part of the Second month, being still occupied in attending to my dear wife, I concluded to write some incidents, experiences, and reminiscences of my life, that were not immediately connected with the development of my character, but which still possessed some points that I thought might be of interest, and place them as an appendix to my Autobiography; but before these were quite finished, the precious invalid was taken from me (Fifth month 1st), and I felt unable to continue the employment. But, thanks to the benevolent framer of the human constitution, time, the great soother of sorrow, has gradually brought the sad reality to blend harmoniously with my daily thoughts and duties, and I concluded to resume the occupation and finish what was then before me, which is now done.

14

Goods Seized for Militia Fines.

A little over a year after we commenced housekeeping in Alexandria, D. C., in 1824, the captain of the militia of the district presented to me a bill of fifteen dollars for muster fines for the past year, five musters in the year, and a fine of three dollars for absence from each. I told the captain the discipline of the religious society to which I belonged required that its members should be in no way active in anything connected with military affairs, but suffer peaceably whatever penalty the law imposed. He said he would then have to distrain my property for the amount of the fine, and requested me to designate what goods I could best spare. I told him I could say nothing upon the subject, but left it all to him to do what the law required. He then levied on our parlor furniture, taking a large looking-glass, my portable writing-desk, brass and-irons, shovel and tongs, and several other things; goods selling so low at *such* sales, which no respectable people attended, it took more than we could replace for fifty dollars to pay a fine of fifteen. But I cheerfully made the sacrifice to the Society, for the many privileges I enjoyed from it, although our parlor did look very much stripped, and I thought such a stripping every year, which was the prospect before me, would be a severe tax.

At the ensuing session of Congress, however, the Columbian College, of Washington City, petitioned to exempt the President, professors, teachers, and students of that institution from military duty in time of peace, and a bill was laid before the House for that object. While the bill was under consideration, a motion was made to extend the same favor to the officers of George-town College.

Charles Fenton Mercer, who represented the Congressional district in Virginia contiguous to Alexandria, and a warm friend of our school, moved an amendment so as to include "all the institutions of learning in the District of Columbia," which was adopted, and the bill as amended passed. I immediately obtained a copy of the laws of that session, when they were printed, and the next year, upon the collector's presenting his bill of fifteen dollars, I showed him the law, which he had not before seen. After examining it carefully, he said it exempted all persons connected with our establishment from military duty in time of peace, and he seemed to be gratified with it.

The change was greatly in my favor. The law previously required military duty of all males over eighteen years of·age, which would have embraced not only the teachers, but nearly half the students, five days in the year, and a fine of three dollars each time for non-attendance. This would have occasioned no little perplexity, but it was all obviated by this kindness of my friend Charles Fenton Mercer, of Aldie, who, though many years deceased, is still held in pleasant and grateful remembrance.

From principle I could not engage in military training, either as an officer or in the ranks;—not as officer, for the reason that I could not assume the responsibility of commanding a company of men in what may become a case of morals, in which each individual must be left free to act according to the dictates of his own conscience or sense of right, which is the voice of God to his soul, and therefore superior to all law or any *human authority*. For a like reason, I could not be one of the " rank or file," because I believe it would be wrong to place myself under another, in a position where I might be commanded to do what my conscience and sense of right, the supreme authority for *my* guidance, would forbid.

Therefore, independent of any consideration in regard to the hurtful influence of war in all its connexions, I have a testimony against military training as a preparation for war. But I have a high respect and regard for law. I am at heart a law-abiding citizen, never to be active in opposition to law, but ready and willing to comply with the law or suffer the penalty which it imposes for non-compliance.

As a member of civil society, I think it would be right for *me* to pay the penalty which the law imposes for non-compliance in this respect, believing the general effect would be far better than the present mode prescribed by Friends' Discipline, of having the penalty collected by distraint. But estimating very highly the privileges my birth-right of membership in the Society of Friends has given me, and yet gives me, I will not pay such fines while the Discipline of the Society requires its members not to do so. Is this the right course? Do we not blame the Pope and the Roman Catholic Church for a similar thing — for placing the obligations of the citizen to a religious society above his obligations to his country?

Anecdote of a Graduate of West Point.

About 1848 or 1849, one of our former students, whom we highly regarded, came to Alexandria expressly to inform my dear Margaret and myself that he was going to the

Mexican war, and to bid us an affectionate farewell, his return of course being uncertain. My dear wife, on hearing this, remarked to him, "I shall hereafter examine the papers with additional interest, to see if thy name is there." He replied, "If you find it, madam, I hope you will never see 'run' after it." "I would rather see 'run' than *killed*," she answered. "Well," said I, "much as I love him, *I* would not. If he entertains the least conscientious scruples about going to war, I advise him by all means to be faithful to these and not go; but if he has not such scruples and does go, then my earnest advice to him is, to do his duty, stand to his post faithfully, obey the commands given, and do all that is expected of him. His unfaithfulness in running, from cowardice, not *principle*, might cause a panic, throw all into confusion, be the means of sacrificing the lives of many brave men, as well as bringing disgrace on the officers and loss to the country. A true man will always be faithful in the effort to perform any duty he undertakes, and will endeavor to do all that can be reasonably expected of him, to the best of his ability."

After mature and deliberate reflection upon the subject, these are still my honest convictions.

INCIDENTS OF THE WAR, 1861–65.

In the year 1860, seeing that a great sectional strife was approaching, in which my former students, who felt to me almost like my own children, were arrayed on opposite sides, thus seeming to add to the horrors of war, I determined, as far as practicable, to keep my mind and feelings from all participation in it, and I ceased, as far as possible, from reading the newspapers, making inquiry, or hearing anything on the subject, for three years, from 1860 to the fall of 1863, which period, included my six months' journey by private conveyance beyond the Mississippi river. While traveling in the Mississippi valley, I learned that General Lee had crossed the Potomac, and had invaded Maryland and Pennsylvania, and that Harrisburg, Philadelphia, and Baltimore, were in great danger of being overpowered by the Southern army and captured. Although General Lee had been one of my students, in great favor, and a warm personal friendship had existed between us from that time, so that it would seem natural that my sympathies should be all with him and his success, yet when I heard that General Meade had arrested his progress and driven him across the Potomac to his own State, my heart rejoiced! It was impossible to avoid it. It was an instinctive outburst in favor of right, justice, and freedom.

So now (Fourth month, 1875), I wish every success to Governor Hartranft, of Pennsylvania, in his wise and just measures for restoring peace and quiet in the counties at present threatened with lawlessness and anarchy. Bad as we all admit war to be, anarchy and mob violence are much worse than regulated war. Police in cities—indeed, all government — rests ultimately on armed force. In a civilized community, there must somewhere exist a means of securing safety and peace by coercion, if milder efforts fail.

The inquiry has frequently presented itself to my mind, whether persons who refuse to give aid to the Government, to assist in carrying it on in such way as those entrusted with that duty think best, can *consistently* avail themselves of its advantages in recording their deeds, wills, and in all the machinery of civilized life. Can they with propriety employ a magistrate or a constable to arrest a thief that has their stolen horse in his possession, and recover their property?

Taking of his Horse Ande.

In the summer of 1864 a Confederate officer, accompanied by two soldiers, galloped up the lawn at Rockland, and finding my riding-horse fastened in front of the house, they loosed her and took her off before I could get to them.* Seeing that they stopped at the barn, I ran there immediately, and got hold of Ande's bridle rein. The officer endeavored to get my hand loose, and jerked me about for some time. My wife and children, who were looking on, were greatly alarmed. He then presented a pistol to my breast, and said he would shoot me if I did not let go. I looked him firmly in the face, and told him I could not do it; the horse was mine; the Confederate soldiers had taken our three best horses the previous year, and this was the only one I had left, and I could not spare her. I was just as calm and collected during the scene as I am now in describing it.

After a little time his countenance relaxed, and he let go the bridle rein and went to look at the other horses, but found none to suit, and soon after left. I did not regard this as a " special Providence" in my favor, and should not have dared to presume to consider it in that light. Throughout the whole scene my consciousness was all active, and I was closely observant of his countenance and of the muscles of the finger that rested on the trigger, with the determined purpose, having hold of the bridle rein with my left hand, the first moment I perceived the least

---

*It was the horse that had taken me on my long Western journey.

increase of tension in either, to use my right hand and arm to give such direction to the muzzle of the pistol as would cause the ball to pass by me, feeling under no obligation whatever to remain a stationary target for him to shoot at. Before the officer left the premises, he came to me and offered an apology for his conduct, and shook hands with me at parting, in a very friendly manner. He said to some persons in the village, where he stopped, about half a mile distant, "That old Quaker gentleman was very determined, but I liked him for all."

Such men, soldiers though they be, have a higher respect and regard for a person who stands up firmly for his rights, because of its harmonizing with the witness for right and justice in their own hearts. This witness it is that renders truth, justice, and love invincible.

The day on which the scene just related occurred was a trying one, the whole neighborhood being overrun with Confederate officers and soldiers; but we understood in the evening that all had left.

The next morning at breakfast, I told my wife I would walk over and see how our sister-in-law, Sarah B. Farquhar, who lives about half a mile distant, had fared through the disturbed day, her residence being much nearer the roadside than ours, and I was apprehensive she might have been more inconvenienced. My wife said the morning was so very warm (it being in the Seventh month), I had better ride. I took her advice; had Ande brought out, and set off. Before I had gone more than two hundred yards from our back gate on the main road, I met a Confederate officer and two soldiers of a different company from those of the day before. I spoke to them respectfully, and was about to pass on, when the officer commanded, "Halt!" I stopped, and he, after examining my

horse closely, said, "We must have that horse — the
Major's horse has given out, and we were sent to take the
first horse that would suit, and this is just the one we
want." He then ordered me to dismount. I told him I
could not do that — the horse was mine, she had carried
me four times across the Alleghany Mountains, and once
beyond the Mississippi river and back, and had been so
faithful to me that I could in no way be accessory to
separating from her. "You must then," said he, "go with
me to headquarters," to which I cheerfully consented, expecting to find headquarters in a room, where I could
plead my cause, and I hoped, save my horse. We had
gone but a little distance, however, toward "headquarters,"
when we came to a turn in the road, from which we could
see that it was full of soldiers, being General Bradley
Johnson's command, with six pieces of artillery and fifteen
hundred mounted men, besides many on foot.

The officer took me up to General Johnson, who,
with his body-guard and three pieces of artillery abreast
in front and behind him, was riding along, and said to the
General, "This old gentleman is not willing to part from
his horse." The General looked at the horse critically, I
riding along between him and the officer, and then emphatically said to the officer, "*Take that horse.*" The officer
conducted me to the side of the road, which was streaming with cavalry, into the corner of a "worm fence,"
and I felt convinced that "Ande" was gone —that the
command received would have to be obeyed; but I did
not see how the officer was to get us separated. He said,
"You heard what the General said, and I wish you to
dismount." I looked him firmly but mildly in the face,
and told him I had heard it. "Now," said I, "it is
not obstinacy, but as I have already said, this is my

horse; she has been faithful to me, and I cannot in any
way be active in separating from her. I bought her
sire in Montreal, Canada, just because I fancied him, and
brought him home by railroad, canal, and steamboat,
paying duty on him as I crossed the lines, to New York
city, had him shipped to Alexandria, Virginia, where I
then lived. I bought her dam in Loudoun county,
Virginia, and we raised three colts, two of which, with
another of our best horses, the Confederate officers took
last year, and this is the only horse left that I can ride,
and I cannot, by any act of mine, part from her."

I saw from his countenance my remarks had made
an impression, but he had to obey orders. He asked me
if I was far from home, which I thought was with a
view, in case I was, to make this an excuse to the General for permitting me to retain her. This I do not
know, but it manifested a benevolent consideration. I
told him I was not far from home. "Then you can
readily walk there?" I told him I could. "Then
you must dismount." I told him, for reasons I had
already given, and from no obstinacy whatever, *that* I
could not do. I was observing him intently. He looked
perplexed, having his eyes turned in the direction the
army was going, that was still streaming by us. At
length I observed a turn in his thoughts that lighted
up his countenance. He came up to my saddle, coolly
and deliberately unbuckled the girth, took hold of the
saddle with one hand in front and the other behind me,
and pulled it and me over (I resting on his shoulder),
and laid me down at full length as gently as if I had
been an infant; and by the time I could get up, he had
mounted his horse and was leading Ande off, so that I
barely got sight of her, before they came to a turn in

the road, and she was lost to me forever. Poor Ande, she was a true and faithful horse! In consideration of the hard usage to which, in all probability, she would be exposed, the regret I felt was quite as much on her account as my own.

But I never had the least feeling of unkindness or blame towards any of the persons who were engaged in these proceedings, although from myself and my children they took nine of our very best horses (they being excellent judges, and taking none but the best), seeing how completely the whole neighborhood was in their power, and what amount of damage they might have done in our settlement, with six pieces of artillery and fifteen hundred mounted men. In addition to a little personal inconvenience for a few days, the loss of a few horses and rails was all the neighborhood suffered. No building was burnt, no life lost, and no one taken prisoner, except as guide for a short distance.

INTERVIEW WITH A ROMAN CATHOLIC PRIEST.

On one occasion, about the year 1840, while I was President of the Alexandria Lyceum, a member chose for the subject of his lecture " European History," in the early portion of which the history of Rome and of the Pope was necessarily prominent. The lecture bore pretty hard upon some features of the Pope's proceedings and of the Roman Catholic religion, as infringing upon individual freedom and intellectual development, particularly in denying to its members freedom of thought.

It happened that the Roman Catholic priest, resident in Alexandria, was present. The next morning after the

lecture, I was called out of the school-room into my
study, where I found the priest, who had come up to
protest against my allowing such utterances in the
Lyceum as the lecturer of the preceding evening had
used; that, as the presiding officer of the institution, I
ought to prohibit it, as doing great injustice to a part
of the community.   "Besides," said he, "it is not true
that the Catholics are denied freedom of thought.   The
church leaves every one at liberty to think just what
he pleases, and no greater freedom of thought could
possibly be desired.   But no one has a right to tell his
infidel thoughts to another.   If his own mind is poisoned,
it is the duty of the church through its officers to prevent
his spreading the poison, but he is allowed the privilege
himself to *think just what* he pleases."

It was not without some difficulty I refrained from telling him that there was room for some doubt whether
the privilege he mentioned would be long accorded
them, if it were in the power of the Pope or the
church to prevent it; but I treated him and his concern politely and respectfully, reminding him, however,
that *this* was a free country (he being a foreigner), and
that the lecturer had said no more on the subject than
is recorded by those who are considered reliable histo-
rians.   With this view he seemed better satisfied, and
we parted in good and kind feeling.

Now, incidents in my own experience have frequently
reminded me of the Catholic's privilege, and his view of
what constitutes full liberty of conscience and freedom of
thought " to have the liberty to *think* just what he pleases,
but no right to tell his thoughts to another."   Many
times, both in speaking and in written documents, I have
found myself with the Catholic's privilege, allowed to

think what I pleased, but not allowed to express my honest thoughts and deepest convictions to others, without censure from some member of the Society to which I belong.

My idea is, as forcibly expressed by A. W. Stevens, "that it is best for each one to speak frankly what he believes, and to have no concern whatever whether his propositions stand or fall. Stand they *will*, as far as they are *true*, and fall they *must*, as far as they are false.

"The moment a man begins to have any pride or egotism of opinion, that moment his mental and moral eyesight begins to fail, and he looks at truth as a partisan, not as a philosopher.

"Let us have done with personal and dogmatic controversialism, and in our discussions invoke the spirit of calmness and peace. Only thus shall we be able to know the truth and to state it with powerful persuasiveness."

ADVENTURE WITH AN ALDERNEY BULL.

Extract from a letter written to a friend in Philadelphia, the day after the occurrence.

In the forenoon of the 20th of Fourth month, 1872, my dear Margaret and I concluded to make a friendly call on our neighbors, George B. and Eliza Brooke, of Brooke Grove, the road to which place passes through the woods of the Fair Hill property. As we rode along we saw a very fine Alderney bull lying about twenty yards from the road, but with no fence between us.

It has long been my custom, when riding, and I see anything that interests me, as a mineral, a flower, or whatever particularly attracts my attention, to get out and examine it; so on this occasion, prompted by a not very well-defined object, but one of rather a mixed character, prominent in which was a desire to see a very handsome animal on his feet, I told Margaret I would get out of the rockaway and make him get up. She offered some objection to this, on the ground, as I understood it, that it would delay our call, which had been deferred late enough already.

I knew the bull possessed rather a bad character, and moreover, he had a board over his face, an evidence of his not being entirely reliable, but I had not the least idea of any danger, and, thinking it would cause but a few moments delay, I got out, with whip in hand, and roused him up.

I noticed he stood very sulkily, eying me sternly from behind the board as he stood sideways to me, and, on my giving him, with the whip, an intimation to move further away, he rushed on me with terrific violence, threw me down on my back, and, standing over me (an ugly-looking object then), attempted to gore me.

. As is common with this breed of cattle, his horns were comparatively short, and stood nearly at right angles with his head and neck, so that he could not bring either horn in position to gore me, without turning his head very much to one side. This, I was enabled to prevent him from doing, by taking hold of his horns, one with each hand, and applying tolerably great strength, which my position on my back favored, my elbows resting on the ground, and pulling the upper horn and pushing the lower one, thus keeping.them level, so that they could not injure me.

My body and feet were under him, while he was battling at my head, and I holding on to his horns, and endeavoring also to get hold of his nostrils, by which I thought I could obstruct his breathing and induce him to desist, but in this effort I was unsuccessful. At length he gave me a sudden jerk and toss which threw me some five or six feet, but his horns only tore my clothes, and did me no personal injury.

Before I could get up, however, he was over me again, and I felt myself to be in a pretty tight place, from which I could not see how to become extricated. No one was near but my dear wife, and she too feeble even to attempt any assistance. But I succeeded, as before, in getting a good hold of his horns, and being still on my back I had strong power to prevent injury from them. My greatest danger appeared to be from the tread of his feet on my body, he being such a large, heavy animal. He several times stepped across from one side to the other, but I soon observed that he moved his feet with great care, seeming to regard any part of me as unsafe for his feet in his combat, and I was relieved from this apprehension.

After a considerable struggle, he gave me another sudden toss, throwing me about the same distance as before. I fell close to the foot of a pretty large tree, and at once saw that now was my chance of escape, by getting on the other side of it before the bull came up, which I succeeded in doing, and then kept it between him and me, so that I appeared to him to be annihilated. On coming up to the tree and not finding me, he walked quietly off in another direction, and I went to the rockaway, where I found my dear Margaret, who had been a distressed witness of the whole struggle, under feelings of intense apprehension and nervous excitement, more easily imagined than described, fully expecting that I could not get out of the contest alive, and she, although so near, utterly powerless to render any assistance. She was a living picture of true and genuine distress. But, finding I was not seriously injured, she soon became calm.

As may well be supposed, I was much bruised and battered in the contest, but am glad to be able to say that my physician (Dr. Magruder) gives it as his opinion that there is no serious injury. My head and face are very badly bruised and scarred, done in part, no doubt, by the board which the bull had over his horns, and which I noticed as he walked off hung by one end only.

I am now writing with the blackest eye, as shown from the mirror, that I ever saw. My lower limbs are very much bruised, I suppose from the animal's scraping them as he stepped from side to side, and the muscles of my arms and breast are extremely sore from the severe strain on them, in my effort to keep his horns from doing me injury.

Still I do not mind it. I am willing to bear it all patiently, and feel thankful it is no worse. I have nothing whatever to regret. I intended no harm, and wished to do nothing wrong. In getting out of the vehicle I acted entirely in harmony with my general character on such occasions, and it would not have been "me" to have acted otherwise. I have gained much more by getting out in that way, when riding, than I have lost, including my present loss of usual looks and comfort. I retain, however, my wonted cheerfulness and hopefulness, which I regard a favor.

I have not a single feeling of blame, unkindness, or ill-will towards him. He was in his forest range and free, and had a right to take his repose whenever he chose to do so, in which I obtrusively interrupted him for my individual gratification, and he, not knowing how far my obtrusiveness might extend, acted in harmony with the instinct of self-*protection*, and I with that of self-*preservation*.

LECTURES.

My first lecture, as before stated, was delivered before the teachers and scholars of Westtown Boarding School in 1822, to the males one evening, and the same lecture repeated to the females next evening.

The plan the teachers had adopted was to lecture from very brief notes, just the headings of the different topics, and I felt bound to follow it, and have continued this mode in my lectures, all my life since, with very few exceptions.

The experience in these lectures at Westtown was of great advantage to me. I record it for the benefit of others, to make in the first place all needed preparation, by a full acquaintance with the subject of the lecture, and then, however great the embarrassment, make a determined effort, and the energies and powers will rise with the occasion, so that the effort will prove a success. Such has been my experience.

I began to lecture more than half a century ago, and have lectured a great deal; at Westtown, in Philadelphia, in the Medical College, at Washington in my boarding - school at Alexandria, twice a week during the whole school term of nine months, every year for many years, besides at various other places, from a country school-house to the Smithsonian Institution, and have never yet commenced a lecture or an address without a feeling of embarrassment.

My dear wife, who used frequently to attend my earlier lectures, knowing my embarrassment at the commencement, sympathized with me deeply, which reminds me of a pleasant little incident that occurred years ago, soon after the opening of the Smithsonian Institution.

She and I rode up to Washington from Alexandria one evening to attend a lecture by Professor Silliman, on Geology, at that Institution. We arrived there early. When Professor Silliman came in and began to make preparations for his lecture, he pulled out, at one end of the lecture table, a small sliding shelf, on which he placed a tumbler of water to use during the lecture. Colonel Abert came in and took a seat on the step of the platform, nearly under the tumbler. Margaret said to me, in a whisper, " Now, if thee were going to lecture, the first thing thee would do would be to overset that tumbler." She had scarcely finished her remark before over it went, as Professor Silliman was arranging something, the water falling on Colonel Abert, whose look at the Professor, as he brushed the water off his clothes, was very significant.

15

EXTRACT FROM A LECTURE ON CANADA.

While in the neighborhood of Lake Simcoe, which lies to the east of Lake Huron and southeast of Georgian Bay, with which it is connected by the river Severn, we had the great gratification of seeing a band of Indians of the Chippewa tribe, who live on Snake Island in the adjacent lake, about seven miles from the shore. They come annually into the white settlement to make and sell baskets, the material they use being black ash. The whites allow them to get whatever material they wish for making baskets or building canoes, or for any other purpose, wherever they please, considering them to possess a proprietorship for whatever they may need, that dates back beyond the grants of the British Crown. It was truly gratifying to see these manifestly just rights accorded to them by the whites, and to observe the cordial and mutually confiding terms upon which the two races there live as neighbors, and it is greatly to be desired that a similar state of things should exist in our own country. But, alas! alas! with us it is to be feared that the Red Man, with all his noble qualities and heroic virtues, is doomed to extinction, and that the time is not distant when "the places that have known him shall know him no more." The lands of the poor Indians are craved by the grasping ambition and acquisitiveness of our people, and every device is resorted to in order to induce them to do something which shall form a pretext for their murder.

In the graphic and touching language of a poet,—

"We seize the comforts bounteous Heaven has given,
    With strange diseases vex him from his birth;
We soothe his sorrow with no hopes of Heaven,
    Yet drive him headlong from his home on earth.
As shrinks the stubble from the rushing blaze,
    Or feathery snow from summer's tepid air,
So at our withering touch his race decays,
    By whisky poisoned all that war may spare."

But to return to the band of Chippewas we met in Canada. They came on shore in two canoes made of birchen bark and white cedar, which is very light, and of consequence the canoes had but little weight. The largest was fifteen feet long and three and a half feet wide in the middle, tapering exactly alike t ward each end, which was a sharp edge. This canoe was capable of conveying six persons, perhaps more, and yet so light that a man could readily carry it.

These Indians speak intelligible English, and we held considerable conversation with them. They live principally upon fish, with which the lake abounds, and game, which is getting scarce. One of them seemed delighted with his success in shooting a ground-hog, on which we were to breakfast the morning of our visit.

Their chief is an old man named John Snake, and lives on Snake Island, from which circumstance these Indians are frequently called Snake Indians.

As soon as I saw the canoes, I desired to have a ride in one, and by the influence of a little silver, the value of which they seemed well to understand, this desire was gratified.

Two Indian girls, the elder about seventeen, named Phebe Snake, took four of our company in one canoe, and a man took the remainder in another, and they gave us a most delightful and romantic ride on a beautiful narrow bay, amidst a dense forest,

> "Where high in air the cypress shakes
> His mossy tresses wide,
> On Simcoe's stream near the dark blue lake,
> Where the wild duck squadrons ride."

It was a scene and an incident long to be remembered. As we paddled along in our light canoes of birchen bark, in these solitary waters, one of the Indian girls, by request, kindly and modestly sang for us in her own language. We could not of course understand a word of what she said, but her evident embarrassment and effort to brace herself for the occasion, the lofty and noble appearance of her countenance, as her feelings seemed touched by the elevating import of what she was reciting, and the grand display of the works of nature, in the tall cypress, whose overarching branches, with intermingled shade and sunshine, were reflected from the smooth bosom of the bay below,—all these, mixed with deep sympathy for this interesting but vanishing race of people, gave a multiplied activity to our pleasurable consciousness, which is, and I trust ever will be, a source of joy whenever we think of Lake Simcoe, and our kind friends, the Chippewa Indians.

Conclusion of an Article on the Science of Common Things, from "The Children's Friend."

All animals live on vegetable substances ultimately, for although some animals feed on other animals, yet what they thus feed on, fed on vegetables, so that vegetables are the support of all animal existence. And generally, it is the growth of last year that supplies the food for this. Vegetables derive their food from inorganic matter and convert it into food for animals, so that we are truly formed out of the dust of the ground. Our bodies are in this sense "as old as the hills." It is all wonderful.

> "See dying vegetables life sustain,
> See life dissolving, vegetate again.
> All forms that perish, other forms supply,
> By turns they catch the vital spark and die."—POPE.

It has just been mentioned that it is principally the growth of one year that supplies food for the next; there is never enough food on the earth to serve two years; so that, if one single harvest were to fail, and the food be equally distributed, every living being on the earth would necessarily perish. But we have the gracious and unfailing promise that, "while the earth remaineth, seed time and harvest shall not cease."

When I lived in Alexandria, Virginia, many years ago, I was President of the Alexandria Lyceum, and we had a number of distinguished persons to lecture for us, among whom were John Quincy Adams, Caleb Cushing, Dr. Sewall, and Samuel G. Goodrich, or "Peter Parley," as he was generally called.

At my request, "Peter Parley" gave a day lecture for the children of all the schools. The house was filled. It was one of the most interesting lectures I ever listened to.

He had a happy faculty of speaking to the children, and such tact in gaining and keeping their attention, that they did not seem to get tired.

I have two objects in view in referring to his lecture. He gave the children rules, formed for the occasion, which "would prepare them for entering the Temple of Virtue," and told them, if they would come to his residence, near Boston, and recite these rules, it would be a passport to *his kindest attentions:*

> "Ne'er till *to-morrow's dawn* delay
> What can, *as well* be done *to-day ;*
> Nor *do* an act you'd wish *undone,*
> Viewed by to-morrow's risen sun :
> Observe these rules a single year,
> And you shall freely enter here."

The author has been deceased many years, but the good he did *still lives,* and the remembrance of him is sweet.

The other point I wish to recommend to the young readers of "The Children's Friend," is to commit to memory the closing lines of "Junius's Letters," as a *precious gem of crystallized thought.* He says :

"Grateful as I am to that Good Being, whose bounty

has bestowed upon me this reasoning intellect, whatever it is, I hold myself proportionally indebted to *him* from whose enlightened understanding *another ray of knowledge communicates to mine.* But neither would I regard the highest faculties of the human mind a gift worthy of the Divinity, nor any assistance in the improvement of them a subject of gratitude to my fellow-creatures, were I not satisfied that really *to inform the understanding, corrects and enlarges the heart.*" The latter part is what I wish you *practically* to *bear in mind:*

" *To inform the* UNDERSTANDING, *corrects* and *enlarges* the HEART."

Should I ever meet with any of you, the repetition of this quotation will be a passport to my warmest affections.

VIEWS, EXPERIENCES, AND REMINISCENCES, CONNECTED WITH EDUCATION.

Published in the "Journal" in 1875.

A true *system* of *Education* must accord with the principles of freedom and justice. The *muscles* should be educated simultaneously with the *mind.*

Having spent fifty years of my life in active connection with educational institutions, endeavoring to awaken intellect and impart instruction, I hope that no apology is needed, now that education is engrossing so much of public attention, for my publishing somewhat at length, my views and experiences upon the subject.

While I am strongly in favor of the *object* aimed at by the laws of Illinois, Massachusetts, and some other States, on "Compulsory Education and Truancy," the education of all children between the ages of five and fifteen years, I am fearful that the *means* proposed for securing *the end* by these laws will conflict with those principles of freedom and liberty which are held, and should ever be, more sacred even than life itself.

No useful end, for the benefit of man, can *possibly* be attained by means that are not in accordance with the principles of *freedom, justice,* and *love.*

Man cannot be legislated into morality, or into such conduct as society may think best for him and his. This is impossible. If law *could do it,* it would already be done by *Deity,* who does for man everything that is compatible with that freedom of choice on which rest man's responsibility and accountability, which, in his wisdom, he saw proper to confer upon him, without which he would be a mere machine.

So great are the love and condescension of the Good Father, that he has given man power even to *rebel against himself and his laws.*

We must, therefore, in order to be successful, take man as he is, and in all efforts for his elevation and improvement, cooperate with Deity ; work from *within,* not from *without ;* depend upon love, not human law or force.

My ideas upon this subject are so well expressed by Abram W. Lawton, in a lecture on "Morality," recently delivered before the "Moral Educational Society" of Boston, that I will quote from his discourse the following paragraphs :

"We expect society to make the individual *moral* by *laws* and *penalties,* instead of putting our first faith in the moral nature in the individual himself, and its eternal tendency to develop into rectitude.

"Let not society be so vain as to think it is worthy to be the permanent master or keeper of the individual, or to be aught else than his temporary tutor and helper. Let it not presume to create the law for him, but only to help him find it and read it in his own nature, as it is there written by the hand of the Almighty.

"On pain of incalculable sorrow to itself, will society sacrifice man, or any true part of him, to any one of its institutions, its laws, its customs, its fashions, or hinder him from seeking in freedom whatever his mature soul craves.

"As no wise parent will flog his child to school, but only

incite and help him to go there (and remove those causes that render school repulsive), so society, if it be wise, will never undertake to *compel* men to be moral after its own notion, but will offer them every inducement and assistance to be moral after their own individual standard.

"It is a matter of history, as well as of daily observation, that the judgment of what is moral and what immoral varies according to circumstances. It is impossible to make the standard of morals absolute and uniform. Society legislates and administers in vain to do this. No system of police can accomplish it, though a constable of the State should be stationed at the door of every private residence, or be detailed to walk with every individual citizen.

"The high importance of man's being moral rests primarily in the fact that there have been given to his soul an infinite existence and scope. He has a divine life to unfold and to clothe it with the manners of the skies. Sounding in the depths of his soul, he hears a call to come up higher, to lift his whole finite nature into the breadth of infinitude. He sees a finger from afar pointing to the goal of perfection, and this it is which incites him to strive to the uttermost, and bedeck himself with every moral and spiritual grace, that he may sit at last with and among the pure, and move in celestial society without a tell-tale blush or an awkward gesture. So far as society can help him to do this, it deserves his thanks, but he lives his life for far nobler purposes than to secure its favor or escape its censure.

"Not until society learns how rightly to deal with the individual, to put itself into *sympathetic* instead of *antagonistic* relations with him ; to attempt no despotic, but only an educative influence over him ; not until it learns to read and appreciate his nature generously and fairly, ceasing by any means the effort to crush it, but help him protect himself against its fierceness and to unfold its sweetness ; not until society itself perceives, and makes the individual see, that all his interests are identical with its own, and that they cannot be advanced separately, but best together — not until this charming period of mutual good understanding and amity come to pass between society and the individual, shall we have a complete blending of social and personal morality, a beautiful adjustment and harmony of the inward and outward life of man."

The attainment of so desirable and such an advanced condition of society, older and younger, must necessarily be by a slow process, and it will require more than one generation to complete and perfect it, but it is in every way worthy of the effort, and this effort should be commenced immediately, and be continued by means and measures that are in harmony with those principles that rule in the heart of humanity, freedom, justice, and love.

This certainly can be done by a united effort, and when we take into consideration that by the accomplishment of this object both ignorance and idleness, the great opponents of virtue and thrift will be removed, the heart of every philanthropist must be stimulated to the patriotic effort.

But a change is needed in the object aimed at and embraced in the term education. The present aim in the systems of education is to *study books;* to store the minds of the young with the recorded thoughts of the wise, learned, and good who have preceded us.

This is all right in its place, but we must bear in mind that there is a great amount of unwritten knowledge. This knowledge the present system cannot reach. Besides, the young have *muscles* as well as *minds*, which, in this day of imperative practical duties, possess equal claims to careful education and training.

Of the capacity of the muscles for training, we have multiplied evidences. When a girl first commences to knit, how slow and studied is every movement of the fingers, her whole mind being engrossed with the deliberate placing of the needles and the slow adjustment of the yarn, in every stitch, one after another; and often, with the mother's instruction and aid superadded, when it is finished it is but a poor specimen of knitting after all. But during this slow process, the muscles are being educated. By means of the sympathetic nerves, the same movements of the muscles, successively repeated in the same order, through the wise economy of the physical constitution, so trains them that each movement suggests the next, and in a little time the process is carried on without further thought than a watchful consciousness to detect when the natural movement suggested by the nerve is *not* responded to by the muscle, that is, when the suggested movement is *not made.* This break in the natural process at once arrests attention. A readjustment ensues, and the operation proceeds again, seemingly without thought.

The same education of muscles is witnessed in making a pen from a quill, writing with a pen, playing on a musical instrument, and indeed in every process requiring a repetition of movement in the same order. At first every motion must be carefully guarded and directed, but during this process the muscles are educated and trained to the movement, so that, in a little time, the operation can be continued, while the mind of the operator may be engaged in conversation or in improving thought and reflection. What a wise and benevolent provision do we here find in the human constitution !

The muscles, like the mind, are more easily educated when young. They are then more pliable, teachable, and retentive. In processes requiring delicacy of touch or movement, early training is of the highest importance. Unless the muscles are trained, as they can be, to execute either directly or by appliances the most delicate and perfect conceptions of the mind, the human machine is not in harmony, it is not properly balanced. Such a person is not more than half educated. But this defect is not the fault of his original constitution. It is the result of the disproportionate regard to the education and training of his *mind* and *muscles.*

There is no substitute for this *muscular training.* It matters not how much the mind may know, how highly it may be educated — it is a locked-up treasure in every department, until the muscles are trained to give to it active value, by executing properly whatever the mind dictates.

Even speaking and writing — articulation and penmanship — to both of which important processes far too little attention is given, require careful muscular training. If this is done early in life and persistently adhered to for a few years, the enunciation being clear and distinct and the letters well formed, both of these valuable and indispensable needs of pleasant and improving social intercourse can be performed as readily as in the present too general indistinct and hurried articulation, and illegible writing, and more pleasantly.

Some years ago great perfection was attained in Paris in forming *papier mache* representations of the human body, with all its parts, muscles, nerves, organs, viscera, etc., true to nature. Every portion, with the most minute precision, was so arranged that it could be taken apart, piece by piece, and layer by layer, or dissected and then readjusted, so that every part of the human body, internal and external, and its connection with every other part, could be readily seen and deliberately studied. This attainment was regarded with great interest and favor by many benevolent persons, under the belief that it would relieve students of medicine from what was considered the hardening influence of dissecting a subject, by furnishing all needed information without it. Some students of surgery were accordingly educated by using a *papier mache* representation instead of a *real* "subject."

When they came to put their knowledge into practice, however, by using the knife and other surgical instruments, they found that their muscles not having been trained to the requisite delicacy and steadiness of movement, the operation was like "butchering" the patient,—a rough, irregular, and unsuccessful attempt, causing much suffering, which a proper training of the muscles would have avoided.

No trade can be learned by mere *sight* knowledge ; there is no substitute for *using the knife,* the *plane, or the hammer.* It has been tried, and always with the same result as that of the class in surgery.

In order for full success, the muscles must be trained simultaneously with the mind — must be taught to *do* while the mind is learning to *know,* it being the practical part, which is of the greatest service to our fellow-creatures.

The general plan of our institutions of learning is *imported.* Colleges and universities were formerly conducted by priests and clergymen. The principal aim of the colleges of Europe was to educate the students for one of three learned professions, Divinity, Medicine, and Law. School learning, or literary education, was regarded as thrown away upon farmers, mechanics, laborers, and even upon merchants, further than to have a knowledge of Geography and of business accounts.

In the time of Henry the Eighth and Queen Elizabeth, it is said a large portion of the nobility could not read or write.

Times are now happily altered. We see their mistake, and in a measure correct it. We have learned to appreciate the superiority of *intelligent* over *unskilled* labor in every department of industry, and to understand the greatly predominating importance of industrial pursuits, to society and to the country, over those of the "three learned professions," and to see that this relation is becoming more and more marked in favor of industrial avocations.

To the Society of Friends this consideration presents itself with peculiar interest and significance. In such education as it is their concern to impart to their children, which must include a knowledge of the laws of health and of the importance of obedience to these laws, the three "learned professions" may very generally be dispensed with. Instead of preparation for these, the education of the muscles and a knowledge of the use of tools must be substituted, as adapted to the present practical condition of society, and must be acquired simultaneously with the literary and scientific attainments, and skill and superiority in them should be rewarded by similar evidences of approbation.

Two marked and sorrowful results arise from the present mode of pushing the intellectual development in college, to the neglect of training the muscles to some definite, useful end, and learning to use tools with *a purpose* while young.

First, very few college graduates, comparatively, ever engage in mechanical or other producing industrial pursuits. The reason is evident, from controlling principles in human nature, that we will do well to regard.

From constitutional influences, which tend to self-reliance

and progress, and therefore are good, it is unfavorably mortifying to a young person, after having attained an eminence or an advanced position, to be compelled to come down or go back again. Hence, after a college graduate has obtained his diploma for success and distinction in his collegiate performance, if he enter upon mechanical or manufacturing pursuits he has to go back and commence at the very A B C of the business, and with all his college acquirements, have the mortification of being surpassed and thrown into the shade by young and illiterate fellow-workers, who had happily acquired experience and training in using tools. This humiliation the college graduate can rarely undergo, nor ought he to be subjected to it. It is unfavorable to him. His manliness and self-respect suffer, and all this from no fault of his, but from the neglect of those who had the direction of his education.

If he had had his muscles trained and had learned the general use of tools simultaneously with his literary and scientific studies, a very brief *special* training would have enabled him to take a respectable and remunerative position in a manufacturing establishment, or other industrial engagement.

The second sad result from the present mode of collegiate studies is the great number of graduates that become intemperate. This, also, is a result naturally to be looked for from the combination of circumstances brought to bear upon them.

· I have been lately informed that a person who had carefully traced the lives of the graduates of a certain college after they had gone out into the world, had ascertained that a large proportion of them had died drunkards. What a sorrowful termination of a life, from which, no doubt, much was hoped during the sacrifices that were made in order to get the collegiate course completed! The thought is rendered sadder when we reflect that the course pursued towards the student, from want of proper care to adapt his education to his wants and circumstances, tended to produce the result of filling a drunkard's grave, instead of fulfilling the high hopes and expectations that had been entertained of him! It is a sorrowful picture, but it is one that should be looked at, carefully examined, and the practical lesson which it plainly teaches, thoughtfully and carefully treasured up.

Let me state a not uncommon case. A bright youth of a family is selected to have a college education. His *home education* is wholly directed to this end. His brothers perform all the domestic duties, and he is "kept at his books." Father, mother, sisters, all cheerfully make the necessary sacrifices, which are often severe, in order that this favorite of the family may pass successfully and respectably through the college course, and receive his diploma. This obtained, they suppose their labors and sacrifices for him will terminate, and he will be able by his learning not only to do for himself, but perhaps to return to them a part of what they had through many long years advanced.

Now with all his learning and his diploma he is among the most helpless of human beings. The "learned professions" are all fully supplied. That last resort, "a vacant school," does not open to him. He can find no market for his wares. He has no means of converting the knowledge which he has acquired with so much expense and labor into needful food and clothing for himself, much less to make any return to his family for their kindness and sacrifices on his account. This thought saddens him. If he only had a knowledge of the use of tools, he could do *something*. But this he does not possess. This practical part of his education, unhappily for him, was neglected. There is nothing he can do for a livelihood. He is forced into idleness, seeks associates probably circumstanced like himself, wants excitement, takes to drinking, and dies of intemperance, *the natural result of the mistaken system of distorted education!*

Many men of wealth who have not had that practical knowledge of human nature, which would have shown them the necessity of bestowing upon their sons, with their scholastic education, a means of usefully and pleasantly employing their activities (rendered the more necessary by what such education awakens), have had similarly to deplore the premature loss of beloved and promising sons! The son bears the *shame*, the *suffering*, and the *blame;* but if we regard things rightly, the primary fault, although no doubt kindly intended and from want of full knowledge, rests with the parent, in the one-sided education he bestowed upon his son, and the failure to place him in the way of some congenial, remunerative, and useful activities.

Employment is a great preservative of virtue. It is man's natural want. For his safety it must be supplied. Let every youth possess knowledge of a trade of some kind. Of *what* kind the parent or guardian, from his superior knowledge, is best qualified to judge. In learning any trade, a youth gains a vast amount of unwritten knowledge, besides the inestimable benefit of having his muscles educated and trained to the use of tools. Let the first aim be *precision*, and this be *well established*, then rapidity.

But here a practical question arises : Where shall children be placed to acquire this desirable knowledge? The "trades unions" crowd out apprentices in almost every branch, so that frequently the owner of an establishment is not permitted to place his *own son* as an apprentice to the business. The want must be supplied by industrial schools, where different trades and employments will be taught simultaneously with literary and scientific knowledge, which is the present great need in a true system of education. Such schools will assist too in solving the "Labor Question," which has to be met. A revolution in industrial concerns is steadily and rapidly taking place. Proper assistance or help on a farm, or in a family, is even now difficult to procure, and the difficulty is annually becoming greater. This *must* be the case under the present condition of things, and it is the part of a wise forecast to prepare to accommodate ourselves to the new order.

A community cannot be regarded as enlightened while it contains an ignorant or degraded class. Such a class is felt to be a mutual disadvantage. Hence, the benevolent object now is to educate, elevate, and enlighten the whole population. This is all right. We must not even *desire* to check the philanthropic movement, however much the present higher class in society may feel the inconvenience. We will all ultimately be better for the change. But we must prepare to meet it by giving such directions to coming events as will force them to evolve harmonious and favorable results.

When all females become themselves housekeepers with families, and the males conduct business on their own accounts, whence are to be derived hired help and domestics? This is the state to which things are properly tending, and with the diminution of foreign immigration, which must take place, the tendency will be rapidly increased, but there must still be a right way for all to get along *comfortably*.

When this want shall happily be *severely felt*, it will lead to or compel its own supply. It will induce parents at the earliest practicable period to educate and train their children, both sexes alike (and what a blessing to them!), to all duties and labors, in and about a house or family, of which their strength is capable. Every business or employment which has to be done for the comfort, convenience, or health of a family is *highly respectable*. Its performance is praiseworthy, and should be universally so regarded. The unfortunate circumstance that these duties hitherto have been assigned to hired and illiterate help, has caused the offices to be regarded as low and menial. But they are not so in their nature. They are needful, and therefore noble and honorable. The sooner the false notion in regard to them is corrected, the better for us and our children, and for society at large.

In many a family of children at present, and for years past, how heavily the hours hang, many times, just for want of some employment. Of this favor the domestics deprive them. Sufficient time to perform all the household duties is thus worse than wasted. Such occupation, too, would be very promotive of health. How frequently are the domestics the healthiest portion of the family, rarely unable to perform their accustomed routine of duties!

As soon as a child is old enough to carry a plate or a cup to or from the table, it should be trusted and encouraged to do so. Let there be no fear of the child's letting the article fall. Teach it to take hold of it *rightly*. Then there is no danger. This taking a right hold of a thing, and keeping that hold, is the first step to be taught, and a most important one for success and usefulness.

This education of the children will require patience and tact on the part of parents and others having them in charge, and a careful study of human nature, the instructors beginning with themselves. But it will eventually make their own lives easier, and the lives of their children happier, by all being preserved in harmony with well-ordered domestic arrangements and economy, besides preparing children for a sphere of usefulness in society.

As remarked by Elizabeth P. Peabody, who has made the habits and instincts of children a special duty: "There is within children a certain æsthetic sense, or love of beauty and order, which accepts and acts out the *right thing* when it is suggested to them — that is, if it is *suggested* and not arbitrarily *imposed*, for *arbitrary* suggestion is opposed by a child inevitably, just in proportion to the force of individual character ;" which is a hint in the management and education of children well worthy of careful study. Every one can be pleasantly moved if we can only *find* and *touch* the *right spring*. A key exists which patient research will discover, that will unlock every useful energy and impart to it the desired direction.

Children, even when quite small, *wish* to do and *delight* to do what they see others perform, and especially to help father and mother, older sister and brother, in their engagements. If this feeling is properly cultivated, it will develop and strengthen, and become a source of permanent enjoyment. Then, every family would be an efficient kindergarten of the best kind, where the muscles and the mind are simultaneously trained and developed in early life by a true and healthy natural process. This would be the best preparation and foundation for entering the industrial schools already alluded to, where, with the literary and scientific education, different trades and varieties of business occupations would be taught to both sexes.

16

These industrial schools are the present *great want* in a *true system of education*. Institutions of this kind would be attended with the happiest results. Besides the general benefit of each young person possessing the elements of *wealth* in the muscles, together with a *knowledge* of the means of performing intelligent labor, their time would become systematized and all the hours of the day be wisely appropriated, according to the wants and needs of the human system, to useful and agreeable purposes, — literature, science, domestic duties, a practical knowledge of and obedience to the laws of health, astronomy, industrial pursuits on which a livelihood depends, botany, chemistry, drawing, painting, natural history, and every pleasing occupation essential to their full development, in harmony with their being and surroundings. They would find little time or desire for ornamental dress or light reading. Dress would largely lose its relative importance amidst such a multiplicity of higher enjoyments, and it would naturally have fewer hours appropriated to it in the systematic distribution of time. To a mind of elevated culture, objects of higher interest would be seen and preferred.

Also, in the *practical* examination and study of the different sciences, as chemistry, botany, optics, astronomy, they would find intellectual entertainment more enrapturing and elevated than can be imparted by any work of imagination, and would experience the truth, taught by science in the telegraph, daguerreotype, spectrum analysis, and in many other instances, that *modern reality* is far in advance of *ancient imagination*, and that *fact* is *now* more wonderful than *fiction*.

It is believed, after thoughtful examination, that at an "industrial school," under systematic arrangement and judicious management, after getting fairly into harmonious working condition, every young person, in the period from seven to nineteen years of age, could receive a good education and learn a useful trade, by which to earn a livelihood after leaving school *without any expense to the parent or guardian*, and at the same time receive all the beneficial influences of a home education. Then the two years from nineteen to twenty-one would suffice, with the preparation already obtained, to study a profession or to perfect themselves in the *special* branch of business in which they propose to engage.

It would require at least twelve years for such an institution to pass through one cycle of changes and have all its parts brought into harmonious working condition, and a still longer period for the attainment of that perfection of which it is capable, in the distribution of time and running the complicated machine so as to secure the *greatest benefit* to the health and the greatest profit from the industrial employment (which experience alone can suggest), and to render it self-sustaining.

But with that management and tact, which are entirely practicable, there will be a nearer and nearer approximation to this condition every year, and it is my abiding belief, after much reflection, the happy result will ultimately be attained. Be this as it may, a great benefit will arise from even an approach to it.

Such an institution, however, would not meet the *general* want. It would interfere too largely and unfavorably with home comforts and influences. Few parents would be willing to have their children so long separated from them. But for orphans and those children who are destitute of suitable homes, such institutions, under wise and genial government, would be of incalculable benefit. For a shorter period, (as the number of years ordinarily allowed at school), by the hands of the children "ministering to their own necessities," like those of the Apostle, the expense of education could be greatly diminished, while the value of their acquirements, in the combined intellectual and physical education and training they had received, would be incomparably increased.

Every young person, whatever his or her circumstances may be, should, while obtaining an education, acquire the knowledge of a trade or of some industrial employment to fall back upon, if necessary, so as to gain an honest livelihood. Such acquirement would be a great safeguard, and a means of preservation from vice and crime, of a value scarcely to be estimated.

By statistics, recently prepared by General Eaton, the

present efficient United States Commissioner of Education, it is shown that "from eighty to ninety per cent. of the criminals of New England have never learned any trade, nor are they masters of any skilled labor!"

The subject of Industrial Schools commends itself in every feature to the thoughtful consideration of all philanthropists. Such change in the system of education as they would require must necessarily be slow. But parents, and others similarly interested, should be impressed with its importance. Then a commencement can be made, and being once properly commenced, although some privations and inconveniences will be experienced at first, these will gradually be overcome, and it will proceed with an increasing ratio of benefits to the individuals and the community.

Children will be healthier from the harmonious exercises and development of body and mind, neither of these being overworked or underworked so as to produce deleterious effects, and thus mothers would be furnished with stronger constitutions, and a general improvement in the foundation of society be established.

NEEDED MODIFICATION OF THE LAWS FOR A SYSTEM OF FREE SCHOOLS. PROPOSED LAWS AND CURRICULUM FOR A FREE SCHOOL SYSTEM.

The laws proposed for the public school system need a modification in one or two points. Instead of requiring children to attend school for a certain length of time, they should require that they should possess a certain amount of knowledge by specified ages, and let the children and their parents or guardians know what they have to do, and what is expected of them, and leave them at liberty to effect this in their own way, so that it gets done, and then to provide some efficient means of knowing that it *is* done. It would certainly be better and cost less to have examiners to see that the children *do know*, than a police to see that they *attend schools*, for the police would have to be on duty *daily*, while the examiners would be required but a few days at most in a year.

The laws should be made for *all* children, and both sexes should comply with them in every part, including the use of *tools*, which may be made so smooth, light, and delicate, as to suit the softest hand, and then after the *practical* education, as far as required by the common school system, it may be extended as much further and in such direction as the children and their parents or guardians desire.

But, in order that the system of public or common schools shall be successful, the requirements that are made by law should be imperatively binding on all and, cheerfully acquiesced in and faithfully supported by all classes of society.

In no way can a man of the wealthier class confer a more valuable benefit upon his child and upon the community in which he lives, than to have a neighborhood school, at which this foundation for an education can be successfully laid for every child, by the time it is fifteen years old. No better investment can any parent or guardian make than the outlay required to secure the six years of intelligent and skilled labor from fifteen to twenty-one.

I will here present, in order to invite consideration and reflection, such a course for public or free school education as my judgment and experience at present approve, but of course to be subject to such modification as the combined wisdom and experience of practical educators shall approve and adopt. It is presented as only a "block" from which may be hewn what is needed.

The law should be headed : "The State requires the education of all children between the ages of five and fifteen, who are physically and mentally qualified to receive, etc.," and then enact :

ARTICLE I. It shall be the duty of every parent or guardian having charge of children to have his or her child or ward educated by the time it is six years old, so far as to know and draw on a slate the letters of the alphabet, large and small; to spell simple words of three letters; to count one hundred; to know and make on a slate the ten digits and the Roman numbers as far as ten; to copy simple drawings, and to use the gimlet, screw-driver, and hammer with dexterity and precision.

ARTICLE II. By the time the child is nine years old, in addition to the knowledge required in Article I., to spell and read through the Speller and earliest Reader of the district schools; to write on paper; to know the Multiplication Table, and to be able to perform the four primary rules in Arithmetic, Addition, Subtraction, Multiplication, and Division; to make or express the Roman numbers to C (one hundred); to copy more complex drawings; to use the sewing needle in sewing seams, sewing on buttons and working button-holes, and exhibit specimens of his or her work to the Board of Examiners; to use the tools mentioned in Article I., with the addition of a saw, and exhibit to the Board of Examiners a box or some useful article of wood of his or her own make.

ARTICLE III. By the time the child is twelve years old, in addition to what is required in Articles I. and II., to go through an advanced Speller and Reader, adopted in the schools; to write a free, fair hand; to know the Tables in Denominate Numbers, and perform Addition, Subtraction, Multiplication, and Division of Denominate Numbers; the use of tools continued, with some manufactured article by each scholar to exhibit to the Board of Examiners; to draw objects from nature; to commence English Grammar, the elements of Geography and of Natural Philosophy, and to sew on the sewing-machine, with a specimen of the work of each scholar to exhibit to the Board of Examiners.

ARTICLE IV. By the time the child is fifteen years old, in addition to what is required in the three preceding Articles, to continue in advanced Spelling and Reading; to write a free, good hand; to understand Vulgar and Decimal Fractions, the Square Root, Duodecimals, Mensuration of Surfaces and Solids; drawing objects from nature continued; the use of tools continued, elements of English Grammar continued;

elements of Natural Philosophy continued, type-setting and printing with printing-press.

ARTICLE V. School Commissioners who are in sympathy with the State in its great object, *the education of all*, shall be appointed, one from each school district for each county, by the judge or judges of the County Court, to serve three years, any three of whom, at a time, by their own selection and arrangement, shall constitute a *Board of Examiners*, who shall attend at each school, as nearly as practicable, at the commencement and close of each school year, to examine the scholars and see that the object of the State is being faithfully carried out, and to act in all cases in such way as they think best calculated to effect this object.

ARTICLE VI. The Board of Examiners shall be competent to make any abatement in the prescribed studies (except the industrial ones in Articles I. and II.), for certain scholars, or the entire school, which they may think will be promotive of the interest of such scholars or of the school.

The studies prescribed are those to which it is the design of the State that all the children in the State shall ultimately be educated at the ages indicated. When a child cannot pass an examination such as the Board of Examiners prescribes for the age of six years, he or she is to be regarded as *under six*, till the next examination, or until the scholar *does pass* the examination creditably. The same course is to be pursued at any other of the ages mentioned, nine, twelve, and fifteen.

ARTICLE VII. The Board of Examiners shall be authorized to distribute premiums or "graded medals of merit," on behalf of the State or county, to the scholars for observed proficiency and good conduct during the examinations, or on the recommendation of the teacher.

ARTICLE VIII. The School Commissioners shall require each teacher to furnish the Board of Examiners, annually, with a list of the names and ages of all the children between four and fifteen years, within the prescribed limits of that school.

It cannot be too strongly impressed on the mind of the

reader that the foregoing course or plan of study is presented *merely* in order to have *something* before the public in the direction of what is desired ; but the plan must be *matured* and *perfected* by the combined wisdom and experience of practical educators and the friends of "*the education of all children* by the State."

The Board of Examiners will save themselves much labor by securing for each school a *competent, industrious,* LIVE teacher, whose heart is in sympathy with the great object before him.

Although the *teaching* should be free to all, I am strongly in favor of books, tools, drawing materials, etc., being furnished by the scholars. What costs *absolutely nothing* is seldom if ever adequately appreciated.

By the scholars furnishing the things they use, these will be more valued and be likely to have more care taken of them.

With the existence of the Public or Free School system, in order to render its influence fully efficient, there must co-exist Normal schools for the education of teachers, to which no one should be admitted who has not taught for at least one school term, so as to realize any existing deficiency in his or her education, and thus be stimulated to make the necessary effort to remove such deficiency.

All the text-books in the schools of the State should be of the same kind on the same subject, and constitute a regular series, so that one book will not cover the ground occupied by another. Then, at certain periods, say once in ten years, these text books should be revised by a judicious and competent committee, so as to keep up with the new discoveries. The additional matter should be printed in a separate form, and be inserted in or used with the old books, so as not to impose on parents the expense of procuring a new book for a few additional pages.

No new books should be introduced into the public schools except at the time of such revision.

Self-preservation imposes upon our government the duty of educating the people sufficiently to qualify them to exercise intelligently the right of suffrage. Conscious of this, at the commencement of the government, every free State established a system of free schools. So great and beneficent has been the influence of these schools upon the people, that the material prosperity, intellectual and moral development, respect for law, and obedience to it in each State, may be measured and computed by the condition of the free public schools.

In the city of New York it costs more to support the Police and Police Courts, to restrain and punish a few thousand criminals, nearly all of whom became such for want of proper education, than to educate their *two hundred and thirty thousand children!*

In the whole United States the facts are derived from official statistics, that the crimes committed by illiterate persons are ten times the number committed by educated ones. In short, it appears from statistics, that *crime decreases* almost in the same ratio that *schools increase.*

Those unerring guides of the statesman — statistics — *demonstrate* that the most economical, effective, and powerful preventive of crime is the free common school. Universal education tends to universal morality. They also show that as *education increases, pauperism decreases,* and as education *decreases,* pauperism *increases.*

Society may therefore well afford to make liberal provision for universal education, since it thereby not only rids itself comparatively of *ignorance,* but also of the dread and costly attendants of ignorance, *pauperism* and *crime.*

FAVORITE POEMS

FOUND IN HIS SCRAP BOOK AND AMONG HIS PAPERS.

The Book-keeper's Dream.

BY J. W. EDDY.

The day had wearily worn to its close,
And night had come down with its needed repose,
As a book-keeper wended his way from the store,
Glad that his toilsome hours were o'er.

The night was cheerless and dismal and damp ;
And the flickering flame of the dim street lamp,
Went out in the wild rough gust that beat
With furious speed through the gloomy street.

Tired and cold, with pain-throbbing head,
He sank to repose in his lonely bed ;
Still, through his brain, as the book-keeper slept,
Visions of Debtor and Creditor crept.

The great balance-sheet he had finished that day,
And profit and loss in the usual way,
Showed how much money the merchant had made,
Or lost in the preceding twelve months' trade.

And he dreamed that night, that an angel came,
With the *Ledger of Life;* and against his name
Were charges, till there was no room to spare,
And nothing whatever was credited there.

There was life and its blessings, as intellect, health ;
There were charges of time, opportunities, wealth,
Of talents for good, of friendships the best,
Of nourishment, joys, affection, and rest.

And hundreds of others, and each one as great,
All with interest accrued from the time of their date ;
Till, despairing of e'er being able to pay,
The book-keeper shrank from the record away.

But the angel declared the amount must be paid,
And protested it could not be longer delayed ;
The book-keeper sighed, and began to deplore
How meagre the treasure he'd laid up in store.

He would cheerfully render all he'd acquired,
And his note on demand, for the balance required ;
Then quickly the angel took paper and wrote
The following, as an acceptable note : —

"On demand, without grace, from the close of to-day,
For value received, I promise to pay
To Him who has kept me, and everywhere
Has guarded my soul with infinite care,

Whose blessings outnumber the drops of the ocean,
While living, *the sum of my heart's best devotion;*
In witness whereof, to be seen of all men,
I affix the great seal of the soul's *Amen.*"

The book-keeper added his name to the note,
While the angel across the ledger page wrote,
In crimson letters that covered it o'er,
"*Settled in full;*" and was seen no more.

ODE TO DISAPPOINTMENT.

HENRY KIRKE WHITE.

Come, Disappointment, come !
    Though from Hope's summit hurled,
Still, rigid nurse, thou art forgiven,
For thou, severe, wert sent from Heaven,
    To wean me from the world ;

To turn my eye from vanity,
And point to scenes of bliss that never, never die.

What is this passing scene?
   A peevish April day,
A little sun, a little rain,
And then night sweeps across the plain,
   And all things fade away.
Man soon discussed, yields up his trust,
And all his hopes and fears lie with him in the dust.

The most belov'd on earth,
   Not long survives to - day ;
So music past is obsolete,
And yet 'twas sweet, 'twas *passing* sweet,
   But now 'tis gone away !
Thus does the shade in memory fade,
When in forsaken tomb the form belov'd is laid.

Then, since this world is vain,
   And volatile and fleet,
Why should I lay up earthly joys,
Where rust corrupts and moth destroys,
   And cares and sorrows eat?
Why fly from ill, with anxious skill,
When soon this hand will freeze, this throbbing heart
   be still?

Come, Disappointment come !
   Thou art not stern to me,
Sad Monitress ! I own thy sway,
A votary sad, in early day,
   I bend my knee to thee :
From sun to sun, my race will run,
I only bow and say, My God, thy will be done.

At Port Royal.—1861.

J. G. WHITTIER.

The tent-lights glimmer on the land,
  The ship-lights on the sea ;
The night-wind smooths, with drifting sand,
  Our track on lone Tybee.

At last our grating keels outslide,
  Our good boats forward swing ;
And while we ride the land-locked tide,
  Our negroes row and sing.

For dear the bondman holds his gifts
  Of music and of song :
The gold that kindly nature sifts
  Among his sands of wrong ;

The power to make his toiling days
  And poor home-comforts please ;
The quaint relief of mirth that plays
  With sorrow's minor keys.

Another glow than sunset's fire
  Has filled the west with light,
Where field and garner, barn and byre
  Are blazing through the night.

The land is wild with fear and hate,
  The rout runs mad and fast ;
From hand to hand, from gate to gate
  The flaming brand is passed.

The lurid glow falls strong across
  Dark faces broad with smiles ;

Not theirs the terror, hate, and loss
  That fire yon blazing piles.

With oar-strokes timing to their song,
  They weave in simple lays
The pathos of remembered wrong,
  The hope of better days.

The triumph-note that Miriam sung,
  The joy of uncaged birds ;
Softening with Afric's mellow tongue
  Their broken Saxon words.

MILTON ON HIS LOSS OF SIGHT.

ELIZABETH LLOYD.

I am old and blind!
  Men point at me as smitten by God's frown ;
Afflicted and deserted of my kind ;
  Yet am I not cast down.

I am weak, yet strong ;
  I murmur not that I no longer see ;
Poor, old, and helpless, I the more belong,
  Father supreme ! to Thee.

O, merciful One !
  When men are farthest, then art Thou most near ;
When friends pass by me, and my weakness shun,
  Thy chariot I hear.

Thy glorious face
  Is leaning towards me ; and its holy light
Shines in upon my lonely dwelling place —
  And — there is no more night.

On my bended knee,
   I recognize Thy purpose, clearly shown ;—
My vision Thou hast dimmed, that I may see
   Thyself — Thyself alone.

I have nought to fear ;
   This darkness is the shadow of Thy wing ;
Beneath it, I am almost sacred ; here
   Can come no evil thing.

O, I seem to stand
   Trembling, where foot of mortal ne'er hath been,
Wrapped in the radiance of Thy sinless land,
   Which eye hath never seen.

Visions come and go ;
   Shapes of resplendent beauty round me throng ;
From angel lips I seem to hear the flow
   Of soft and holy song.

Is it nothing now,
   When heaven is opening on my sightless eyes?
When airs from Paradise refresh my brow,
   The earth in darkness lies.

In a purer clime,
   My being fills with rapture — waves of thought
Roll in upon my spirit — strains sublime
   Break over me unsought.

Give me now my lyre !
   I feel the stirrings of a gift divine ;
Within my bosom glows unearthly fire,
   Lit by no skill of mine.

The Closing Scene.

T. BUCHANAN READ.

"I think this is one of the most suggestive and touching
little poems I ever met with. Every line seems to awaken
tender and touching memories, and the last stanza is beyond
description.   B. H."

Within the sober realms of leafless trees
   The russet Year inhaled the dreamy air;
Like some tanned reaper in his hour of ease,
   When all the fields are lying brown and bare.

The gray Barns, looking from their hazy hills
   O'er the dim waters widening in the vales,
Sent down the air a greeting to the Mills,
   On the dull thunder of alternate flails.

All sights were mellowed and all sound subdued;
   The hills seemed further and the stream sang low;
As in a dream, the distant woodman hewed
   His winter log, with many a muffled blow.

The embattled forests, erewhile armed with gold,
   Their banners bright with every martial hue,
Now stood, like some sad, beaten host of old,
   Withdrawn afar in Time's remotest blue.

On sombre wings the vulture tried his flight;
   The dove scarce heard its sighing mate's complaint;
And like a star slow drowning in the light,
   The village church vane seemed to pale and faint.

The sentinel cock upon the hillside crew;
   Crew thrice, and all was stiller than before;
Silent, till some replying warbler blew
   His alien horn, and then was heard no more.

Where erst the jay, within the elm's tall crest,
 Made garrulous trouble round her unfledged young,
And where the oriole hung her swaying nest,
 By every light wind, like a censer swung ;

Where sang the noisy masons of the eaves,
 The busy swallows, circling ever near,
Foreboding, as the rustic mind believes,
 An early harvest and a plenteous year ;

Where every bird which charmed the vernal feast,
 Shook the sweet slumber from its wings at morn, —
To warn the reaper of the rosy east ;
 All now was songless, empty, and forlorn.

Alone from out the stubble piped the quail,
 And croaked the crow through all the dreary gloom ;
Alone the pheasant, drumming in the vale,
 Made echo to the distant cottage loom.

There was no bud, no bloom upon the bowers ;
 The spiders wove their thin shrouds night by night ;
The thistle-down, the only ghost of flowers,
 Sailed slowly by, passed noiseless out of sight.

Amid all this, in this most cheerless air,
 And where the woodbine shed upon the porch
Its crimson leaves, as if the Year stood there,
 Firing the floor with his inverted torch ;

Amid all this, the center of the scene,
 The white-haired matron, with monotonous tread,
Plied the swift wheel, and with her joyless mien,
 Sat like a Fate, and watched the flying thread.

She had known sorrow : he had walked with her,
 Oft supped, and broke with her the ashen crust ;
And in the dead leaves still she heard the stir
 Of his thick mantle, trailing in the dust.

While yet her cheek was bright with summer bloom,
 Her country summoned, and she gave her all ;
And twice War bowed to her his sable plume ;
 Re-gave the sword to rust upon her wall.

Re-gave the sword, but not the hand that drew,
 And struck for liberty the dying blow ;
Nor him who, to his sire and country true,
 Fell 'mid the ranks of the invading foe.

Long, but not loud, the droning wheel went on,
 Like the low murmur of a hive at noon ; —
Long, but not loud, the memory of the gone
 Breathed through her lips a sad and tremulous tune.

At last the thread was snapped ; her head was bowed ;
 Life dropped the distaff through her hands serene ;
And loving neighbors smoothed her careful shroud,
 While death and winter closed the autumn scene.

ADDRESS TO THE SUN.— *Ossian.*

"Oh thou that rollest above, round as the shield of
my fathers! Whence are thy beams, oh Sun — thy everlasting light? Thou comest forth in thy awful beauty ;
the stars hide themselves in the sky ; the moon, cold
and pale, sinks in the western wave ; but thou thyself movest alone. Who can be a companion of thy
course? The oaks of the mountains fall ; the mountains
themselves, decay with years ; the ocean shrinks and
grows again ; the moon herself is lost in heaven ; — but
thou art forever the same, rejoicing in the brightness of
thy course.

When the world is dark with tempests, when thunder
rolls, and lightning flies, thou lookest in thy beauty
from the clouds, and laughest at the storm.

But to Ossian thou lookest in vain ; for he beholds thy beams no more; whether thy yellow hair flows on the eastern clouds, or thou tremblest at the gates of the west. But thou art, perhaps, like me, for a season ; thy years will have an end. Thou shalt sleep in the clouds, careless of the voice of the morning.

Exult then, O Sun, in the strength of thy youth! Age is dark and unlovely; it is like the glimmering light of the moon when it shines through broken clouds, and the mist is on the hills ; the blast of the north is on the plain, and the traveler shrinks in the midst of his journey.

The Prayer of Agassiz.

The Christian Union (H. W. Beecher), speaking of the speech of Professor Agassiz at the opening of the Anderson School of Natural History, says, "After a few opening words, felicitously suited to put all their minds into fellowship, Agassiz said, tenderly, and with touching frankness, 'I think we have need of help. I do not feel that I can call on any one here to ask a blessing for us. I know I would not have anybody pray for us at this moment. I ask you for a moment to pray for yourselves.' Upon this, the great scientist — in an age when so many other great scientists have concluded that praying is quite an unscientific and very useless proceeding — bowed his head reverently ; his pupils and friends did the same ; and there, in a silence that was very solemn and very beautiful, each spirit was free to crave of the Great Spirit the blessing that was needed."

For our own part, it seems to us that this scene of Agassiz and his pupils, with heads bowed in silent prayer for the blessing of the God of Nature, to be given to that school, then opened for the study of nature, is a spectacle for some great artist to spread out worthily upon canvas, and to be kept alive in the memories of mankind. What are coronations, royal pageants, the parade of armies, to a scene like this? It heralds the coming of the new heavens and the new earth,— the golden age, when nature and man shall be reconciled, and the conquests of truth shall supersede the conquests of brute force.

How to Break a Bad Habit.

Understand clearly the reasons, and all the reasons, why the habit is injurious. Study the subject till there is no lingering doubt in your mind.

Avoid the places, the persons, the thoughts, that lead to the temptation.

Frequent the places, associate with the persons, indulge in the thoughts, that lead away from the temptation.

Keep busy. Idleness is the strength of bad habits.

Do not give up the struggle, when you have broken your resolutions once, twice, ten times, a thousand times. That only shows how much need there is for you to strive.

When you have broken your resolution, just think the matter over, and endeavor to understand why it was you failed, so that you may be upon your guard against a recurrence of the same circumstances.

Do not think it a little or an easy thing that you have undertaken.

It is folly to expect to break up a habit in a day, which may have been gathering strength in you for years.

This, in brief, is our answer to a question which is put to us by anxious inquirers from ten to twenty times a week.

THE INDIANS.

The following is of interest as showing the first steps taken to give systematic aid to the Indians.

"On the 16th of 2d month, 1869, the following letter was received by the Secretary of the Standing Committee on the Indian Concern of Baltimore Yearly Meeting of Friends, which committee was organized in 1795, and has been engaged, from that time, with an unbroken organization, in endeavoring to promote the interests and welfare of these people:

> "HEADQUARTERS ARMY OF THE U. S.
> WASHINGTON, D. C., FEB. 15, 1869.

BENJAMIN HALLOWELL, Sandy Spring, Md.

SIR :— General Grant, the President elect, desirous of inaugurating some policy to protect the Indians in their just rights, and enforce integrity in the administration of their affairs, as well as to improve their general condition, and appreciating fully the friendship and interest which your Society has ever maintained in their behalf, directs me to request that you will send him a list of names, members of your Society, whom your Society will endorse, as suitable persons for Indian Agents.

Also, to assure you, that any attempt which may or can be made by your Society, for the improvement, education, and

Christianization of the Indians, under such agencies, will receive from him, as President, all the encouragement and protection which the laws of the United States will warrant him in giving.

Very respectfully, your obedient servant,

E. S. PARKER, ·

Brevet Brig. Gen. U. S. A. and A. D. C.

A letter of similar import was sent to the other branch of Friends in Philadelphia. A convention of delegates from several Yearly Meetings of the Society was held at Lombard Street Meeting House in Baltimore, to take action in what was regarded as a very important matter. A circular was issued, giving information of the qualifications desired in the Agents, as follows:

1st. A prayerful heart, and a firm trust in the power and wisdom of God — and not in man or military force — for guidance and protection.

2d. Industry, economy, firmness, vigilance, mildness, and practical kindness and love.

3d. A knowledge of farming and gardening, ability to superintend the construction of buildings, and to see that the schools are properly conducted.   .

4th. Tact in managing or influencing persons, so as gradually to induce the Indians of his agency voluntarily to join in the various employments of farming and gardening, and in mechanical operations.

Lastly, high in the scale of qualifications, to be possessed of strict integrity, and to be perfectly reliable in financial matters, and to know how to employ with economy, and to the best advantage, the funds entrusted to him by the Government for the use of his agency.

On the 5th of Fourth month, 1869, a committee of Friends read to the President and Secretary of the Interior

a memorandum upon the subject, from which the following extracts are taken:

"The nearer we approach the time for practical action on the request of the President to recommend suitable persons, members of our Society, for Indian Agents,
the more weighty appears the responsibility of encouraging our members, in the prime of life, to isolate themselves for a number of years from the moral protection
and social intercourse of our religious organization, and
subject themselves to the hardships and privations of an
Indian agency and a frontier life. This consideration
has awakened no little anxiety and concern.

"Under the belief, however, that there is always a
right way to attain a right end, an effort has been made
by us to devise some means of alleviating in a measure
the separated condition of those of our members who
may think it right to engage in the undertaking.

"Upon much reflection, it is believed that this can
be done by having an entire superintendency placed
under the care of Friends. Each agent should be allowed
to name the farmer, teacher, mechanic, and other employees of his agency, subject to the same recommendation by the Society that he himself receives, and confirmation by the appointing power. Then all these,
together with their families, which some of them would
have, would form at each agency a little community of
Friends, where they could continue their social and religious privileges. By such means, we believe they
would be preserved in that mental and moral condition
which would be most favorable to the performance of
their duties, in the civilization, enlightenment, and moral
and physical improvement of the Indians.

It is proposed also to have a committee of three or

four older judicious and experienced Friends, who have the welfare of the Indians at heart, as well as the faithful performance of their duties by our members who are in their employment, to visit all the agencies of the superintendency placed under our charge, at least once a year, and to spend some time amongst them, so as to see how things are working, what wants exist, what improvements might be made in their plans of action, and how the benevolent objects of the Government might be more efficiently carried out, if such a contingency should exist."

The President and Secretary of the Interior having, in accordance with this request, assigned to us the Northern Superintendency, which embraces six agencies in the State of Nebraska, it was in fulfilment of the duty implied in the last paragraph above, that the delegation who made the following report was sent out during the past summer.

When a committee of the Friends presented to the President the names of the persons they had selected for Superintendent and agents of the Northern Superintendency, they, on behalf of the Society, read to him an address, from which the following is extracted:

"We are highly gratified with the desire announced by the President to inaugurate some policy to protect the Indians in their just rights, and enforce integrity in the administration of their affairs, as well as to improve their general condition. We hail this announcement with gladness. We see in it evidence that a benevolent and righteous effort is to be made by the National Government to raise the small remnant of the once numerous and populous tribes of our red brethren from that depth of misery, wretchedness, and impending extermination to which they are so sorrowfully sunk by the mal-administration of our Indian affairs.

"In this work of humanity and justice we are willing and desirous to render every aid in our power. As promotive of this end, we have desired that the persons whom we may recommend for Indian Agents may not only be efficient business men, who have the interests of the Indians warm at heart, but such as are really representative men, — of fixed principles, sterling integrity, liberal and expanded views, free from sectarian prejudice, and such as recognize the fatherhood of God and the brotherhood of all men, and are deeply impressed with the filial and fraternal obligations which the recognition imposes."

SANDY SPRING, MD., 12th Mo. 24th, 1869.

ARTICLE CONTRIBUTED TO THE "BALTIMORE AMERICAN" TO SHOW THE SPIRIT IN WHICH THE SOCIETY OF FRIENDS ACCEPTED THE TRUST OF CARING FOR THE INDIANS.

Upon the commencement of the present Administration, a general belief existed that the Indian Bureau was in an unhealthy condition, and a desire for its improvement prevailed in the mind of every friend of humanity and justice. Hence the announcement of President Grant, in his inaugural address, that he would "favor any course toward them which tends to their civilization, Christianization, and ultimate citizenship," was read with universal gratification throughout the country.

It is acknowledged by all who have had most practical experience with the Indians, that the great difficulty to be overcome is to *gain their confidence;* first in the individual who approaches them, and then in the Government which stands behind him, afar off. This is the great point; and the Indians having been so long deceived, it will require time and tact to attain it.

It is believed that President Grant, in looking to the Friends for some assistance in the improvement in the Indians, which he so much desired, was not led thereto by any belief in the superiority of *theirs* over *other* religious organizations, or that the right of membership in that Society would impart any qualification for an Indian agency; but that it was because the entire record of the Society of Friends towards the Indians, from the time of William Penn to the present day, was an unbroken one of kindness, justice, and brotherly friendship, which is traditionally known to the different tribes of Indians at this time.

President Grant's sagacity led him to see that *these traditional facts* will give the Society of Friends a prestige with the Indians, which, if properly used, might tend to restore that confidence in the National Government, which has been so sorrowfully impaired by the mal-administration of our Indian affairs.

The request made to the Friends by the President was regarded by them in this light solely. It was entirely for the benefit of the Indians. They took no credit to themselves. The object appeared to them to be to use the *traditional reputation acquired by those who have preceded us* in the Society, as a means of producing a favorable influence upon the Indians, by giving them confidence in us and then in the Government, which selects our members for Superintendents and Agents amongst them. It is to be hoped that a corresponding kind, just, peaceful, and brotherly conduct towards them afterwards by Superintendents and Agents who are appointed, will continue and deepen the impression, and convince them that the spirit that actuated William Penn still lives in those whom their Great Father, the President, sends to reside amongst them and assist them.

The positions to which the Friends were invited in the Indian service, with the hardships and privations necessarily attendant upon a frontier life, were, when first proposed, very uncongenial to our people, and the acceptance of them was regarded as involving a great sacrifice of comfort and convenience, and as assuming heavy and precarious responsibilities. But the promotion of the interests and welfare of the Indians had been for over a century an object of concern and active labor with the Society, and now, when they were invited to a wider field of usefulness, they did not feel at liberty to refuse to enter it. We hailed with gladness the announcement of the President's desire "to inaugurate some policy to protect the Indians in their just rights, and enforce ̄integrity in the administration of their affairs."—(Letter from Gen. E. S. Parker.) We saw in it evidence that the benevolent and righteous effort was to be made by the National Government to raise the small remnant of the once populous tribes of our Red Brethren, who, as one of their number recently expressed it to us, " are fast dwindling away! falling like the leaves of the forest, *to rise no more*" from the depth of misery, wretchedness, and impending extermination to which they have been so sorrowfully sunk.

In this work of humanity and justice we are willing and desirous to render every aid in our power. We accepted the invitation so kindly extended to us; and it was the concern and aim of the Society that those whom they should recommend for Superintendents and Agents should not only be possessed of efficient business qualifications, and have the interests of the Indian warm at heart, but be *really representative* men — of fixed principles, sterling integrity, liberal and expanded views, free from sectarian prejudice, and such as recognize the *fatherhood of God*, and the *brotherhood of all men*, and are deeply impressed with the filial and fraternal obligations which this recognition imposes.

The following portion of the advice recently issued by the Society to the Superintendents and Agents, although written with no prospect whatever of its being published, is appended as an evidence of the feelings and concern with which the Friends are actuated in their practical proceedings in this very interesting engagement:

" We feel a deep solicitude that there may be no collision, interference, or difficulty in regard to the Missions or Mission schools established on the reservations to which you are assigned. These Missions, as we are informed, are under the immediate charge of the Indian Department and report directly to it, and not through the Agent or Superintendent. While there is need therefore of great caution that no feeling of jealousy or unfavorable criticism be permitted to arise, there is at the same time a relief from responsibility from their not being placed under your charge, so that you may conscientiously feel privileged to *let them entirely alone.*

"Although a concern or uneasiness may arise from an apprehension that the course pursued at these Missions or in their schools may not be the one which you think is best calculated to subserve the interests and promote the welfare of the Indians of your agency, yet any manifestation of opposition, hostility, or controversy, among the professors of the religion and civilization for the sake of which the Indians are invited and urged to leave the long - cherished traditions and customs of their fathers, would be far more unfavorable and deleterious, and highly calculated to mar the work from which so much is hoped.

"It is therefore our *earnest desire and concern* that there may be an unslumbering watch maintained upon this important point, that, like Abraham and Lot, there may be "no strife between you and them," for the precious reason that "ye be brethren;" but, on the contrary, that all due and faithful friendship, cordiality, kindness, and harmony of effort between them and you may be maintained on your part throughout, thus indicating that we had been successful in what we have stated should be our aim, in selecting those whom we should recommend as Agents.

"The comparative success of your labors and theirs must and will be the test as to which of your plans and systems possesses the greatest merit.

"And it can be predicted in advance, that this will be the one which practically rests upon good works — kindness, love, candor, justice, charity, good - will, and brotherly friendship to *all* — to the Indians and to those whose lots may be cast amongst them."

BENJAMIN HALLOWELL,

Secretary of the Committee on the Indian Concern of Baltimore Yearly Meeting of Friends.

SANDY SPRING, MD., 6th mo. 21st, 1869.

LETTER OF H. B. WHIPPLE, BISHOP OF MINNESOTA.

FARIBAULT, *April 10th, 1869.*

"MY DEAR FRIEND: — I am very glad that your Society have decided to take hold of this Indian business. You will have trials and difficulties beyond anything you have ever met, but God will help you. You ask my advice. I can only say, Do not allow any one to be concerned with you, unless you are assured, beyond question, of his integrity. Many of the old Indian rings will profess such love for the poor Indians and such respect for Friends, that Satan would seem to have put on the dress of an angel of light. You cannot afford the risk of taking counsel, or employing any one you do not know. *Be sure of this.*

The Indians have been so long deceived, it will take time to regain confidence ; but your people will do it.

The first requisite in civilization is authority to give to every Indian a piece of land to be his own. You must be able to do it. Men have no manhood until they have personal rights.

2d. You need to teach them to labor. The Indian men are unused to it ; the muscles of their arms are poorly developed, much less than their women. It should be gradual— say a given number of hours a day ; and those who work should be encouraged by small gifts in payment, as tea, sugar, coffee, etc.

3d. You would do well to teach the boys or young men the use of tools. A rude table, or chair, or trunk, or bedstead, made by them, is worth more than the most valuable furniture. It may be a question where you are to begin. If your people have selected no place, I would have advised you to be sure to select a people who have good land, which will repay effort. I should have been deeply grateful to have you come to Minnesota. The Chippewas have an excellent country at White Earth, at Leech Lake, and at Red Lake. But you will decide best.

The things necessary to elevate the Indians:

1st. Knowledge of God and duty to Him.

2d. Personal rights of property.

3d. Protection of law.

4th. Habits of industry.

5th. Education.

The whole matter is one of simple common sense. The same rule is good with Indians as with whites. It may be a heart-aching work, but if one soul is saved, if the load is lightened from one poor heart, you will be overpaid. Praying God to bless you,

With much love, yours faithfully,

H. B. WHIPPLE.

RELIGIOUS VIEWS.

FROM ARTICLES PUBLISHED IN " FRIENDS' INTELLIGENCER."

Copy of a letter in reply to one from a Friend living in the Ohio Valley, whom I have never seen, and who took some exception to part of my communication in " Friends' Intelligencer," volume 31, No. 48, as " tinctured with Universalism," and inquiring what I understand and do with the text, Matthew xxv., verses 45, 46: " These shall go away into *everlasting punishment*, but the righteous into life eternal."

SANDY SPRING, MD., *3d Mo. 2d, 1875.*

DEAR FRIEND :—Thy favor of the 3d ult. was duly received, but having had a press of writing on hand, with other duties, I have not till this morning been able to acknowledge its reception and notice its contents.

I am much gratified with the tenor of thy letter, and

particularly with the affectionate manner of which thou speakest of thy "wife and two dear little daughters," to whom please extend the love, *warm from the heart* of an old man who knew and loved thy children's grandfather, and their great-grandfather, who lived for many years only about three and a half miles from where I am now writing this letter.

It is evident our *hearts* are together, both drawn into the Good Father's love, even though our judgments or understandings may not coincide on some points. It is thought by some that if the *heart is right, that is all which is needed.* I do not so regard it. The *whole man* must be perfect. The heart *knows nothing.* It *feels*, and is the seat of the emotions and affections, but it has no *knowledge*, no *understanding*, no *judgment.*

The affections, as benevolence and parental love, may prompt to a liberality and an indulgence that will involve an expenditure *"beyond the means,"* and will thus violate the principle of justice, and it will need the healthy restraint of the understanding or judgment. *Truth* is more in harmony with man's nature than *error*, and is therefore always to be preferred ; and truth brings into harmonious exercise and united healthy action *all* these gracious powers, the emotions *and* the *judgment*, the *heart* and the *understanding* or *reason*, which are both illuminated by the same glorious effulgence, and both are the good gifts of the same Eternal Father. I have long regarded the closing sentence of "Junius's Letters" as a pure gem of crystallized thought : " To inform the *understanding corrects and enlarges the heart.*"

When a person makes a communication to the public, spoken or written, he must depend upon any *truth* such communication may contain to *make its own way*, by meeting the *witness* for truth in the minds of his hearers or readers. Therefore thou needst entertain no apprehension whatever of my "feeling hurt" by thy writing as thou didst. Far from it.

But while I do not feel that it is required of me to attempt to explain any particular passages of Scripture that may be presented, such a one for instance as thou hast given me (Matthew xxv., 45th and 46th verses), I feel willing to give thee my views of the required preparation of the heart and understanding for reading the Scriptures to profit, which may be gathered from the following.

To the object of man's worship, there is naturally a tendency to conform his life and assimilate his character; that is, man will endeavor *to be like what he loves.* Hence, the more elevated, pure, lovely, merciful, kind, just, and true is the object of man's worship (his God), the higher will be his aspirations and aims, and the more elevated, pure, lovely, merciful, kind, just, and true will be his life effort. "With the pure, Thou wilt show Thyself pure."—Psalm xviii., 25 and 26.

Different persons call the object of their worship by the *same name* — God, — while their ideas of the *attributes* of their objects of worship may be very different, taking their coloring from the reflex of their own hearts. They are then in this sense worshiping different Gods, and endeavoring to be like and conform their lives and characters to very different conditions of existence.

As the Psalmist inquires, xciv., 4, "He that planteth the ear, shall He not hear? He that formed the eye, shall He not see?" so He that implanted the principles of justice, love, mercy, compassion in the hearts and judgments of men, shall not He be everlastingly just, loving, merciful, and compassionate, — even far more so than the tenderest earthly parent?

Now, couldst thou reconcile it to thy ideas of justice and mercy to keep one of those precious little daughters to whom thou refers, and towards whom my heart yearns in tenderness, in torment or suffering for a year, for an error of a minute, let alone *eternally* for the *brief span* of *man's life?* or that the suffering and torment should continue any longer than they are required as means of reformation? Would it not rather be vindictive and cruel to do so? Now, the God that *I* worship will not permit me for a moment to entertain such an idea of Him. He tells me He never gave life but for enjoyment; He never created but to bless, and He being infinite in justice, wisdom, love, and mercy, it is impossible that any of His purposes shall fail of their accomplishment.

18

Any person who believes that the All-Father inflicts *everlasting punishment* for a finite offense, and without affording opportunity for amendment and repentance, does not worship the same God that I do, however nearly our hearts may be drawn together in love and charity.

Thy sincere friend,

BENJAMIN HALLOWELL.

On Prayer.

EXTRACT FROM A LETTER TO A VALUED CORRESPONDENT.

SANDY SPRING, MD., *6th Mo. 21st, 1875.*

DEAR FRIEND: — * * * * I am made willing to relate some of my experiences. If ever a person had received *supernatural aid* by prayer, I think I would have been favored by it. For over thirty years of my life, "prayer on bended knee" was my great dependence. I would wander out into the woods and other solitary places, and wherever I would find a secluded spot, I would kneel in supplication for that *supernatural influence*, which, although I had never experienced it, I was educated to believe was communicated to some ; and I still hoped for it and believed I would yet some time be favored with it, if I continued devoted and faithful.

In my long journey West in 1863, on several occasions, when a concern would be before my mind for several days previous to reaching a meeting, so that I would follow out the connections of the concern, and somewhat mature the subject before me, I was sensible that I would speak to better effect on the audience, and with more satisfaction and comfort to myself. But I did not draw from this fact that instructive lesson which I *now* believe, it was calculated to teach. I still persisted in being *afraid to entertain* a subject before meeting, thinking, in accordance with my education as a Friend, it would *then* be presented, with Gospel authority to communicate it to the people, and I continued hoping, looking for, and praying for this supernatural assistance, which I have never yet received.

This condition, however, had its use. The integrity of purpose was blessed. Things would be presented to my mind in meeting that I would feel uneasy not to attempt to express, and I found a comfort afterwards in having done so. This condition of not feeling easy without making the attempt, and the attendant satisfaction when I did, was the highest authority I was favored with in the ministry. I was kept humble and watchful *to do the very best I knew*, which I regarded as the most favorable condition to obtain the assistance I desired, and which I still hoped and prayed for.

Throughout all this exercise, which was strong and deep, I was favored with a continued sense of the Good Father's preservation, and the comfort of His love, overflowing in my heart, with a perfect trust in His wisdom and goodness, and an entire willingness to do anything and everything that was in my power to please Him, so that I could say from my heart, "Thy will be done in all things." Still, I did not receive the *help* I so ardently looked and hoped for.

At length, a new view gradually unfolded to my mind. It seemed to me as if the Good Father was kindly speaking to me, saying, "I have given thee of *my spirit*, as a continual guide, *and an understanding*, capable of comprehending all my works and laws, and adapting them to thy purposes, physical, intellectual, and spiritual. What more can I give thee, or thou reasonably desire?" I was wholly unable to reply, or to say in rational terms what it was I had been wanting and looking for.

I came to the full conviction that the *spirit and the understanding* are the *tools*, so to speak, graciously imparted to us, with which we are to work our way through life, confident of His aid, in every effort under their direction, to do good. He imparts to every soul that is willing and able to receive them, all His communicable attributes, love, justice, truth, purity, holiness, etc., which constitute His spirit in man, that is always *striving* to speak, to raise man *spiritually* so as to be "at one" with the Father, man's will becoming merged in the Divine will. The consciousness of this is the basis of *true faith*, which is the "gift of God." Then we must *do;* we must add to our faith virtue, knowledge, temperance, patience, godliness, brotherly kindness, and charity or Divine love, the crowning labor, that, with the others, brings man to be "at one" with God. These seven principles render their full possessor enlightened or wise. "Wisdom has builded her house; she hath hewn her seven pillars."—Prov. ix., 1.

What appears to me now to be right, in regard to *any duty*, is in the first place, to endeavor to dwell near God, continually, through obedience to the gracious influence of His spirit, — that is, to "walk humbly with God," which is recorded as one of the three divine requirements for which ability must be afforded. Micah vi., 8. Then, to have the heart so open to the needs, frailties, and infirmities of humanity that it will overflow with Divine love, in active desire for their supply and amelioration, urging me to use all the means the Good Father has furnished to effect this end,— always to be cheerful and pleasant to old and young, but never light or trifling in word or manner, these being incompatible with the habitual consciousness of the Divine presence that I entertain.

Nothing Created in Vain.

Dear —— : — Thou sayest, "Will it do for us to conclude the life-giving stream is ever useless, valueless, and wasted, even though it be hidden in its flowings? We cannot so believe in reference to the outward world and its resources, some of which are still deeply hidden from man's eye. May we not rather look upon these as a reserve force, so designed by Infinite Wisdom? A hidden stream surely has its service.".

My conviction for a long time has been that nothing

the Good Being ever created or bestowed was useless. As recorded in the early history of creation, so in all time, "God saw everything that He had made, and behold, it was very good." But the point before my mind when I wrote to thee was the needed co-operation of man in the Divine economy, or, as a part of it, to render the gifts and blessings of Providence more practically and abundantly serviceable than He leaves them, and to which He invites us, as, for instance, by the spring gushing forth, showing that the waters are in the earth, and could be found beneath the surface if sought for. We should not leave Providence to do all, nor we in our own wisdom and strength undertake to do all, but man should employ the powers with which he is endowed, in harmony with the Divine mind, to render the good gifts within his reach of more service to himself, and consequently to the higher glory of the Supreme Good. I will endeavor to render my meaning clearer by illustrations.

Our settlement is very much on a ridge, and of course has few streams and but little water-power. A friend and neighbor, seeing the difficulty in the neighborhood of getting sawing and grinding done, dug a large well and erected a steam saw and grist mill. Then, using his knowledge of the properties with which the Good Being has endowed water, and properly and wisely adapting means to ends, — all of which proceed from the one source, — he makes part of the water of the well raise another part, to saw timber with which to build houses, make fences, and for many other conveniences, and also to make flour for the whole settlement, etc. Moreover, the cattle drink of the waste water, chickens, ducks, and birds sip at the little pools, and the whole neighborhood seems benefited by his rendering *active* what was before hidden and comparatively valueless, though no doubt good. No known disadvantage or inconvenience in any way arises from his thus tapping the hidden stream and employing part of it for these purposes.

This illustration is from near *my* home; a more interesting one, and on a larger scale, is near *thine*, in the

Schuylkill river. That beautiful stream formerly passed on directly, to mingle its waters with those of the Delaware, and thence to the ocean, until some mind, under the enlightenment of Divine Wisdom, as I fully believe,—for all that is good comes from the one source, — by employing His laws and the properties with which he endows matter, makes a part of it raise another part to a mound, whence it is conveyed and distributed, by its own force, to the different families, all over your city, bringing comforts, conveniences, and blessings through your houses. The Delaware does not suffer, nor does the Atlantic; nothing suffers, and yet how many are blessed.

How great the contrast with what would have been, had the river continued to flow on uninterruptedly, as it would have done but for these active and enlightened minds. In my view, there are many spiritual Schuylkills passing quietly on as to the greater river and the ocean, the waters of which, by using accessible means, under the direction of the wisdom and power that will no more be withheld in the spiritual than the physical world, might be *distributed* to comfort, strengthen, and bless many. The clay, sand, and marble had their uses in their quiet beds ; but how much greater since the enlightenment of man has placed them in the beautiful and comfortable structures of your city. Also, coal in its bed fills undoubtedly its place so far in the Divine economy ; but when employed as a means adapted to useful ends, how much more has it performed to comfort and bless man, and thus to glorify God, during the last century, than during the thousands of years it had lain quietly in the mines.

If thou wilt not tire of my illustrations, which seem to crowd upon me, I will refer to iron in the ore, contrasted with its use in the needle, the axe, the plough, and the innumerable other useful purposes to which it is directed, by enlightened intelligence using those laws and properties, which are among the good gifts of Providence, the better to adapt some of His other gifts to the wants of His rational creatures. Oh, were there the same life, the same faith, the same effort and industry in the spiritual realities and laws, as in the physical, with the collection that might and should be made of facts and principles furnished by experience, with the adaptation of them as means to ends, beginning in early life, and pursuing as steadily in the one as the other, what a different condition of things, in my view, would exist. But I am by no means discouraged. I think there is a tendency and a progress in this direction. The Great Spirit is continually at work. As in the physical world, according to the conclusions of those who are most deeply learned in the Book of Nature, the vast mountain ranges, such as the Andes, Alleghanies, and Rocky Mountains, have been raised, little by little — perhaps not over three or four feet in a century, and even more slowly, — but still raised by the means He has adapted to that end, always acting in the same direction, through a period of past time which no one can estimate, — so is He raising little by little, higher and higher, the mountains of Truth, Justice, Love, and all the elevated and ennobling virtues, to be more and more conspicuous, and to be beheld in their loveliness and beauty, from greater and greater distances, till, *in time*, they will be seen, loved, admired, and practiced by all the families of the earth ; so that in a shorter period than has been employed in bringing our physical world to its present condition of adaptation to the wants of its inhabitants, will the moral and spiritual world of the human family, now *comparatively* so entirely in its in_fancy, be brought to fully as advanced a condition. Deity never fails of His purpose. He must have intended a higher moral condition of mankind generally on this earth than now exists ; and that purpose will ultimately be and *is now being* effected, *slowly*, as comparable to a few feet a century, but is destined to go on, until, using a figure of Scripture, "Righteousness shall cover the earth as the waters do the sea."

REFLECTIONS ON THE WISDOM, POWER, AND GOODNESS
OF GOD.

From very early life I have been a lover of nature
in all its phases; and being impressed with love and
veneration for the Author of nature, and possessing a
fondness for tracing evidences of his three great attributes, Wisdom, Goodness, and Power, throughout all his
works, I was frequently perplexed to reconcile some
things with these attributes; but on waiting reverently
for light and instruction, they were always afforded to
my entire satisfaction. Two instances of this kind I feel
at liberty to mention, to illustrate my meaning. First:
— When I came to live in the country in 1842, I was
very much interested in the birds, and wished as many
as possible to build and remain around my residence.
Among other birds which commenced building was a
wren; and to my surprise and dissatisfaction (it not
harmonizing with my ideas of the goodness of the
Creator to impart such an instinct), I observed her
fretful and quarrelsome disposition, driving all the other
birds away, and thus preventing them from building
where I wanted them to build. I did not like it. But
the impression attended my mind, from a conviction
that *all* was in wisdom, goodness, and love, that this
apparent discord was "harmony not understood;" so I
continued to be observant of her.

> "All nature is but art, unknown to thee;
> All chance, direction which thou canst not see;
> All discord, harmony not understood;
> All partial evil, universal good."— *Pope.*

I noticed that she followed the other birds, in driving
them away, only a short distance. After a time she

laid her eggs and hatched her young, some eight or ten of them. Then came the feeding time. For a few days this was an easy task, but as her progeny grew, and required a greater supply, and the food probably becoming a little scarce by her daily draft upon it, she was most incessantly employed from early morning till late evening; and I became fully convinced that if the other birds had been gathering for *their* young also, from the same area, as would necessarily have been the case, had she not with instinctive prudence driven them away and prevented them from building near her, she would not have been able, with all her industry, to have kept her young family supplied.

Here was manifestly not a cross or quarrelsome disposition, as I had supposed, but an instinctive observance of the law of self-preservation, regarding her offspring as part of herself, by obedience to which she did a kindness also to the other birds. In my observation I discovered to my entire satisfaction that many traits in animals and birds which are often regarded as quarrelsome or vindictive, exhibited between males of the same species, and in parents with their young, arise simply from instinctive obedience to laws connected with the continuance of the species and self-preservation.

Second: — A similar difficulty attended my mind in relation to a hawk taking the chickens, and in reconciling birds and beasts of prey generally with the wisdom and goodness of a benevolent Providence, until I was favored to see that *all* the animals that are annually produced cannot continue through a succession of years to be sustained by what the earth produces. *Some must die.* The amount of support which the entire produce of the earth will yield to the animal creation is limited; only a certain amount annually grows, and this will afford only a certain amount of animal subsistence; *more* when the fertility of the earth is *greater, less* when it is less. Hence if all the animals were permitted to live and feed immediately upon the produce of the earth, as in the case supposed, without animals of prey, they must necessarily do, — that is, upon growing and mature vegetables, — since the amount of these is but little more in any one year than it was in the preceding, while the animals multiply rapidly, the result must inevitably be that many or all would eventually die of starvation.

To illustrate this point, suppose one of the best farms to be fully stocked, and every animal and fowl produced on it permitted to live. They might get through two, perhaps three or four years, with what it produced, but in the fourth or fifth year at furthest, every green thing would be eaten up to support life during the summer, and in the succeeding winter *all would starve to death.*

Our earth is only a large farm, and if all the animals produced on it were permitted to live through their natural lives, the same consequences would necessarily follow; in a few years all would starve to death! Hence we see the wise and benevolent introduction of beasts and other animals of prey, in the economy of Providence, in places remote from the dominion of man, or before he was placed upon the earth, in order that, with the existence of those animals which feed immediately upon the produce of the earth, other animals which feed on these may co-exist, thus preserving a beautiful harmony by what frequently is regarded as an evidence of cruelty.

Every animal which feeds on vegetables is, in the natural state, food for some beast or bird of prey, or has what is wrongly called its "natural enemy;" hence, when any species of those animals which feed immediately on vegetables increase in numbers, food is rendered more abundant for its "natural enemies," and these, therefore increase more rapidly; thus preventing the exhaustion of vegetable food, and preserving a wise and harmonious equilibrium.

This is by no means an evidence of cruelty of disposition in the animals of prey; far from it. It is their nature, imparted to them for the most benevolent purpose — the *preservation*, not the *destruction*, of all races of animals.

They cannot live at all on vegetable food; they cannot digest it; but they require by nature food which has undergone both vegetable and animal organization, before they can assimilate it for the support of their systems. They are the benevolent instruments of a wise Providence acting through instinct, till man, guided by enlightened reason, was prepared to take their place to prevent the accumulation of an animal population beyond what the earth could support, and thus avoid the alternative of death by starvation, perhaps the most painful of all deaths. Naturalists agree that a beast or bird of prey always strikes its victim in the most vital part, so that they cause the easiest possible death. In a state of nature, a beast of prey never goes for food till urged to do so by hunger; he then kills immediately and eats; afterwards he lies down and sleeps till hunger again arouses him. His enjoyments are consequently of the lowest kind; but still, "wherever there is life there is some degree of enjoyment." Hence it is seen, since the animals which feed on vegetables have *their* life and enjoyment, while the animals that feed on these have *theirs also*, the sum of happiness by this wise provision is multiplied; the same vegetable growth giving successive support and consequent enjoyment to different races of animals.

Here we have a striking instance of the falsity of first appearances, to which I may have occasion to refer, and the beautiful harmony that is unfolded by observation and reflection. At first view, one animal appears to be cruelly and malevolently preying upon another animal, bird upon bird, fish upon fish, insect upon insect, and some upon all, till the whole world seems like one great slaughter-house, all in disorder and confusion. Investigation removes the great apparent blot upon the harmony of creation, and discovers in this arrangement of Providence an evidence of the highest benevolence and wisdom, the same that are always manifest in the works of Deity when understood.

I can gratefully acknowledge that I have met with no apparent incompatibility of anything in the works and dispensations of Providence with the great attributes of wisdom, goodness, love, and mercy, but what, as I dwelt in confiding and watchful patience, has been entirely removed, to the satisfaction of my own mind.

The next attribute of Deity which I was brought to love, and I might say reverence and worship, was *Truth*. If I found He said yea to-day, I came to know He said yea for all time. If He said nay to-day, He said nay eternally. This pervaded all nature, in every branch of research. To illustrate:

The properties of a circle, large or small, are *always* the same; — chords equally distant from the centre are, in the same circle, or in equal circles, *always* equal; the radius can be laid around on the circumference *precisely* six times; the circumference of different circles are in exact proportion to their diameters; and their areas to the squares of the diameters. These truths, and thousands of other similar ones, are eternal, past and future. Man has only discovered what previously existed, though hidden, till revealed to his researches.

This is further illustrated by the fact that the circumference and the area of the circle can neither of them be exactly measured in terms of the diameter; that is, when the diameter is known, the *precise* circumference or area cannot be stated, notwithstanding a near approximation to it. Such an approximation is thus stated by Peacock, in his Calculus, page 70: "Some notion of the prodigious accuracy of the determination of De Lagny, extending the value of the circumference when the diameter is one, to one hundred and twenty-seven places of decimals, may be formed from the following hypothesis: If the diameter of the universe be a million of million times the distance of the sun from the earth (which is ninety-five millions of miles), and if a distance which is a million of million times this diameter be divided into parts each of which is the million of millionth part of an inch; if a circle be described whose diameter is a million of million times that distance, repeated as many times as often as each of those parts of an inch is contained in it; then the error in the circumference of that circle, as calculated by this approximation, will be less than the million of millionth part of the million of millionth part of an inch." Yet with all this inconceivable nearness, the result *is not the truth.* Further labor might approach still nearer to it, but can never arrive at it. All this can be tested by any intelligent person.

While the length of the circumference of a *circle* cannot be computed with precision, the length of a curve of a *cycloid*, which is much more complicated, and is generated in the revolution of a circle by a point in its circumference, is *precisely equivalent to four diameters of the generating circle.*

Also, although the area of a *circle* is incommensurable in terms of its diameter or any other of its dimensions, the area of a *parabola*, one of the conic sections, and more complex than the circle, is precisely three-fourths of the rectangle or product of its base by its altitude.

These truths are not revealed to one person and hid from another, but they are revealed to all, in every age, in the same way; the reply of nature to every true inquirer is the same unvarying, intelligible, eternal truth.

The same thing obtains in every department of nature. Subject water to certain temperatures under similar circumstances, in any part of the world, and it begins to freeze at one temperature and to boil at another, *always the same.* In crystallization, the primitive form of the same substance has *precisely* the same angle *always;* so that the most certain method of distinguishing some substances is by measuring the angles with the goniometer, these being in the same substance invariably of the same dimensions, with mathematical precision.

Place a certain amount of pure marble or pure chalk in dilute sulphuric acid, and a *fixed amount* of carbonic acid gas will be liberated, and a fixed amount of plaster of Paris or sulphate of lime will be formed, both of which amounts can be previously calculated *with precision* from the quantity of marble or chalk used.

Burn six grains of diamond or pure charcoal in sixteen grains of pure oxygen gas, and *precisely* twenty-two grains of carbonic acid gas is formed, the gas being the same kind of substance which was obtained from the marble or chalk ; and when this gas is of the same temperature as the oxygen gas was, it will be of *precisely* the same bulk.

It can therefore be foretold, with *unerring certainty*, what answer Nature will give to any question intelligently propounded to her. Her language cannot vary, because it is *always truth*. The needed intelligence is to know what answer Nature has once given to the question.

Every branch of knowledge adds its weight of testimony to the wisdom, power, and goodness of God. Geology gives striking evidences of wisdom and benevolent design in the gradual preparation of the earth for the habitation of sentient existences through countless ages, and its adaptation to the residence of man, not only as it respects his conveniences and comforts, but the development of his physical energies, and his intellectual, moral, and religious capacities.

The records of Geology, intelligibly written upon tablets of rock by Deity, conclusively inform the intelligent reader that the time since the earth was inhabited by man, compared with the whole period of its existence is less than an hour to a thousand years. The race of man is *very young*, compared with the time this residence was being prepared for him, and one who has full confidence in the ability of Deity to accomplish all His gracious designs, will feel no fear that man will be able to frustrate these ; nor will such persons be discouraged by witnessing conduct comparable to the convulsions which our earth has experienced while it was being

prepared for its present habitable state, which preparation
is in some parts of the globe still going steadily on, and
the process gradually tending to improvement and amelioration.   Inasmuch as unmistakable evidence exists
that those great convulsions of the earth, by which whole
continents were raised, the rocks melted and contorted,
when lava flowed in great streams and buried large
tracts and all that was upon their surface, filled up river
beds and formed lakes, when immense tracts of land sunk
in one place and were raised in another, till Plato and
Beattie could say,

> Earthquakes have raised to Heaven the lowly vale ;
> And gulfs the mountain's mighty mass entombed ;
> And where the *Atlantic rolls, vast continents have bloomed ;*

I say, inasmuch as all these were not the result of the
blind conflicts of contending elements, but were, with
harmonious wisdom and benevolent design, the Provi-
dential adaptation of means to ends, in order the better
to fit the earth for the wants and purposes of man,
bringing within the reach of his enterprise and industry
the coal, metals, marbles, and other rocks, which had
been laid up in store-houses, like a good parent providing for the future wants of his beloved child, when
otherwise their existence · would never have been known
to him, or if known, would have been entirely beyond
any power of his to procure them,— so these convulsions
amongst communities of men may have had their place
of compensating advantage and instruction in the moral
world, under the direction and control of a wise and
good Providence.

The contemplation of the wisdom and benevolence
in nature awakens my gratitude, love, and reverence for

a Being whose wisdom, by so astonishingly simple means, has made such ample provision for the production, protection, sustenance, and enjoyment of his sentient creatures, evidencing the abounding everywhere of his wisdom, goodness, love, and mercy, and inspiring a confiding trust in him.

> "All are but parts of one stupendous whole,
> Whose body nature is, and God the soul,
> That changed through all, and yet in all the same,
> Great in the earth as in the ethereal flame,
> Warms in the sun, refreshes in the breeze,
> Glows in the stars, and blossoms in the trees;
> Lives through all life, extends through all extent,
> Spreads undivided, operates unspent;
> Breathes in our soul, informs our mortal part;
> As full, as perfect in a hair as heart;
> As full, as perfect in vile man that mourns,
> As the rapt seraph that adores and burns."—POPE.

I entertain an abiding conviction that it was the design of the Good Being that man should enjoy the faculties with which he is endowed in examining carefully and reverently into the works of his Maker; explore the secret recesses and mysteries of nature, and become an enlightened witness of the beauty, order, harmony, wisdom, love, kindness, goodness, and truth which everywhere abound in God's works. This conviction rests upon several facts and considerations:

First — The positive enjoyment which attends any well-balanced mind upon the discovery of a new truth, and the stimulus it imparts to a healthy industry, in an effort to discover others.

Second — The first appearance of things being invariably false. The earth *appears* to be still, and the sun and stars all in motion. Observation and experience prove that the opposite of this is the truth,—the earth is in motion, and the sun and stars relatively still.

Now, it cannot be supposed that the Good Being would thus present to his children a false appearance first, without a kind and benevolent design therein to invite investigation, and the exercise of those faculties, the legitimate use of which renders him a wiser, a better, and a happier being.

Many as are the evidences of wisdom and benevolent design in the world of dead matter, as it is called, they are much the most numerous and striking in the organic world of both the vegetable and animal kingdoms. The structural arrangement and functions of the different parts all excite wonder and reverence in a healthy and intelligent mind, and these intensify with every advancement in the knowledge of them. I leave out the marvels of growth and development themselves, as wholly beyond comprehension, and shall only refer to some special points of interest and instruction,— taking Indian corn as an illustration:

From every point of the growing cob, on which a grain of corn is to set, a tubular fibre of silk begins to grow close along the side of the cob to the end of the husk, where all these fibres of silk unite, there being just as many fibres in the whole number as there are to be grains of corn on that ear. Then, some pollen from the tassel must fall on every fibre of the silk, be absorbed by it, and conveyed through its tubular structure, to the point at which the silk began to grow, otherwise there will be no grain at that place. The pollen need not come from the particular stalk upon which the ear is growing; that from a neighboring stalk will answer the purpose just as well. Experience has proved that it is best to plant Indian corn in a body of adjacent hills, in order that the atmosphere may become filled with the floating particles of pollen, the continual falling of which deposits some on every fibre of the silk, thus fertilizing it; whereas, where a single stalk exists, the wind may blow the pollen away, so that but few fibres of the silk will become impregnated, and consequently but few grains will become perfected in the ear. Now, the point is, what causes the silk to begin to grow in a tubular fibre at that point, and continue its growth to the end of the ear, and when it has received the pollen, conduct it back to the point at which the growth of the fibre commenced—all unerringly and everlastingly the same?

Again, when there comes a storm about earing time and blows the corn down, it will be found in a little while that growths are putting out at different points some distance above the root, and on the side of the stalk toward the ground, growing longer and longer downwards, till they reach the earth, where they fix themselves firmly, and then lengthen out, thus pushing the stalk up, raising the ear into the air and light, and favoring its maturing. What wonderful wisdom and design!

The interesting inquiry is, what makes it thus put out these stays just at those points, and then, when fixed on the earth, lengthen them, to push up the stalk, and this over the whole field, with all the skill and efficiency which the most ingenious workman could devise with his attention confined to a single stalk? Inquiry might proceed on and on interminably.

> "All we behold is miracle ; but seen
> So duly, all is miracle in vain."

Some persons attempt to explain all these wonderful phenomena and processes in the animal and vegetable kingdoms by attributing them to the obedience of the particles of matter to *Law* — the "Law of Matter" — "Law of Life" — "Law of Development" — "Vital or Organic Law." But matter possesses in itself no *power* to obey a law. Nothing can obey a law in such sense which has not the power to disobey it. Matter can not work intelligent obedience and design such as are manifested in those operations. *Obedience* is *active* and positive compliance with what is required. Hence, with the existence of power to obey must necessarily co-exist power to disobey. No such power is possessed by matter in any form, whether organic or inorganic, nor is it *capable* of receiving and retaining it. It is wholly passive under that great controlling Power and Intelligence which created, regulates, and sustains all things, and is the life of all that lives and the mover of all that moves. No adequate agency, other than the immediate and continued action of the First Great Cause of all things, can be assigned for the exercise, control, and direction of such varied, important, unerring, benevolent, and wise movements and processes as exist throughout the whole range of vegetable and animal economy.

> " Some say that in the origin of things,
> When all creation started into birth,
> The infant elements received a law
> From which they swerve not since. That under force
> Of that controlling ordinance they move,
> And need not His immediate hand, who first
> Prescribed their course, to regulate it now.

But how should matter occupy a charge,
Dull as it is, and satisfy a law
So vast in its demands, unless impelled
To ceaseless service by a ceaseless force,
And under pressure of some *conscious* cause?
The Lord of all, Himself through all diffused,
Sustains, and is the Life of all that lives.
Nature is but the name for an effect,
Whose cause is God. *He* feeds the secret fire,
By which the mighty process is maintained,
Who sleeps not, is not weary ; in whose sight
Slow circling ages are as transient days ;
Whose work is without labor ; whose designs
No flaw deforms, no difficulty thwarts ;
And whose beneficence no charge exhausts."—COWPER.

As all these varied, important, and unerring movements and processes are the result of Deity acting immediately upon matter which does not possess sensation,
so instinct in animals is Deity acting through sentient
matter. No other adequate cause can be assigned for
the phenomena presented by it. It is manifestly not
the result of education, of tradition, or of reason. It
is certain in its adaptation of means to ends. Each
kind of insect deposits its eggs on such plants or substances as will nourish its young. Although man may
deceive animals by mixing poison with their food or
drink which disguises it, yet in a state of nature animals never eat too much, nor partake of that which
would injure them, although such things abundantly exist
in their range.

Instinct is perfect in its offices. When uninfluenced
by human disturbances, it never runs into excess. It
never falls short of its full requirements. It does not
vary, it has not varied, to improve, increase, or diminish

from generation to generation, through the entire period of authentic history. "The bee of modern times forms the cells of its hive exactly of the same shape as the bee of the remotest antiquity; each species of birds builds its nests after the same unalterable pattern, and sings the same invariable melody."—*Cavallo's Philosophy.*

The keenest powers of human intelligence, aided by the highest and most reverential conceptions of delegated agencies, have never been able to assign any adequate cause for these multiplied and complicated instincts, save the immediate action of Deity through or upon sentient matter.

As all his operations are the simplest possible adaptation of means to ends, and "with Him is one eternal now," He supplies only the present felt want of animals, like the "daily bread" to the hungry, obedient soul, without imparting to them any foreknowledge of results or consequences. The bee when forming its cell, or the bird when building its nest or sitting on its egg, is only gratifying thereby a felt present want, and possesses no more object or design in such processes than the pea-fowl, when eating its food, has a design to paint itself with those bright figures of unequalled regularity and beauty on the ends of its long feathers. We see the same principle manifest in children; they eat in order to supply a present felt want, and not in order to live or to grow, or to become strong or useful, or with any ulterior object whatever.

The bee forms its cell to gratify a want with which Deity impresses it, and which can in no other way be gratified. The bird feels an unrest from the same source, which cannot be removed except by certain actions which result in gathering suitable materials and placing them in a position to form its nest. It sits on its eggs, and cannot feel at rest away from them for any length of time, until the peeping of the young bird gives it a feeling of liberty to withdraw. Then a round of new occupations commences, all induced by corresponding influences.

The newly-born lamb feels a want which leads to activity and motion, and moves.about its dam uneasy and restless, but without any design or knowledge of what it is searching for, until it finds its natural food, when soon its want is supplied, and it is at rest for a time.

A belief has long attended my mind that all these processes, and many others of a similar character called instinct, are the result of the immediate impress of Deity, without any prospective object, design, or result being entertained by the recipient of the impression. This is all they require for their reproduction, comfort, and self-preservation.

Hence, animals are not furnished with a capacity to receive more extended impressions. When the sportsman's gun is aimed at a doe, whose fawns, which are dependent on her for sustenance, are playing around her, she possesses no capacity by which she could be impressed with a sense of the existing danger; her sight and hearing, which are wisely given her for this purpose, and are ordinarily sufficient, entirely failing her now, through the superiority of the powers of reason arrayed against her. This is all in wisdom. Compensations for this want of capacity are more than counter-balancing.

No impression can be interpreted or revelation made to any sentient existence of a more advanced intelligence, or a higher and purer spiritual character, than corresponds with the capacity or endowment possessed by

the recipient, to interpret them.   Hence the higher,
purer, and more intelligent the recipient of an impression or revelation may be, the more pure, expanded, elevated, and divine will the interpretation be which he
will be able to give.

Beasts and birds in their wild or natural state are
always shown by the Good Being, through what is
called instinct, what will nourish and what will prove
injurious to them; so that while those animals of which
man has the government, and to which he measures out
and distributes their food, will frequently eat too much,
so as to cause injury or death, this is not the case in a
state of nature, when left entirely to instinct, or the
guidance of Deity.   The important and instructive inference from this is, that if man were *as* obedient, and his
will as entirely given up to conform to the Divine will
and teachings, as the fowls of the air and the beasts
of the field, there can be no question that he would
be guided and cared for with at least equal certainty
and security.   The attentive, humble, dependent, and
faithful soul will always be shown the nature of anything
proposed or presented to it, either outwardly or inwardly,
whether in doctrines, by the imagination, or the cogita-
tions of the mind.   If it is suitable and proper to
nourish and strengthen the spiritual nature, the Good
Being, always present, in His love and mercy will instantly make this manifest, telling it, in the language
of impression, "Partake of this, it will nourish thee;"
whereas, if it is hurtful, He will say with equal clearness, "Let it alone, it will be injurious to thee."

"How are thy servants blessed, O Lord !
  How sure is their defence !
  Eternal Wisdom is their Guide,
    Their help, Omnipotence !"

If God is so immediately present, directing the
growth of the plants of the fields, and most wonder-
fully and bountifully providing for and protecting the
insects, birds, and beasts, and every sentient being of
the lower animals, how much more will He be present
with, guide, protect, bless, and sustain, in life and 'in
death, His humble, devoted, dependent, and obedient
children, the world over! Of this, for myself, I entertain
no fear whatever, if only I can maintain the requisite
humble, obedient condition. Then, as with migratory
birds, it is my full belief that

" He who from zone to zone
  Guides through the pathless sky 'their' certain flight,
In the long way that I must tread alone,
    Will lead my steps aright."

All the foregoing facts and considerations become,
when incorporated as they are in my constitution, the
foundation for a true and substantial faith in God and
His providence. We cannot have faith at will; there must
be a basis for it. It is a truth, that " by grace are we
saved; through faith, and that not of ourselves, — it is the
gift of God." But the gift of faith must harmonize
with our consciousness, or we cannot receive it. These
facts and considerations, manifesting His love, mercy,
kindness, and care over everything, and all sentient existence, give us ground for faith to believe He will do
as much for us, and that we will be able to receive His
saving grace, which consists of a *knowledge of His will*,

an *injunction* to *obey* it, and *ability* to *perform* it. Here
is the whole matter: *Obedience* to the *manifested will of
God.* "The grace of God which bringeth salvation, hath
appeared unto all men, teaching them that, denying un-
godliness and the world's lusts, they should live soberly,
righteously, and godly in this present world." All this
beautifully harmonizes. This saving grace is the manifest imparting of a clear knowledge of the will of God,
accompanied by an injunction to obey it, and an ability
to fulfill all its requirements.

Nevertheless, no one will experience the benefits of
this saving grace, or know salvation, who does not comply with *his* part by strict watchfulness, and yielding
faithful obedience to every manifested duty.

I have noted these things as they have presented
while writing, and as they and a vast variety of corresponding beliefs exist abidingly in my consciousness, constituting a part of myself as an accountable being, it
would be impossible that I could be without them and
be myself.

The impress arising from the facts and considerations
of the immediate presence of God in everything, of His
infinite power, wisdom, love, mercy, truth, and justice, and
the evidence of the exercise of these attributes where-
ever they are required, — first in inorganic matter, causing it to assume all the variations adapting it to His
multiplied purposes, and the most wise and benevolent
ends; then in the vegetable kingdom, where there are
stronger and higher evidences of all these; and still
stronger and higher in the animal, — becomes in me the
foundation of an unshaken faith that He is equally as
kind, to say the least, to His last, highest, and noblest
work, man; and that He will guide and care for him,

for the fulfillment of all the purposes of his being, as simply, as unceasingly, and as perfectly as he does any other animals, on the simple condition of *man's being obedient to what is manifested to him.*

> "God marks the bounds which Winter may not pass,
> And blunts his pointed fury ; in its case,
> Russet and rude, folds up the tender germ,
> Uninjured, with inimitable art ;
> And ere one flowery season fades and dies,
> Designs the blooming wonders of the next.
> From dearth to plenty, and from death to life,
> Is Nature's progress, when she lectures man
> In heavenly truth ; evincing as she makes
> The grand transition, that there lives and works
> A soul in *all things*, and that Soul is *God.*
> Happy, who walks with Him ! Whom what he finds
> Of flavor or of scent in fruit or flower,
> Or what he views of beautiful or grand
> In Nature, from the broad majestic oak'
> To the green blade that twinkles in the sun,
> Prompts with remembrance of a present God.
> His presence, who made all so fair, perceived,
> Makes all still fairer. As with Him no scene
> Is dreary, so with Him all seasons please."—COWPER.

Man being endowed with a higher capacity, he is capable of a higher inspiration and revelation, — that is, of recognizing and giving a more elevated and more Divine interpretation to the spiritual impressions made upon his consciousness; and as he is faithfully obedient to these manifestations, his spiritual conceptions become more and more quickened and pure, till he becomes able to comprehend the whole mind and will of God concerning him, and to be clothed with (or led by) the Spirit of God. Everything needful for him to know is clearly manifested to him.

From the wisdom, justice, and goodness of God, it is incontrovertibly deduced, and all experience confirms the truth, that every duty required of man is made clearly manifest to him through his consciousness, by the Light of God, or Spirit of Truth, as he is watchful and faithful; and this manifestation is always accompanied by ability to fulfil every requisition. In what *particular way* this ability may be furnished, is a matter of no consideration whatever. The fact of its existence is the great point. It is a "good gift," and we therefore know it comes from God, the alone Source of Good; and we are called upon by gratitude to give Him the glory, honor, and thanks, which are His due.

The Scriptures are full of testimony to the truth of this great point, although sometimes in figurative language. It was preached to Adam before he transgressed, and repeated to Cain, and to every intelligent member of the human family to the present day. "It is shown unto thee, O man, what is good; and what doth the Lord thy God require of thee, but to do justly, to love mercy, and to walk humbly with thy God?" "Thou wilt keep that man in *perfect peace* whose heart is stayed on Thee, because he *trusteth in Thee.*"

The whole of the incomparable Sermon on the Mount recognizes and sustains the same glorious truth. It is incontrovertible.

Much, however, as I love and value the Scriptures, and great as has been, and still is, the comfort I derive from them, any portion or interpretation of them which does not harmonize with this reverential consciousness of Deity and His attributes, which is impressed, as I believe, by God Himself upon my spiritual being, is of no moment, or value, or consideration to me whatever.

I see portrayed in the Scriptures, as the experience of
holy men of old, and particularly of the blessed Jesus,
evidences of the truth of the highest convictions or
conceptions, which have been revealed to my consciousness, in corresponding truths and convictions there recorded. The other parts I leave as not needed by me,
and giving me no concern whatever. This I regard
as fulfilling the wise and comprehensive injunction of
George Fox, to "mind the Light."

Every appetite, desire, affection, and capacity for enjoyment with which we are endowed, is good in itself —
is a good gift of a wise Providence; but it requires to
be kept under the regulating and restraining influence
of the same wise and good Providence, shown us by the
illuminations of His Spirit. The possession of any faculty or talent is God's permission to use it; but always
in harmony with his requirements.

He must be held pre-eminent in all things. *His* will
must be *our delight*. The heart must be kept watchfully
devoted to Him. His language, which must be obeyed
in order to know peace, is, to every one, "My son, or
my daughter, give *me* thy heart." With obedience to
this, a harmonious condition of consciousness is constantly
maintained, which is the "peace" that attends "the work
of righteousness." In watchful attention to this consciousness is the voice heard, saying, "*This* is the way,
walk thou in *it*," when we turn to the right hand or
when we would turn to the left.

When any gratification becomes too engrossing, so as
to interfere with other duties, injure the health or usefulness, or disturb the harmonious condition of our consciousness in any manner, it should be immediately
relinquished; and if we heed our consciousness, and it

is in a healthy condition, we shall always find that an intelligent demand for this relinquishment is there made.

Man will be preserved, not only from all *sin*, but from all *evil*, as Noah and Lot were; that is, from everything which would not be best for him, or in accordance with the Divine will and purposes in regard to him, spiritually and physically; for, in a state of obedience, being endowed with the capacity of a sensitive, enlightened consciousness, a disturbance would exist, and be immediately perceived in every condition or position which was not in harmony with the Divine mind, or in any manner not safe and best for him; and he would be favored not to know peace until in a place of safety. Thus is the arm of the Almighty *always* round about them that love Him, and who put their trust in Him; they are *always* in *His* keeping, and always safe. To Him and to His justice, goodness, love, and mercy I am favored to feel perfectly willing to trust myself—my all—in life and death.

One other subject presents, which has been partially touched upon, but I will explain my meaning more fully.

A religion is needed among men, in which they can have a basis for their faith. They manifestly are becoming more and more dissatisfied with an educational, traditional, or scriptural faith, which is all that is proposed to them. It does not and cannot satisfy an enlightened soul. Neither can we have faith at will, or of ourselves; it is the gift of God; and He always bestows it in harmony with His nature and with existing realities. He does not inspire us with a faith which positively contradicts our reason, such as to believe we are somewhere else than where we know we are. It is impossible.

True religion must be simple; it must be plain, reasonable, and it must admit of being tested by consciousness as a basis of true faith. In all other departments in which belief is required, experimental evidence is attainable by enlightened research, to attest its truth wherever any doubt may exist; and certainly this cannot be less the case in the highest of all concernments, those which affect the welfare and eternal interests of the soul.

Spiritual influences and instincts are no less realities and powers than any which come under the cognizance of the external senses. No force is superior to spirit-force. All the great powers in the universe, producing the great round of mighty influences, since their Author and Controller is a spirit, are spirit in action or spirit forces. The Spirit of God is a power, and all his attributes are spirit-forces, the full and vast efficiency of which few (comparatively) know, because few believe, for want of a living faith which possesses a true foundation.

Nothing is known to us by its abstract, inherent nature. Matter is known by its properties alone; its inherent or abstract nature is wholly concealed. So it is with attraction. The same is true of heat, light, electricity, magnetism, — everything with which we are acquainted; they are known *only* by their properties, qualities, capacities of influencing and being influenced, and affecting those senses through which we hold communication with the external world, thus revealing themselves to us.

Speaking with deep heartfelt reverence, the corresponding fact exists in relation to Deity. He is known to us only by His attributes. But then we reverence, love, and adore *Him* as the embodiment of these attributes — the Giver of all good. He *reveals Himself* through these attributes by impressing them upon the soul, thereby imparting to it their nature.

As an instance: He imparts the impress of truth to the soul, which brings it into a knowledge of truth, and of course so far to know God; and with this knowledge of truth He imparts also an intelligent admonition to obey all its requirements, or to act in harmony with its nature, at the same time affording requisite ability to obey the injunction.

Through willing obedience to these manifestations, the spiritual perceptions become more and more refined and acute; the field widens in which the ramifications of the principle of truth extend its influence, through the corresponding increased delicacy of the sensitiveness of the Divine perceptions in the soul, until, so far as it respects truth, it approaches nearer and nearer the Divine nature. This obedience to truth, through the power which accompanies its impress and is thus made known to the soul, saves it from all departure from it, and from all the consequences which flow from every form of a departure; hence such soul has experienced true salvation, and knows the power and grace of God whereby it was saved.

The same saving power is a redeeming power, so that when one who has departed from the government of truth comes humbly and faithfully to yield obedience to its influence upon his soul in all things, he is brought back again into the Divine harmony and favor; he has thus experienced redemption from sin through the grace and power of God, and knows salvation, and that his Saviour and Redeemer liveth, — the wisdom of God and the power of God.

A person whose soul is thus circumstanced living up

humbly, reverently, and faithfully, day by day, to his highest conceptions of the requirements of all those attributes, or to the most pure and elevated interpretation which he can give to the impressions of them upon his consciousness, is clothed with or governed by the attributes of God; he is a *manifestation* of God, or "God manifest" in man; he is "led by the Spirit of God;" he is "a son of God."

All this is to be learned, experienced, and practiced *within* by careful and constant attention to our individual consciousness, which has its laws of disturbances and influences, and its capacities for discipline, regulation, advancement, and purification. It is to this great field of labor we must look for spiritual and religious advancement in the human family. And this, as I understand it, is the *doctrine of Friends, or true Quakerism,* all being embraced in the comprehensive injunction of George Fox, "Mind the Light;" or the still more concise one of the blessed Jesus, "Watch."

I shall close with the solemn prayer of Thomas à Kempis, which I can truly say contains the sincere and earnest cravings of my heart also. "Oh God! who art the truth! make me one with Thee in everlasting love! I am oft-times weary of reading, and weary of hearing (and weary of writing). In Thee alone is the sum of my desire. Let every teacher be silent! Let the whole creation be dumb before Thee; and do Thou only speak unto my soul!"

QUAKERISM.

SANDY SPRING, MD., *2d Mo. 18th, 1870.*

DEAR FRIEND:— * * * * The article thou lately enclosed, headed the "Radical Club," etc., from the "Springfield Republican," suggested ideas worthy of careful examination and reflection. The editor of the Anti-Slavery Standard gives a definition of "Quakerism," with which I fully accord. It is beautiful and true:

"The distinctive doctrine of Quakerism," he says, "is the immediate teaching of the Holy Spirit in the human soul." * * * Added years have only tended to strengthen my faith in this fundamental doctrine which distinguishes Quakerism, and my admiration for the more important features of its historical record.

The estimate of human nature which the doctrine of the "Inner Light" necessitates is an exalted one. Logically it subordinates everything else.

The witness within sits in judgment upon every message, verbal or written, and upon every thought and action as well. There is no room left for a Bible of *absolute authority;* none for the functions of an *exclusive* Mediator and Savior. All are children of the Father and joint heirs in His divinely human household.

The practical requirements of this fundamental doctrine of Quakerism are, to "mind the Light," that is, to be *obedient* to its teachings,— to live up, faithfully day by day, in all our intercourse with our fellow creatures, to the *highest convictions of right and duty* which are manifested to our watchful consciousness. It recognizes the fatherhood of God and the brotherhood of *all men,* and demands the faithful fulfillment of all the varied filial and fraternal obligations which this recognition imposes. No room exists in it for sectarianism, or prejudice against race, class, or caste. As a rule of practical life it is full and complete. Nothing can rise above it,— nothing go beyond it. As has been said of it, "It is as high as the heavens and as holy as the Lord."

It is adapted to all mankind, and to every condition of mind and of life,— high and low, rich and poor, strong and weak, learned and unlearned,— the duty of each individual being *simply*, as has been already said, to live up, day by day, to the highest convictions of right and duty which are revealed to the watchful consciousness.

Every such revelation of duty is necessarily accompanied by ability to perform it; for, God being just, He must give the requisite power to perform every requirement He makes of His creatures.

This is the doctrine of Quakerism; not as anything peculiar to its purposes, but as the privilege of all mankind. George Fox founded no sect. His platform he regarded (as it is) sufficiently broad and strong to hold and support the whole human family. And so does every true Quaker.

"THE GOD-GIVEN POWER TO SEE OR RECEIVE A TRUTH, IS GOD'S COMMAND TO IMPART IT."

I regard all *truth* as coming from God, hence eternal, universal, always good, and from its nature incapable, when rightly used, of being anything but good, to any person, in any place, or at any period.

There is, and can be, no new truth. Every truth, however recently discovered, has existed through all time. Every mathematical or philosophical principle, every property of the triangle, the circle, or material bodies, is eternal. No matter when or by whom it was discovered, it pre-existed in the Divine mind and is the embodiment of a Divine thought. The mind of the discoverer is brought in harmony with, and to understand the Divine mind, so far as to be able to receive this impress or revelation from it.

Hence, all that the mathematician or philosopher can

do, is to *discover what previously existed*, although *unknown*. When Dr. Herschel and Professor Leverrier each discovered a "new planet" as it was termed, to which the names of Uranus and Neptune were applied, they were only favored to see what had existed from the time of the creation. The *discovery* was new, not the *object discovered.* So of each principle and property in every department of physical science.

The same I believe to be true in relation to spiritual truths, which are as much realities as physical truths. They are from the same eternal source, and communicated in like manner, whenever a mind or soul is *prepared* — that is, sufficiently enlightened, expanded, and purified — to see or receive them. And every such revelation, spiritual or physical, is for good to mankind — is a blessing. Witness the happy influences of the physical discoveries within a century past, upon the comforts, conveniences, and interests of humanity; the sewing-machines, mowing and reaping machines, and various other labor-performing inventions, that so expedite operations in the houshold and upon the farm, and lessen muscular exertion; also the truths or principles upon which these rest, as well as other God-given ministers to man — the laws governing steam, so as to adapt it to the supply of so great a variety of our wants and greatly to lengthen our lives, if measured by what we are enabled to perform; the sunlight to paint the pictures of our absent friends, and scenery, and objects of interest in foreign lands, and thus "bring a distant country into ours," with a reliability that no human delineation can equal; and the same agent in spectrum analysis, rendering such great aid in understanding the composition of terrestrial substances, and giving a better acquaintance than was previously possessed with regard to many bodies in the planetary and stellar regions; the truths or laws of electricity and magnetism, in their application to that wonder, the telegraph, to electrotyping, and many other valuable and labor - performing processes; all of which, and many others, may be regarded, as far as their general practical benefits are concerned, as the gifts of the last one hundred years.

But unquestionably, these laws and principles have all existed from the epoch of creation. Then whence come they into use? And why at this time?

I have just now called these truths or discoveries "God - given ministers," for they are certainly "good gifts," and minister greatly to man's convenience and comfort, and we have the assurance that "every good and every perfect gift *is from above*, and cometh down from the Father of lights, with whom there is no variableness, neither shadow of turning," He "being the same yesterday, to - day, and forever."

Now, as we have the assurance of the Apostle, which we all believe, that *God does not change*, and these "good gifts," though existing from the period of the creation, have been withheld, or rather not imparted to His children, beneficent as they would have been, till within the last one hundred years, and far the greater number of them, and the most valuable, till within the last half century, there must exist *some cause* for this; *something* must have changed. I think it is *man*. There has been a progress in humanity. So far from man being a fallen being, and his *highest condition past*, so that we must *look back* for the most elevated and favored types of humanity, the human family has been continually advancing, taken altogether, from the first creation,

so that man has come to occupy a higher plane than ever
before. He has come nearer to God, and been enabled
to partake more of His image, both in the creative
faculty, so to call it, and in the diffusion of blessings to
his fellow - creatures, so as to be capable of apprehend-
ing, receiving, and propagating the great truths that
have long been waiting to burst forth in a revelation
to bless mankind, as soon as a mind should be prepared
to receive it.

But this *preparation* must be by man. The *means*
are furnished him, but he must industriously use them.
He must diligently put inquiries to Nature, and atten-
tively and patiently await her answers. It is interesting
to note how *gradually* all these revelations have been
made. One person discovers a truth and makes it
known. This raises the mind one step towards the object. Then the same person, or some one else, discovers
another, and so on, until the present elevated degree
has been attained, in all the sciences and the arts resting upon them. This grand result has arisen from each
discovery of a new truth, when made, being thrown into
the common stock of knowledge, thus bringing up all
well - informed and thinking minds to that level, and
preparing them for further advances.

Not that the highest possible degree, or one near it,
is yet attained; great blessings no doubt are still in
the Divine treasury waiting till some one is sufficiently
advanced or elevated to receive them, and add them to
the already long list of "good gifts" from above.

Now let it be observed emphatically that these revelations, as I term them, or the knowledge of these
truths or laws that have proved of such incalculable
benefit to man, have not been made to or obtained by the

idle and the thoughtless, but they are the reward of the industrious, patient, devoted *worker*, the close *observer*, the man who questions nature with an unshaken confidence in the uniformity of her laws, which are the laws of God, and partake of His unchangeableness, wisdom, and goodness.

All this, in my confident belief, is equally true of spiritual realities and the revelations of spiritual truths. Every God-given truth is good.

These truths make up the heart or condition of humanity. Every added one expands the mind or soul, and increases its enlightenment. Their being successively imparted is interesting evidence of the progress of humanity. They are revealed to the industrious and devoted seeker into the depths of his spiritual nature, watchfully observing the changes in his moral consciousness, inquiring into the causes by which these changes are produced, and by the aid of that light which is freely furnished to all, discovering spiritual truths never before revealed. By this means he becomes deeply instructed in spiritual things, learns the nature and power of spiritual influences and forces, and that they are as real and as invariable as those governing material bodies. When not restrained by considerations of policy arising from society organizations, there is the same noble impulse to impart what has been discovered,— to share with others the treasure that has been found, and place it in the common stock of knowledge. Such devoted workers were the venerated George Fox, Fenelon, Luther, Calvin, Wesley, and no doubt many others. George Fox, in the fields and woods, in retirement,— Newton in his observatory,— Luther and Calvin and Wesley in places of silent meditation,— Davy in his laboratory,—and others who have made discoveries in their respective provinces of research, were all industriously and devotedly engaged in studying those laws established by Deity, through which man may acquire a higher and fuller knowledge of His works, spiritual and physical, and of Him, and become a more enlarged recipient of His bounties and blessings.

A succession of these laborers, astronomers, chemists, and other physicists, and also of the explorers and expounders of spiritual truths, has been steadily maintained, but their labors have been attended with very different results.

In every department of science, whose votaries make known every discovery, or what is believed to be such, as soon as it is made, there has been a great and steady advance,—an advance proportioned to the industry, devotedness, and skill with which they were pursued. One discovery prepared the way for another. Recognizing the unvariableness of the Great Father and of His laws, that He was no respecter of persons, had no favorites, but that He rewarded humble and thoughtfully directed industry and research alike in all, it was seen that what one man had done, others could do by the same means, and by using the additional knowledge his industry had gained, other laborers in the same field could even surpass. This important fact was continually verified in their experience, and herein lies the source of the successive and important discoveries and developments in the last hundred years, in every department of scientific pursuit.

In the *spiritual* department, if so it may be termed, the case has been very different. The field has been largely occupied, but the advance, if whatever change has been produced could be called an advance, has been comparatively very slow. For this difference there must be some cause, and this cause must be with *man*, not *God*. *He* would assuredly reveal truths connected with man's higher life, and eternal interests, as freely and fully as He has revealed those in the other departments which He has enabled man to explore.

The hindering cause or causes appear very clear to me, and I feel free to express my views in regard to them. They are principally two. Among the generality of the people from whom it would be expected such investigations and advancement would be made, a conviction has obtained that all revelation has ceased; that the whole mind and will of God, respecting man, is contained in the Bible; that every spiritual discovery or illumination must conform to what is therein recorded, thus regarding any advance as unhoped for and impossible; and that the *only* means of progress in a knowledge of spiritual truths is to study this book. Oh! if only all had been led to study the book of their own lives and experiences, the varying influences of their moral consciousness, with the same zeal and industry that they have studied the Bible (for I believe them honest), what progress would they have made in the knowledge of spiritual realities! — even greater and of incomparably more benefit to man than has been made in any department of physical science.

With Friends, who nobly maintain that God is unchangeable, and that consequently the blessing of His immediate revelation to man has not ceased, its benefits are yet not fully realized, from the belief which too generally prevails, that it was, in its fullness, made to George Fox, William Penn, and other early Friends, and that nothing therefore can be in advance of what was made known to and recorded by them, to which all doctrines and beliefs of members of the Society are expected to conform.

The second impediment is a prevailing belief that a knowledge of spiritual truths is not obtained through devotedness, inquiry, and observation directed to the influences of our consciousness, but that God reveals these truths not naturally, but supernaturally to a favored few; and also, that there must be great discrimination when and to whom these truths are imparted; so that those who have been enabled to see more advanced and elevated truths, are restrained from disseminating them, lest they should thereby disturb the harmony of the religious organization of which they are members. In this respect, society organization, though possessed of so many advantages, has been as a bond or restraint, preventing its development and growth.

Moreover, no two religious societies agree in what they maintain to be the fundamental doctrines essential to the soul's salvation, and ignoring reason and practical evidence, because it is feared they will conflict with supernatural revelation and some other received doctrines, no means are left by which to arrive at certainty in their conclusions on these most important subjects. In Astronomy, Chemistry, Mathematics, and all the sciences, certainty prevails; but in spiritual realities, the most important of all, there are uncertainty and mystery, bigotry and superstition.

Now with these views, which I honestly entertain, it will be seen why I regard the "God-given power to see or receive a truth, to be God's command to communicate it," believing it to be for the benefit of the race, and not of the individual alone; and that every truth that the Father reveals is a *universal* truth, and needed to bring up or complement the heart or mind of humanity to the present period in its progress.

A great loss, in my view, has been sustained by our Society for want of a fuller and more honest expression of the deepest convictions of the soul, which I regard as the revelations of God to that soul, with authority to proclaim them. This revelation is by the language of impression. This language must then be interpreted to others, and the interpretation can only be as high and pure as accords with the highest conceptions of the recipient of the impression. But it is so much an advance in the right direction. By thus making it known, one of two benefits may arise. If erroneous, it may be corrected by more advanced minds; and if true, it may correct and enlarge the opinions of others, and like the discoveries in science, lead to a still greater discovery.

Doubts have a right place in the mental and spiritual economy. They lead to a deeper and more careful examination of the subjects in search of evidence to establish the truth. An honest doubt, that one cannot remove, had better be expressed than withheld.

The expression may lead to the removal, not only from the mind that expressed it, but from many others; but if withheld, it may prey upon the soul like a canker.

It is my full belief that less danger may exist, if there is any, from the free and honest expression of the deepest convictions of the soul, than has arisen from that "withholding more than is meet, which tendeth to poverty." Truth is to be preferred in all things, because it is more in harmony with man's nature than the error it displaces.

The truths imparted by the Most High are *universal* truths, and like His laws, are of *universal application*. With regard to *special* utterances, injunctions, encouragements, or reproofs, it may be different. Such truths I understand to be referred to by the blessed Jesus in the quotation, " I have many things to declare unto you, but ye cannot bear them now." These evidently were not *universal* truths, but something *especially applicable to them* — some deficiency to point out, reproof to administer, or instruction to impart, which they were not then able to bear.

In the very instructive parable, when the servants proposed to gather the tares from among the wheat, the injunction was, " Nay, *let them alone, lest while ye gather up the tares ye root up the wheat with them*." The plan of the servants, as seen from the reply, was to " root up" the tares. But the wise and effective way is to " root up" nothing, contradict nothing, but to plant and nourish the *true seed*, plant truth, propagate and cultivate truth, and then, in accordance with the theory of " natural selection," that the strongest will prevail, truth, being stronger than all opposing principles, and possessed of greater vitality and power, will flourish and spread, overshadowing and causing to decay and die everything of a contrary nature, till " the mountain of the Lord's house shall be established on the tops of the mountains, and exalted above the hills, and all nations shall flow into it ;" *which mountain is truth.*

FRIENDS IN GREAT BRITAIN.

It is our privilege to draw practical instruction from the trials and sufferings of others, even when our hearts are tendered in near sympathy with the sufferers. The fact of the suffering is evidence of feeling, and hence of life; and, if only it is regarded in the light of that "wisdom which is from above, and is profitable to direct" in all things, a way of relief will be manifested, which will lead to a higher condition than had been previously known.

These reflections were awakened by reading the editorial in the "Friends' Intelligencer" of Tenth month 28th, and the articles in the same number, headed respectively "Hardshaw East," and "Hardshaw East Monthly Meeting," to which the editorial refers; and they have been recently revived by articles upon the same subject in the "British Friend" of last month (Eleventh). The "British Friend" states that "the protracted agitation in the Monthly Meeting (Hardshaw East) has at length culminated in the disownment of one member and the resignation of twelve more." The original cause of the disunity was entirely in relation to *doctrines*, and is stated by the "British Friend" to have been "the denial of the God-head of Christ, of His atoning, mediatorial offices, and of the Divine authority of the Scriptures."

The person who was disowned for holding and expressing these views, David Duncan, appears to have been a man of unblemished character, and to have lived a life of strict uprightness and integrity. In a solemn "protest" against his disownment, signed by over forty members of the Monthly Meeting that disowned him, and presented to that body, they state two of their objections to his disownment to be:

"Because, seeing that the Society of Friends, instead of according the ordinary prominence to a creed, has ever held as its most cherished doctrine the enlightening influence of the Spirit of God as the guide into all truth; and believing that our late beloved Friend accepted this truth, and endeavored to live up to the measure of light received, we therefore contend that, in disowning him, the Monthly Meeting separated from its fold one of its most useful and estimable members. And

"Because we believe that differences of opinion upon matters which are beyond the reach of human power to solve, must be allowed to remain open questions. Were this admitted, no harm could result from the calm discussion of religious subjects; on the contrary, much good; — whilst to attempt to stifle inquiry, by the exercise of a merely artificial authority, as in the case of our deeply lamented Friend, is a discredit to the cause of truth, and a dishonor to the profession of religion."

The readers of the "Intelligencer" will do well to give these two articles of the "protest" a careful and studied perusal, and endeavor to enter into sympathy with a Monthly Meeting of Friends, against the proceedings of which forty-four of its members thus solemnly protest, and in consequence of which proceedings, twelve others had previously resigned their rights! What comfort in social religious worship, what power for good, can possibly exist in a meeting whose members are in such a divided and alienated condition? I feel near and tender sympathy with them all, as brethren and sisters,— both the members of the Monthly Meeting who issued a testimony of disownment, and those who protest against the proceeding. I have no doubt all are equally honest in their convictions of the duty required of them, and that they would all rejoice to have harmony and love restored amongst them on a basis which truth would sanction.

To such restoration, the distress and suffering that must necessarily exist in such a state of alienation and estrangement, significantly point. How wise and comforting, if they take heed to these pointings! and what a blessing, if others imbibe the instruction which the lesson so impressively imparts!

If we examine the cause of this unhappy disturbance, we find it was an attempt to suppress inquiry; to fetter the mind and conscience; to enslave, by the authority of man, what God, in His infinite wisdom, love, and mercy, left free. Such attempt has ever been the bane of Christianity, and the fruitful source of persecutions, schisms, and separations in religious organizations.

I repeat, in tenderness of feeling, as a historical fact, that the attempt to enslave the mind, and bring it under human authority of whatsoever kind, or however established, being in its nature unjust, and out of the Divine harmony, like the personal slavery that existed in our own country, is withering and hurtful to the oppressor and the oppressed. But the unfavorable influence is naturally most marked in the oppressor. He assumes the accusing spirit of judging a brother, and lording it over God's heritage, which induces spiritual decline and death; whereas the oppressed, on the principle that "truth crushed to earth will rise again," if they are only favored to abide in the spirit of humility and meekness, have nothing to fear. They will partake of the beatitudes pronounced by the blessed Jesus.

But through the weakness of our nature, some thus oppressed, being conscious they are wronged, will, under this feeling, be more earnest and emphatic than they otherwise would be in proclaiming their peculiar views, and maintaining what they believe to be their inherent rights and privileges, to their own spiritual hurt and the injury of the cause of truth. Such are some of the evils that naturally spring from an attempt to enslave the mind and bring it into submission to human authority.

The cause and the unhappy influence of the disturbance being thus apparent, the remedy immediately suggests itself. This remedy is toleration — spiritual freedom — liberty of conscience — the very principles our earliest Friends, and all advanced advocates of truth in every age, contended and suffered for. No disadvantage can possibly arise from liberty of conscience — the right freely to think and to express the highest thoughts and deepest convictions of the soul, at all comparable, in their hurtful effects, to those which have been witnessed from an attempt to enslave it, because it is a God-given right.

Any apprehensions on this point, like those entertained in regard to according to slaves their right to liberty, by setting them free, will never be realized. An act of justice can do no harm. When the principle is yielded, all contention in regard to it ceases. All is peace.

We need not be afraid of "doctrines." What is requisite is a fuller and more perfect trust in the enlightening and protecting power of God, and His unceasing watchful care over all His rational children.

The effect of attaching paramount importance to "doctrines" and "beliefs" has always been, as it ever must be, to "divide in Jacob and scatter in Israel." What is now taking place in Hardshaw East Monthly Meeting is no new thing. It is but a repetition of what took place among the Friends of Ireland from the same cause towards the close of the last century, and the disastrous consequences continued active till late in the year 1803. This difficulty appears to have originated in different views being entertained in relation to the Scriptures by the elders of the Monthly Meeting of Carlow, producing ultimately an estrangement of feeling among the members generally; and a great number of disownments ensued of some of the most exemplary, enlightened, and worthy members, for different causes, among which was that of not rising in time of prayer. The reading of this deeply interesting "narrative of events" is very instructive and suggestive. Like causes produce like effects. What has been, may be again. We can there see of what great benefit a little toleration would have been towards prominent members of the Society, of spotless, exemplary lives, who fully and practically believed in the "grand fundamental doctrine of the Society," "the inward principle of light and grace, which, if attended to, they believed to be sufficient to lead all in the way they should go," and yet, because they held different views of certain portions of Scripture, they became separated from the Society.

Now we cannot believe at will. Belief is not a thing of *choice*, but of *evidence*. With sufficient evidence, belief is a matter of necessity. There is then no *merit* in *belief*; no *demerit* in *disbelief*. The same evidence, on minds equally sincere and honest, will not necessarily bring them to the same conclusion. When a judge was impeached before the United States Senate, during General Jackson's administration, Senator Taze-

21

well of Virginia, and Senator Livingston of Louisiana, who were of the same political party, had both been judges of courts, and (I think) Governors of their respective States, had each written upon jurisprudence, and would be supposed to possess minds as likely to be similarly influenced by the same evidence as possible, under oath, came to *exactly opposite conclusions.* One pronounced the judge on trial "guilty," the other "not guilty."

This invites us to toleration in honest differences of opinion, where it rests solely on evidence. Hence such a course is eminently essential in regard to *portions* of Scripture. It is a great and very common error among the devoted advocates of the perfection of the present version of the Scriptures, that the rejection or disbelief of one portion necessarily involves the rejection or discredit of the whole. The good and wise Newton, to whom the poet Cowper, also a devoted lover of the Scriptures, makes this apostrophe:

> "Such was thy wisdom, Newton, childlike sage!
> Sagacious reader of the works of God,
> And in His word sagacious!"

even Newton "clearly shows that the text, I. John, v., 7, 'For there are three that bear record in heaven, the Father, the Word, and the Holy Ghost, and these three are one,' was engrafted upon the Scriptures about the fourth century, to favor the doctrine of the Trinity." He adds, "For a long time the faith subsisted without this text, and it is rather a danger to religion than an advantage to make it now lean on a bruised reed. There cannot be a better service done to the truth than to purge it of things spurious." Yet the rejection of this, and some other portion of the Scriptures which his re-

searches and learning showed him were not in the original, did not in the least degree diminish his confidence
in, and love and veneration for, the great truths contained
in the Bible.

Now, these facts all point to the propriety and
necessity of forbearance and toleration for differences of
opinion and belief, under different degrees of experience
and development in regard to *those portions* of a work
written in "an unknown tongue" to most, many hundred years ago, and of which we have, and necessarily
can have, no other evidence than the authority of this
book; and very especially when its strongest advocates,
and those best qualified to judge, admit it contains
errors; and particularly when we reflect that the *facts
would be just as they are*, let our *beliefs* in regard to them
be what they may. Our beliefs would not affect the truth,
nor our relation to it. We have a practical work to do,
for which we feel and know we are responsible. This
work is, to place ourselves in harmony with God; to be
obedient to the manifested will of the Creator and Sus-
tainer of the universe, for which purpose He graciously
furnishes us with wisdom and power, light and strength.
Here all is centered.

To what will this direct the mind of one who loves
humanity, and particularly the Society of Friends?—in
which I include all its various "branches" or "divisions,"
who, while holding the same fundamental practical doctrine of the sufficiency of the enlightening influence of the
Spirit of God to guide into all truth, and the precious
testimonies which are the outgrowth therefrom, are yet
kept apart by unpractical "beliefs." It points to the
necessity of another test. It directs to a return to the
practical test of qualification of membership with Friends,

to the criteria given by the blessed Jesus Himself: "*By their fruits* ye shall know them." "A good tree cannot bring forth evil fruit, neither can a corrupt tree bring forth good fruit." The Apostle John bears testimony to the same point: "Let no man deceive you; he that *doeth righteousness is righteous.*"

What plain, practical tests are these! How wise, efficient, and sufficient! How easily applied! No danger of misunderstanding them.

If the fruits of making "doctrines" and "beliefs" the tests, are invariably schisms, divisions, and alienation among friends and brethren, and the multiplied disownments of persons of great worth and spotless lives, —as witness the trouble referred to in Ireland, the deplorable separation in this country, and the present unended difficulty and suffering at Hardshaw East, in Great Britain,—they always have been, and still are, of that tree which cannot be good.

On the other hand, if the acts and deportment of a member of Friends' Society are kind, good, true, lovely, and pure, such member "doeth righteousness," and by the test is "righteous," and every way worthy of being continued a member.

This, from the nature of man, must necessarily be the true test. Here permit me, in order to be understood, although it may be some repetition, briefly to state my convictions upon this point.

Man was created with many animal desires, appetites, and propensities, all good in themselves, but tending to run into excess, and requiring that the garden of his heart should be diligently "dressed" and "kept." "God breathed into man the breath of life, and he became a living soul." This breath of life is the Spirit of God, which is breathed into every rational creature. God could only breathe forth of His own nature. He breathed into man the spirit of truth, justice, love, kindness, mercy, purity, and holiness, and all His communicable attributes, which are in man *living powers* or *spirit forces*, to regulate and restrain all the animal appetites, desires, and propensities, and preserve them in the Divine harmony. We all know what truth, love, and justice are, and when we know these, we so far know God. For (I speak it reverently) we can know God only by or through His attributes, in accordance with the Scripture truth, " What is to be known of God is manifest in man " — the " breath of life " that was and is breathed into him. Then the conscious existence in which all these blessed attributes, in infinite perfection, reside, and which the soul feels to be ever present with it, is God.

The watchful and enlightened soul feels not only that He is ever present, but that the welfare, safety, and peace of the soul depend on preserving a harmonious relation to Him ; and this can only be secured by acting in perfect obedience to all His manifestations. These manifestations to the soul being wisdom and power, light and strength, are always accompanied by ability to perform or fulfill all their varied requirements.

Let us individually, by example and precept, urge to faithful, practical obedience to these blessed and pure principles, as the one thing essential to a holy life, and a child of God.

There is no way in which we can possibly fulfill the requirements of justice but by the spirit of justice, or the requirements of love and truth but by the spirit of love and truth.

And these are the gifts of God to every soul. They are the "grace of God which bringeth salvation," — a knowledge of His will, with power to obey it. " All have heard, but all have not obeyed."

This, to my understanding, is the true doctrine of practical Christianity, and the primitive and fundamental doctrine of Friends. Friends, without any regard to how or why, accept the simple fact of the " light within," the manifestation of the will of God to the soul, with power to obey it. In support of this truth there is an abundance of Scriptural testimony. But we require no other evidence than our own experience furnishes. We know that if we diligently watch we shall see or hear, and if we *will*, we *can obey*. Then are we saved from sin through obedience, for "sin is a transgression of the law," and with the obedient soul there is no transgression.

How beautiful, how simple, how practical! Love God; love man; recognize the fatherhood of God, and the brotherhood of all men. Every one knows the duty he owes to a father and to a brother; and he must observe faithfully, day by day, the varied filial and fraternal obligations which this recognition imposes, and these God, in His love and mercy, will impart ability to perform. He watches over us continually, with all the tenderness and care of a loving Father. "He works in us, both to *will* and to *do* of His good pleasure." Our wills, as we are faithful and obedient, are merged into His will, till the abiding desire of the heart, in all things, is, "Thy will, O God, be done."

He calls upon and assists us to work up, day by day, to the highest convictions of right and duty which are revealed to our watchful consciousness. Then all is peace,—all is brought into the Divine harmony.

What more can God give or we desire, than results from simple obedience to known duty—the voice of God manifested to the soul?

Here is a platform large enough and strong enough not only for all the divisions into which the once united Society of Friends is unhappily separated, but for all peoples. That we may all profit by the lesson which the facts that have been stated so impressively teach, is the ardent aspiration of my heart.

SANDY SPRING, MD., 12*th* *Mo.* 23*d*, 1871.

SOME THOUGHTS CONNECTED WITH THE FUNDAMENTAL PRINCIPLES OF FRIENDS.

Practical Quakerism consists in faithful obedience to the "still, small voice," which is the voice of God speaking to the soul.

Friends do not believe that they, as a Society, possess any privileges from the Good Father that are not equally tendered to all the rest of mankind on the same conditions. The Friends bear emphatic testimony to the beauty of holiness, the riches of Divine love, and the universality of the grace of God—this grace being a knowledge of his will, with a power to obey it. The Society of Friends has no creed. A creed is necessarily fixed, and does not admit of growth, expansion, and progress, which they regard as inherent characteristics of humanity, by which man is distinguished from all other animals.

They regard as of binding daily obligation the fundamental injunction of George Fox, "Mind the Light,' "Hear and obey," "Let obedience keep pace with knowledge," all meaning the same thing, which is to live day by day up to the highest convictions of right and duty that are revealed to our watchful consciousness, recognizing the fatherhood of God, and the brotherhood of all men, with the filial and fraternal obligations which this recognition imposes.

This is the simple doctrine of Friends, to which they invite *all people.*

Friends do not ask nor desire other people to join their *outward religious organization.* This, of itself, will do no good. But their earnest desire is that every individual shall become practically obedient to the everyday teaching of the Spirit of God in their own hearts, and thus become members of the Church triumphant, experiencing a foretaste of heaven.

A heart that is obedient to the Spirit of God, is under the government of God; God reigns in that heart; and where God reigns, there is His kingdom — there is Heaven, and there is joy now and forever. "Behold the kingdom of God is within you."

It is recorded, "They shall not teach every man his neighbor, and every man his brother, saying, ' Know the Lord;' for they shall all know me, from the least of them to the greatest of them, saith the Lord; I will put my laws into their hearts, and I will be to them a God, and they shall be to me a people. For I will be merciful to their unrighteousness, and their sins and their iniquities will I remember no more."

Wonderful privileges! glorious promises! and they are *all* "yea and amen forever!

These encouraging truths of Scripture harmonize

beautifully with the highest conceptions we are capable of forming of the goodness, justice, love and mercy of God, and His fatherly care of His rational children.

But we have other confirmation of the important fact, that God guides, instructs and aids *His children* — all who are willing to be guided and instructed by Him.

According to right reason, the infinitely wise, good, just and omnipresent Father would not bring His helpless child into existence, and then, notwithstanding the great and important responsibilities resting upon it, leave it without access to a reliable guide and helper in every case of necessity and emergency. When Queen Victoria, the present good sovereign of England, permitted her oldest son, heir to the throne, to visit this country, she selected the wisest statesman and the best physician of her kingdom to accompany him, with earnest commands and instructions to take the best possible care, in every respect, of her beloved child.

Could the sovereign of the whole world, the eternal and universal Father, the loving and tender parent, do less for every child He sends forth on the journey of life, through its varied perplexities and dangers, than this mother did for her son?

Now, a perfect guide, such as is needed in life, must be able to take in a view of the whole journey, not only the *past* and *present*, but the *future*. This cannot be man. It cannot be a book or books. Such guide can only be the Omniscient God.

That man is favored with the privilege of having such a guide — " the light within "— accords with the experience of the wise and good of all ages, as well as with the Scriptures, as already shown.

The same important fact finds further confirmation in the phenomena of animal instinct.

> "Reasoning at every step he treads,
>   Man yet mistakes his way ;
> While meaner things whom instinct leads,
>   Are rarely known to stray."—COWPER.

How great are man's privileges! How dignified and noble the position he occupies! He is the active recipient of the attributes of Deity, and invited and empowered to co-operate with the Eternal Father in diffusing blessings and dispensing good to His creatures; "made a little lower than the angels," "crowned with glory and honor," and having dominion over the works of the Divine hand. These are man's privileges and capabilities, to be attained by watchfulness and faithful obedience. He then becomes a "ministering spirit," under the guidance of the Father, and with the power from the Father, doing the Father's work. The Father works in these obedient ones, both to will and to do of His good pleasure, and what they thus do, He does. The work is His and the power is His, and to Him be all the glory ascribed. The instrument he will fully reward.

A person in a stream of deep water and unable to swim, or in any outward difficulty or danger, cannot be extricated without the practical human aid of himself or others. His own prayer (I speak it reverently), or the united prayers of all mankind cannot save him without human aid. Let us keep this in mind, and with it our responsibility consequent thereon, and maintain a state of due watchfulness. God works by instruments in the outward affairs of men. He has created us social beings, and placed in our hearts a feeling of kindness and sympathy, that prompts to immediate action whenever occasion may require. He puts it into the hearts of His watchful, obedient children, to be hands and feet for Him, and minister to the relief, assistance, or necessities of those who need aid. Thus such obedient ones become agents or ministering angels of the Most High. What a dignified position!

This is the means appointed by Deity for conveying special blessings and favors to mankind, thus binding them more closely in a common brotherhood, cemented by love and practical good will. The instrument, whether ministering in word or deed, will frequently be wholly ignorant of the favors and blessings transmitted through his instrumentality, they being known only by the heart of the recipient and the Good Being who confers them.

All the *special* blessings and comforts extended to the different members of the human family — assistance to the poor and suffering; help to the widow and the orphan; care and instruction to the young; kindness and counsel to those setting out in the business of life, — proceed from man acting under Divine illumination and government, and I am comforted in the belief that the number of these willing instruments, these ministering angels of the Most High, is increasing, although probably giving little external sign in any other way.

If we can only be brought fully to recognize this important fact, the increase will become more rapid.

In order to become His true and efficient instruments we must first labor to be brought into entire harmony with the Good Being in all respects, clothed with the Spirit, and then, abiding in a state of sensitive watchfulness, act promptly in conformity to every impress or manifestation of duty.

On the other hand, much of the special suffering, cruelty, injustice, misery of all kinds, endured by the different members of the human family, proceed from man — one's self or others — when in a state of disobedience or rebellion against the Most High.

The Good Being, in His marvelous condescension, in the freedom which He has bestowed upon man has imparted to him the power even to *rebel against His Maker and disobey His known commands.*

Hence proceed all the special evil, misery, and suffering in the world. May these thoughts claim our deepest reflection, and may this reflection tend to individual profit!

Every desire and effort to act right and do good is practical prayer; and every feeling of happiness and enjoyment from the blessings of which we are partakers, is practical and acceptable thanksgiving and praise; but these active and healthy engagements of the soul are greatly intensified when they are designed for an intelligent being, who, we are strengthened to believe, smiles upon and blesses the effort, and accepts with approbation the grateful emotions of the heart.

When the Apostle John was "in the spirit on the Lord's day," which is the time whenever *we are willing* the Lord shall reign in our hearts, he wrote, "He that hath an ear, let him hear what the Spirit saith unto the churches: To *him that overcometh* will I give to eat of the tree of life that is in the midst of the Paradise of God;" and this it is the high privilege of every one to enjoy.

SOME REFLECTIONS IN RELATION TO PEACE AND WAR.

In the editorial notice (No. 42 of *Friends' Intelligencer*) of Dr. Miles's report of the conference held at Geneva, Switzerland, in Ninth month last, in the interests of universal peace, the editor says, "We believe there is no subject of equal magnitude now claiming the attention of the civilized world, and we trust every member of the Society of Friends will do his part to help bring about so desirable a result as is contemplated by this organization."

These remarks, together with the following in the "scrap column" of the same number: — "There surely is a tendency with some to *keep* whatever of good *they may have*, or that *may come to them*, and in so doing, they impoverish themselves. Let us be stimulated to examine our storehouses, whether of the memory or of the desk; peradventure we will find there that which is of value, *in danger of becoming mouldy*. Let us bring it forth,"—took strong hold of my mind, and induces me to bring forth the following, which has lain in my "letter-book" since 1871.

At our late Yearly Meeting (1871) I was one of a committee to embody the exercises of the meeting in a suitable minute, and I wrote the following paragraph on the subject of war: "This advancement of the cause of peace will not be effected by aiming at impracticable ideals, but by recognizing existing facts, and, under the influence of Divine wisdom, endeavoring by the unchanging principles and laws that govern the heart of humanity, to shape and direct the course of events in such manner that *peace shall be evolved as a natural and harmonious result. Then* will peace be permanent. *Then* will man hold sacred not only the *life*, but the *rights, interest,* and *happiness* of his fellow-man everywhere."

In the original draft of the minute was this sentiment: "Bad as war is, it is not the *worst* of evils. Anarchy, riot, and mob violence, in which innocent women and children indiscriminately suffer, are even worse. Hence the necessity in our large cities of a *police, sustained by military force,* to check these in their early stages, to which arrangement the inhabitants are indebted for their quiet and security."

This passed the committee, but, on being read in the Yearly Meeting, it was objected to by some Friends, and I, having written it, proposed that it should be omitted, which was accordingly done.

Believing the sentiment to be a correct one, however, I am encouraged, by the extracts I have quoted at the commencement of this article, to revive it at this time, and express something further on the subject.

It is not by legislation, or any external means, that war, intemperance, and such like corruptions of human nature are to be healed, but by an action or power *from within* —" making clean and pure the inside of the vessel."

Then the *spirit of man* being purified and peaceful, *man's spirit* will *co-operate* with the *spirit of God in man,* which is always striving to bring man into a closer union and oneness with God.

The value of peace and harmony, when they proceed from the *spirit of peace* or the *spirit of God in man,* without which no peace can be permanent, cannot be computed; therefore it is worthy of every effort and of all needed sacrifices to obtain them. Virtue and intelligence are their true foundation.

But when the *spirit of war exists,* a practical experience of the hurtful consequences to which this evil spirit leads may be a means, in the Divine economy, of correcting and purifying the spirit, and teaching its possessor wisdom by what it causes him to suffer.

I once had a lesson that has been of great value to me on this point.

In the Seventh Month, 1849, with some of my family, I made an excursion for recreation and improvement, and in passing from Niagara to Montreal, we took passage in the "British Line" of steamboats.

The boat was much crowded. Before we reached the outlet of Lake Ontario a difficulty arose between two Irish gentlemen, and it was evident that a fight would ensue unless there was some intervention. They were fine, large, noble-looking specimens of humanity, with benevolent countenances, and well dressed, and my sympathies were all aroused to prevent the abuse they were both in danger of receiving. I went hastily to the captain, told him there was a fight brewing between two of his passengers, and asked his assistance in an effort to prevent it, with which request he promptly and cheerfully complied. He invited one of the party to walk with him to the after part of the boat, and I asked the other to go with me to the upper deck, which he did. It was a most beautiful evening, and we were just passing among the "Thousand Islands" of the St. Lawrence. I found my companion to be very intelligent and appreciative of the beauties of nature, and we spent an hour or so in agreeable conversation.

When all seemed calm, and reason entirely enthroned, we gradually separated. He went down to the lower deck, I following at a little distance, and being pretty tall, I was able to keep my eye on him in the crowd. At length his eyes and those of the one with whom he had had the difficulty met, and in less time than I can write it, they had their coats, cravats, and vests off, and began to beat each other in such manner as I had never before seen or imagined! I felt sick at heart! Neither seemed to gain any advantage over the other. At length they straightened themselves up and looked each other sternly in the face. Then at it they went again, with the same result, and a pause as before. After a little while they had the third round, more severe and lasting than either of the others, but with a similar result; by which time each found he had a worthy antagonist, and on straightening up and looking squarely at each other, both stepped backward simultaneously, then retired. They soon returned. Never probably were two men more changed in appearance in so short a time! I would not have known them to be the same! One had an eye badly bruised and entirely closed from the swelling. The other had a large piece gouged out of his cheek, and both were scarred and bruised beyond description, their shirt bosoms and clothes badly torn, till they appeared to be mere wrecks of the persons they were half an hour before.

But the change in their outward appearance was not all. Owing to a very dense smoke from burning forests that prevailed, the captain had to stop frequently, so that we were two days on board, all the passengers mingling together; and there were not two more *calm, polite, and gentle men on board,* and they were *particularly kind and respectful to each other.* They had evidently been benefited by what they had experienced, and had learned wisdom by what they had suffered. When the *bitter spirit remains*, such practical results may be a means of pacifying and purifying it. "Great and marvelous are Thy works; just and true are Thy ways!"

An appeal to the *reason of men in a passion* is simply futile; because by the rise of passion, reason is disenthroned, and can only be restored to authority by some check from circumstances — by some pressure of environments.

For the peaceful adjustment of difficulties between nations, as we must hope, there will be a sufficiently large number possessed of their reason, to direct the counsels of the state in a course so obviously to its interest.

A few months before the Yearly Meeting referred to (1871) the subject had weighed heavily on my mind, that our Government might embrace the favorable opportunity then existing, to advance the interests of peace, and thus of humanity, and I wrote a private letter to President Grant, with the view of delivering it in person and explaining my views to him. Before this was done, there were communications on the same subject in the "Friends' Intelligencer," and a meeting of the Representative Committee of Baltimore Yearly Meeting was called, which decided to memorialize the President on the subject, and into this my concern became merged.

In accordance with the suggestion in the "Intelligencer," I have examined the storehouse of my desk, and now produce the letter I wrote to President Grant, and the memorandum I made to read to him, containing a *mode of proceeding*, in order to have a true and permanent peace between nations, *without looking to a resort to forcible or warlike measures in any contingency.*

22

It will be remembered that this subject claimed the solemn and active attention of that great apostle of peace, William Penn, and in 1695 he wrote what he entitled "An essay towards the present and future peace of Europe, by the establishment of a European diet, parliament, or estates," from which I will quote the entire fourth section, as showing the views on the subject of that great statesman and philanthropist: —

"SECTION 4. *On a general peace or the peace of Europe, and the means of it.* In my first section I showed the *desirableness* of peace; in my next the truest means of it, viz., *justice, not war;* and in my last that this justice was the fruit of government, as government itself was the result of *society;* which first came from a reasonable design of men of peace. Now if the sovereign *princes* of *Europe,* who represent that society or independent state of man that was *previous* to the obligations of society, would for the same reason that engaged men first in society, viz., *love of peace and order,* agree to meet, by their stated *deputies,* in a general diet, estates, or parliament, and there establish rules of justice for sovereign princes to observe one to another, and thus to meet yearly, or once in two or three years at farthest, or as they shall see cause, and to be styled 'The Sovereign or Imperial Diet, Parliament, or State of Europe,' before which sovereign assembly should be brought all differences depending between one sovereign and another, that cannot be made up by private embassies before the session begins, and that, [if any of the sovereignties that constitute these Imperial States shall refuse to submit their claim or pretensions to them, or to abide and perform the judgment thereof, and seek their remedy by *arms,* or delay their compliance beyond the

time prefixed in their resolutions, all the other sovereignties united as one strength shall compel the submission and
performance of the sentence, with damages to the suffering party and charges to the sovereignties that obliged
their submission].

"To be sure, Europe would quietly obtain the so much
desired and needed peace to her harassed inhabitants;
no sovereignty in Europe having the power, and therefore cannot show the will, to dispute the conclusion ; and
consequently peace would be procured and continued in
Europe."

It is clearly to be seen, by the part enclosed in
brackets, "*if they refused*, all the other sovereignties,
united as one strength, *shall compel* the submission "—
the plan proposed by William Penn contemplated the
possibility of an ultimate resort to force.

Since the time William Penn wrote, now well nigh
two centuries ago, a *new power* has arisen, as an *aid to
induce* and *regulate* peaceful relations between nations
— that is, the financial one, or the benefits of trade and
commerce, as I endeavor to show in the following
"memorandum," which I prepared to read to President
Grant after he had read my letter.

SANDY SPRING, MD., *8th Mo., 1871.*

ULYSSES S. GRANT, President of the United States :

DEAR FRIEND : — The present is a remarkable period in
the world's history. Events of the highest significance, in some
of which thou hast been a prominent actor, succeed each other
with unprecedented rapidity. This rapid succession demands
coincident and unremitted vigilance, lest the opportunity to
impart that wise direction to these events of which they
are capable, and which the best interests of humanity re-

quire, shall be permitted to pass unimproved. Every individual, however humble and limited his sphere of action, must be faithful in the performance of whatever part may be required of him in the great work which is manifestly in progress, in order that all may proceed with that healthful and harmonious regularity which is beneficial to our people and our race.

The successful termination of the convention in Washington City, which thou wast instrumental in procuring, by which a mode of adjusting the pending questions of difference between the United States and Great Britain was amicably agreed upon, by the "Treaty of Washington," to the satisfaction of the governments and peoples of both countries, thus giving the joyous promise of peace and fraternity, where the horrors of war were so imminent, has imparted to the friends of humanity additional ground to hope that the same wise, peaceful, and Christian mode by which this happy issue was consummated, may be adopted to settle all difficulties and differences that may in future arise between nations.

In view of the existing political condition of Europe, the present time appears eminently propitious for a favorable consideration of such a measure.

In contemplating this momentous subject with deep and reverential feeling, confidently believing that the "Unseen Hand," whose workings have been so marvelously witnessed in the removal of slavery from our beloved country, is now outstretched to lead on to the greater and more widespread blessing of permanent peace between the nations, to the saving of a vast number of lives and amount of misery and treasure which cannot be computed, the undersigned believes it to be his duty thus respectfully and privately to suggest to thee the propriety of thy bringing the subject before the Congress of the United States at its next session, either in thy annual message or in a special communication to that body, in such form as thou mayest think most likely to effect the desirable object, recommending that measures be taken to make a proposition, in suitable terms, by this Government to the governments of other nations, to unite in adopting some measure by which all national difficulties and differences may be peacefully and amicably settled, so that "nation shall not lift up sword against nation, neither shall they learn war any more."

If thy mind has already been turned to this subject, with a view to taking action thereon in the direction already indicated, as is most probably the case, then it is earnestly desired that thou mayest be encouraged to proceed in the good work, which from the great benefit its accomplishment would be to His children, cannot fail to receive the blessing and favor of the good and merciful Father.

With the greatest sincerity, the undersigned feels at liberty to add that he believes there is no one with whom the inauguration of this important message could, with as much propriety, originate as thyself; regarded by the people as amongst the greatest of generals the world has ever produced, and at the head of what is acknowledged to be one of the most powerful, prosperous, and enlightened nations of the earth, *and yet* whose continued effort has been, and is, for an amicable settlement of all disputes and difficulties; one who recognizes the "Golden Rule" of measuring our duty to others by what we would desire them to do to us, as being equally obligatory among nations, whether strong or weak, as among individuals; and whose pleading entreaty to all people on all occasions is, "*Let us have peace.*"

Very respectfully thy sincere friend,
BENJAMIN HALLOWELL.

MEMORANDUM

to accompany the preceding Letter, and to be read to the President.

A great difficulty exists in devising a working plan, by which such a measure as is suggested in the foregoing letter, should it happily be adopted, can be consistently carried out; that is, in devising a mode of proceeding by which the terms that may be agreed upon by a convention or congress of the representatives of the different nations, and adopted by their governments, *shall be enforced* or *maintained*, without looking to compulsory or warlike measures, should a party to the peaceful arrangement fail to comply with its provisions or requisitions.

There is, however, good reason to believe that *there is a way*, and a *right way*, to attain every *right object;* and with the guidance of that "wisdom which is from above," and which will surely not be withheld from the sincere actors in such a heaven-inspired movement, a *means can certainly be devised* to secure peacefully all that will promote the best welfare of nations and of mankind.

One element of action has been suggested to my mind as being calculated to contribute to this important end: that is, in regulating the commercial intercourse between different countries. Should peaceful relations be secured between all civilized nations, an immense amount of annual expenditure for the army and navy would become *unnecessary*, and thus be *saved*, to be employed in advancing the national prosperity and the interests of peace and enlightened civilization.

Such nations therefore as may fail to come into the peaceful measures agreed upon by several governments, and any one of these that might subsequently violate the promised support in the maintenance of them, would be the *cause* of making it necessary for those governments which are disposed to preserve peaceful relations with all peoples to maintain a military and naval power, and hence they would be the cause of imposing these war expenditures upon these governments.

A discrimination therefore could very properly and justly be made in establishing commercial relations between the different governments, by which the means of paying these war expenditures should be drawn, in whole or in chief, from those governments which render them necessary,—the anti-peaceful ones,—by laying heavy duties upon their exports, and high rates for all postal and telegraphic communications; while between the peaceful nations the fullest freedom of intercourse and of trade might safely be permitted to exist, such as is now happily in operation among the different States of our Union, and the privilege always to be secured to any anti-peaceful State to become a member of the peaceful fraternity of governments, and partake of all its benefits and immunities.

It may be queried how under such arrangement would the expenses of the National Government be paid? To this it is answered, in the same manner that those of the States of the Union now are. *All the vast expenses of the National Government are* NOW *paid by our people.* In the proposed peaceful arrangement the army and navy expenditures, including those for fortifications, their maintenance, etc., which together constitute a very heavy item in the annual expenses, would immediately be greatly diminished, and we trust in time removed entirely, so that the amount to be raised annually would be far less than now. There would also be a large diminution in the Custom House expenses. Therefore, there would be *much less* national expense than at present, and of course *less money to be paid by the people in direct or in indirect taxes.*

The only difficulty would be in the *mode of assessment*, and the wisdom of the national legislature, with such important consequences pending, can certainly make that equitable, just, and satisfactory to the mass of the people.

Should any species of manufacture be of sufficient national importance to render it a proper object of Government encouragement, in order to bring it up to the full condition of perfection and usefulness of which it is capable, and to become self-sustaining, such aid could be furnished by Government as now, the aid to terminate when the manufacture shall become self-sustaining or its relative national importance ceases.

In a civil community, where an unruly person or a body of lawless people act in such manner as flagrantly to violate the peace, safety, and rights of those around them, such person or people *must* be secured or confined as a *protective measure*, even though lives are lost on one side or the other, or both, in obtaining this result.

This must be done in order to prevent a continuance or spread of the evil, to stay further lawlessness and aggression, and the probable loss of a far greater number of lives, including those of innocent women and children, than would be sacrificed in checking it, as well as to maintain that good order which the security, happiness, and healthy condition of society imperatively demand.

It is vain to look, on such occasions, to a *special* interposition of Providence for protection, or the removal of the scourge. Deity acts, in human affairs, *only* through instrumental means; and He has already furnished mankind with the means of self-preservation and

protection from outward aggression, in the physical
power with which, in His wisdom and goodness, He
has endowed him; in the reason he has bestowed
to direct these, and to discover and use all his material
laws, to protect from wild beasts and from men whose
passions have dethroned their reason and made them
more dangerous than wild beasts; and also, in the
moral power, or spiritual influence, to restrain from
every wrong action, and preserve all in harmony with
the eternal principles of right, justice, and love.

But all efforts to secure permanent peaceful relations
in communities, should be continually and wisely made
by increasing virtue and intelligence among the people;
and every renewed opportunity, such as at present exists,
to advance the righteous cause of peace among nations,
should be promptly embraced, in order that the welfare
of humanity may be secured, and the noble aspiration,
"Let us have peace," be fulfilled.

"Whence is Evil?"

The beautiful extract from "Augustine's Soliloquies,"
in "Friends' Intelligencer" of Twelfth month 30th (No.
45, current volume), making the inquiry, "Whence is evil?"
touches a subject upon which there has been much
discussion and controversy in different ages; and the
subject is revived with renewed energy and great learning in recent times,—"How came evil and wickedness
into the world?"

Seeing the much evil and great wickedness which
man, the highest and noblest of God's works, commits,

it is maintained by some, in order to explain the mysterious phenomenon, that Deity abrogated His omnipo-
tence, omnipresence, and benevolence, in favor of man,
and leaves him free to rule and act independently for a
limited space and time.

I take an entirely different view of the subject, which
I feel it right to endeavor to present.

Everything that can be known of Deity leads the
thoughtful mind to the necessary conclusion that He is
all wise and all good, so that evil or wickedness could
not originate with or proceed from Him.

Now, Deity, in His wisdom, has endowed man with
freedom of choice, which endowment is essential to the
happiness and advancement of a rational being. Consequently, if man is free to choose the good, he may
choose the evil; if he is free to obey, he must be free to
rebel. The highest evidence to my mind of the goodness and condescension of the Almighty, is seen in the
astonishing fact, that He has conferred on man, the
creature, the power even to rebel against his Creator.

The commission of wrong is, by a wise, benevolent,
and immutable law of the good Providence in the constitution of man, always attended by suffering. By this
suffering we are taught wisdom. We are all at school.
The whole human family are scholars, learning and
growing wiser, some very rapidly of latter times. The
progress of a people or a community in civilization and
enlightenment is in proportion to, or is measured by, the
suffering, distress, and misery which such people or community experience, all events tending ultimately to elevate, purify, and benefit them, and render them more
intelligent and happy.

It is not in the power of Deity (I say it reverently),

to compel a man to be happy against his will or without his co-operation. If a man could be made obedient and happy by compulsion, every rational creature, such are the love and care of the good Father, would now be wholly under the Divine government. But while Deity invites all, He compels none; He leaves all free to choose.

The Creator never formed a creature that He could not control. He knew just what man was when He brought him into existence; and he is just the being that an intelligent existence, possessed of freedom of choice, with various desires, appetites, and propensities, and placed amidst objects by which these can be excited and gratified, must naturally be.

But, while man is free to choose, if he violates the laws of truth, justice, and love, the penalty is attached, that he must suffer. This is an immutable law, as all human experience testifies; and the suffering becomes greater and greater, until ultimately it becomes so great that he is brought voluntarily to yield to the invitations of Divine love, and come under the government of the spirit of truth, in which state he finds peace, because his spirit is brought into harmony with the spirit of God.

Hence it is seen that evil and wickedness came into the world by man's disobedience, and that suffering is the great means employed by Deity for man's improvement and progress. It acts as a check or curb to his evil ways. All the desires, appetites, and propensities are in themselves good and pleasure-producing, when wisely used,— that is, when used in healthy moderation. It is only when indulged in to excess that they become hurtful or produce suffering. And the knowledge of

the limit between due moderation and excess is to be
gained by observation and experience by ourselves or
others; so that our own observation and experience,
united with that of others, are the great sources of
knowledge in moral training.

By these, man is brought to see that in his state of
disobedience he was ignorant of what would have pro-
moted his true welfare and peace.

This brings us to the important practical point, to
see how evil and wickedness are to be overcome or removed, which is by the extension of this knowledge by
the removal of ignorance, and securing the universal
education and enlightenment of all classes of society,

Discouraging as may be the outlook in our country
at present, there are still many evidences of a steady
progress and improvement during the past century in
the whole civilized world, and this improvement is still
going on.

Human life is held to be more sacred by the great
mass of the people; kindness, justice, and right are more
regarded, and the import of the fact, as stated at the
close of an address by Samuel Longfellow, is more clearly
and instructively seen, that "a wrong thing is never a
success, nor a right thing a failure, seem things as they
may."

Some Results of Reflection and Meditation.

I entertain a full belief that what was written formerly was written for our instruction, and that with what
was recorded, there was frequently associated in the mind

of the author a spiritual meaning of instructive significance, which may be opened to the contemplative mind.

Of this kind, I have thought, are the expressions of
a wise king, as recorded in Canticles II., xi. and xii.,
" Lo! the winter is past; the rain is over and gone;
the flowers appear on the earth; the time of the sing-
ing of birds is come, and the voice of the turtle is
heard in the land."

There seems in this beautiful description to be implied such a sweet revivification after a winter of cold,
wet, darkness, and decay (a spiritual condition which,
no doubt, every traveler Zionward at times experiences),
after which all nature breaks with beauty and joy, and
the soul is enabled to see and feel that the clouds and
vapors in which it had been enveloped were all from
the earth—a mental doubt or bodily infirmity—so
that if the soul will arouse its inherent energies, it may
rise above all those mists, and bask in the beams of
Eternal Love, corresponding to the outward sun, which
is always shining, however dark and dreary the day
may be.

It contributes greatly to man's happiness and to
the staidness of his religious feelings to have a clear
and settled conclusion in regard to his relation to the
Supreme Being — his Creator.

Deity created man for happiness. God never gave
life but to spread the enjoyment of existence. He
never created but to bless. He is always ready and
willing to help, save, bless, and bring into the kingdom. " Fear not, little flock," said the blessed Jesus,
"it is your Father's good pleasure to give you the
kingdom." God is no " respecter of persons." It must
therefore be His " good pleasure" to give the kingdom

to every soul, and every individual may consider this language addressed to him or herself: "It is the Father's good pleasure to give thee the kingdom." When any one in true humility and truthfulness breathes the aspiration, "If Thou wilt, Thou canst make me clean," the response is immediate, "I will: be thou clean," and such soul is instantly cleansed of its maladies as far as it respects Deity. But we must bear in mind that these maladies may have been the results of long-continued errors or habits that have been increasing in strength, and it will require a long-continued effort wholly to overcome them. But if persevered in, craving Divine help, this overcoming will ultimately be effected, because all the powers for good in the universe are acting with such striving and aspiring soul.

In the pathetic lamentation of the blessed Jesus over Jerusalem: "How often would I have gathered thy children, but ye would not;" the same as if He had said, "The good Father would have saved you, but your wills resisted the wisdom and power of God." And thus it is with any who are not gathered and saved, in all time. Deity, by His spirit or His good angel in the soul, desires and strives to save all, but the human will resists the proffered salvation.

It is a great truth that God breathed into man the breath of life, and man became, and is, a living soul. By the term "soul" is meant the conscious moral being, or that part of the human constitution which is capable of being impressed and enlightened by the spirit of God, and of controlling the will, when the soul and will are both in a healthy condition. This "breath of life" thus breathed into man must be of the Divine nature — the communicable attributes of Deity — justice, truth, love, mercy, purity, and holiness; and when these are impressed on the soul and control the will, they bring man more and more into the "image of God," governing his will, and bringing it into harmony with the Divine will. As has been beautifully and figuratively said, "All the powers of God are winged, being always eager and striving for the higher path which leads to God," bearing the soul upward and onward, nearer and nearer to Him, not in place, but in condition or state; more and more godly in life, more just, kind, true, pure, and holy; these principles manifesting themselves by regulating all the conduct. Being influenced by the spirit of truth, such "are guided into all truth" and righteousness.

These Divine attributes, with which it is man's privilege to be endowed, are all spirit forces; they control his will, so that it becomes his life, his meat, and his drink to do the will of God. He is clothed with righteousness as with a garment. All that we can see of him, in word or conduct, gives evidence of the Divine principles by which he is governed. He is a "son of God," for he is led by the spirit of God.

Together with those great and eternal principles, the good Father has endowed man with an understanding capable of comprehending all His laws, physical, intellectual, and spiritual, and of adapting them to His various purposes.

These two guides — the Spirit of God and the Understanding or Reason — must always be in harmony with each other, because they both proceed from the same bountiful source, and are both enlightened by the same glorious effulgence.

It is by the combined influence or assistance of these

Divinely furnished powers that man is to perform everything of good that he may attempt in life. He need not look for special direction or help. God is always ready and willing to help, bless, and prosper every effort to do good in harmony with these powers.

Of this truth let every one be assured (not waiting for anything special), and the truth will be confirmed by practical experience. Let him be "up and doing," with the ability with which God in these powers has furnished him, embracing at the same time frequent opportunities for silent meditation and retirement, in order to have a renewal of strength, and he will find a growth in wisdom, experience, and peace.

Truth is more in harmony with man's nature than error; right than wrong; virtue than vice; and truth, right, and virtue would always be chosen in preference to error, wrong, and vice, if men were wise and enlightened, and understood the real nature of what they were choosing and doing. Most of the errors of men arise from ignorance, which is very inconvenient as well as very hurtful. Hence the pathetic imploration of the blessed Jesus, "Father, forgive them, they know not what they do." And the nearer men come to that pure, enlightened state that Jesus occupied, the more earnestly does a similar aspiration for the erring rise from their hearts. The disastrous criminal offences of which nearly every day brings us a report, involving not only the authors of them, but their families and near friends, in deep trouble and suffering, it cannot be believed would take place, were not the perpetrators of them ignorant of the sad consequences that result from them, did they possess this one great truth: "A wrong thing is never a success, nor a right thing a failure, seem things as they may."

A wrong thing connects itself with everything that is wrong in the universe; while on the other hand, what is right connects itself with universal good, and thus with God, and must triumph, for His power is above all other powers combined.

Now, if young people would only bear these facts in mind, and avoid taking the first step in wrong, knowing that that course will certainly lead to darkness, distress, and misery, deeper and darker the further it is pursued, and be firm in the right (and then they will always be certain of having the help of the good Father), they will have acquired a practical lesson that will enable them to pass safely and happily through the various vicissitudes of life.

The consequences of ignorance being so hurtful, and, in many cases, at present unavoidable, would seem calculated to induce a feeling of discouragement, did we not remember that

> " He, our gracious Father, kind as just,
> Knowing our frame, remembers we are dust."

The Scripture injunction is, " Add to your virtue, knowledge," and this is the standing and universal obligation of every one. Become enlightened, scientific, acquainted with the laws and truths of nature! Science is classified knowledge. There can be no just conflict between science and religion. They both proceed from the fountain of all knowledge, truth, and goodness. Both are gained and increased by silent meditation, with the mind and will attentive and obedient to the influences of the Good Father.

23

There is a great amount of very valuable knowledge to be gained by reading, making us acquainted with the thoughts of other men, and with facts and events of past times, which possesses many advantages; but truth and new discoveries must be labored for — must be sought in patient, silent meditation and retirement, with the soul ardently aspiring after the All-good.

In this condition of silent meditation the truth was revealed to George Fox that there was no need for men to go to Cambridge or Oxford for qualification to preach the gospel, but that all which was required was obedience to the manifestation of truth in their own hearts.

By the same means (retirement and meditation) was it revealed to Isaac Newton that the force which imparts form to the planets and retains them in their orbits, is the same force that "moulds the starting tear, and makes it trickle from its source," from which he deduces the law of universal gravitation.

By the same silent meditation, and an abiding confidence in the wisdom and unchangeableness of the Creator, it was revealed to Charles Lyell that all the changes which have taken place in the earth in past times were produced by causes or agencies which are now in operation. So of the important discoveries of John Tyndall in relation to light; Joseph Henry, of the Smithsonian Institution, in regard to magnetism (of which the magnetic telegraph is one of the outgrowths); and so of many other persons who have made useful discoveries in truth, the requisites in all being the same.

These facts or truths which have thus been discovered have existed "from the beginning." Why, then, being so useful to man, have they not been discovered before? This is from no change in Deity. He is unchangeable. Deity has always been as ready and willing to reveal them as He is now; but man was not prepared to receive and properly interpret the revelation.

Herein we see evidence that the "thoughts of men are widened with the process of the suns."

We naturally love those who have benefited us by their labors and discoveries. We have strong affection for George Fox, William Penn, Newton, Henry, and many others, by whose labors and discoveries we are enjoying many blessings, and deriving numerous daily advantages which, but for their labors and discoveries, we should not have possessed.

They made many and great sacrifices, each individual being led to labor in his own field of discovery; and they are rightfully entitled and permitted by the Good Father to share with Him the gratitude of those that can appreciate the blessings they enjoy through the labors of these worthies.

It will be a day of great and beneficent progress of the human mind, when men rid themselves of the superstition of special providences, and come to understand practically that Deity is unchangeable, "the same yesterday, to-day, and forever;" that with God "is no variableness, neither shadow of turning;" that He "is no respecter of persons."

All who have ever lived, however wise and distinguished they may have been, were not supernaturally enlightened, or spontaneously endowed with the great ideas they possessed; but on the contrary, every individual of them, including Abraham, Moses, George Fox, William Penn, has been the product of the age that preceded him, together with his own environments and experiences.

Besides unjustly attributing partiality to Deity, this view of special endowment for certain positions and callings in life detracts much from the regard and affection we are naturally led to feel for those devoted servants of God. When their qualification for useful labor is attributed to special preparation by Deity, they fail entirely to be an example to us. Whereas, by regarding it, as it truly is, as being due to their individual devotedness and faithfulness to the light of Divine truth in their own souls, they proclaim a loud invitation to all of us to follow in the same path of obedience — to the "light," which is always accompanied by power. For the fact cannot be too frequently or emphatically impressed upon the mind, that the wisdom and power of God — light and strength — are ever united,— the ability to see being always accompanied by the power to do.

No person who is free from superstition, and who possesses a just idea of the attributes of Deity, particularly of His impartiality, can ever consider himself or his people to be special objects of Divine favor.

Deity, being unchangeable and impartial, undoubtedly has, from His first teachings to humanity, which is always done by impressions upon the soul, spoken in the same pure, peaceful, just language to the souls of the people that he did to George Fox and William Penn; but the outward teachings and environments of the preceding ages had not prepared men to give that interpretation to the impression received that these worthies did.

When William Penn, in the year 1680, came into possession, by a grant from the King of England, of a large tract of country in America, which it devolved upon him to govern, his thoughts were naturally led to study the principles of government; and his mind (already expanded by travel and experience, and being of a logical turn), together with the eternal principles of right and justice inculcated by his religious profession and his environments, soon enabled him to see, and to say, as he did in his first letter to the inhabitants of Pennsylvania :

"It hath pleased God in His Providence to cast you within my lot and care. It (government) is a business that, though I never undertook before, yet God hath given me an understanding of my duty, and an honest mind to do it uprightly."

Penn was thus led to see "the desirableness of peace," that the "true means of maintaining peace are right, justice, and kindness, not war; that this justice was the fruit of government, as government itself was the result of society, which first came from a reasonable design of men of peace, and the love of peace and order.

This revelation to the mind of Penn of the nature and requirements of true, just, and peaceful government, and his faithful obedience to the manifestations as they were gradually unfolded to him, as had been the case with that faithful and devoted fellow-laborer, George Fox, naturally inspire feelings of affection and reverence, that are due to them from us, who enjoy so many blessings and privileges in freedom, intelligence, and good government, as the result of their sacrifices and labor. And the principles of right, justice, and peace, which shone out from them so brightly, have been a beneficent light, not only to the Society of Friends, and to our beloved country, but to the whole civilized world.

But while we enjoy these blessings and privileges, and feel that they to whom we are indebted for them are rightfully entitled and permitted by the Good Father to share with Him the gratitude and joy of a heart that is capable of appreciating them, let us not arrogate to ourselves, either individually or as a Society, any claims to superior merit or favor for their services and sacrifices. As has been admirably said by my highly esteemed friend, Richard J. Bowie, Judge of the Court of Appeals of Maryland, "We cannot live on the reputation of our progenitors. He is a pauper indeed who adds nothing to his patrimony in fortune or fame. Degenerate sons of noble sires are the most pitiable objects of moral existence. The hollowest pretension of human pride is descent from distinguished ancestry, while devoid of noble thoughts or noble deeds."

They performed their work well and faithfully, and we must do ours at the present time in like manner. Unless we advance upon what they did, we are spiritually dead. A living tree grows every year,—puts out new branches, new leaves, and new fruit. And it is equally true of spiritual development, the powers becoming more and more pure and refined, enabling the soul to perceive advanced and advancing truths and duties, until, in the beautiful and highly figurative language of Scripture, "The light of the moon shall be as the light of the sun, and the light of the sun shall be seven fold, as the light of seven days."— Isaiah xxx., 26.

In this Centennial year, 1876, it seems particularly appropriate that the sincere convictions should be clearly and emphatically set forth, to which obedience to the comprehensive injunction of George Fox, "mind the Light" (which, as just stated, is progressive), has brought some members of the Society of Friends, as a basis or platform, upon which it is believed all members of Friends' Society — indeed, all peoples, may confidently rest. For George Fox founded no sect. He invited all mankind to those universal and eternal principles of truth and righteousness, which are as pure as divinity, as broad as humanity, and as enduring as eternity. These principles are all active powers — spirit forces — each winged as a good angel, bearing the soul upward and onward in purity and holiness, nearer and nearer to the Good Father.

A knowledge of God cannot be imparted or received by words. It cannot be described. It cannot be written. It must be communicated by the immediate impress of the spirit of God upon the souls of His rational creatures. In this manner is obtained, unmistakably, a knowledge of His attributes.

The best preparation or condition for receiving this knowledge I believe to be reverential, silent worship. Worship is an act of the soul. It is an effort to attain a state of greater and greater perfection, striving, with humble and earnest aspiration, to assimilate itself to Deity by becoming of the Divine nature — to be "perfect, even as the Father is perfect" — crying, Abba, Father, deep calling unto deep. For the soul of man is a great deep, which nothing short of Deity can fill. The possession of the greatest wealth, learning, power, and other outward things, still leaves an aching void in the soul. King Solomon's experience proved them to be, not merely vanity, but vexation of spirit. While at the same time, a single wave or pulsation of the Father's love not only fills the soul, but causes it to overflow to all mankind, accompanied by the feeling of peace and joy.

The humble, earnest desire and effort for a higher, purer life, a closer walk with God, persisted in day by day, raises the soul to a higher plane, on which its possessor is further removed from earth, or the government of his animal nature, so that the attraction and power of worldly things are diminished, and he is brought wholly within the sphere of heavenly influences and enjoyments.

Here is a state of peace and rest, or a time for one " encampment " on the spiritual journey, where the " Guiding Angel " halts for a season. But, after a little time, the " Good Angel," by inducing a feeling of unrest, summons the traveller to further labor on his spiritual journey, when the desire and effort are again brought into exercise to raise the traveller on to a still higher plane, and in this manner he will proceed in successive labors and rests, or halts, each, when accomplished, bringing peace of mind and joy ; until, ultimately, his " peace shall flow as a river, and his righteousness as the waves of the sea," continual and refreshing. Here is the state required for true labor, as an instrument of good in the Divine hand.

Prayer is not words, nor are the best of words prayer. Prayer is an earnest aspiration or yearning of the soul after the highest good, in harmony with the spirit of God in us, this spirit making intercession with our spirits with feelings that cannot be uttered. Whatever is petitioned for in such a state of the soul, with a continuous, calm, steady, undisturbed, watchful consciousness, will be in harmony with the Divine mind and will, and it will be received, for such is the "asking" to which the promise applies, "Ye shall receive."

EASTERN TALE.

BY THE LATE MOSES SHEPPARD, OF BALTIMORE.*

Gonzalmo, in early life, was strongly impressed with the importance of the trust confided to him, of securing a happy perpetual residence for an immortal spirit of which he was the recipient. His labors and researches were stimulated by the magnitude and duration of the object to be obtained. He studied the Scriptures, and consulted the opinions and productions of the wise and pious. He acquired a knowledge of the Oriental languages, and thus arrived at the fountain from which Christianity flowed, to direct probationers here to future bliss in the region beyond the valley of the shadow of death.

Having acquired a correct knowledge of Christianity by ascending to its source, he practiced its duties with undeviating constancy. Alive to the fatal effects of error in the momentous requirements of religion, he felt anxious for the happiness of his primogenitors, as ignorance might produce direful consequences to them. Stimulated by pious solicitude and filial affection, he prayed for a corporeal resurrection of his forefathers, that he might examine them personally in regard to their religious beliefs.

---

*B. H. was much interested in this allegory, from the moral it contained.

An angel descended and addressed him, "Gonzalmo, your prayers are heard, and your petition is granted. To-morrow your progenitors shall be arranged at your *right hand*." Gonzalmo directed his descendants to place themselves at his *left* hand.

When his forefathers were arranged in a line, he was astonished at their grotesque appearance. He beheld a *turbaned Turk*, a *Red Cross Knight*, with a group of nondescripts! But his object was to ascertain the safety of their souls, and he began an examination. The Turk vociferated, "Praise to God! I am the slave of Ali!" The knight declared that he who gave neither money nor personal services to rescue the Holy Land from the infidels, was himself an infidel. A priest held up a cross, exclaiming, "You deny the *Real Presence*, and although you are my descendant, for this heresy I would consign you to the stake." A doctor of the Sorbonne gave him a severe lecture for his apostasy. By another he was vehemently denounced for denying the doctrine of electors.

Knowing that *they* were *wrong*, and being certain that *he* was *right*, he felt irritated; but sympathy softened his resentment. He informed them that, since their time, researches had enabled sincere Christians to correct many errors, and replace them with truth; new lights had arisen and dispelled the obscurity in which Christianity had been shrouded.

Although his ancestors did not agree among themselves, they all agreed that he was a heretic, and regretted they had an apostate descendant.

Grieved at the fatal errors of his progenitors, he turned with anticipated joy to his posterity, to whom he had imparted the unchangeable doctrines of Christ in their purity; but he was overwhelmed with sorrow to find that they had abandoned the saving doctrines he had taught them. To his remonstrances they replied, "*Researches have enabled sincere Christians to correct many errors and replace them with truth. New lights have arisen, and dispelled the obscurity in which Christianity had been shrouded.*"

Grieved and agonized at the thought of being the parent of an apostate race, and at the awful consequences of their fatal errors, he was inconsolable. But they were his offspring; and, notwithstanding their startling aberrations, he desired to rescue them. He therefore offered up a fervent prayer for their admission into heaven. The angel again descended, and announced to him that his prayer had availed. "Your children are accepted. Had your prayer been *general, yourself* would have been admitted also. But, as it was confined to *your* descendants, *you* are excluded. *The selfish and uncharitable are not admitted into Paradise.*"

SKETCH OF THE LATTER DAYS OF
BENJAMIN HALLOWELL.*

Two months only after writing the preceding Autobiography, our dear father was called on to part with
the loved companion of more than fifty years. Though
bearing up with wonderful fortitude and cheerfulness,
it seemed to us who were near that life was never
again the same to him.

He performed all his daily duties, visited his friends
while strength permitted, took a deep interest in the recently discovered truths of science, and in the events
of the day, and communed more closely than ever
with nature and his Heavenly Father; but he constantly missed her who had been his beloved in early
manhood, his helper and counsellor in his prime, and
the object of his tender and constant solicitude when
disease dimmed her bright intellect and benumbed her
busy hands. She was well worthy of all that he bestowed upon her. Much as he had accomplished in
his passage through the world, he knew that her encouragement when he was depressed, and her calm and
restraining influence when unduly aroused, were most
valuable supplements to his more impulsive character.

She placed before us an example of industry, economy, patience, purity, and truthfulness, and a charity

---

* From the close of the Autobiography. By his son **Henry**
C. Hallowell.

that kept her silent as to the failings of others. She passed quietly from us on the 1st of Fifth month, 1875.

From this time father continued as nearly as possible in his accustomed habits, the faithful Bridget Murray (who had lived with them since 1858) providing his meals as usual, which he preferred taking at the same table where he had so often eaten alone during mother's sickness. The son and daughter-in-law, who occupied the same home, would have been glad to have him at their table, but the necessary confusion of little children, and his difficulty of hearing, made him feel more comfortable in his own part of the house. He wrote considerably for "Friends' Intelligencer," and to his numerous correspondents, and passed much of his time in reading, walking, and reflection. Many of his friends called to see him, and numerous visitors to the neighborhood came to pay their respects, either for their own sake or for that of friends who had known and loved him. He went out twice a day, when suitable, to take his "sun-bath," his walk being either to a neighboring clump of pines, "around the square," as he called it, when he went out of one entrance and returned by the other, or up and down the lawn, where there were seats placed, upon which he might rest as his strength became less and less. He had always been remarkably strong in his limbs, so that long after a stranger would have thought him too weak to walk, he would go down the lawn to his little "observatory," though it was a painful sight, toward the last, to see how his walk shortened and his once active frame drooped from the weakness of disease.

He had from childhood been a close observer of nature, and on his seventy-seventh birthday a weathervane, rustic seat, etc., were put up on an adjacent hill, where he could command an unobstructed view of the heavens, and such of his children and grandchildren as could be present, with some other dear relatives, were invited to come to "dedicate" it.

It was a most pleasant evening, and he several times afterwards alluded to it as one of the happiest occasions of his life. He had pleasantly insisted several times on one of his children making an address, or "little speech," as he called it; so the following lines were written by a son, just before going out, and were read while we were all standing near, he and his loved sister-in-law, Phebe Farquhar, being seated on the bench:

> One by one the years glide by,
>   Shod the while with silken feet;
> We sleep, we wake, we smile, we sigh,
>   And lo! life's circle is complete.
>
> Yet how *long* the days we live,
>   Measured by the work we do!
> We toil, we mourn, we take, we give,
>   Ever met by labors new.
>
> Long, our father, is thy life,
>   Spent in working for thy race,
> Never lagging in the strife,
>   Ever found in duty's place.
>
> Soldiers on the distant plain,
>   Teachers, striving for their kind,
> Sailors on the stormy main,
>   Toilers with the hand and mind,
>
> Turn with tender thoughts to thee,
>   Shaper of their life's career,
> Thy loved form in memory see,
>   Hold thy precepts ever dear.

Dwellers on the prairies vast,
  By the mighty rivers' flood,
Tell how, in the years long past,
  Came the Preacher, doing good.

He, whose form shall soon be found
  On the breezy plain no more,
Who seeks the "happy hunting ground,"
  To shun the "Christian's" ceaseless war,

Knows thy labors for his race,
  On the Cattaraugus stream,
And where on his dusky face
  Omaha's broad prairies gleam.

All around thee thou dost love,
  Sea and sky and grassy sod ;
Earth below, and heaven above,
  Raise thy heart to Nature's God.

Fitly on thy natal day,
  Here we place this token slight ;
Clouds and stars and sunny ray,
  Meet thy unobstructed sight.

Gently may the breezes blow,
  On thy cheek upon this hill ;
May thy steps, though weak and slow,
  Long to it be guided still.

When thy Father calls thee home,
  Gives thy tired spirit rest,
Thy children, wheresoe'er they roam,
  Will seek this spot and call it blest.

Mother's love we here will know,
  And thy precepts learn anew,
Stronger to our tasks will go,
  After musing here with you.

This walk soon seemed too far for his strength, and the observatory was removed to a point in the lawn at the foot of the hill, where his beloved form would oftentimes be seen, watching the clouds, which were an unending source of pleasure to him, and studying the meteorological aspects of the sky.

A great source of pleasure to him for some years had been the love and correspondence between the "three Benjamins," viz., Benjamin P. Moore of Fallston, Maryland, Benjamin Rodman of New Bedford, Massachusetts, and himself. They were nearly of the same age, Benjamin P. Moore having been seventy-seven years old, Benjamin Rodman seventy-four years, and he sixty-nine years, when the correspondence began. Benjamin Rodman was a schoolmate and friend of Benjamin P. Moore's, and through the latter became interested in and opened a correspondence with Benjamin Hallowell, which continued with unabating vivacity and interest until death.

In the fall of 1872 the three met in Baltimore; Benjamin Rodman and Benjamin Hallowell being mutually pleased on coming "face to face." The former (with his daughter Susan) made a visit to us at Rockland, shortly after this interview, the memory of which helped to gild the declining days of both.

In 1875 Benjamin P. Moore passed away, in his eighty-fourth year, and in the spring of 1877 Benjamin Rodman followed, aged eighty-three years, and father felt that those of his generation were nearly all assembled on the "other shore." He still kept cheerful, but happily as he often said he was situated as regards this life, he longed for the summons that would reunite him to the many that had preceded him, when it should be his Father's pleasure to call him.

In the fall of 1876, though very weak, he expressed a desire to visit Baltimore Yearly Meeting, to see once more his almost life-long friend Lydia Jefferis (then herself very feeble, and who survived him only a few weeks), and some few other friends. He accomplished the undertaking with comparative comfort, remaining one night. His heart was overflowing with love for the whole human race, even the driver of the carriage that took us to the depot receiving his hand and cordial "farewell."

He had long been a sufferer from a chronic disease, and few can ever know the agony endured at times during the latter years of his life. On his memorable journey to Iowa in his own carriage, in 1863, he "shed tears and blood in every State from Maryland to the Mississippi." Many times when his intellect seemed brightest, and his conversation most interesting, he would be suffering pangs almost unendurable. He had frequent attacks which would confine him to bed for days and weeks, but his wonderful physical powers triumphed again and again over the severity of his disease. Strange as it may seem, these spells of sickness were periods of deep interest to his attendant and himself. He was so tender and affectionate, so desirous of giving as little trouble as possible, so cheerful, animated, and altogether lovely, that the writer even now at times longs inexpressibly for those sweet though sad days. He held that the mind could overcome physical pain, and some of his most interesting conversation was during the intervals between his spells of suffering.

He had been so long an invalid, and so often, as he thought, near his close, that while we noticed his declining strength, we did not realize that we were at last to lose him, although he himself often remarked that he was "running down hill rapidly."

During the spring and summer of 1877, he grew perceptibly weaker, and had scarcely any appetite. The faithful Bridget tempted him with everything her ingenuity could devise, and his daughter and daughter-in-law suggested various modifications of his diet, with very little success.

His nephew, James S. Hallowell, would often call on his return from Washington, bringing early fruits, vegetables, fish, or other delicacies, that he hoped would be enjoyed, and for which kind attentions he always received grateful acknowledgments.

In the spring of 1877, he was very much gratified by a visit from his old and loved student Edward C. Turner of Fauquier county, Virginia, who came with William Williams of Loudoun expressly to see him once again. Edward had been a great favorite with him and with our mother, and was one of those who had helped bear to their graves the two sons, James and Charles, that they had lost from scarlet fever within a week of each other, in 1831.

He was always associated in their minds with these precious children. All were interested in the visit, and in the renewal of the love of the old Alexandria days.

Every alternate Sixth-day, when nothing occurred to prevent, his brother-in-law, William Henry Farquhar, came to take tea with him, and to talk over such subjects of scientific, literary, or religious interest as had attracted their attention during the intervening time. These occasions were always looked forward to with pleasure, and were much enjoyed.

During the last year of his life he found much to

interest him in his visits to Norwood, the home of Joseph T. and Anna L. Moore, with whom Patience Leggett resided. It was at a pleasant distance to ride, and Patience and her daughter Anna were always glad to see him. Much was talked of that afforded him gratification at the time, and gave him occupation afterwards, in copying poetry and other things that had been under discussion. His children will always remember with gratitude the many delicate and kind attentions bestowed upon him so long and so constantly by the Norwood family.

His interest in his country, and in the advance of freedom in all things, grew and strengthened with advancing years. He had much interesting correspondence with friends of liberty and humanity, and his mind and heart expanded with length of days, so that it was remarked to the writer, on one occasion, by a distant admiring friend, that "Benjamin Hallowell had taught him that one need not necessarily grow conservative and despondent while growing old."

During the summer his weakness increased, and he found great difficulty in conversing long at a time.

On the 2d of Eighth month he was very much interested in the erection of a new pole, sixty-two feet high, for his weather vane, the old one not having been sufficiently tall to be unaffected by the surrounding trees. His son Benjamin, who, with his wife Lydia T., and daughter Margaret, were making their summer visit to Rockland, undertook the superintendence.

Father enjoyed it for a brief period, pleasantly associating his absent son with it when looking out, as he so often did, to watch the changes of the weather.

On the 9th the writer took him to see Eliza Kirk,

at Woodburn, who, with her daughter, Mary B. Kirk, was much beloved by him. We also called at Stanmore, but he found the exertion much more fatiguing than usual.

On the 10th his granddaughter Mary took him for what proved to be his last visit. They stopped at Stanmore, where his daughter Caroline was distressed to see how weak and poorly he appeared to be.

They then went to Norwood, making a brief call, his strength scarcely holding out until his return. He went to bed on reaching home, and his last sickness may be said to date from that time. He suffered extremely, some days not getting up, but on others trying to come down a little while if possible, for the sake of the change. During this time he had a most touching and memorable visit from a former beloved pupil, Manning F. Force. Manning had been five years at his school in Alexandria, entering very young, and after graduating at Harvard, had studied law, settled in Cincinnati, and become prominent as a lawyer, a general in the Union army, and as a judge, yet he was still only "Manning," and father was "Benjamin."

We received a note saying he was in Washington, and would come out and dine with us on the 27th. The visit was looked forward to by the dear invalid with deep interest.

It gave a pleasurable excitement to the daily dressing and preparation for coming down stairs. He wore a white vest, because "Manning always saw him with one on when lecturing." He put on his "best clothes," had his spectacles in the breast pocket of his waistcoat, and everything as nearly like "old times" as possible. Weak and wasted as he was, he straightened himself to his full height when "Manning" entered, gave him the warm grasp and kindly greeting as of yore, and was indeed "every inch a man."

He could only remain with him half an hour, and returned to his bed. On saying farewell, he looked Manning in the face, and with a voice tremulous with affection, asked him "if he could give an old man a kiss?" We felt that it was a parting for eternity.

For a few days he came down stairs, both in the morning and afternoon, and would walk a little in front of the house, leaning a hand upon the shoulder of one of the grandchildren, whom he called his "other cane."

On the 3d of Ninth month the writer took him for a short ride, going a little beyond the front gate and around the outbuildings, "to see how things looked," and we had strong hopes that, as on other occasions, he would now get comparatively well. During the night, however, he was worse, and had a most distressing time. Dr. Wm. E. Magruder gave him all the relief possible, with the tender affection of a son; and his son-in-law, Francis Miller, spent the night of the 5th assisting Dr. Magruder in attending upon him.

The passage from life was to him mentally but a pleasant journey to home and friends, and he made all his preparations with business-like precision and cheerfulness.

He gave his oldest son, who had been his constant companion and attendant, excepting at night, full directions as to all things, as they occurred to his mind. He had at different times been his own executor, and had distributed various mementoes and gifts to his children, grandchildren, and friends, including his dear daughter-in-law, Anna T. Hallowell, of Philadelphia, and her children, and William S. Brooke, his daughter Mary's husband, and their two children.

On the 5th, however, scarcely thirty-six hours before his close, he remembered several little things he wished given to different individuals, and particularly to his grandsons, Frank and Robert, who had been attentive to him during his sickness, the former at night and the latter during the day, especially in assisting him to shave the last time, only a few days before his death. Having decided upon two mementoes, he asked his son to write a few lines for him, which he heard read, and then attached his well-known signature to each, with the little familiar flourish, it being the last time the dear hand traced that name, which had been so often written during a long, weary, yet most useful life.

All through the day of the 6th, we knew he was dying; still he retained his intellectual brightness, for which he expressed himself grateful. On Francis Miller's entering the room, he stretched out his hand and shook hands with him as usual.

Much as he was suffering, he begged us not to administer anodynes, or to try longer to give him relief, but to "let him die in peace."

About 3 p. m. his sufferings began to diminish, and he became gradually unconscious. He had remarked while suffering most, that he would not "turn his hand over to have it less," as it was all in accordance with fixed laws, and "must be right." He also said, "Dear children! I would rather see you smiling than weeping! All is so bright—so *glorious* before me! My Heavenly Father is near me,—in this very room,—and He has *promised* me that He will never desert me if I am only *faithful*, and *that* I will try *hard* to be!"

His daughter Caroline, Dr. William E. Magruder, his daughter-in-law Sarah M. Hallowell, his much-loved namesake Benjamin H. Miller (whom we sent for to watch with us that last night), and his son Henry, were in the room with him. Not long before his close, in a faint voice he asked us to kiss him, feebly motioning with his lips. Soon afterwards, and very near the end, he opened his eyes wide, and they seemed filled with a mysterious depth and reverential awe, as he gazed fixedly at something unseen by us ; then a glory, as of the new day that was dawning upon him, rested on his grand countenance, and with scarcely a struggle, on the morning of the 7th, at a quarter before four o'clock, his spirit took its flight, and he who had been so much to us, our pride and protector, and of latter years our beloved charge and care, lay calmly beautiful after his long, weary march through life, during which he had battled bravely for truth and right, and had suffered almost a martyr's death, the disease having been aggravated by his devotion to what he believed to be his duty.

As teacher, lecturer, philanthropist, and Friend, he had filled a wide sphere of usefulness, had earned his long-desired rest, and attained the victor's crown.

His son-in-law, Francis Miller, Dr. Wm. E. Magruder, Benjamin H. Miller, and the writer, prepared him for his final sleep. Many of his friends had called during his sickness, and now again came to offer their services and to express their sympathy. Mary S. Lippincott, his only sister, and his playmate in childhood, came on the 8th to see his face once more. His son Benjamin and wife came also on the 8th.

On the afternoon of First-day, the 9th of Ninth month, 1877, a most lovely and beautiful day, we carried him to the meeting-house at Sandy Spring, where was gathered a large and solemn assemblage of friends from far and near, many of whom looked for the last time on that countenance, majestic even in death.

Appropriate and beautiful remarks were made by his sister, Mary S. Lippincott, Samuel Townsend, Rebecca Thomas, Hadassah J. Moore, and his most faithful friend and physician, Dr. Wm. E. Magruder. Then his oldest and only living daughter closed the lid of his last home, and we went out into the beautiful sunshine and laid him by his beloved wife, under the branches of a spreading tree. All was quiet, solemn, and lovely. Those who carried him to his grave were Henry Stabler of Roslyn, Richard T. Bentley, George E. Brooke, Mahlon Kirk, Robert R. Moore, and Charles Abert, all old and valued friends.

These were the closing scenes in the life of our father. His autobiography seemed incomplete without some account of his latter days.

Time, while it softens the severity of the loss, reveals more and more the grandeur of his character, the singleness of purpose with which he endeavored to serve his Creator, and the wide influence he had exerted among his fellow-men.

Letters, touching and earnest, and public notices far and near, indicated the hold he had upon the hearts of his former pupils and friends.

The city of Alexandria, where he labored so long for the good of others, placed his likeness upon some of her bonds, and his views upon education are quoted as the highest authority.

His example of unselfish devotion to the highest views of usefulness will long be felt.

LETTERS RECEIVED.

After our father's death many sympathizing letters were received, and the following have been selected as representing the tone of almost reverential love that pervaded them all:

From S. M. Janney.

LINCOLN, VA., *9th Mo. 8th, 1877.*

DEAR FRIEND: — Thy card was received yesterday afternoon, bringing the mournful intelligence that thy dear father had been removed from the trials of time to the rewards of eternity. I regret that I cannot be with you to-morrow, to join you in the solemn duty of attending his remains to their last resting place.

My thoughts will be with you, and I trust that the consolations of the gospel of Christ will be granted to the near relatives and friends who mourn the departure of one so greatly beloved.

I shall always cherish an affectionate remembrance of thy father, as having been one of my most valued friends, and his name will be registered among the wise and good.

Thy cordial friend,

SAM'L M. JANNEY.

From Edward C. Turner.

MONTROSE, FAUQUIER CO., VIRGINIA, *Sep. 11th, '77.*

MY DEAR HENRY: — The sad news of the death of your honored father had reached me before the receipt of your card, and I was on the eve of writing to you when it came. I was not surprised to hear of his death, as I saw plainly, when I visited him in May, that his time on earth could not be long.

No day has passed since I was with him that I have not recurred to the delightful visit; and now that he is gone, it is a source of real comfort to me that I made it.

He knew that his time was near at hand, and seemed so happy in the prospect of rest and peace so soon to be enjoyed. He told me he was ready to go, but in no hurry, and that he intended to enjoy to the full all of life here that it might please his Master to give him. I shall never forget his sweet, gentle, affectionate talk to me. "Give my love to thy wife and children, and tell them all that I love them for thy sake," etc., etc.; and I have felt since I left him that the good I derived from hearing him talk, and the softening influence of his noble spirit, were worth the trouble of a dozen such trips. Few men have died leaving behind them better monuments of their disinterested usefulness, and no man whose memory is more cherished by those who knew him best.

He has gone to his reward, and it makes me happy to think that we may meet him and know him intimately again on "the other side." I know, dear H., that my poor words can give you no comfort, but rest assured you have my sincere sympathy.

Sincerely yours,
EDWARD C. TURNER.

FROM F. E. ABBOTT.

BOSTON, MASS., Sept. 13th, 1877.

MY DEAR SIR: — I am indeed grieved to learn the sad news of the decease of my dear and venerable friend, your father. It is true I never saw him in the flesh; but I have seen, and learned to love, the beautiful spirit that revealed itself in his letters. The name of Benjamin Hallowell will always be tenderly cherished by me, as that of one who extended to me his constant sympathy and aid in the objects of my highest aspiration.

Truly, he was a saintly man, not alone in his "close," but in his life; for he testified of the Spirit, and the Spirit testified of him.

With respectful and sincere sympathy I am,

Most truly yours,

F. E. ABBOTT.

FROM BISHOP PINCKNEY.

Sept. 14th, '77.

MY DEAR SIR : — I do most deeply sympathize with you in your great sorrow, for, although your father had lived beyond the three score and ten, he was fresh in heart and fresh in mind, and was therefore able to contribute largely to the pleasures of the household.

A father's smile possesses a fascination that few things else on earth possess. The withdrawal of it is like an eclipse on the soul. You have, however, bright memories to soothe you. He lived to illustrate the higher walks of life. As a mathematician he ranked among the foremost, while as an instructor of youth he had no superior.

The urbanity of his manners and his sterling integrity won for him the admiration and respect of the whole community, while his active charities endeared him to the poor.

These shadows admonish us that we have no continuing city here. They teach us that we must seek one to come.

The images that are hung upon the walls of this earthly tabernacle are eloquent in speech. They exemplify the beautiful and the true, while they stimulate us to aim to secure a like nobility of soul.

There is, I know, a sacredness in grief, on which a stranger should not intrude; and yet there is, in the sympathy of the poorest, a something that saves it from intrusion.

Affectionately,

W. PINCKNEY.

From Mary G. Moore.

Mosswood, *9th Mo. 8th,* '77.

My Dear Friend : — My heart feels the blank that has
been made, — thy precious father, father and companion to thee
as few fathers are to their sons, has passed to the higher
life, and the void that is made I know something of, and
I have sat with thee and his children in deep sympathy.
Gradually you have been prepared for the separation, and I
have imagined, judging from my own experience, that you
have almost rejoiced that the weary spirit had cast off the
shackles of mortality.   There can be such a feeling when
the heart is lonely and bowed under the loss of sweet companionship.   But what a rich inheritance is yours! And it
will be increasingly rich as you live over the past life of
your beloved, venerable parent.   All who came within his
influence felt that they had gathered something of value
from him ; and how unostentatiously he gave out his stores,
whenever he saw it would give pleasure or would be useful.
Truly the law of kindness dwelt in his heart ; and when I
follow in thought (as I always do those I love) to the invisible world, and feel that upon all speculations as to the
unfolding and development of the material and spiritual
world to those so interested in such subjects here, there
must ever be a veil, till we too are unrobed of mortality,
I turn to that which *I do* know for a certainty, that the
loving heart that overflowed to all, is joined to the great
Source of love.   The more I contemplate thy dear father's
character, the more I am in admiration at his rare qualities.

His attainments are known to the outside world, and
his life of usefulness receives the acknowledgment of appreciation ; but to those who were admitted to a closer intimacy,
the admiration was constant of his benevolence of feeling.
He interested himself (even when engaged in the mental
pursuits which so largely occupied him) in all classes.   A
large portion of those who shared his friendship, or upon
whom he bestowed his attention, could not share with him
the pleasures of science, or reach to the heights that he
had attained.

I am the richer for having known him and shared his friendship, and I feel that another of my closest ties of friendship is severed, though only for a time; for at my age and with my infirmities, I feel that the time of abiding here cannot be long.

I feel the loss, not only for myself, but I think of my husband's last and most intimate friend, gone too, to the same home, the home that awaits us all, if we too walk as he walked, in the fear and love of God.

You have been blest in the past in no ordinary degree with the companionship of one of the greatest minds of the age; but you have been blest in a higher degree with the example of great intellectual attainments, sanctified and devoted to the Giver of them all.

May his mantle rest upon you, and the blessing of Him in whom he placed his trust be with you all, and be your stay and support through all, even to the end.

Thy attached friend,
MARY G. MOORE.

From W. W. Corcoran.

WASHINGTON, Sept. 18th, 1877.

DEAR SIR: — I received, with deep regret, the intelligence of the death of your father, who deservedly held so high a place in the estimation of the public, and whose intellectual endowments and moral worth attracted my sincere regard. I regretted also that indisposition prevented me from attending his obsequies, and rendering this last sad tribute of respect to his memory.

I avail myself of the present occasion to say that my valued friend, General Robert E. Lee (who had long known him), expressed to me, in most emphatic terms, his admiration of the pure and elevated character of your father.

Accept the assurances of my sympathy in the loss you have sustained, and believe me

Truly yours,
W. W. CORCORAN.

From General Manning F. Force.

POMEROY, OHIO, *Sept. 23d, 1877.*

My DEAR HENRY : — I have just learned of the death of your father, in looking over the mail that was kept for my return.

How rejoiced I am that I had an opportunity of seeing him once more. It was a great privilege to be within his influence. It is when he leaves us, and the void is perceived, that we feel sharply how much more character is worth than station, and how cheap and vulgar is ambition for rank and office, compared with the purpose to do always that which is right. The great concourse that assembled to do honor to his memory, shows that reverence for virtue has not died out.

Very truly yours,

M. F. FORCE.

From J. F. W. Ware,

SWAMPSCOTT, MASS., *17th Oct., '77.*

My DEAR SIR : — A short time since, I heard of the death of your honored father. I count it one of the privileges of life, that I knew him somewhat in my pleasant visitings to Sandy Spring, and that I had two or three letters from him.

Descended myself from Friends, and having most of the warmest intimacies of my life in that Society, and sympathizing in a good deal of their doctrine, I was the more drawn to a man whose character and personal bearing would of themselves have attracted me. The mingling of sweetness and strength with the mellowing serenity of years, the spirit enshrined in a tenement of so much dignity, and what is best in manly beauty, made him a sort of "beau ideal" of Christian manliness, a portrait to hang in my chamber of memories.

I am sure, that while you will hardly mourn, you will greatly miss him, while you can only be grateful for so long a life and so priceless a legacy.

Very truly yours,

J. F. W. WARE.

FROM MONCURE D. CONWAY.

HAMLET HOUSE, HAMMERSMITH,
LONDON, ENGLAND, *October 22, '77.*

MY DEAR MRS. MILLER: — I have just heard of your beloved and revered father's death, and I cannot forbear writing you to say how deeply I feel this event. All sorrow at the death of such a man as Benjamin Hallowell is over-arched with a bow of hope. He remains so immortal in our grateful hearts, that we cannot think of his life as closed and ended ; he only rests from his labors as we knew them, and, where our own weak wisdom valued him so much, we cannot think the Great Wisdom will value him less, but much more !

I would like, on this soft October day, to be able to pluck that last white rose in my garden, and kneel and plant it on his grave, — emblem of his pure simplicity, the light that clothed him, the sweet fragrance of his beautiful life.

After long years of contact with sects and their dog-mas, I find that I have a creed, and it is written in such lives and hearts as your father's. The faith that can pro-duce such men is the faith for me. With one Benjamin Hallowell, I will outweigh all the theology ever written.

I often think of you, and of our talks on great themes. Dear old Sandy Spring — how I love it! I have over my table in a frame, sent from India, one leaf of the "Holy Bo tree" — the tree under which it is said Buddha sat down a prince and at last rose up "an enlightened teacher," five hundred years before Christ. As I look at the leaf, it seems to be transformed to many, — to an old grove, with Sandy Spring meeting-house in the center. There I sat down a Methodist preacher, and rose up with faith in the inward light. We must all have our own Bo tree before we can reverence that of another, and though I am not very "enlightened," I can see the light, and, as Paul says, "follow after."

Heartily your friend,
MONCURE D. CONWAY.

Extract of a Letter Received From Prof. Joseph Henry in 1876.

"It is one of the principal pleasures of my life to have the kind regard of men of the character of your esteemed father. He has done a good work in life, and the seeds he has sown in the minds of the youth of this region, will germinate and bring forth fruit long after his departure from earth. Give him my affectionate regard."

J. H.

NOTICES OF THE PRESS.

Among the many notices of his life and character that appeared in the journals of the day, the following have been selected.

From the Baltimore American.

It is idle to speculate as to what the singularly gifted scholar who was yesterday laid to his rest in the Friends' burial ground at Sandy Spring might have been if he had chosen to become a leader rather than a teacher of men. His career might have been that of a great publicist or jurist, if his cultivated tastes had not led him to prefer "the cool, sequestered vale of life." His talents were of the highest order, and if they had been associated with even a moderate amount of ambition, his name might have been as conspicuous among statesmen as it is among mathematicians and philanthropists.

But he will be remembered, not for what he might have been, but for what he really was. If he did not attain the highest place in the temple of fame, he certainly was the centre of a circle of devoted

friends, that expanded with his ripening years. His
large philanthropy took in the freedman and the Indian,
and both will remember him as a wise benefactor.
In the religious denomination to which he belonged
(the Society of Friends), he exercised a commanding
influence.

ELIZABETH P. PEABODY, IN FRIENDS' INTELLIGENCER.

I want to speak a word to somebody who knew the venerable Benjamin Hallowell, for I cannot keep perfect silence
when he has just died — just been translated, rather ; for
such, death must have been to him, who was *all life*.

I became acquainted with him first in 1851, when he was
keeping school in Alexandria, and I called on him with a note
from Elizabeth Foster, I think, to communicate to him an idea
which I had received from a Polish friend about memorizing
chronology in such a manner that it should really be an aid to
the memory of history, instead of its being, as usual, a burden and extraneous.

I cannot now remember the details of that conversation, but I remember the impression I received of his
extraordinary intelligence and personality. I never forgot
him, and, as I found afterwards, he never forgot me ; and
on my first putting into " Friends' Intelligencer " an article
upon the identity of Froebel's and George Fox's method of
proceeding from that point within, at which God and man
meet, and living out from that, he wrote to me, and expressed
his unity with the kindergarten method.

In a year or two after (1871), when I was in Washington,
at the Bureau of Education, for a few months, to answer questions and to make explanations to those who had been interested by my paper on kindergarten culture (which appeared
in the report of the Commisioner of 1870), he sent a carriage
from Sandy Spring to bring me there to talk to the people at

the Lyceum on the subject, and at his request my article in the "Friends' Intelligencer" was inserted again, as I had revised it when I put it into the first series of the Kindergarten Messenger.

He was one among the several aged men who welcomed that effort of mine to introduce the subject of Froebel's reform to the thoughtful of this country. Since his death, I have been hunting for a long letter he wrote me about it; and he subscribed for many copies, which he asked me to send to mothers in Montgomery county, Md., paying for them himself one year, thinking that they would afterwards keep up the subscription.

Perhaps it will quicken many minds to know how Benjamin Hallowell felt on this subject, for I think everybody in the Society must believe that his was a foremost mind on educational subjects. In their mathematical cast of mind, Froebel and he were similar. They both felt that in mathematical truth the human and divine were purely *at one;* and both showed that the most tender and profound hearts were compatible with the keenest exercises of the pure intellect, and could obey the command in its fullness of loving the Lord with all the *mind,* as well as heart and might; that the Christian communes with the Eternal Reason, as well as the Infinite Love and Power.

It is at this point, I think, the Quaker creed (for, though unwritten, they have one) somewhat fails. The followers of George Fox are not quite up to the high point of vision of Fox himself. Like all *followers,* they rest upon his testimony, instead of, like him, returning to first principles.

But Benjamin Hallowell did not embody with the principles of George Fox the inevitable limitations of that day. He did not need to rest on the traditions of even the *Saintly Fathers,* because, like those Fathers, he held immediate communion with God. He was indeed the ideal Friend.

I know Friends do not like the word Quaker, but it is consecrated to me by a few whom I have known of that denomination, who had no narrowness, and it seems to convey a certain characteristic.

I feel as if they themselves did not realize in their imagination all that they are, that they give to others a greater ideal than they define to themselves. No body or bodies of people are conscious of what is best in them, but God knows and mankind profits by it.

E. P. PEABODY.

Cambridge, Massachusetts.

A. G. RIDDLE, IN NEW YORK TRIBUNE.

To the Editor of the Tribune:

SIR : — Several years ago, when Benjamin Hallowell was only a name to me, I was a guest at a beautiful home near Sandy Spring, the seat of the Montgomery Friends. My host, a prominent Marylander, was of the community, and I accompanied him on Sunday to the Quaker meeting-house, an old structure of brick, in the margin of a primitive forest of considerable extent. Most of the congregation were in their places when we entered. I had hardly taken my seat when my attention was arrested by one of the most striking-looking men I have ever seen. Almost in front, facing me, on the raised platform against the wall with the elders, sat a man of seventy, of just less than gigantic mould, with a grand, massive head, scantily crowned with longish white hair, a lofty brow and noble features, bowed in reverential reverie, with closed eyes, with his shoulders almost above the heads of the men about him. I was not familiar with the leading names of the Friends, but knew I was looking at an extraordinary man. I glanced from him over the silent assembly of serene, silent men and women, and back at the noble form before me, in moulding which nature had reverted to the great primitive type, which she now so rarely produces. The spirit and presence of the silent worship stole upon me.

It was a June morning, and the notes of the thrushes and robins came to me from the surrounding forest. Suddenly, little twittering sounds, like the first notes of a bird's song, fell on my ear, and I turned just as the form I so admired was rising. He rested his trembling hands on the back of the seat before him, with a little stoop in his shoulders, and a bending of the head, revealing deep-set but very fine blue eyes. The voice was sweet, tender, and flute-like, a little monotonous, but could never have wearied. The sermon, if such it might be called, was a sort of lofty and beautiful chant. It was an expression of the depth, purity, and peace of that holiness of heart and life to which man may attain, and its outer manifestation of love, benevolence, and widest charity. The language was nervous, happily chosen, simple and pure, and beyond the power of the mere rhetorician. The matter was so arranged that its clear statement was a great and beautiful argument, while a trill of the voice rendered it touching.

The delivery of this rare homily may have occupied fifteen minutes.

As the preacher was sitting down, another train of thought opened to him, when, with the same little murmur, he arose to his full height, and spoke perhaps five minutes longer — not in continuance of the first discourse, but of a germane topic, which illustrated and supplemented it. He sat down, observed a moment's silence, turned and shook hands with the man next to him, — a signal that the service had closed.

That was Benjamin Hallowell. As he passed out, men and boys, matrons and maidens, gathered about him, followed him to his carriage, and did not part with him till he drove away. He was of them, lived their daily life, went in and out before them, ministering, beautifying, and elevating their lives; helping to improve and adorn their homes and fortunes, lighting and conducting them along the upper paths of virtue, culture, and beneficence; yet so natural and common, that, in a way, they lost the power of appreciating the more striking of his remarkable qualities and powers.

I came to know him well all these years since I first saw him. He was a man rarely endowed, and doubtless, in his philosophy of life, he secured as much of real value from the world as it is capable of yielding. Nature had given him most of the striking qualities of intellect, will power, and the rudiments of the strongest human passions, and clothed them with a form of dignity, beauty, and grace. Seemingly he had but to choose his career, and will his own fortune. Among his gifts the religious element was large, and this, with his early training and surroundings, determined his course. In history there was but one model. The spirit of Mary's Son he made his own. It restrained his ambition, opened his pathway, enlightened his studies, formed his manners, and informed his life. Politics and the government of the nation, all great enterprises, were very much to him, and he kept well informed of them. The unfolding and fashioning of the minds, the frame and structure of the character of the chosen young men of the land, were to him much more. To that he dedicated himself with a devotion and unreserve which marked his appreciation of its importance. No youth was ever under his care who did not carry with him through life something of the bent and bias imparted by his hand; as none approached him without reverence or left him without love.

His work was that which lay nearest his hand. Emphatically, he loved his neighbor. His neighborhood was the universe, and all living things were the objects of his care. As his manners were the manifestation of his heart and spirit, he was naturally the most graceful and polished of cultured men. The servants, the coachman who drove him to the railroad station, always remembered his consideration for them. If a man may apply the term "lovable" to a man, that was eminently his due. Nothing bearing life ever came under his care, that did not love him as it was capable. It was beautiful to see him break from a clinging group of lads and maidens, and hear him say, "Farewell, now, I must go to my Margaret," toward whom he manifested the same ardor of love and tender observance at seventy-five as in the first days of wedded bliss.

If his life was lovely beyond usual, his last illness and death were beautiful and touching beyond earth. His Margaret passed away nearly two years before his exit, and it was a sore trial of his faith that he must remain longer. That the example of his life might lack no perfection, that illness was a protracted bodily torture, gradually growing more intense, till the sources of life were exhausted : yet, such were the strength and fortitude of the spirit, that all was endured with a serene smile, calling forth assurances of the mercy and goodness of God. Sometimes when the anguish was at its greatest, he said to his attendant, "Thee must allow me to groan a little." He refused anodynes and anæsthetics, saying, "if permitted, he would retain his faculties unclouded." He wished to note the shades of on-coming death, which were also to be the opening dawn of immortality. Such an intellect could never be shattered. Once it seemed to wander, making a luminous track.

As if his sufferings might disquiet the faith of a favorite daughter, in the mercy of Providence, with clearness and energy he demonstrated two or three mathematical problems; concluding with, "So thee sees, daughter, that it is all clear and right." His method of clarifying and refreshing his mind, even in this illness, was by the solution of a problem. As the end approached, the glow of the perfect faith became a luminous nimbus, on the almost transfigured countenance — instances of which many have read of, but few ever witnessed. His last words were assurances that the way was clear, the light broad and steady, and the glory serene.

A. G. RIDDLE.

Washington, Sept., 1877.

MEMORIAL OF SANDY SPRING MONTHLY MEETING OF FRIENDS, CONCERNING BENJAMIN HALLOWELL.

Benjamin Hallowell, an approved minister, was born the 17th of the Eighth month, 1799, at Abington, in Montgomery county, State of Pennsylvania, and died at his late residence, near Sandy Spring, in Montgomery county, Maryland, of which meeting he had been a consistent and useful member many years. When such a character has been "called away to be seen of men no more," we think it due to his surviving friends and to future generations to commemorate such a portion of his valuable life as might give them encouragement and a stimulus to go forward in their travel over the rough places in the journey of life.

In all his transactions this dear friend endeavored, through the spirit of love and trust and obedience, to make the Divine harmony his rule of self-government — entitling him to the fulfilment of the Scriptural promise, " He that overcometh shall inherit all things, and I will be his God, and he shall be my son, and shall have a right to the tree of life which is in the midst of the paradise of God." He devoted a considerable share of the unusual energy and capacity with which he was gifted to the advancement of true science, and he was enabled to contribute largely to its diffusion, though he never sacrificed any of the least of his moral or religious duties to its cultivation, but made *them* his chief concern. It does not seem requisite that we should here expatiate on his scientific or literary pursuits; his labors in that field have indelibly written their own memorial, which has long been before the world, showing conclusively how science and religion may be blended without a clash. The most prominent features in this noble character were his humility, self-denial, and willingness to labor in the cause of humanity, righteousness, and truth; and while he occupied such an eminent position in the world of mind and culture, no class of people were too lowly to escape his warm greeting and sympathy when brought in contact with him; and it was always his effort, in his intercourse with others, especially those of youthful age, to give an instructive turn to the conversation, and it was noticeable that these sought his companionship as though he were coeval with themselves; and rarely did any associate with him, we believe, who did not receive a blessing from the overflow of his genial spirit, that would go with them even beyond this period of existence.

Volumes might be written of his deeds of love, charity, and benevolence, to which there are living testimonials; but we will not attempt that theme. His countenance seemed to be continually illuminated with that kind of peace and benignity that has fully realized the Fatherhood of God and the brotherhood of man; and in striking emulation of his Divine Master, when he was reviled, he chose rather to suffer affliction for a season than to revile again. But on some occasions, when these encounters would be too acrimonious, and his failing earthly tabernacle would give way, he immediately sought repentance, even in tears, and was soon ready in the meekness of a little child to make any necessary concession or reparation for the vindication of righteousness and truth.

Exemplary in all the relations of life, he was never wholly satisfied unless something of a practical benefit was kept in view. His exhortations were mainly directed to impress this great object of existence, and his own life was a continued illustration of the doctrine he taught.

When disease came upon him in his latter years, in a most painful form, he was enabled to prove the sustaining power of these life-long principles by wonderful resignation under the severest suffering. These seasons of protracted agony were often periods of deep interest to his attendants and himself. One of them writes that "he was throughout tender and affectionate, desirous of giving as little trouble as possible, cheerful, animated, and full of love. At length his powerful constitution gave way under attacks of disease continually repeated, and when it was evident that he was dying, his son and daughter manifesting their grief by tears, he said, 'My children, I would so much rather see you smiling. My way is all clear; it is all so bright, beautiful, glorious.' Feebly moving his thin hand, he added, 'I would not turn my hand to remove a single throb of pain; it is the will of the Heavenly Father, and His will is right. He is so near—He is in this room; He will never forsake me while I keep right, and I will try so hard to keep right.'" Not long before his close he opened wide his eyes, which seemed filled with a mysterious depth, a radiance and reverential awe, gazing fixedly on something not visible to his attendants, and without a struggle his spirit took its flight; and thus finished his earthly course with the anthem of praise on his dying lips, on the 7th of the Ninth month, 1877, in the 79th year of his age.

Read in and approved by Sandy Spring Monthly Meeting of Friends, held Ninth month 4th, 1878.

BENJAMIN H. MILLER, }
MARY E. MOORE,   } *Clerks.*

Read in and approved by Baltimore Quarterly Meeting, held at Gunpowder, Ninth month 9th, 1878.

THOMAS H. MATTHEWS, *Clerk.*
ELIZABETH G. THOMAS, *Clerk for the day.*

Read in and approved by Baltimore Yearly Meeting, Tenth month 31st, 1878.

LEVI K. BROWN, }
MARY C. CUTLER, } *Clerks.*

———

Our work is finished. In his Autobiography and the extracts from his writings, our beloved father has himself told the story of his life.

Allowing for the infirmities inseparable from humanity, we may truly say, "Mark the perfect man, and behold the upright; for the end of that man is peace."

www.ingramcontent.com/pod-product-compliance
Lightning Source LLC
Chambersburg PA
CBHW031959120726
47898CB00004BA/1356